# ABOUT THE AUTHOR

From an early age, Martin was enchanted with old movies from Hollywood's golden era—from the dawn of the talkies in the late 1920s to the close of the studio system in the late 1950s—and has spent many a happy hour watching the likes of Garland, Gable, Crawford, Garbo, Grant, Miller, Kelly, Astaire, Rogers, Turner, and Welles go through their paces.

It felt inevitable that he would someday end up writing about them.

Originally from Melbourne, Australia, Martin moved to Los Angeles in the mid-90s where he now works as a writer, blogger, webmaster, and tour guide.

**www.MartinTurnbull.com**

This book is dedicated to

**SUELLEN OAKLEY**

because our friendship has prevailed
through the rises and falls of life's pavlova.

ISBN-13: 978-1985449152

ISBN-10: 1985449153

# CITY OF MYTHS

a novel

by

Martin Turnbull

Book Eight in the Hollywood's Garden of Allah novels

# CHAPTER 1

Marcus Adler vaulted onto the stone balustrade at the eastern rim of the Trevi Fountain and twisted the zoom lens on his camera. Louis Jourdan sharpened into view as the early afternoon sun reflected off the white marble, highlighting the actor's aristocratic face. Marcus waited for a movie-star smile and knew right away his photo was a keeper.

Jean Negulesco, the director on *Three Coins in the Fountain,* had kept a sure hand through long days toiling in the relentless Roman summer. But September was around the corner, which meant that in four days the cast and crew would be boarding a Pan Am flight back to the States.

Everybody else would be resuming their lives and tackling the next film, but for Marcus, it meant picking up his life again.

Goodbye blacklist.

Goodbye graylist.

Hello Garden of Allah Hotel.

Hello career.

Today they were shooting the final scene where the three couples reunited around a deserted Trevi Fountain to what Marcus guessed would be the swell of the movie's theme song—the on-set rumor was that Frank Sinatra was going to record it.

But two rolls of film and only one usable photo was not a great ratio.

Negulesco walked out from behind the enormous Technicolor camera and approached Jourdan with a beckoning hand. As Marcus lifted his Leica to readjust the zoom, he heard a metallic clattering at his feet. One of his cufflinks bounced off the stone and plopped into the water swirling eight feet below.

It wasn't just any cufflink; it was half of his favorite pair, two gold studs embedded with three tiny emeralds apiece.

Strictly speaking, they weren't his; they belonged to someone he'd been avoiding ever since he arrived in Italy.

Not that Marcus wanted to see Oliver Trenton. Of course, he *wanted* to, but Marcus knew it wasn't healthy, so he'd avoided walking past the seminary where Oliver had enrolled in the Jesuit priesthood nearly three years before.

Filming had taken them all over the city, but never near Piazza Colonna. They were there right now, a couple of blocks from it.

*Four more days,* Marcus told himself, *then you'll be out of here and you can put this behind you.*

The cufflink glinted on the concrete bottom of the fountain. He jumped down from the balustrade and skirted around the fountain's edge until he was close enough to dip his fingers; the water was refreshingly cool in the stifling August heat. Marcus thought of the pool at the Garden of Allah, and how this time next week he'd be able to dive in any time he wanted. God, how he'd missed that.

"Ladies and gentlemen," Negulesco announced to the crew gathered around the Piazza di Trevi. "We have dust in the camera. Mr. Krasner and his team will need several hours to clean it all out, so I'm calling an early lunch until two o'clock."

Marcus turned back to the water. It didn't look too deep. Knee height, maybe? Waist deep at most. With any luck he could slip off his shoes, wade in, collect the cufflink, and wade out again before anyone objected.

"Marcus?" Negulesco curled a finger. "May I have a word?"

He joined the director in the doorway of a gelato store. "I got a great shot of Louis, and another of you two just before the camera clogged."

"We need to talk."

Jean Negulesco was an urbane Eastern European who eschewed shouting in favor of expressing himself with an air of genteel authority that brooked little opposition. However, in Marcus's experience, no pleasant conversation ever started with the words "We need to talk."

"Sure. What's up?"

Negulesco took a long pause, heavy with apprehension.

"Let's walk." He led Marcus out of the piazza and into one of the narrow lanes that made up the labyrinth of Rome. "*River of No Return* has been a rough shoot. Otto Preminger and Marilyn Monroe have not gotten along very well and evidently it shows. Zanuck has decided that a number of scenes require reshoots, and he wants me to step in."

"For no screen credit, I assume?" Marcus asked.

"'Take one for the team' is how he put it."

They turned onto a wider thoroughfare, Via del Corso, where a long newsstand hawked an array of European and international newspapers. The headline straddling *The New York Times* was about the Korean war. Marcus ached to find out what was happening back home, but Negulesco pressed on. This was no casual stroll.

"Does this mean you want me to accompany you on the set when we get back?" Marcus asked. "Kathryn Massey wrote to me the other day. She told me that Monroe—"

"Zanuck has plans for you."

"Some other movie?"

*Demetrius and the Gladiators* and *Prince Valiant* were currently shooting on the Fox lot. Did either of them have a troubled script?

Negulesco remained silent for half a block. "He wants you to stay in Rome."

Marcus halted out front of a basket store. "Nope." He shoved his hands down his pockets and rattled the loose change inside. "I took this job so that I could get off the graylist. And when we've finished, I get to go back to LA and start my life over."

"I know," Negulesco replied quietly.

"I'm getting on that Pan Am flight and neither you nor Zanuck can stop me." The edges of the lira coins dug into Marcus's fingers. He pressed them harder until they hurt. "I've been counting the days since we got here. He can't snatch this away from me."

Negulesco wrapped an arm around Marcus's shoulders and pulled him farther along the sidewalk. "There are worse things in the world than having someone like Darryl Zanuck owe you a favor."

Marcus shrugged away the director's arm. Its intended intimacy wasn't lost on him, but it felt like a heavy yoke. The two men veered into a side street. It was a relief to step away from the unsettling bustle. "What were his words, exactly?"

"It was a P.S. at the end of his telegram. He said that he had extra duties for you to complete."

"But he didn't say what?"

"You're to expect a telephone call sometime next week."

"Don't those trans-Atlantic calls cost a fortune?"

"They do, which means it must be important. And that means he trusts you. Trust is not a quality that comes easily to the Zanucks of this world."

"So I'm supposed to wave you off at the airport, then sit around until the telephone rings?"

"Think of it as enjoying the Eternal City on someone else's dime," Negulesco advised. "And while you're here, maybe you'll have to run a few errands."

They were standing at a pasta store window that held fifty different sorts, composed like a Picasso cubist sculpture. The arrangement was astonishingly clever, and must have taken hours to assemble.

*I'm a forty-seven-year-old messenger boy.*

"You won't be off any list, gray or black, until Zanuck says so." Negulesco pulled at Marcus's elbow. "Let's take a breather on that bench over there in the shade."

It was noticeably cooler on the south side of the street. Marcus felt the tension slip from his shoulders. "If you were to take an educated guess about what these errands might be . . .?"

The director watched an old lady dressed from bonnet to shoes in widow's black shuffle past, dragging a shopping cart behind her. Every dozen steps or so, she stopped to fan herself with her purse or nod to a storeowner she knew.

"Movie audiences are getting more sophisticated. Fake backlot versions of the Spanish Steps and the Colosseum don't cut it anymore. For pictures like *Three Coins in the Fountain*, the studio is selling Europe as an authentic shooting destination. I imagine Zanuck's going to want lots of scenic pictures of Rome."

"That's not something he needs to place a trans-Atlantic call for."

"I know, which is why I'd put my money on Bella Darvi. She's one of his new protégés. Her name came up a few times in that telegram. With *The Robe* poised to clean up at the box office, I think he's looking at casting her in *The Egyptian*."

*The Robe* was Fox's first picture in the new widescreen CinemaScope format and was set to premiere in LA the following week. In her most recent letter, Kathryn had told Marcus that Zanuck was expecting the movie "to out-DeMille DeMille."

But it was Marcus who had originally planted the idea for *The Robe* in Zanuck's head. Hope warmed his chest as clues started to fall into place.

"Does Zanuck want to film *The Egyptian* at Cinecittà?" he asked Negulesco.

"The studio still has a mountain of frozen funds locked up over here—but that might be an excuse."

"For what?"

"If they film in Italy, he might have to make a trip to ensure the cast and crew are happy."

"He didn't do it for *Three Coins*."

"Ah, but our picture doesn't feature Bella Darvi."

Another puzzle piece. "She isn't just a protégé, is she?"

"You asked for an educated guess, Marcus. And if life has educated me about one thing, it's that men like Darryl F. Zanuck can think with only one part of their anatomy at a time."

Halfway down the block, a church bell announced that it was one o'clock.

Negulesco got to his feet. "There's a place not far from here that serves the best saltimbocca alla Romana in the whole city. Care to join me?"

"Thanks," Marcus said, "but I need time to think. I'll see you at the Trevi."

Negulesco headed back the way they'd come, dissolving into the crowd of hungry locals emerging from doorways in search of lunch. "Ciao!" and "Benvenuto!" echoed off the walls as cafés and bars started to fill.

Marcus stood up and pulled his shirt away from the sweat that coated his back. He thought more clearly when he was in motion, which usually meant swimming laps, but the Garden of Allah pool was 6,327 miles away, so he'd have to make do with walking.

He turned left and headed toward the church. The bell was silent now; it had done its duty for another hour. But as he drew closer, a growing sense of trepidation rose in his throat.

*Jesus H. Christ on a bicycle built for two, you've got to be kidding me.*

For more than a month, Marcus had done everything he could to avoid standing in this exact place. Every time he'd found himself close by, he'd gone out of his way to steer clear of the Jesuit seminary off the Piazza Colonna. And yet here he was ten steps from the matching pair of ornately carved doors that separated him from Oliver. His fingers instinctively reached for the edge of his left sleeve to fiddle with the gold-and-emerald cufflink that now lay at the bottom of a fountain.

A burly man wearing a dark blue suit swept past Marcus; their shoulders brushed as he marched toward the church door. He grasped the circular brass doorknocker and pounded it against the wood.

"APRA QUESTO PORTELLO!"

During his time in Rome, Marcus had picked up a fair smattering of Italian. *Open this door!*

"ORA!"

*Now!*

The man tightened his grip and assaulted the door. "APRA QUESTO PORTELLO!" His bellowing brought no response. He pulled off a shoe and struck the door with the heel. The sharp sound made café patrons look up and pigeons take to the air.

"DEVO PARLARE CON QUALCUNO! OGGI! ORA!"

*I must speak with someone! Today! Now!*

He struck the door again and again until a chunk of weathered wood broke off and fell at his feet. The man gathered it up off the cobblestones, took a couple of steps back, and threw it at the doors.

"NON SIETE UN SANTUARIO! SIETE UNA PRIGIONE!"

*You are not a sanctuary! You are a prison!*

His face now flushed bright, he turned and stomped past Marcus, muttering a stream of Italian too heated for Marcus to catch. The lunchtime crowds parted for him as though his fury were a contagious disease. Soon he was out of sight and the street gradually resumed its customary hubbub.

Marcus walked to the doors of Oliver's seminary. The chunk of wood was an angel, about the size of his palm.

Three years ago, when he'd first arrived in Rome to work on *Quo Vadis*, Marcus had been a refugee. He had seen the Eternal City as an escape hatch from the Hollywood blacklisting that had killed his career.

But now it felt different.

Dusty. Dirty. Decaying.

The magazines might have dubbed it the center of the burgeoning jet set, but to Marcus it felt like a city stuck in its Roman Empire glory. It was the past, and he wanted to get on with his future. He felt like taking off his own shoe and banging it against the doors. That nutty guy was right. *You are not a sanctuary. You are a prison.*

# CHAPTER 2

Gwendolyn Brick sat at a worktable in the corner of Twentieth Century-Fox's costume department. It was a vast rectangular room with a row of long windows near the high ceiling that allowed California light to stream in. Eight tables sat in two rows, each offering a luxurious expanse on which to spread a seventeenth-century wedding dress or a gypsy skirt. A wall ran parallel to them, packed with bolt after bolt of the finest fabrics Gwendolyn had ever run her fingers along: Armenian needlelace, Crêpe de Chine, worsted wool, softer-than-soft mohair. Loretta Young had given Gwendolyn carte blanche to design anything she wanted, so it was all there for the taking.

She contemplated the sketches laid out in front of her: a floor-length ball gown in white lace; an organza shin-length tea dress; a Chanel-esque woolen suit; an ankle-length duster in shot silk. Gwendolyn didn't know Miss Young well enough yet to anticipate what she'd say, so all she could do was wait.

Everyone in the department said she was one of the most professional actresses in Hollywood. The woman had a television show to put together, so she wasn't likely to be sitting at home leafing through magazines.

Gwendolyn pulled Marcus's latest letter from her purse. He opened with "Buona sera di Roma" in uncharacteristically wobbly penmanship—a sure sign that he had been tipsy when he wrote it.

"So sorry!"

Loretta Young sailed through the swinging doors looking chic in a dark plum pencil skirt and matching jacket, perfect hair and makeup. She held out her hand. "You must be Gwendolyn Brick?"

Gwendolyn shook it. "It's so nice to meet you in person, Miss Young."

"We're going to be working closely together so you must call me Loretta." She half-turned to the teenager trailing behind. "This is my daughter, Judy." The girl forced a tight I-don't-want-to-be-here smile.

Loretta pulled off her gloves and stowed them in her handbag, which she deposited on Gwendolyn's chair. "I'm dying to see what you've come up with."

Gwendolyn laid out the four sketches on her table and stood back to let the actress study them. Gwendolyn looked over at Judy, who'd parked herself in a chair next to the water cooler. She pulled out a paperback and started reading it with an air that fell somewhere between resigned and resentful.

Loretta tapped a freshly lacquered nail to her pointed chin and tsked. "I'm afraid none of these will do."

Two days to complete four sketches for someone she'd never met was like driving at night with the headlights switched off. Not an insurmountable hurdle, but hardly the best way to get the job done.

Gwendolyn ran her finger back and forth along her collar until she had stifled the urge to scream. "When we spoke on the phone, you said I had carte blanche to create anything—"

"I don't think I said *that*," Loretta broke in.

Gwendolyn looked down at her sketches, unsure how to respond.

"But you did, Mother." Loretta's daughter dropped *The Snake Pit* into her lap. "I was there when you took that call."

"Judy," Loretta warned.

"Those were your actual words: carte blanche. So you can't—"

"That's enough." Loretta turned to Gwendolyn. "There's going to be a door. I'll open it onto the set and sweep through, make a little turn to close it behind me, and then I'll walk directly toward the camera. What I want is something that will catch the lights, flare out as I spin, and swirl about me as I move."

Gwendolyn pointed to the ball gown sketch. "Ball gowns are made to sweep and swirl."

"The set is a cozy little den, as though I'm inviting the audience into my home. Nobody wears a ball gown in a den."

*And that's the sort of information that would've been handy forty-eight hours ago.*

"In addition to which—" Loretta flicked the swatch of white lace "—the dress can be anything but white because the door I sweep through is white, so I don't want to be lost against it. But other than that, I want you to feel free to create whatever you wish."

*But not a ball gown, a tea dress, a suit, or a duster. Or anything in white.*

Loretta bit down on her lower lip as her large gray eyes narrowed in concentration. "What I meant was, anything but an empire cut. I do not look good in high-waisted dresses."

There was nothing in Gwendolyn's sketches that remotely suggested empire cuts.

"And when I say anything but white, I mean nothing light-colored. Nothing pale, so no pastels, either. Any sort of neckline is fine but I'd prefer no halter necks and nothing squared. One-shoulder designs are acceptable, and while I'm not a fan of Queen Anne necklines, let's not discount them altogether. As for patterns, polka dots are rarely flattering, in my opinion. Tiny dots might be okay, but no larger than a dime. Other shapes, like stars or leaves or feathers, can work wonderfully well. That is, of course, unless—"

"Oh, Mother, please!" Judy tossed her paperback onto her chair and started crossing the room. "Like it or not, your movie career is behind you."

Loretta looked around, relieved to see they were alone. "I hardly think you're qualified—"

"Look who they paired you with on that last picture at Universal. John Forsythe is a nice guy, but he's just a TV actor. Virtually a nobody."

"Must you remind me?"

"Have you heard about Betty Grable?" Judy persisted. "I sat next to a couple of secretaries in the commissary yesterday and one of them was saying that Betty's next movie is called *Three for the Show*, and they're casting some guy called Jack Lemmon. Another TV actor."

Loretta pressed her lips together and scratched the back of her neck, careful to look anywhere but at her daughter.

"You're forty now, Mother. Your leading lady days?" She snapped her fingers. "Pffft!"

Loretta raised an eyebrow at Gwendolyn. "My daughter, the psychic."

"I'm just a realist," Judy said. "If you want to continue acting, your future's in television. You may as well embrace it instead of putting up all these restrictions."

Loretta and Judy glared at each other in a way that told Gwendolyn they'd had this quarrel before.

A trio of seamstresses entered the room laughing about Robert Wagner's ridiculous wig, their arms filled with medieval costumes from *Prince Valiant*. It didn't take them long to read the tension. They deposited the leather tunics and chainmail armor on the nearest workbench and hurried away.

Judy returned to her chair. "They're doing retakes for *River of No Return* on Stage Seven and I'm going to watch."

Loretta jammed her hands on her hips. "I doubt that Mr. Negulesco—"

"He told me I was welcome at any time." Judy threw her book into her purse, and strode to the swing doors. "I'll see you at home."

"I'm sorry you had to hear that," Loretta told Gwendolyn. "And on our first day together."

"I've heard worse."

Loretta ran a fingertip down the side of the tea dress sketch and along the bottom. "What do *you* think?"

"I think your daughter has a thing or two to learn in the art of diplomacy."

Loretta smiled weakly. "She's been at a loose end since graduating high school. I thought perhaps if I brought her with me to the studio, she might find . . ." She fluttered her eyelashes and let out a little sigh. "Everything changes when an actress turns forty." Her voice took on a fragility she usually saved for the emotional scenes in her movies.

"It's not fair, is it?" Gwendolyn said.

"If you're Gary Cooper or John Wayne or Jimmy Stewart, who cares if you're forty—or sixty? Those roles keep on coming down the pipeline. But once a woman steps over a certain line in the sand, they're looking at the twenty-year-old who just stepped off the bus from Omaha. They look at you and think to themselves *We could get her to play the mother.*"

"This is a big change for you," Gwendolyn said gently. *You and me both.*

Not too long ago, Gwendolyn had been running her own Sunset Strip boutique, famous for its signature fragrance. But then she fell afoul of a squalid rag called *Confidential.* She had been relieved, therefore, when Fox's leading costumer, Billy Travilla, had hired her to work at the studio's costuming department. He wanted her on hand to help wrangle an increasingly erratic Marilyn Monroe, as well as assist on pieces for other movies. All this on top of designing for *Letter to Loretta.*

What she hadn't counted on was having to deal with a capricious star unprepared for the transition out of romantic leading roles in feature films and into hosting a television show.

"May I be frank?" Gwendolyn ventured. *For my sanity as much as yours.*

"By all means."

"I believe your daughter's not far off the mark."

"I probably don't want to hear this, but go on."

"I think you've been handed an opportunity. Look at Lucille Ball. The other day I read in *TV Guide* that more people watch *I Love Lucy* every week than saw her last seven movies combined. If this show is a hit, you could be seen by millions. And if that's the case, you get to make a wow of an entrance every week and countless people will see it."

"The big entrance at the top of the show? That was my idea."

"And it was a good one." Gwendolyn brushed her sketches off the table and onto the floor. "Let's start from scratch." She took a blank sheet and drew two vertical lines down the page, then wrote YES at the head of the left-hand column, NO in the middle, and MAYBE on the right. "We make a list of what looks good on you, and what doesn't, and what's up for negotiation."

Loretta's shoulders slumped. "What if I change my mind?"

"That's what erasers are for. We've got ten days to create an eye-catching gown that will allow you to make such an entrance that America will be forced to tune in the following week to see what you'll be wearing. So tell me, what goes at the top of the YES list?"

Loretta stared bleakly at Gwendolyn's paper. "I'd prefer my career was based on acting ability and not how I looked in a new frock."

*And I'd prefer to be designing Marilyn Monroe's wardrobe in* There's No Business Like Show Business, *but we'll take what we can and be happy with it otherwise we'll go nuts wishing for a life that used to be. If I can say goodbye to Chez Gwendolyn, you can say goodbye to movies.*

Gwendolyn tapped the tip of her pencil on the YES she'd printed across the first column. "Shall we begin?"

# CHAPTER 3

The alabaster tower of the Carthay Circle Theatre blazed like a Roman candle under the four searchlights trained on its whitewashed walls.

Kathryn handed her car keys to the parking valet. *Roman candle,* she thought. *That's not bad.* She pulled out her notepad and jotted it down.

When she'd first heard that the director of *Roman Holiday* had cast a newcomer called Audrey Hepburn, she had made the rookie mistake of dismissing the unknown out of hand. Casting nobodies in starring roles wasn't unprecedented, but the idea flopped more often than it flourished.

The chances of this European greenhorn making good opposite Gregory Peck, who was coming off his *David and Bathsheba* smash were slim at best. Kathryn had taken to calling her The Other Hepburn in her column until she'd learned that the girl had starred on Broadway in *Gigi* and that her mother was a Dutch baroness, so her role as a European princess wasn't too much of a stretch.

Chastened for her curt assumption, Kathryn had paid more attention as production photos of the movie started to circulate, showing a poised Hepburn blooming under William Wyler's astute guidance. By the time the movie was ready for its unveiling, the entire world was primed to see what this swan was all about.

Kathryn waved to the rowdy moviegoers installed on wooden bleachers. An usher in a black-and-red uniform pulled the door open and welcomed her with a program. She accepted it with a nod and stepped inside. The face of her beau, Leo Presnell, loomed above the heads of invitees assembling around the crowded foyer.

He kissed her cheek. "You're right on time." He seemed surprised.

"You make it sound like I'm not punctual!" She swiped him across the shoulder with her program. "I'll have a manhattan, and make it snappy."

Leo pointed to the bar, where a matching pair of cocktails was set up next to a bowl of peanuts.

"Does this mean you're thoughtful or that I'm predictable?"

He pressed his hand to the small of her back and nudged her toward the bar. "It means we know each other very well."

The manhattan wasn't as chilled as she liked it, but the bartender had blended the bourbon and vermouth perfectly. Kathryn took a second sip and exhaled slowly with a low groan, letting the tension of the day leak out of her.

She knew she had taken a risk earlier that afternoon when she rode the elevator to the seventh floor of 510 Spring Street, where the National Council of Negro Women kept their offices.

A month ago, when Kathryn had stepped in front of a radio microphone to sabotage evangelist Sheldon Voss's scam to bilk thousands of dollars from unsuspecting believers, the Council had been the first worthwhile cause that came to her mind. It was run by a formidable no-nonsense type named Mrs. Cornelia Wyatt, who welcomed Kathryn with a hug to her substantial bosom and insisted they share a cup of "the best damned coffee you'll find west of Little Italy." Alongside the coffee, Mrs. Wyatt had set down a slice of rhubarb pie big enough to choke the last four winners at Santa Anita.

"It must have taken you ladies a week to count all those quarters," Kathryn had told her.

"The grand total came to $8,137.25—you should have seen our faces."

"I wish I'd been here to witness it for myself."

"Miss Massey, you can't begin to know the good that money will do among black folk all over the state."

As heartwarming as that was to learn, Kathryn had been there to test a theory. "You should tell Sheldon Voss."

Mrs. Wyatt sneered. "Oh honey, the decision to donate those funds had nothing to do with that no-account hustler."

Kathryn swallowed a chunk of melt-in-the-mouth deliciousness. "You think Sheldon Voss is a charlatan?"

"I know it, and I know you know it." Mrs. Wyatt spooned sugar into her coffee and stirred it leisurely. "We don't often receive manna from heaven, so when it comes our way, we're not disposed to question the whys and wherefores. But between you, me, and my rhubarb pie, we knew that money was intended for the eighth floor."

Kathryn knew a rat when she smelled one and she'd been smelling one since she learned where Voss's Quarter Cans were supposed to be delivered. "The eighth floor is why I'm here. It houses the FBI, doesn't it?"

Mrs. Wyatt closed her office door; the chatter of typewriters and telephones dropped away. "Officially, the eighth and ninth floors of our building are unoccupied, but we hear them walking around, sometimes yelling fit to wake Beelzebub himself. Those agents, they're all cut from the same cookie mold. They think they blend in, but they don't. When you're riding the elevator with a Bureau boy, you know it."

"Do you ever speak with any of them?" Kathryn asked.

"We ain't nothing but a bunch of black women, but I'll tell you something for nothing: word around the building is that the FBI's LA office has gone rogue."

Kathryn pushed away the rest of her pie; she simply couldn't finish such a huge wedge. "You don't say."

"The week ahead of Voss's broadcast, this building was swarming with Voss Vanguards mixing with them Bureau boys. They were in cahoots and ain't nobody going to tell me any different."

"Has Voss ever shown his face around here?"

The woman's mouth flattened into a determined line. "I'm not about to let some two-faced hustler like that claw back one single quarter. Not that that's likely, considering what's happened."

After Voss's Sea to Shining Sea March, which had culminated in a tent revival meeting in MacArthur Park, Kathryn had expected Voss would announce a new venture. Perhaps another march from California back to Washington, DC, or a radio show, or maybe he'd build his own church. But instead, the most publicity-hungry media celebrity of 1953 had disappeared like he'd been nothing more than a mass hallucination.

Both the public and the press—Kathryn included—began to speculate whether Voss's vanishing act was a replay of Aimee Semple McPherson's "disappearance," when she resurfaced a few weeks later with a patently phony kidnapping story.

But Voss was too wily, too greedy, and far too egotistical to stay out of sight for long. Kathryn hoped Cornelia might have had a Voss sighting she was keeping to herself—Kathryn was desperate to find the guy. Minutes before she'd walked on stage to announce his "donation," Voss had admitted to Kathryn that he'd helped frame her father's conviction for treason. As far as she was concerned, Voss was the reason why Thomas Danford was in Sing Sing and only he held the key to getting her father exonerated.

Voss going to ground was a wrinkle she hadn't counted on. But nor was this information that the LA office was playing outside the FBI rule book. Could she use it as leverage?

"Bad day?" Leo asked, snapping Kathryn back into the present. She hadn't shared with him what she'd learned since the night of the meeting. She felt like she was wading into a murky pit of morally questionable quicksand. The more she shielded him from it, the quicker he could claim ignorance in case the situation became dire.

"Kathryn, my darling! How *are* you?"

Edith Head emerged from the crowd, her arms outstretched.

"I hear your work on *Roman Holiday* is Oscar-worthy," Kathryn said.

"We'll see," Edith responded, feigning indifference. "That girl is all bones and long limbs, so it was a challenge to camouflage her flaws."

"If the production stills are anything to go by, I'd say you've pulled it off."

"Only if it works on screen." Edith permitted herself an inscrutable smile. "Of course, I've encountered no such problems with Grace on *To Catch a Thief*."

The other big news over the summer of '53 was how Alfred Hitchcock had lured Cary Grant out of self-imposed retirement. Cary had declared that the rise of Method actors like Marlon Brando meant that moviegoers were no longer interested in seeing his style of screen acting. Six months later Hitchcock cast him opposite Grace Kelly.

"As soon as Grace walked into my office," Edith went on, "I had inspiration for half a dozen outfits. If I couldn't use them in the movie, I knew any of them could be part of her press junket wardrobe. We're a match made in heaven. Her words, not mine."

The front doors of the Carthay Circle Theater swished opened and a thick knot of people marched in. At its center stood the svelte figure of Audrey Hepburn in a white strapless dress.

"She really is like a swan, isn't she?" Kathryn commented. "That beautiful, long neck." Now that she could see The Other Hepburn in person, Kathryn felt bad for having dismissed her so cavalierly.

"She's a sweet little thing," Edith said. "How she'll survive the minefields of Hollywood is anyone's guess."

A semicircle of flashbulbs besieged Hepburn.

"Someone needs to hand her a cheeseburger." Kathryn took out her notebook again and scribbled down a few observations. "Look at those collarbones."

"She confided in me how hard it is for her to keep the weight on. Chronic starvation during the war, apparently."

Hepburn caught sight of Edith and gave a little wave. She glided her hand down the white tulle and gave Edith the thumbs-up. She looked like she wanted to stop for a chat, but the momentum of her entourage propelled her into the auditorium.

Kathryn finished off the last of her manhattan, bid Edith farewell, and took Leo's arm.

Paramount had allocated them seats in the eleventh row, directly behind James Mason, who was about to start work on Judy Garland's *A Star is Born* remake at Warners. He was keenly aware that he'd gotten the part of Norman Maine after more than a dozen actors had knocked it back, including Bogart, Flynn, and Peck. He'd told Kathryn he was going to give the best he could to what was probably a thankless role in the shadow of a towering talent like Garland making her comeback.

They were still chatting when the house lights went down and the credits began to roll. The travelogue of images around Rome—the Colosseum, the Forum, Vatican City—reminded Kathryn how deeply she missed Marcus.

To anyone who didn't know him better, his frequent letters told of an enchanted life: three-hour lunches of mouth-watering pasta and smooth chianti, sunset walks through the gardens of the Villa Borghese, people-watching on the Piazza Navona. But she also knew of a recent trans-Atlantic phone call. Marcus's frustration over being trapped in Rome seeped between the lines.

Around about the scene where Gregory Peck shocks Audrey Hepburn by pretending to have lost his hand in the Mouth of Truth, Kathryn's attention began to splinter from the charming romantic comedy unspooling on the screen.

A four-word phrase repeated over and over in her head.

*To Catch a Thief.*

*To Catch a Thief.*

*To Catch a Thief.*

Sheldon Voss was a thief. She didn't believe for a minute that he was gone for good. Ruthless shysters like that aren't easily thwarted. But he had hidden himself away so well that nobody could find him. If Kathryn was going to get her father exonerated, she had to do it by either luring Voss out of hiding or sending someone on his trail. A job like that took a professional.

Her mind turned to the private eye she had employed to look into Voss's murky past. When she'd first met Dudley Hartman, she hadn't been immediately impressed. She'd been hoping for a bulldog, but he'd struck her as more of a basset hound. He did come up with the goods, though.

"It's time I paid Mr. Hartman another visit," she muttered to herself.

Leo leaned over. "What's that, dear?"

"This movie makes me want to go to Rome for another visit."

*Maybe it doesn't take a thief to catch a thief. Perhaps it only needs a clever trap.*

# CHAPTER 4

Darryl Zanuck had called Marcus right after Fox launched *The Robe*, still euphoric from how his first CinemaScope movie had already grossed a record-breaking $35,000. Then he'd sobered up and told Marcus to take notes "because this is costing me five bucks for every ten seconds."

As Negulesco had predicted, Zanuck wanted photos of Rome. "Tons and tons. Every part of the city, every time of day; scenic panoramas, fountains, piazzas, parks, Roman ruins, as well as any old-time building you see with atmosphere. Give me local color, too. Outdoor markets, pretty girls, Italian lovers, handsome slickers—but not any of those greaseball types. Make sure they're good-looking, like Rossano Brazzi. Beefcake for the gals and cheesecake for the guys."

Marcus assured him he knew exactly what he wanted. "Anything else?"

The pause that followed set Zanuck back nearly five bucks. "I need you to find an apartment."

"Any specific area or size?"

"It's gotta be in a classy area, preferably not too far from Cinecittà. But I want a penthouse, y'understand? I can't stand to hear people walking around above me."

"How many bedrooms?"

A three-dollar pause. "Two bedrooms, two bathrooms."

"That might be tricky. Most places have a shared bathroom down the hallway."

"When money is no object, trust me, doors always open."

"Sure," Marcus said. "When do you think you'll go into production?"

"What?"

"Isn't this for *The Egyptian*?"

"How the hell did you figure that out?"

Marcus didn't want to get Jean Negulesco into trouble for blabbing outside school. "I pal around with Kathryn Massey. She gives me the inside scoop from time to time. And with your *Robe* success, I put two and two together."

Zanuck grunted. "Start shopping around for possibilities."

"Certainly." Marcus let two dollars' worth of trans-Atlantic static fill Zanuck's ear. "And then do I get to come home, free from the blacklist *and* the graylist?"

Another grunt came down the line, but it was more of a begrudging *Yeah, okay.*

Marcus was midway through his thanks when Zanuck hung up.

The next day a telegram advised Marcus that a wire transfer for three hundred dollars awaited him at the American Express office near the Spanish Steps. Three hundred bucks bought a hell of a lot of linguini. He could easily afford better accommodations than Signora Scatena's modest pensione, but how long was this money supposed to last? A week? A month? Until Christmas?

With this much uncertainty and very little left in his Hollywood bank account, Marcus elected to stay put. His closet was perfect for a darkroom, and nobody made stuffed zucchini flowers like the signora.

He spent the next couple of weeks capturing the damp San Callisto catacombs on the Appian Way, the countless columns of the Vatican City, and every breathtaking vista and charming nook tucked into secluded squares in between. Each day he'd venture out with ten rolls filling his Florentine leather courier bag. If Zanuck wanted magnificent shots of Rome, Marcus would make sure his publicity department got a proverbial embarrassment of riches.

But for all his zigzagging, he saw few signs that anybody had a penthouse for rent. The few that he found turned out to be converted attics—a far cry from the lavish penthouse where Zanuck was planning to stash his "protégée."

But no matter where he was—strolling the gardens of the Villa Borghese or sampling every café that dotted Trastevere—he avoided Piazza Colonna. That is, until one warm Thursday afternoon late in September when, after he'd visited every fountain, outlook, and temple worth photographing, Marcus had once again felt the magnetic pull of those ornately carved doors.

He told himself he'd walk past once and once only. And he'd give the doors a quick glance to see if the priests had reattached that broken angel.

The street wasn't as busy as it had been the day he and Negulesco had wandered by. Most of the cafés had survived the lunch rush and were now catering to tourists looking to revive their spirits with a plate of cannoli.

The angel was back in place, but fragments of wood had splintered away, allowing gobs of dried glue to dribble onto an eight-stringed lyre directly below.

A deep longing to see Oliver overcame him.

*One more time. I need a final goodbye – no, I deserve one.*

He lifted the hinged brass doorknocker and banged it, hard as he could, three times. When that drew no response, he cupped his hands around his mouth.

"C'è qualcuno dentro?" *Is anybody inside?*

He knocked again. "Voglio parlare con qualcuno." *I want to speak with someone.*

The doors remained closed.

"You must shout more loud to get the attention."

The guy Marcus had encountered the last time was dressed in the same dark blue suit, but now he wore an altogether different expression. More bemused, less furious.

"Excuse me?" Marcus said.

"You must make the noise with all your muscles."

He was more handsome when he wasn't scowling. He possessed the full face of a man who enjoyed his fettuccine Alfredo, but was saved by a well-defined jawline and a Kirk Douglas cleft in his chin.

"You mean with my shoe?" The guy pulled his brows together until Marcus fingered the broken angel. "I was watching when you did this."

"I was very angry."

"Two people can make more noise than one," Marcus said.

The guy stared at the door, the angel, then back at Marcus. He leaped the four steps that separated them. "If we are together, we can make two times more sound. If you hit the – what is this called in English?"

"Doorknocker."

"*Si!* You bang-bang-bang with the doorknocker, and I—" he pulled off a polished black leather shoe "—bang-bang-bang with this. Together we will be very loud!"

"Try not to break an angel," Marcus said. "It might be bad luck."

The man's face lit up. Marcus had never encountered such vibrant hazel eyes flecked with moss green. "Ha! No breaked angels today. My name is Domenico."

"Marcus."

They shook hands.

Marcus lifted the heavy brass handle and started beating a slow, regular rhythm. Domenico grappled his shoe like a hammer and struck it against the wood in time with Marcus. After a dozen blows, he called out, "FACCI ENTRARE!" *LET US IN!* "Faster!" he told Marcus, and accelerated the pace.

"FACCI ENTRARE! FACCI ENTRARE! FACCI ENTRARE!"

They'd been going at it for a few minutes when the left-side door squeaked open and a horse-faced monk with a shaved head squinted through the crack. He whispered at them, too hoarse and low for Marcus to catch, but the *GO-AWAY!* tone needed no translation.

Marcus shoved his foot into the gap. He pushed past the startled monk and stepped inside a stone foyer dense with dank, stale air. A single naked bulb lit the space; its woeful light barely reached the corners.

"Questo è un oltraggio," the monk protested. "Dovete andare immediatamente!"

"Speak English," Domenico said. "This gentleman is from America."

The monk sneered at Marcus and then turned back to his fellow Roman. "You are not welcome here. This is sacred ground. You must go!" He reached for the iron door handle but Domenico brushed his hand away.

"I am here to see Jacopo Galano and I will not leave until I have. My American friend is here to see—" He looked at Marcus expectantly.

"Oliver Trenton," Marcus said, crossing his arms.

The monk strained to achieve an ingratiating smile. "When our students enter this seminary, they change their names. Whoever they were out there—" he poked a bony finger over Marcus's shoulder "—it makes no difference in here."

Marcus asked, "How many Americans have you accepted in the past five years?"

Comprehension filtered through the monk's dark eyes. "Ah! L'americano! Si."

"Where is he?" Marcus's eyes had grown used to the murky light. He spotted a narrow staircase made of the same cold, gray stone curving upwards to the left. He dashed to the foot of the stairwell. "OLIVER! OLIVER TRENTON!" The heavy stillness of the place swallowed his voice.

"Silencio! Your friend is no longer here." The monk fluttered a patronizing eye toward Domenico. "And your friend is also not here."

"How can you be sure?"

"The seminary closed at the start of summer. All students and graduates have been moved to other monasteries."

"But you must have a record of where each man was sent," Marcus said.

"The decisions come from a department within the Vatican. We receive the orders and we obey them."

Domenico wore a hangdog expression that Marcus wouldn't have suspected possible a few minutes ago. "We are too late."

"So that's it?" Marcus asked.

"They could be any place in Italy."

"Any place in the world where God's work is needed." The sliver of light hitting the gray stone floor widened as the heavy door squeaked fully open. "Your friends are in God's care now."

Marcus shielded his eyes from the bright afternoon light as Domenico drew in a lungful of fresh air. He let it out slowly as he pointed to the four-story column standing in the middle of the square. "Do you know the name?"

Marcus shook his head.

"In Italian we call it *La Colonna di Marco Aurelio*."

"The Column of Marcus Aurelius?"

Domenico rubbed his palms together. "And on the other side of the square, past *la colonna*, do you see Café Aurelio? They serve the best *ZABAGLIONE IN THE CITY. I WILL BUY YOU ONE AND YOU WILL SEE FOR YOURSELF HOW delizioso* it is. And we will wash it down with a macchiato—no!" He snapped his fingers and grinned. "A *caffè americano*! Come!"

Marcus knew when he was in the presence of a fellow queer. He felt a sense, almost a vibration, and this guy oozed it from every pore. He followed Domenico to the café and sat down next to him in a pair of matching red-and-white chairs. Keeping his eyes on the Marcus Aurelius column, he cleared his throat. "So, this Jacapo guy you wanted to see, is he your brother?"

"He is my lover."

The Catholic Church dominated every aspect of Italian life, shaping its rhythms, guiding its habits. Its teachings on homosexuality being what they were, Marcus had noticed a stealthy furtiveness to the local queers. The exchange of intense looks was still there, lingering a heartbeat longer than was polite, but it was rarely taken further than a discreet smile and backward glance. However, this guy didn't hesitate to state the facts, plain as day.

Domenic smiled. "But you guessed that, no?"

"I did."

"And Oliver, he is your boyfriend?"

"Was."

"Hmmmm. I suppose we should use the past tense now."

Their waiter arrived with zabaglione served in an oversized martini glass. Domenico lifted his metal spoon. "This was Jacopo's favorite dessert. In his honor, and in the honor of Oliver, we bid farewell!" He tapped the glass three times.

Marcus sat up. "Why did you do that?"

"Do what?"

"The way you hit the glass three times."

Domenico's eyes widened. "You know the word *amore*, yes? A! Mo! Re!" He pinged the glass stem three times again. "We did it when we were alone."

"Oliver and I had something similar." He thought about the cufflink he'd lost at the Trevi Fountain.

Domenico laid his spoon next to his coffee cup and fixed Marcus with a penetrating look. "You *americanos*. You take it most serious."

"We do?"

"Life. Money. Food. Time." He laid his hand on Marcus's wrist, wrapped his fingers around it, and gently squeezed. "Love."

*Admit it,* Marcus told himself. *His hand feels nice.* He said, "I don't know about that," and immediately regretted it when Domenico withdrew his hand.

"When was the last time you saw your lover?"

Marcus could feel his face flush. "Three years, give or take."

Domenico almost choked on his coffee. "*Years?*"

"I know. I must learn to let go."

An awkward silence followed until Domenico said, "I have made you feel uncomfortable. Please accept my apologies."

Marcus tasted his first mouthful of zabaglione. "This is custard!"

"Yes, but zabaglione sounds better, no?"

Marcus wished the guy would return his hand to his wrist but the moment had passed. "So tell me, Domenico," he said, "what do you do for a living?"

"I work in the movies. I am the man with the big mouth who orders extras to line up over here and spread out over there."

"I have a sister who does that same job."

"In Hollywood?"

"Columbia Studios."

"Rita Hayworth and Glenn Ford!"

The Zabaglione was velvety smooth and not too sweet. "Have you worked at Cinecittà?" Marcus asked.

"I have."

"I was working there this summer."

Domenico slowly pulled his spoon from between his full lips. "Three Coins in the Fountain."

"How did you know that?"

"I noticed you around. Always with your camera. Always so intent on your job."

Marcus blushed like a virgin at the senior prom. He'd forgotten how it felt to have been noticed from afar, and experiencing it again gave him a warm, floaty sensation.

# CHAPTER 5

Gwendolyn held up the organdy gown printed with snapdragons. "What do you think?"

Judy Lewis nodded. "Mom adores everything you've made for her. But you must know that, the way she gushes."

Gwendolyn threaded a mahogany hanger through the gown's shoulders. *Gushes?*

When Loretta had seen the gown for week one, her mouth said "yes" but her eyes said, "Perhaps this'll be okay, after all."

Week two's gown—a full-skirted tea dress in dark apricot—had brought a smile tinged with hesitation.

Gwendolyn's third gown was a tight sheath in puce wool. It didn't flurry around her like the previous two, but it displayed Loretta's hard-won figure in all the right places. It had earned an enthusiastic nod, but no gush.

"You've got a good eye for what works on her." Judy held a stray organdy off-cut in front of her mouth like an Arabian veil. "Do I look like Mata Hari?"

*With the bottom half of your face hidden, you look like your father.*

The true paternity of Loretta Young's "adopted" daughter had been the topic of conversation around poolside canasta at the Garden, but the discussion always ended with "But of course I'm certainly not going to be the one to tell the poor girl that her father is Clark Gable."

"Scheherazade," Gwendolyn said.

"Even better!"

Judy twisted the organdy through her fingers. It was a nervous habit she succumbed to whenever she hung around the costuming department waiting for her mother.

Gwendolyn started collecting loose threads. "No college for you?"

"I don't think it's necessary for what I—" She caught herself with a sharp inhale.

"What do you want to do?"

"Promise you won't tell her?"

"If you can't tell your mother what you want to do with your life, perhaps you ought to rethink your plan."

"I have to pick the right opportunity." She discarded the material. "We're always fighting, or making up, or maintaining a tentative truce until the next argument."

Gwendolyn rested a hip against the worktable. "My friend Kathryn and her mother are like that."

Judy snuck a peak at the far end of the room where a clutch of seamstresses hunched over Egyptian slave girl costumes. "You know what it's like, then."

Gwendolyn bent forward, creating a more intimate space. "In a second-hand sort of way."

"I want to be an—actress." She pushed the word out like it was *hooker* or *murderess*.

"I'm guessing from your tone that your mother won't approve."

"Not for a second."

Gwendolyn rested her chin in her palm, the way she often did whenever Kathryn came to her, wailing about Francine. "She seems to have done pretty well out of the acting game."

Judy frowned. "She'll see me as competition."

"I doubt that," Gwendolyn said. "She's got this TV show now, and it's rating its patootie off." Loretta's gambit to spend a sizable chunk of the budget on her entrance had proven to be astute. Each week the show pulled in more and more viewers keen to see what she wore. "And besides, you're eighteen. You're hardly likely to be going up for the same roles."

"Actresses don't think that way. Every pair of legs in a tight skirt is viewed as competition."

A studio messenger rushed into the room, "Gwendolyn Brick?" He deposited a note in front of her without saying a word and left as briskly as he had arrived.

> *Free for lunch? Please say yes. Meet me in the commissary? 12.30? Don't be late. I hate sitting there all by myself. MM xoxoxo*

Gwendolyn grabbed her purse. "If your mother shows up while I'm gone, tell her the dress is nearly done but if she wants to try it on, she should watch for pins. And if you want my opinion, she might not be overjoyed about the idea of you giving acting a go, but I doubt it'll be for the reasons you think."

Gwendolyn found Marilyn Monroe seated at a table in the middle of the bustling commissary trying to avoid spilling beef broth on her glittering red-and-gold costume.

She spotted Gwendolyn and pointed to a second bowl. Gwendolyn was hungry for more substantial fare, but the wistfulness in Marilyn's face made her rush right over.

They exchanged a brief kiss.

"It's wonderful to see you," Marilyn exclaimed, "I've been back from Canada for three weeks and we haven't had a chance to catch up!"

"They keep me real busy." Gwendolyn sampled the soup. It was the thinnest broth she'd ever tasted; the bowl probably didn't have more than twenty calories.

"Isn't it nutso?" Marilyn said. "You and me working at the same studio?"

Whatever trouble Marilyn had experienced on the Canadian location shoot for her next movie didn't seem to have left a mark. She glowed like a klieg light.

"How's *River of No Return* going?" Gwendolyn asked. "I hear you and Otto Preminger didn't get along so good."

Marilyn rolled her eyes. "Frankenstein with dysentery would be a gentleman compared to Preminger. I was not looking forward to the reshoots. When I learned that he's moved on to *Carmen Jones*, I almost sent his leading lady a note. 'Good luck, Dorothy Dandridge!'"

"What's next for you?"

Marilyn pushed away her bowl. She was only halfway through it. Surely she was still hungry. Or, cinched into a dress like that, maybe peeing was too hard to risk eating more.

"That's what I wanted to see you about. The *How to Marry a Millionaire* premiere is coming up and I desperately need something to wear."

"But surely Billy Travilla will be—"

"Word has come from high above that he's only to work on my screen costumes. I was distraught until I heard that you were on board. Do you think I could come over to your place and bounce around some ideas?"

Every photographer in town would be jostling to capture Marilyn's arrival. If she wore a Gwendolyn creation, it might be enough to lift her profile inside the studio.

"Hello!" Loretta materialized in front of them like Constance Bennett in *Topper*. "Sorry to interrupt, but I was so thrilled with the new dress that I had to come find you. We haven't met yet, have we?" she asked Marilyn as she laid her tray on their table. "I'm Loretta. Mind if I join you?"

Even in a room packed with people used to seeing stars all day long, the sight of Loretta Young and Marilyn Monroe seated together made heads turn in their direction.

"I'm sorry that I haven't seen your television show yet," Marilyn told Loretta. "I hear it's very good."

Loretta lifted a bowl of the same beef broth from her tray and set it in front of her. "It was a bear to get off the ground, but now that we have, it's skipping along nicely."

Sitting across from an It Girl of the past trying to impress an It Girl of the future, Gwendolyn realized that, even inside the citadel, women like these two still played the game.

Gwendolyn thought about Judy. Growing up in the shadow of a movie-star mother, surely she'd witnessed the price that Hollywood exacted from its women. At least she knew first-hand what she was letting herself in for.

"Haven't you?"

Gwendolyn blinked at Loretta. "I'm sorry, what?"

"I was saying you've probably already conjured a bunch of ideas for Marilyn's premiere."

"Yes, I have." *No, I haven't. See? Even I play the game.*

A twenty-year-old kid with a nervous twitch approached their table. "Miss Monroe?"

Marilyn knitted her brows. "Ready for me so soon?"

"Makeup'll need you in about ten minutes."

"Thanks, T.J. Tell Ben I'll be right over." She turned back to Loretta and Gwendolyn. "Sorry ladies, but with reshoots cutting into the budget, poor Mr. Negulesco is under pressure to get them done as quickly as possible." She made a point of shaking Loretta's hand. "It's been a pleasure, Miss Young."

Loretta smiled but did not ask Marilyn to call her by her first name. *Every pair of legs in a tight skirt is viewed as competition.*

Marilyn pulled at her corset and set off for the exit, oblivious—or pretending to be—to every eye in the cafeteria following her.

"Gracious!" Loretta exclaimed. "That lass sure is something."

Gwendolyn wanted to reassure Loretta that she herself was still something, but another messenger appeared at their table.

"Can I help you, young man?"

"I'm here to see Miss Brick."

"Oh." Loretta's gray eyes lost their focus.

"I'm the new messenger for Mr. Zanuck," the kid said. "He wants to see you this afternoon."

Gwendolyn could feel Loretta scrutinize her face for signs of surprise. "When?"

"Five o'clock sharp. His office."

"I'll be there."

The two women watched the messenger boy retreat.

"Why, Gwendolyn!" Loretta exclaimed. "Is your luncheon table always this eventful?"

"Hardly."

"Are you and Zanuck . . . *close*?"

Loretta tinged the brief hesitation near the end of her question with bitterness.

"We've met a few times, but I'd be surprised if he could pull my name out of the air."

Marcus had put pen to paper as soon as he'd hung up from Zanuck, detailing how he was tasked with finding a secluded penthouse where Zanuck could schtup his mistress. The mistress had an odd name. *What was it? Belle? Delle? Is that why I'm being summoned?*

"Apparently he *can* pull your name out of thin air." Loretta filled her face with a sweet smile. "Perhaps you could do me a favor?"

"If I can."

"There's a picture in pre-production called *A Woman's World* with Jean Negulesco directing. High gloss, very classy. There's a part I'd be perfect for. I got my agent to let it be known that I want the role, but it appears to have gone nowhere. Perhaps you could bring it up when you see Zanuck this afternoon?"

"I don't even know why he's summoned me."

"In case you can find a way, I'd appreciate it so very much."

Gwendolyn admired Loretta's refusal to be tossed aside in favor of fresher faces, but if Zanuck cast her in a movie, it wouldn't be because some peon like Gwendolyn Brick suggested it. On the other hand, Loretta had been at this game since before *The Jazz Singer*. At the very least, Gwendolyn would be doing her boss a favor.

"I can try."

* * *

Darryl Zanuck was selecting a pipe from a chrome rack behind his desk as Gwendolyn walked through the redwood door that opened into the mogul's huge office. "Miss Brick, always a pleasure." He indicated she could take either of the chairs in front of his desk.

She smoothed her dress as she lowered herself into the closest one.

"I need you." His candor made the hair on the back of Gwendolyn's neck stand up. "You and Monroe are friends, right?"

"We were having lunch together when your messenger—"

"I know. Here's my problem: she's becoming difficult to manage. *River of No Return* has been a nightmare."

"The reshoots with Jean Negulesco have gone smoothly, so I don't know that you can hold Marilyn solely responsible—"

"She's heading down the same goddamn road that every actress with great tits and a modicum of success heads down. She's already started showing up late, or not at all. She stumbles over her lines or blanks on them, fusses over her hair and makeup for hours." He lit his pipe. "I need her to quit draining the budget of every movie I put her in."

"You want me to give her a talking-to? I can certainly try, but I doubt—"

"I need someone reporting every move she makes as soon as she makes it."

Gwendolyn had played enough poker to know that Zanuck was consciously refusing to blink.

"You want me to spy on her."

During the war, the FBI had approached Kathryn to inform them if the people she worked with showed signs of falling prey to Communism. After one particularly stressful encounter, Kathryn had told Gwendolyn, "You don't know how it feels to be forced to squeal on people you love and admire." Gwendolyn was getting a taste of it just now, and it made her chest tighten.

"Don't think of it as spying." Zanuck used a gentler tone but he still hadn't blinked.

"A rose by any other name, Mr. Zanuck."

"Quoting Shakespeare now, are we?"

The guy played with his gold cigarette lighter. He was using it as a prop to control the conversation, and Gwendolyn resented how well the tactic worked.

He picked from his tongue a loose sliver of tobacco that she suspected wasn't there. "*Confidential* magazine ran an article that was so damaging, you had to close your store. The merchandise you couldn't sell was offloaded at a highly discounted rate, which failed to cover what you owed your suppliers. Consequently, Miss Brick, you're in debt. Quite deeply, I believe."

He pulled a long draw on his pipe and blinked his eyes with infuriatingly slow deliberation.

Everything Zanuck said was true. Her holding a regular job at Twentieth Century-Fox had helped convince Gwendolyn's bank manager to agree to pay off a fraction of her debt each week. It was going to take years, but at least it saved her from the ignominy of declaring bankruptcy.

Was Zanuck threatening to fire her? Or blackball her from the industry? After watching Marcus struggle for so many years, Gwendolyn knew the consequences of non-cooperation.

"I guess you leave me no choice."

"Oh, come now." He jumped to his feet again, but stayed on his side of the desk. "Don't look at me like I'm the Gestapo and you're the French Resistance. I'm just asking you to keep your eyes and ears open. Especially DiMaggio. If you catch wind of her marrying that wop, you tell me immediately. And I want you to talk her out of it."

*If Kathryn could worm out of her enforced obligations with the FBI, I can get around this egomaniac without losing my job.* "I'll do my best," she told him, "but I'm not her mother."

Zanuck's eyes crinkled with victory. "I hope not—I hear she's crazy."

Gwendolyn propelled herself from the chair. "I can't make any promises."

"Did I ask for any?"

It was a fair point, but Gwendolyn was in no mood to concede defeat. "By the way, Loretta Young wants you to consider her for the lead in *A Woman's World*."

Zanuck snorted. "Her? For a theatrical feature?"

"She's made over ninety pictures!"

"In the eyes of the public, she's now just a television actress.

"You cast Jack Lemmon opposite Betty Grable and he's a television actor."

"That's different. Jack's on his way up. Don't worry, Miss Brick. You've done what you promised. You can assure your boss that you pleaded her case."

Gwendolyn took a step backward. The carpeting in Zanuck's office was unusually plush and as she turned to go, her heel sank into the thick pile. She managed to recover before she stumbled back into the chair like a messy drunk at Ciro's. With her back now turned to Zanuck, she wasn't sure if he'd seen the expression on her face. She made a straight line for the exit and didn't breathe again until she closed the massive redwood door behind her.

# CHAPTER 6

It was now a week since that DAY in the Piazza Colonna and the idea that someone had noticed him around Cinecittà still made Marcus smile. It was thrilling to be on the receiving end of such a flattering confession, but it also made him realize how rusty his flirting skills were.

Seeing him redden like an ingénue, Domenico changed the subject. Was Cary Grant as handsome in real life as he was on the screen? Had Marcus ever danced with Ginger Rogers? How were the thick shakes at Schwab's? He had listened attentively as Marcus described premieres at Grauman's, parties at the Cocoanut Grove, and Hollywood Bowl concerts. Then without warning, he announced that he must take his mamma shopping for new shoes. He shook Marcus's hand warmly, assuring him it had been a pleasure, and set off across the piazza.

Seven days later, almost to the hour, Marcus was in his makeshift darkroom developing a roll of film that he'd discovered in his satchel, so he wasn't sure what might appear. Signora Scatena knocked on his door and said that a Signore Beneventi was here to see him. When he told her that he didn't know anyone by that name, a deep voice called out, "Zabaglione!"

Marcus cracked open the door. THE pint-sized signora wore an unsure expression over her usual scowl as she kept a grinning Domenico at bay. Though towering over her by two feet, he knew that to reach Marcus, he'd have to get past the signora first.

Marcus thanked her and asked Domenico to join him in the darkroom. It was a tight fit but as long as Domenico didn't move much, there was enough room for Marcus to do what he needed.

Domenico studied the contents of Marcus's developing tray. "What is this?"

"I'm not sure. So how did you find me?"

"You said you lived in a pensione on the Via Anzio so I started knocking on doors until your *proprietaria di casa* frowned at me like I was a Nazi spy and I knew I had the correct address." He peered more closely at the emerging photograph. "Is that Rossano Brazzi?"

About halfway through the *Three Coins* shoot, Negulesco had pulled Marcus aside and told him to take as many shots of Brazzi as he could. Joe Mankiewicz wanted to cast him in *The Barefoot Contessa* but was having trouble convincing Zanuck. If Marcus could get some great shots "of Brazzi in his natural habitat," Zanuck would see why he was perfect for the role of Count Vincenzo and Mank would be grateful.

It seemed to Marcus that his professional life consisted largely of accumulating favors for people with little hope that he would be in a position to cash any of them in.

Marcus let the solution run off the photograph and pegged it to the string rigged up overhead. The image showed Brazzi at the Colosseum. His light-colored suit contrasted with the curved shadows of the ancient arches in the background. Marcus had caught him midway to a belly laugh with his on-screen love interest, Jean Peters, throwing his hands in front of him as though preparing to catch a falling damsel in distress.

"You took this?" Domenico asked.

Marcus dropped the second photograph into the tray. "I did."

Domenico drew his face closer to inspect it. They were pressed shoulder to shoulder now; Marcus could feel the heat of Domenico's skin through his shirtsleeve. A heady blend of sweat, hair tonic, and cigarettes exuded from him.

"Your work is as good as Emilio Conti."

Marcus pegged the second photo and immersed a third. "Who's that?"

"Rome's most well-known *scattino*."

"*Scattino*?"

Domenico pulled his face away from the Brazzi portrait. "If you want to know this city, you must experience it in the gutters."

Marcus wanted to find Zanuck a place to hide his mistress and return to Hollywood; diving into the gutters was not part of the plan.

"What is the English word that means to take photographs very quickly?"

"Snap?"

"Si! A *scattino,*" Domenico explained, "means snapper. Someone who snaps a photo. *Scattini* are street photographers who take photos of people on the street, but also of movie stars drinking cappuccino and sipping Campari. They sell them to new movie magazines and make many monies."

"And this Emilio Conti, he's one of the biggest *scattini*?" Marcus asked.

"*Si,* but you could give him a run for his money. This expression is correct? A run for his money?"

"That's right," Marcus told him, "but I won't be in Rome for much longer. I'm not interested in giving anybody a run for any money."

Domenico moved on to the second photo, in which Brazzi and Peters sat on the edge of the Trevi Fountain waiting for Negulesco to set up their shot. Brazzi held his fingers together like he was describing an especially delicious meal. Marcus had taken that shot just after he lost Oliver's cufflink. Days later, when he waded into the water, it was gone.

"Where did you learn to take photos like a *scattino*?" Domenico asked.

He was staring at Marcus now in that open-eyed way that made Marcus's heart quicken. "On the set of *Quo Vadis,* I guess."

Domenico's lips parted. "You worked on *Quo Vadis*?"

"I helped patch the script together, but once that was done, the director got me to shoot production stills. It was the first time MGM had shot over here so they wanted it documented."

Domenico let out a whooping laugh. "I cannot believe it!" He planted his hands on Marcus's shoulders, his mouth pulled into a wide smile. "I have found him!"

"Who?"

"You are the famous mysterious *scattino*!"

"I doubt that very much."

"Sophia Loren!"

The name meant nothing to Marcus.

"Mamma mia! She is a new actress. Very exciting. Beautiful! So fresh and new. So Italian. Everybody is wild for her." He took in Marcus's blank face, then cast an eye over the undeveloped photos. "You finish these later?"

Domenico pinched the end of Marcus's collar and tugged him out of the darkroom.

* * *

The tall apartment buildings that lined Via Tuscolana sped past in a blur as their taxi headed north toward the old city. The tiny Fiat was a pre-war rattler that probably qualified as a jalopy. Domenico's right leg pressed against Marcus's left, from the hip right down to the ankle.

"Where are we going?"

A self-satisfied smile spread across Domenico's face. "When MGM made the premiere for *Quo Vadis*, we said, 'It is like Hollywood!' A red carpet. The huge lights that shine into the sky."

"Searchlights."

"*Si, si*. Everybody wanted to know about making the big Hollywood movie with the big Hollywood stars. Every detail about *Quo Vadis* was news. We have many magazines now, but the most popular is called *Epoca*. They published four pages of photographs taken on the set and it caused a *tumulto*."

"What was so special about these photos?"

"There was one in particular. A girl resting against a column, smoking a cigarette, with her arms crossed. But this girl had a large bosom, so when she squeezed them together, it looked even bigger."

Marcus could picture the girl quite clearly. She was probably not long out of high school, but she balanced her cigarette between two long fingernails like a young Greta Garbo or Hedy Lamarr. Not in looks, but in the sort of attitude she projected: *This movie-making game? I could take it or leave it.*

They skirted past the long Rome train station. Marcus asked, "The photo of this Sophia Loren—it caused a sensation?"

"Suddenly everybody is saying, 'Who is this beautiful vision?' But nobody knew! *Epoca* said that they bought the photos from the *Quo Vadis* production office, but it closed down after the *americanos* went back to Hollywood. So the mystery became a puzzle. Eventually, they found the girl in Naples and her career makes the explosion. But still, everybody is asking, Who was the *scattino*?" Domenico clapped his hands out of sheer glee. "It is YOU!"

The taxi came to a halt on a curving street, lined with trees whose thickly leafed branches formed a shady canopy. Domenico paid the driver and they unfolded themselves from the cramped cabin.

Cafés spilled onto the sidewalk, filling every square inch with iron tables and stiff-backed chairs. One café had black-and-white striped tablecloths; another had red-and-blue checks. The nearest one featured long-stemmed carnations sitting in metal tubes, but Domenico headed for a place a little farther along whose ashtrays were shaped like the Colosseum. He asked the waiter for a specific table, second from the end, facing the street.

"This is Via Veneto," Domenico replied. "And this place has the best rum baba in the city."

They pulled out their cigarettes and lit up.

"Why are we here?" Marcus asked.

"I was at this table when the editor of *Epoca* sat down at the one next to me and pulled out an early copy of the magazine and showed it to his friend. He opened it to the page with your *Quo Vadis* photos and pointed to the *bellissima* young girl. They were very noisy about it and all the customers wanted to see. The editor passed around the magazine and everybody made their opinion." Domenico pointed to himself. "Including me!"

The waiter arrived with their order. A rum baba was a small tube of golden-colored sponge cake saturated in so much rum that it glistened in the sun.

Domenico stubbed out his cigarette. "I pointed to the photo of Sophia Loren and told the editor, 'This is the photo everyone will be talking about.'"

Marcus had always been content to spend his days putting words in the mouths of the people who couldn't leave their house without causing a commotion. For the very first time now, he felt the lure of fame. He hated to admit how appealing it was.

Domenico jabbed at the rum baba with his fork. "*Epoca* sold the photos to other magazines. They were seen all over Europe—your photo of Sophia Loren is very famous now. You should stay in Rome and become a *scattino*!"

Back at the pensione, Marcus had a stack of letters from Kathryn, Gwendolyn, Doris, Bertie, and Quentin confessing their jealousy of his Roman sojourn, but he felt cut off from everyone and everything he cherished. Being held at the whim of Darryl Zanuck was merely a temporary situation that would be fixed as soon as he found the right penthouse. Then he'd be free to head stateside. But stay in Rome? For an indefinite length of time? No thanks.

Marcus took a bite of the cake. Slick with rum, it slid down his throat like a sweet oyster. "There are dozens of pensiones all over my neighborhood. Why did you come looking for me?"

Domenico delayed his answer by lighting up another Gauloise. "I was determined to find you."

"What I'm asking is why?"

Domenico's sheepish grin dimpled his cheeks and revealed a row of teeth whiter than they should have been. "I was watching my mother try on comfortable old-lady shoes and thought to myself, Look at her. She was not even thirty when my papa died and every day she puts on her black dress and black stockings and black shoes. Every day she is reminded of how she lost him. Every day she mourns him. Thirty-five years! I looked at her and I thought, I do not want to become like her!"

"I thought *I* was the one who took love too seriously. That's what you said."

"Jacopo and I were together for nearly twelve years."

"Not so easy to let go, huh?" Marcus stubbed out his cigarette and crushed the empty packet. He dropped it into the Colosseum ashtray. "But you were right. Jacopo and Oliver have let us go. We need to do the same thing."

"Why do you think I knocked on eighteen doors until I found you?"

For the first time since the *Three Coins* crew had left Rome, Marcus felt he wasn't completely alone. "Because I made you realize that hanging onto the past does nobody any good, and you need some help letting Jacopo go."

Domenico nodded. "And you, Signore Marcus Aurelius? Do you need help too?"

"My life is in Hollywood. I will be returning to it sooner or later. Could be next week, could be next month."

"We have only today."

A whirlwind of emotions roiled inside Marcus; fear battled hope while relief fought off guilt.

Domenico rapped his knuckles on the back of Marcus's hand. "If we spend the night together, will your *proprietaria di casa* throw us out in the morning?"

Signora Scatena was a four-foot-ten fireplug who'd witnessed so much in her lifetime that Marcus doubted the prospect of a couple of queers sleeping together would rattle her.

"I think we'll be safe," he said. "My bedsprings don't squeak."

# CHAPTER 7

Kathryn wiped down her kitchen counter. It was already clean, but she'd run out of distractions while she waited for Dudley Hartman.

She checked her watch.

It was two minutes past eleven.

She opened her front door and peered out. A new management team had recently bought the Garden and hired a contractor to repaint the entire place. The team of four men was working their way around, patching and painting each villa, and now they were working on Kathryn's. She knew it was silly to think that house painters would have the slightest interest in her hushed whispers, but at some point during the past month, she had stumbled from 'rational' to 'ridiculous' and wasn't sure how to get back again.

She didn't want to face Hartman alone. Nor did she want to involve Leo—should anything go wrong, she wanted to give him deniability. And Gwennie was working sixty-hour weeks at Fox and had enough on her plate.

It was Marcus she wanted by her side today. She kept expecting a cable saying that he'd be arriving home in a couple of days, but no missive had arrived. She'd have to do this alone.

Scanning the exit from the main house, she spotted a neighbor, Bertie Krueger, carrying a bag of Schwab's bagels. She was probably looking for someone to share them with, and normally Kathryn would beckon her inside, but not today.

She closed her door with an unambiguous thump.

What was customary when entertaining a private eye? Surely not a drink? Not on a Saturday morning.

She lit the gas underneath her coffee pot and pulled out a matching pair of cups from her cupboard. They rattled in their saucers as she laid them on the tiled counter. "This is where procrastination gets you," she admonished herself. "A whole month to work yourself up like a dithering ninny afraid of her own shadow. What's wrong with you?"

Four weeks had crawled by since the *Roman Holiday* premiere, when the title of Hitchcock's new movie had inspired her to catch a thief named Sheldon Voss.

But she kept putting off placing that call to Hartman. *I won't need to if Voss resurfaces*, she kept telling herself. When that didn't happen, she decided to give it until Marcus returned from Rome. But after a month, Voss still hadn't shown up and Marcus was still in Europe, so she'd had to put an end to this insufferable dilly-dallying and called Hartman.

The three sharp knocks shook her.

She pulled open the door and nearly laughed. It was the tension, of course, but unprofessional—not to mention cruel. She remembered now that Marcus had told her Hartman wasn't the sort of private eye who resembled a character conjured from the pages of Dashiell Hammett or Raymond Chandler. Marcus's description—"Moon-faced, with a blandly pleasant smile"—was close, but to Kathryn he looked like a cross between Porky Pig and S.Z. Sakall, with a dash of Peter Lorre thrown in for good measure.

She hid her blush by turning toward her living room. "Mr. Hartman, come in, please. I've put on some coffee."

Hartman sized up Kathryn's living room. "Black, no cream or sugar, thank you."

What details was he picking out? She pointed him to her dining table. "I thought perhaps sitting here might be more comfortable in case you want to take notes."

"Much obliged." He deposited his black briefcase on the table and withdrew a pad and pen. He took a seat and waited silently until she set his coffee in front of him and took the seat opposite. "So, Miss Massey, exactly what am I here to take notes about?"

"Sheldon Voss."

His eyebrows cleared the top of his wire-rimmed glasses. "I'd have thought you'd be happy he's disappeared."

"I grew up without a father, Mr. Hartman, but recently I learned that during the war he was imprisoned for treason under the Smith Act."

Only a handful of people knew her humiliating secret. Sharing it with one more person increased the chances of it getting out—an especially dicey move in a town that ran on the juice of a thousand rumors. Confessing to a virtual stranger took considerable nerve; the coffee occupied her hands and prevented a severe case of dry mouth.

"Conviction under the Smith Act is no small potatoes," Hartman said.

"I think about Ethel and Julius Rosenberg all the time."

"Is your father under the death penalty?"

"No, but he's in Sing Sing like they were."

"And what does this have to do with Sheldon Voss?"

The lanky painter in the spattered overalls propped a ladder against the wall next to her kitchen window. The way he whistled "You Can't Get a Man with a Gun" as he scraped away the cracking paint grated at Kathryn's nerves.

"Voss and I got into a heated confrontation and he admitted that he had my father framed."

"That's quite a confession to make in what I assume was a crowded backstage area."

"Imagine how I felt!" Kathryn gripped the delicate handle of the coffee cup and wished it held something stronger. "I was about to go on national radio in front of twenty million listeners."

"Do you recall precisely what Voss said?"

"He told me, 'I waited years to exact my revenge on your father.'"

"But did he admit to framing him for treason? Did he say those specific words?"

"Not precisely, no."

Kathryn watched Hartman jot down notes until it was too much to bear. She got up from the table and wiped down her counter.

"What *did* Voss say?" Harman asked.

The thought occurred to her that it might help if she didn't start acting like Lana Turner in *The Bad and the Beautiful*, but it was too late for that now. She slapped the rag into her sink.

"He started raving about how premarital fornication is a mortal sin, and about my father's wanton desires. My father got my mother pregnant without the benefit of marriage, so being the fire-and-brimstone preacher he is—or pretends to be—he jumped onto his moral high horse and—"

"May I ask your father's name?"

Kathryn fought against the disappointment sinking through her stomach. Hartman wasn't buying any of it. At least, not on her say-so. *And if my own private eye doesn't believe me . . .* "Voss may not have made a clear-cut confession, but it was a confession nonetheless."

"I merely asked your father's name."

A few feet away, on the other side of the wall, the whistling painter scratched and scoured, interrupting his tune with raucous grunts of effort.

"Thomas Danford."

Hartman looked up from his pad. "The candidate for Massachusetts governor?"

"You've heard of him?"

"Purely by chance. My sister is married to a political science professor at Amherst. He's a bit academic for my tastes, but an okay sort of chap. I only have to put up with him once a year over the Thanksgiving table so I sit and smile as he drones on and on about New England politics. One year it was all about the gubernatorial race and how some political neophyte was going to give the entrenched incumbent a run for his money. He seemed unstoppable until some sort of scandal blew up in his face and that was the end of that."

"The political neophyte was my father."

Outside, the irritating scraping and whistling stopped.

Skepticism still filled Hartman's face. "What do you wish me to do for you, Miss Massey?"

"Find Sheldon Voss."

The scraping started up again, followed by a knock on her door. Kathryn answered it to find Bertie standing there, her button eyes bright with hope.

"I guess you didn't hear me when I called out," she said. "Doris and I were going to have bagels and lox but she got called into the studio, so now I'm stuck with more bagels than—" She blinked. "Have I caught you at a bad time? It's not Marcus, is it?"

No, Kathryn assured her, Marcus was fine, but no, this wasn't a good time. Perhaps later? I'll call you. Bye-bye, Bertie.

Kathryn returned to her living room and sipped her coffee; it had grown cold. "Where was I?"

"You want me to find Sheldon Voss, but that's easier said than done, Miss Massey."

"But with the resources at your disposal—"

Hartman's wide-open face took on a darker mien. "Men like Voss, they're the slipperiest of snakes. They know how to cover their tracks, and if they don't want to be found, it can be extremely difficult to do so."

"You mean 'impossible.'"

"Let's call it 'unlikely.'"

"But I needed dirt on him, you came up with the goods."

"That was back when Sheldon Voss was in the business of ensuring everybody in America knew who he was. When an attention-seeking slippery snake hasn't been seen for more than a month, it means that he has gone underground. Even for someone like me, that's a tall order."

In the movies, a private eye contends with red herrings, a femme fatale or two, plus maybe a motive that turns out to be different from what it first appears to be. But the gumshoe always gets to the bottom of things, even if he has to take a bullet in the arm or a slug to the jaw.

"You're turning me down?"

"What I'm saying is that it could take weeks, or months, and it could very easily result in nothing. Even on a retainer basis, my bill could stack up."

"How much are we talking here?"

"Anything up to a thousand dollars a week."

*Gulp.*

Kathryn had willingly paid Hartman's fee back when she was digging around for dirt on Voss, but that had averaged out to less than fifty dollars a day. It was expensive, but he'd done the job.

One positive consequence of Voss's Sea to Shining Sea March was the huge boost in ratings it delivered to Kathryn's *Window on Hollywood* radio show. The NBC execs were delighted with the blaze of publicity the evening had incited, but Kathryn and Leo knew the ratings bonanza was temporary. With television annexing more and more of radio's territory, everything was temporary these days.

"I don't think I can afford that," she told Hartman.

"We can look at alternatives."

"What? That I go to Boston myself and—and—" She slapped her sides. "I wouldn't even know where to start."

For a few moments, they listened to layers of old paint being scrubbed away.

Kathryn could tell he was giving her defenses a chance to cool down, so she let him, and said nothing more.

"From what I've been able to gather," he employed a more measured tone now, "you are no stranger to the head of the FBI."

"That's quite a butterfly net you've got there, Mr. Hartman."

"In my experience, it pays to be thorough with the subject of your investigations *and* your client."

Kathryn wasn't sure if she was supposed to feel protected or violated. "My last encounter with J. Edgar Hoover was dicey, to say the least. I have no desire to tangle with him again."

Hartman poked his tablet of notes with his fountain pen. "Your father was accused of treason, which is more than enough justification for the FBI to start a file on him. Whatever evidence the prosecution employed to win a conviction, it must have been substantial."

"Or circumstantial."

"The two are not mutually exclusive. The FBI's file on your father will contain everything: police reports, newspaper clippings, court documents, telephone conversation transcripts—both legal and illegal."

Between the painter and his scraping, Bertie and her bagels, and now mention of Hoover, Kathryn could feel her nerves unraveling at the edges. "What exactly are you saying?"

"The reason my fee is so high is that I would need to close my office and take you on as my sole client. But if I could fly to Boston and gain access to Danford's FBI file, everything I need would be right there in one place. Even if it's thick as a phone book, I could be back within a week to ten days. Two weeks tops. Could you afford that?"

Even if her radio show folded tomorrow, a couple of thousand bucks was within Kathryn's means. She nodded.

"Given that your father's freedom and reputation are at stake, how do you feel about calling Hoover?"

"You want me to stick my hand back into a fire that's already burned me?"

"I do."

"Assuming he would even take my call."

"Not unless he was curious to learn why. The trick is to make him *want* to take your call."

Kathryn fell back in her chair. "And how do I do that?"

"Miss Massey, my job isn't about pulling out a magnifying glass and fingerprint kit. It's about understanding human nature and finding a way to use that understanding to extract the information I'm after."

"Are you about to tell me that Hoover is human?" As soon as she said it, Kathryn wished she hadn't. This guy was about to impart useful information and here she was running off at the mouth.

He continued as though she had said nothing.

"People respond better when you've done them a favor. First you do the favor, you let some time go by, and then you approach them again. You say, Hey listen, I'm sorry to bother you but do you think you could help me out?"

He laid his hands on the table, palms toward the ceiling, as though to say *So what kind of favor could you do for the head of the FBI?*

A loud crack rang out from beyond Kathryn's living room window. The handyman called down to his coworkers that he'd broken his last scraper, which meant they'd have to go to the hardware store on Santa Monica Boulevard and buy a dozen more. And while they were at it, some more paint "on accounta this job was bigger'n I planned."

Kathryn listened to him fuss and cuss down the ladder until she heard his boots crunch on the gravel path leading toward the pool. It was all the time she needed to come up with something that might tempt Hoover to take her call.

# CHAPTER 8

Marcus sat at a sidewalk table in front of the Ristocaffé Colosseo wishing he'd thrown on a thicker sweater. The afternoon sun flooded the Colosseum in languid light but very little warmth.

He had contacted the popular rental agencies in Rome but their meager list of penthouses had run out days ago. Back in Hollywood the Zanuck name opened all doors, but over here, it merely induced a blank look and a Continental shrug.

In his recent "No penthouses for love or money" cable, Marcus had added "and money is running low." He hoped Zanuck would tell him to return to California, so he was disappointed when he arrived home to a scribbled message that American Express had called again.

He was desperate to get back to the Garden, to Kathryn and Gwendolyn, and to his old life. But on the other hand, there was Domenico Beneventi.

What a name! It rolled off the tongue like the guy was a Renaissance sculptor. He liked to whisper it over and over when he was alone.

It'd been late when Marcus had brought him home. They'd tried to tiptoe in without catching the signora's attention, but the squeak of a floorboard and a chianti-induced giggle triggered her curiosity. Her door cracked open and a quizzical eye squinted at them. Domenico told her that he was ashamed to admit that he was too drunk to go home to his unforgiving mamma, so Marcus had offered him a rug on which to sleep it off. She'd closed her door and left them to mount the stairs to Marcus's room, where they had fallen into bed and unleashed pent-up cravings that caught them by surprise.

It wasn't like Marcus hadn't bedded anybody since Oliver. There had been some dalliances here and there, and a few fumblings in the dark. But the following morning, he'd woken up with Domenico's wrist fitted neatly into the cleft of his chest, and a pinkie finger resting lightly on a nipple. They'd made love—an unhurried, sensual encounter. When it was over, Marcus had expected the guy to jump out of bed, pull on his clothes, toss off some sort of half-hearted thanks for helping him over the hump of putting Jacopo past him, and hurry out the door.

But instead, Domenico had pulled the blankets over them and woven his legs around Marcus's as they drifted back to sleep. Marcus dreamed that they were at the ornately carved seminary door. They walked through it and onto the Garden of Allah's poolside patio where a party was in progress. It was a languid dream where everybody was in soft focus, like movie stars past their prime.

Later, they'd rolled out of bed for a late breakfast of strong espresso and fresh croissants. Soon, they were spending most evenings together once Domenico was finished corralling legionnaires and villagers at Cinecittà.

And now it was three weeks later and, sitting at a café overlooking the Colosseum, Marcus realized that being stuck in Rome might not be all bad.

He lifted the camera to his eye and adjusted the zoom lens until the crumbling amphitheater sharpened in his viewfinder. He pressed the shutter as a flock of pigeons took to the sky amid a cacophony of squawking.

A nearby diner caught his attention—or, rather, her familiar curly, ash-blonde hair. He bowed to the left to get a clearer look at the woman's face. It was angled down as she leafed through a copy of *Look* magazine. She stopped at something that made her blink with surprise, then giggled to herself.

*Christ almighty, it's her!*

The Hollywood actress denounced on the floor of the US Senate as "a powerful influence for evil" was sitting ten feet away from him, reading a magazine while soaking up the last of the Italian summer sun.

Marcus thought about Domenico's assertion that the European magazines would pay him handsomely. Zanuck's second wire transfer had been half of the first. Domenico hadn't clarified exactly how much "handsomely" amounted to, but it was probably enough for another couple of weeks' rent.

Even without the benefit of studio makeup and lighting guys, Ingrid Bergman looked every bit as natural as she had in *Casablanca*. Marcus had always felt she hadn't deserved to become the target of the relentless accusations thrown at her by Americans outraged that she'd left her family and career to pursue an affair with a foreign director. *Stromboli* was an escape hatch from an unhappy marriage with a controlling husband, as well as from a creatively stifling career. The American public didn't care. They saw her as Sister Mary Benedict in *The Bells of St Mary's* and wanted her to remain that way.

Guilt overcame Marcus for invading the privacy of a woman who'd lost so much. Who was he to take what little solitude she had left?

As he hesitated to release the shutter, the sun slipped behind a wisp of a cloud, softening the light. The Ingrid Bergman that filled his viewfinder became so achingly beautiful that Marcus couldn't resist. *Just because I take some pictures, doesn't mean I'll sell them.* He managed to click off eight frames before his conscience reasserted itself. He lowered his camera to the table just as the waiter approached and handed him a folded note. "Dalla signora al tavolo dietro." *From the lady at the back table.*

At the rear of the café, tucked away in the shadows, was a woman in a wide-brimmed hat of black straw. Under it, she wore a turban of dark red felt, and on her nose sat an oversized pair of sunglasses.

He unfolded her note and read the single word written there:

*skybound*

Marcus wove through the tables until he stood in front of the mystery woman.

"Melody?"

She tipped her sunglasses forward to confirm that she was Melody Hope, the former MGM star whose booze-sodden fall from grace had been humiliatingly documented in the entertainment press. Several years later, she had popped up in his life with the idea for a vehicle that could serve as a comeback for both of them: a biopic about the life of Amelia Earhart, called *Skybound*.

As Marcus took a seat, Melody ordered Negronis. "I couldn't believe my eyes when I saw you."

Marcus wished she'd take off those ridiculously huge sunglasses so that he could get a better look at her. "Were you sitting here this whole time?"

"Long enough to see you take those sneaky snaps of Ingrid. Oh, sweetie, I'm just so gosh-darned pleased to see you! How long has it been?"

The last time Marcus had seen Melody was the night she and Trevor Bergin stopped by the Garden of Allah to announce they'd each been cast in Italian movies after a propagandistic booklet called *Red Channels* had killed the careers of hundreds of people.

"Three years." The Negronis arrived and the two of them clinked glasses. "We didn't hear from you after you left Hollywood. So how are you?"

"Let's see. I came over here to make *Titus Flavius*. I played a Judean queen who was mistress to the Roman emperor who built that." She tipped her glass toward the Colosseum. "It wasn't a big role, but I must have made an impression because they gave me my own movie, *Queen of Judea*. And that did so well, I was cast in *Rome Burns*, playing Poppaea Sabina. She was the wife of Nero and such a bitch, but of course a hell of a part."

Marcus smiled to himself. *Ask an actress how they are, and they give you their résumé.* "It's a shame none of your movies made it to the States."

She gave an apathetic shrug and peeked over the top of her sunglasses to get an unfiltered view of him. "You have a glow about you."

"I do?"

"It's exactly the sort of glow someone told me I had after I took a lover."

Her eyes widened.

"Marcus! Have you taken on an Italian lover?" She thwacked him across the arm. "Aren't they the best? So passionate! So sensual! They're like a goddamned friggin' tidal wave, am I right?" She pushed her sunglasses back up her face.

"Yes to all of the above," Marcus said. "It's made my time here much more bearable."

A ruckus erupted off to the right. A striking woman—all breasts and curves and short dark hair—sauntered into view. Her blindingly white dress hugged her hips then flared out, cascading around her knees as she sashayed along the cobblestones in stiletto-heeled mules.

A thicket of men followed her like a pack of ravenous wolves. To snag her attention, they called out a word over and over, but Marcus couldn't catch it.

"Are those guys the *scattini* I've heard about?" he asked.

"They sure as hell are."

"Do they go after you?"

"Why do you think I'm all covered up like an Arabian concubine? But I don't blame them. We're all trying to make a buck. And they can help you get noticed when you're an up-and-comer like Miss Va-Va-Voom Italian Style over there." The woman in white was now leaning against a low marble fence, a study in nonchalance with the Colosseum behind her.

"That's not Sophia Loren, is it?" Marcus asked.

"She's the other one, Gina Lollobrigida. She made a movie with Bogie called *Beat the Devil.*"

"What are they calling out?"

"La Lolla. It's her *scattini* nickname."

Forming a semicircle around her, they jockeyed for the best angle, gently elbowing each other in the ribs and laughing when one of them pretended to fall at her feet. But the mood changed when a new guy, dressed in a linen suit dyed pastel yellow, thrust himself through the group.

"Oh God," Melody muttered, "here comes trouble."

The new photographer shouted out "GINA! GINA!" in a loud, almost angry tone.

"Who's that?"

"He probably sells more photos to more magazines than the rest of those guys combined."

"Emilio Conti?"

"Sure is."

Conti positioned himself at the front. He started directing Lollobrigida—*Turn your hips to me and twist your shoulders in the opposite direction*—while the others yelled at him in rapid-fire colloquial Italian that Marcus couldn't catch. Conti paid no attention.

Melody opened her purse and pulled out some lira. "Let's go." She led him into a maze of streets bordered by two- and three-story houses in varying stages of dilapidation. "I'm starting a new movie soon. After much campaigning—some may call it 'nagging'—they're finally letting me play a modern woman."

"No more togas?"

"And I couldn't be more excited. It's called *Metropolitana* and it's about a group of World War II French resistance fighters who live in the Paris subway, which they call the Metro. I play a plucky French girl who recruits an Italian to fight for them."

"You'll be shooting in Paris?"

"Get this: *Metropolitana* is a French-Italian-American co-production, set during the war in Paris but shot at Cinecittà, and staffed largely by Americans from—are you ready?—MGM! How's that for irony? Well, here we are."

They had turned off a deserted backstreet and onto an alley. An arched wooden gate stood at the top of a short flight of steps. Craggy from years in the sun, strips of weathered paint hung in jagged ribbons. Flakes of it lay scattered among a layer of vivid purple petals that carpeted the stone steps.

Melody twisted a black iron ring to the left. The gate opened inward, revealing a large bricked courtyard shaded by a lattice of vines. She pointed to an especially thick creeper whose tendrils curled around an explosion of bougainvillea. "The gardener told me it's older than Garibaldi. Amazing, huh?"

"This is where you live?"

"And I thought Hollywoodland was nice."

She led him through the courtyard to the entrance of a six-story building Marcus wouldn't have guessed was there. "Only two apartments per floor, except at the very top."

"There's a penthouse?" His hopes beginning to climb, Marcus shaded his eyes to catch a glimpse of the top floor. "Does anybody live there?"

"One of those surly old ladies, always dressed in black, always rubbing some old crucifix around her neck. Crabby as all get-out and never says hello, goodbye, or kiss my ass."

"Has she lived here long?"

Melody took him through the marble foyer—its walls were painted off-white and hung with horrific scenes of medieval torture—and down one flight of stairs. "She looks ancient enough to remember opening day at the Colosseum. Come to think of it, I haven't seen her in ages. She's probably too decrepit to leave the house."

The living room was bigger than Marcus's entire pensione and filled with light that poured in from three sides. Through the broadest window, Marcus could pick out the tops of columns dotting the Palatine Hill.

"You've landed on your feet," he told her.

"Don't I know it." She ditched the sunglasses on the dining table, plucked off the sun hat, and unwound the red turban. Her hair was lighter than Marcus remembered, almost sandy blonde. She wore it longer now; its natural curls framed her face like a halo.

She handed a bound movie script to him with a single word centered in the middle of the first page.

*METROPOLITANA*

"Do me a favor and read it?"

"Right now?"

"The screenwriter arrives tomorrow."

In Marcus's experience, the writer seldom went on location. His place on the chain gang was in a cramped cubicle, swallowing too much Benzedrine until the script was done. "Lucky guy."

"Not really." Melody threw herself onto a long sofa handsomely upholstered in damask that looked like a Venetian tapestry. "I demanded that they send for him because the story doesn't quite work. I can't figure out why, but I don't want to come off like some birdbrain. You could finish it in an hour and a half."

Marcus fanned the pages through his fingers. It sure felt good to be holding one of these babies. "What would you have done if we hadn't bumped into each other?"

She coiled a lock of hair around her finger. "I probably would have faced him sounding like some birdbrain."

Marcus dropped onto the sofa next to her. "So make with the coffee already."

From the very first page, the script reminded Marcus of his days laboring in MGM's B Unit where they'd had a stack of twenty scripts that recycled the hero into a heroine, the racetrack location into a baseball stadium, the greedy banker into a greedy developer, and the whole thing—abracadabra!—into a brand-new movie.

But at the halfway mark where *Metropolitana*'s heroine, Ursula, meets the Italian love interest, Marcus stopped reading.

"Finished already?" Melody called from her balcony, where she was chain-smoking.

"Does this movie end with Ursula staying underground to live permanently and Alfredo climbing a ladder to the surface?"

She joined him on the couch, stinking of harsh cigarette smoke. "You think they're going to climb back up to civilization together. He goes but she stays. It's a total letdown. They keep telling me 'But it's neo-realism.' Yuck! I know what moviegoers want and it ain't that."

Marcus tossed the script onto the coffee table. "About twenty years ago, I wrote a short story called *Subway People,* which got published in *The Saturday Evening Post*. MGM bought the screen rights and sold them to Cosmopolitan Pictures, who wanted to turn it into a movie for Marion Davies called *Ursula Goes Underground*."

Melody gaped at the script, then back at him. "I don't remember any picture like that."

"The script was deemed subpar and the movie never got made." Marcus flipped to the front page and read the name of the screenwriter: Wendell Pitt. "Is this who they're flying over to meet with you?"

"Nah. They're sending a script doctor." She reached over to the narrow table standing against the back of the sofa where a stack of telegrams sat in a messy pile. She flicked through them. "Vernon Terrell."

"Seriously?"

"You know him?"

"Back in the day, we called him 'Hoppy' on account of how he wanted to play Hopalong Cassidy, but he lost a leg in the first world war so that was the end of that. It was a tough break, but he reinvented himself into a damn fine screenwriter. The last time I saw him, he was working at Columbia."

That was the night Jim Taggert had handed Marcus the job of running MGM's writing department while celebrating the bombing of Hiroshima. Boy, what a week that had been—and what a day this had turned into. Marcus couldn't wait to share all this with Domenico.

"When does he arrive?" he asked Melody.

"Tomorrow."

"And when are you meeting him?"

"Production starts soon and the script isn't set, so they're losing their minds. He's coming straight from the airport. He'll be here this time tomorrow."

"Mind if I gatecrash?"

* * *

Twenty-four hours later, Marcus was back at Melody's front door. She pulled him inside. "Remember Old Lady Crabapples I was telling you about?"

"In the penthouse?"

"She fell down the stairs! She and her horrible son—he looks like a second-string Mafioso gun-runner—they had a terrible row. Screaming, yelling. At one point, she opened up her front door, leaving us no choice but to eavesdrop."

"He pushed her down the stairs?"

"*She* pushed *him*—or tried to, but lost her balance and ended up ass over teakettle all the way down. And they're made of marble so you can imagine the state she was in by the time she hit the bottom."

"Where is she now?"

"They carted her away in an ambulance." She rubbed her hands together. "I've had my eye on that place since the week I moved in."

Marcus looked around at Melody's apartment. Compared to what he was used to, it seemed palatial. "But this is lovely. Do you really need anything bigger?"

She gave him a friendly swat. "I can move in up there and you can move in here. We'd be neighbors. Wouldn't that be terrific?"

"Yes," he replied, guardedly, "but what might be even more terrific is if you were able to do Darryl Zanuck a favor."

Melody pulled an *Ugh!* face. "Why would I do that?" Her doorbell rang. She ran to the door and pulled it open. Hoppy wore his professional pleased-to-meet-you smile. It dropped away when he spotted Marcus.

The intervening ten years had scored deep creases into each side of his mouth and across his forehead. What was left of his once-luxuriant brown hair was now thin and gray, and hovered over his scalp in wisps that caught every draft. The skin under his chin hung like old elastic and his teeth had yellowed from too much smoking.

But his eyes were clear and his smile genuine.

"Marcus!"

"Hoppy!"

The two men wrapped their arms around each other while Melody clapped her hands like a little girl. She sent them to the sofa to catch up and headed into the kitchen to make coffee.

Marcus's exit from MGM after his HUAC testimony in Washington and his inclusion in *Red Channels* had been so public that Marcus didn't need to fill Hoppy in on much more than his circuitous route to Rome via *Quo Vadis* and *Three Coins.*

"And what about you?" he asked Hoppy. "I guess you're not at Columbia anymore. Are you freelancing? And Jim? How's he doing?"

Hoppy's face crumpled at the name of his long-term partner. "You didn't hear?"

"After I left MGM, those studio friendships sort of fell away."

"Poor old Jimmy. He loved heading up the writing department, so life was never the same after he quit."

There had been aspects of the job Marcus enjoyed, but it was hardly a bed of rose petals—especially when Hurricane HUAC hit town. "What happened?"

"He got some jobs here and there, but they petered out once he started hitting the bottle."

"He was always a drinker."

"But not a scotch-in-the-morning-coffee drinker. It went from bad to worse until he was diagnosed with cirrhosis. I thought he'd give it all up but he went on one suicidal binge after another. By that stage, it was just the two of us; no social life, no friends. Him drinking and me wishing he'd stop, but he never did."

"God, Hoppy, I'm so sorry to hear that. I wish I'd known. I'd have called."

Melody set down a tray with coffee and butter cookies. "People like that don't stop unless they want to," she said. "I ought to know—I was one of them."

"After I buried him, I tried to get my old life back on track but it wasn't the same game anymore, so I put my shingle out as a script doctor."

Marcus sipped Melody's coffee. It was dark and bitter—not unlike her Hollywood experience. He added three lumps of sugar and forced it down. "Has the doctoring worked out?"

Hoppy clamped a hand on Marcus's knee.

"That's what you should do. The screenwriters who didn't get their throats slit by the blacklist are okay, but the new ones coming up, they're not so hot. You and I used to churn out script after script, learning on the job what worked, what didn't, and why. You wouldn't believe what they pay me now to fix their pile of dog turds."

Marcus held up the *Metropolitana* script. "Like this?"

"I read it for the first time on the flight over." Hoppy pulled a pained face and looked at Melody, who was perched on the edge of the occasional chair at the end of the table. "You were right to put your foot down."

"Thank you!" She turned to Marcus. "Go ahead, tell him."

Hoppy met Marcus's eye warily.

"This screenplay," Marcus said, "doesn't belong to MGM."

"But I picked it up from them en route to the airport."

Marcus took Hoppy through the circumstances from twenty years ago.

"They never renewed the copyright on your story?"

"Nope."

Hoppy started to giggle. "Two of the biggest players in the movie business in both America and Italy, and you've got them over a goddamned barrel. You've made this trip worthwhile, Marcus! I wouldn't miss this for the world."

He hooked an arm around the back of his chair.

"Here's what you need to know: like so many movies being made today, *Metropolitana* is a complicated web of financing. MGM is footing forty percent of the film in exchange for one hundred percent of the non-European distribution rights. The other sixty percent comes from an Italian film company called Fratelli di Conti."

"As in 'Emilio Conti'?" Marcus asked.

"Yep!" Melody toyed with the ruby ring around her right-hand pinkie. "He's the fourth Conti brother. The other three are the Conti triplets, whom the newspapers dubbed 'miracle babies' because they were born to a woman who was declared infertile. They've been famous all their lives and now have this production company. They're aggressive as hell."

"And you've got 'em with their pants down," Hoppy added. "Are you sure nobody ever contacted you about renewing the copyright?"

"Yes, but maybe we should double check?" Marcus thought of Arlene Curtis back at the Garden. "I know the girl who is the secretary to MGM's chief attorney."

"A guy by the name of Tanner?" Hoppy asked.

"I think so."

"He had an acrimonious falling-out with Dore Schary and left the company. I wonder if he took your friend with him."

"She's only a cable away."

"But if you're correct," Hoppy said, "they're in flagrant violation of copyright. MGM and Fratelli di Conti are about to start shooting a picture they have no right to film. This is priceless!" He slapped the expensive upholstery; a plume of dust motes shot into the air. "You could take them to the cleaners."

"Everybody hates the Conti brothers," Melody added. "They're the Warner Brothers of Italy. The rule is, Never trust a Conti. Those pricks will turn on you using anything that comes to hand. Most people here would love to see someone stick it to them."

"You're planning on staying in Rome for a while, aren't you?" Hoppy asked.

Marcus thought of Signora Crabapples. Getting into Zanuck's good graces would be a smart career move. "I've got a few details to tie up."

"Good, because you'd have to stay here until all this gets sorted out."

"Isn't that what lawyers are for?"

"Hoppy's right," Melody said. "The case will go before an Italian judge. You're a foreigner, so you'll have a hard time convincing the court to find in favor of you over the Conti brothers. It'll be almost impossible if you're not there in person."

Marcus forced down Melody's coffee—it was like drinking liquid asphalt.

"You need to make these fuckers pay through the nose," Hoppy persisted. "And I mean every goddamned nickel you can squeeze out of them."

*But I'm one penthouse away from flying home and picking up my life again.*

Marcus thought of the hell that the studios had put him through since the HUAC decided to rout out suspected Commies with a scorched-earth policy. And not only the humiliating televised hearing in Washington, but the blacklisting, the graylisting, *Red Channels*, and the McCarthy witch-hunts.

*And who's to say that Zanuck will have anything waiting for me back home? Only one thing in Hollywood is guaranteed – and that is that nothing is guaranteed.*

He snapped his head up with a knowing wink. "I'm in."

# CHAPTER 9

Gwendolyn thrust her fingers into the patch of bare earth outside her villa. She angled her face over her right shoulder and told Arlene, Doris, and Bertie, "I haven't done this since we had the victory garden. I forgot how cold the soil is."

Bertie lowered the bag of bulbs onto the gravel path. "I like a cocktail party as much as the next girl, but when we were all working together in the victory garden, I loved the camaraderie. Neighbors getting together, growing vegetables, watching them sprout, getting muddy as hell. God, it was fun! I'm so glad you suggested this."

Gwendolyn wiped the sweat off her forehead, leaving a wide swath of dirt across her face. The loamy smell filled her lungs. "We've left it so late in the year. I feared nothing would grow in November."

"Tulips are a hardier flower than they look." Doris peered into the hole Gwendolyn had made. "It needs to be deeper; otherwise, they won't survive the winter."

"The guy at the nursery promised me that we'll be treated to a whole rainbow come March and April." Bertie opened the brown paper sack and started laying each bulb out on the lawn like it was a precious egg.

Gwendolyn excavated more earth, not daring to look at her nails. They were going to take forever to clean, but that's what Sunday afternoons were for. Twentieth Century-Fox had extracted more than their pound of flesh for one week—especially after Loretta Young and Billy Travilla started battling for her time.

"I am your number one priority," Loretta instructed. "You tell him, 'No, Mr. Travilla, I'm sorry but first I must finish Miss Young's gown.' You must be firm with people like that. Otherwise, they'll walk all over you."

But how was Gwendolyn supposed to respond when Fox's top costume designer had said, "Marilyn's being difficult about a dress I'm working on for her next movie. Could you spend this afternoon with her and try to talk her into this design I've come up with?" Especially when the boss had specifically asked her to keep tabs on Marilyn.

Gwendolyn had managed to juggle both camps so that each of them got what they wanted, but only by disobeying an unbreakable commandment: *Thou shalt not take work home with you.*

At first it was only panels of material that needed stitching together, but as the *Millionaire* premiere loomed closer, her smuggling escalated to full dresses.

Life became a marathon session at the sewing machine followed by hours on her knees in front of the dress form. As the Indian summer of October started to cool, Gwendolyn became preoccupied with the thought of feeling dirt crumbling through her fingers, to smell its rich fertility. She wanted to take a seed or a bulb or a twig and watch it flower.

She had all but forgotten the old victory garden patch until one day it caught her eye. Six years after wartime rationing had ended, it was now an abandoned expanse of weeds with a single shriveled, undernourished cucumber sitting among the foliage like a Japanese soldier who refused to believe the war was over.

A plan to reconnect with Mother Earth took hold, and now they were on their hands and knees, scraping away the soil with their bare hands, filling their nails with dirt, and staining their clothes.

"Hey Gwennie," Bertie said, "when do you think—holy mackerel!"

Gwendolyn dug into the ground again. "Don't tell me you found something else you hid during the war. I thought we got everything."

All three girls stiffened into place, their eyes glomming onto a tall figure in a gray Homburg sauntering down the path. Gwendolyn clambered to her bare feet.

Clark Gable took a step closer. "The guy at the front desk said I'd find you here." He gave the others a cursory glance. "He didn't mention that you were in the middle of—"

"We're planting tulips!" Doris blurted out.

"How can I help you?" Gwendolyn asked.

Hesitation played on his lips. "I was hoping for a moment of your time. In private?"

Each of the three girls looked at Gwendolyn with the same *What the hell?* expression.

"Ladies, if you'll excuse me, please." Gwendolyn picked her way out of the flowerbed, brushing away the dirt. They had taken the trouble to moisten it first, so it clung to her dungarees and one of Marcus's old flannel shirts. By the time they reached her door, she wasn't much cleaner, so she told Gable to take a seat on the sofa. "I should at least wash my hands and face."

"Not on my account, please."

She pointed to the gown hanging on the dress form in the corner of her living room. "On the account of that."

After a mountain of discarded sketches, Gwendolyn and Marilyn had decided on a strapless dress made from nude crêpe, overlaid with white lace. Marilyn didn't mind that it was made of leftovers from a dress June Haver had worn in *The Girl Next Door*, but she did protest that it didn't dazzle enough. So Gwendolyn had brought the gown home and spent the previous day embellishing it with enough sequins to give the girl a hernia.

Travilla would have a conniption fit if he knew it was here, but the gala was less than a week away and Marilyn would be showing up on Monday for a final fitting. Gwendolyn couldn't take any chances that it might get dirty; the smallest speck of muck would show up like an ink stain. Maybe this wasn't the best weekend to go burrowing around in the dirt, after all.

In the bathroom mirror, a filthy street urchin from one of Dickens' more depressing novels stared back at her. "Won't be long!" She scoured as much grime from her hands and face as she could inside fifteen seconds and ran her fingers through her hair. She went to apply a smidge of lipstick, but the guy had already seen her at her worst, so what the hell.

Gable sat on her sofa, his Homburg balanced on one knee, a foot jiggling up and down. She joined him, but not too close. His easy smile had a nervous edge that even an actor of his skill couldn't mask.

"What can I do for you, Mr. Gable?"

"First off, it's Clark, okay?"

His aftershave balm had a dark, musky scent. It had been so freshly applied that she could tell he'd only shaved in the past hour or two—and she'd hung around enough actors at the Garden of Allah to know that not having to shave on their one day off per week was a luxury.

"I've come to see you about a delicate matter." He curled his lips to start talking but the right words failed him.

"I've got whiskey and vodka," she said, "or I could probably scrounge up some scotch if that's your preference."

"Thank you, but I need to do this sober." It took him a couple more attempts to gather himself together. "I hear that you work at Fox, making gowns for Loretta Young's television show."

"That's right."

"And you've become friendly with her daughter, Judy."

Neither Victor Marswell in *Mogambo*, Blackie Norton from *San Francisco*, nor Rhett Butler would be sitting here with his right leg bouncing in agitation. All three of them would have been able to meet Gwendolyn's eye, but instead, Clark kept his gaze averted.

*So those rumors are true.* "Yes, that's right," she told him. "Judy decided college wasn't for her so she's been at the studio. Between Loretta and Travilla, I'm run off my feet, so she's been quite a help to me. Why are you asking about her?"

She tried to keep her face neutral but it proved difficult with that sardonic glimmer in his eye.

"I suspect you know." The strain in his voice told Gwendolyn that this wasn't about what she needed to hear but what he needed to say. "Judy Lewis is my daughter."

The three girls outside started to giggle and yip from what sounded like a mud fight.

"Are you sure you don't want that drink?"

His mouth stayed mute but his eyes begged for a whiskey.

"Four Roses on the rocks?" By the time she returned holding a pair of tumblers, a trace of Rhett Butler had returned to his face.

"Does everybody know?" he asked her.

"About you and Judy? I remember some gossip when Loretta announced that she was adopting a baby girl. But you know how it is—there's always one rumor or other doing the rounds and it usually turns out to be so far removed from the truth that it's barely worth the breath it took to repeat it."

"But you knew what I was going to say."

The guy wasn't here because he was passing by and thought he'd drop in, so Gwendolyn set his drink down on the coffee table and closed the space between them. It was a trick she'd learned from Kathryn to encourage more intimate confidences. "I will confess that when I met Judy for the first time, I did look for signs of you in her face."

"Did you see any?"

Gwendolyn nodded.

"I'm glad." He smiled gently.

"Clark, you've obviously got something on your mind."

He gulped down half his bourbon in one mouthful. "I have a pal who works in lighting at Fox. He was at MGM for years. Great guy. Solid as Plymouth Rock. We sometimes get together to shoot the breeze. He told me Judy's been hanging around the studio and that she's often seen with the knockout who does her mother's wardrobe. The two of them have lunch together at the commissary."

As a forty-three-year-old woman who worked in an industry where thirty was considered passé, Gwendolyn was flattered that someone had called her a knockout.

"You've sought me out to . . .?"

The Rhett Butler smile faded as his dark eyes took on a granite veneer. "Loretta has kept Judy and me at arm's length. She's had her reasons and I understand them, so I've kept my distance. Reluctantly, I want you to know, but I've tried to be respectful."

"You've spent no time with your own daughter?"

"We had one shot at it a few years ago. It was a nice visit. I could see she was a good kid even though she was a bit unnerved by having me in her living room."

"Well, you *are* Clark Gable," Gwendolyn chided him.

He shot back a look that said, *It's as much a burden as a blessing.* "We jawed for a while, nothing deep and meaningful, but I left thinking it was a nice start and maybe we could develop a relationship farther down the road."

"But it didn't happen?"

"It unnerved Loretta and she forbade me to see Judy again. 'Forbade' is too strong a word; more like 'dissuaded.' I didn't put up a fight because I thought I could live with that."

"But you can't."

"When Judy was a youngster, sure, but now that she's becoming an adult, I want more. That's not so bad, is it?"

In the time that Gwendolyn had worked for Loretta Young, she'd grown to admire how much control the woman exercised over her career and her image. She was that rare Hollywood actress who actively battled against ceding all her power to a husband, agent, manager, or boss.

Gwendolyn could see that Marilyn was trying too, but with sporadic success. She had once lamented to Gwendolyn how she lacked Loretta's steel backbone. Gwendolyn had tried to point out that she also lacked Loretta's thirty years dealing with men like Zanuck and Cohn. She may have missed out on *A Woman's World*, but she was in there fighting. If Loretta kept her career, image, figure, and stardom under tight control, she probably kept her daughter on an equally short leash.

"No," Gwendolyn told Clark, "it's not bad at all." She thought about the lengths Kathryn was prepared to go to in order to bring about her father's exoneration. "I think every girl deserves to know her father."

"I'm glad you think so."

"But if Loretta's spent twenty years keeping you two apart, I doubt she'll be a pushover when it comes to letting you into their lives."

He started rubbing the palms of his hands down the tops of his legs. "I've never insisted on my rights as a father so I don't know that I can start making demands."

"What *do* you want?"

"I thought that maybe you could get us in the same room. It'd give me a chance to watch her being herself."

"You want me to sneak you into the costume department at Fox and hide you behind a sewing machine?"

"No, not that. But something. I dunno." He ran a hand over his chin. "I haven't thought this through very well, have I?"

Gwendolyn's first instinct was to reach out and hold his hand, but this was Clark Gable sitting next to her, and she wasn't sure where the lines of etiquette were drawn around a star of his stature. "The problem is that you could walk into a room the size of Gilmore Stadium and everybody would notice."

"I knew it was a tall order." He thrust forward and got to his feet. "I'm sorry to have bothered you on your day off—"

"It *is* a tall order," she cut in. "But not an impossible one."

"You got an idea?"

"No, but that doesn't mean I won't."

When Gwendolyn stood up, she spotted three heads silhouetted against the lace curtains pulled across her living room window and wondered how long they'd been watching.

# CHAPTER 10

Kathryn felt the blade of the ax press against her neck as she walked into the NBC studios. It was just a hunch, but she was fairly sure she knew the cause of the tension.

Kathryn waved to the guy behind the tobacco counter and passed through the stage door. Musicians and sound technicians went about their business, wishing her a good show as usual, but apprehension prickled her arms.

She set her bag on the dressing-room counter and pulled out her notes to reread the joke about how two studios were premiering big movies on the same night: *How to Marry a Millionaire* and *Calamity Jane*. She said out loud, "How's a girl supposed to choose between the charms of Fox's bombshell and the appeal of Warners' songbird? Wouldn't it have been easier if they'd collaborated instead and made a movie called *How to Marry Calamity Jane?*"

It had been funny when she'd written it this morning, but with this unnerving anxiety crowding the studio, she wasn't so sure now.

At thirty minutes till airtime, the flurry of activity intensified. A studio messenger stuck his head in the door. "Mr. Reed wants you to know that Jerry Lewis and Dean Martin have sort of arrived."

Kathryn pulled out her hairbrush. "Sort of?"

The kid contorted his face. "They had a huge fight in the limo on the drive over."

Lewis and Martin were guest-starring on her show at the insistence of their producer, Hal Wallis. Their next movie was the first shot in color *and* 3-D, so it was a big deal to Paramount, but evidently not to either of the stars.

*Is that what I've been feeling? Lewis-and-Martin hostility?*

"Where are they now?"

"Circling the block."

From what Kathryn had heard, those two fought with the heat of an atomic bomb, but once it was out of their systems, everything was fine. It was twenty minutes until show time; that ought to be enough.

* * *

The fight in the limo must have been a humdinger because Lewis and Martin pulled into the parking lot with only seven minutes to spare. Kathryn wasn't entirely certain she even had guest stars for tonight's show until she heard the cry fire along the human chain of ushers from the Vine Street corner, through the foyer, into the backstage area, and up the corridor.

Kathryn waited in the left wings of the stage; Leo took his usual place on the right-hand side. He mouthed the word "Okay?"

Kathryn gave him a double thumbs-up before she noticed Leo's counterpart at Betty Crocker standing next to him.

Kathryn had met Thurgood Pace a handful of times. He struck her as a typical corporate automaton: conservative suits, thicker around the middle than was healthy, not easily given to humor. But he recognized a beneficial promotional opportunity when he saw one, and was happy to let Leo call most of the shots.

Leo's taut smile gave her pause. Had they been fighting too?

A third figure stepped out of the shadows behind Leo and Thurgood. Kathryn had met the West Coast head of NBC only once. Seeing Thurgood Pace had taken her by surprise, but the appearance of Mr. Erickson shook her down to her foundation garments.

But she didn't have time to worry about him. Lewis and Martin's new movie, *Money from Home,* was set in the world of racetracks, mobsters, and bookies. For tonight's appearance, Hal Wallis had conscripted the picture's screenwriter to come up with an extended skit that hinted at the plot but gave Jerry Lewis opportunity to improvise, and Dean Martin the chance to bounce off his partner's wild ad-libs. All Kathryn had to do was keep up—a tall order that was going to take all of her nerve.

Lewis and Martin joined Leo, Pace, and Erickson. Kathryn watched Leo's face as the five men shook hands—it was his everyone-play-nice face. Dean Martin nodded; Jerry Lewis did too, although with less conviction.

From the control booth at the rear of the audience, her producer held up his index finger. It was her one-minute cue.

*Here goes nothing.*

* * *

Nobody listening to *Window on Hollywood* would have imagined that Kathryn's two guest stars had been screaming at each other on the drive to the studio.

The two men hit the stage all smiles, backslaps, and larger-than-life mugging, throwing kisses and insults to the audience with even-handed dexterity.

Kathryn walked off the stage as though she was being carried by winged angels. *If only every show was like that.*

The honeyed scent of an enormous bouquet of red and white roses filled her dressing room. She searched for a card, but found nothing in the glass vase or among the blooms.

"Terrific show, Kathryn."

Leo and Thurgood crowded her doorway, but neither of them was smiling. They parted like curtains to reveal Mr. Erickson, whose face was parked in neutral. The three men stepped inside; Erickson closed the door behind him with a measured click.

"What's up, gentlemen?" She addressed all three but looked at Leo.

Erickson was a tall man and athletically built. He showed no sign of a paunch testing the limits of his double-breasted suit, and retained a full head of hair even though he had to be north of sixty. If he smiled more, he'd almost be considered a catch by women of a certain age.

"Miss Massey, I have some news, and I wanted you to hear it directly from me." He interlaced his fingers. "Our two most popular radio shows, *Amos 'n' Andy* and *People Are Funny*, are moving to television. However, *Window on Hollywood* will not be joining them."

"Bad ratings, I take it?"

"They came in last night and your most recent show charted at thirty-seven."

Kathryn fell back against her makeup counter, where the rose bouquet brushed up against her back, its soft petals caressing her skin.

"We would have been happy to continue the show if it rated above twenty-five; thirty-seven is unacceptable. *Window on Hollywood* has been cancelled."

*Shows don't last forever*, she told herself. It was one thing to expect this news eventually, but it was another to hear it delivered with such indifference. *God forbid he should sugarcoat it.*

She pushed herself away from the suffocating bouquet. "I appreciate you taking the time to tell me in person. I have only one question: when will my final show be?"

"Kathryn," Leo said with a gentleness that was clearly beyond the reach of Mister NBC, "tonight's show was the final one."

"That's it? I'm off the air? Effective immediately? And you didn't even tell me?"

"We decided," Erickson said carefully, "that informing you beforehand might negatively affect your performance."

"I was going off the air anyway. What did it matter?"

"Martin and Lewis's appearance was very important for all parties concerned. NBC has entered into negotiations with Dean Martin's management for a variety show that—"

"A chance to say goodbye to my listeners would have been nice."

Kathryn itched to turn on Leo, but that scene would have to wait until after this pokerfaced windbag scurried back to his pencil sharpener.

"Like I said Miss Massey, we felt—"

"Thank you for the last five years. I'll be vacating this dressing room shortly. Good night."

After Erickson backed out of the room, Kathryn wanted to give the dark mood time to dissipate, so she started counting backward from ten. Pace closed the door and revealed a smile filled with huge milk-fed Midwest teeth. "This is terrific!"

Kathryn turned to Leo with a questioning look.

"This is what we've been waiting for!"

She crossed her arms. "For NBC to can my show?"

"Your contract had nearly seven more months to go," Leo said. "But it carried an escape clause for them to get out of it if they wished. We were hoping your ratings would crater—"

"Jesus! With sponsors like you—"

"We commissioned a consumer study of women working in newspapers, radio, and television. We learned there are three who are considered the quintessential American women."

"The first is Adelaide Hawley," Thurgood took over. "Women know she's an actress playing Betty Crocker, but they don't care. We like to think it's a testament to how well she does her job, and it suits our purposes."

"And the second?" Kathryn asked.

"Betty Furness from the Westinghouse ads."

"Isn't she an actress too?"

"She is, but like Adelaide Hawley, she's permanently linked with refrigerators in the minds of American housewives."

"And, by extension, is an American housewife, too." Leo was smiling as widely as Pace now. "And guess who made the Top Three."

"You've got to be kidding."

"We commissioned our research in the hope that you'd rank Top Ten. But Top Three? We were stunned."

Pace gave out a surprisingly high-pitched giggle. "You're in the Holy Trinity of American womanhood."

Kathryn couldn't help but scoff. "How the hell do I fit into all that?

"Adelaide is viewed as the unruffled, capable housewife they wish they were, whereas Betty is associated with household products. Even though she's an attractive actress, they wish they looked like her."

"So who am I?"

"They see you as genuine and trustworthy," Leo said. "You stand in for those women who *wish* they could work, but can't. You're the woman who made it out of the constraints of being a housewife."

"You're the working woman who is too busy to bake a cake from scratch," Pace added. "They envy that."

Kathryn snorted. "Not if they ever tasted my baking." She patted Pace on the knee. "Thank God for Betty Crocker cake mixes."

"Even better," Leo continued, "you're the one whom our market relates to the most. The other two are actresses, but Kathryn Massey is who she appears to be."

Kathryn wondered how those housewives would feel if they knew that she was the illegitimate daughter of a convicted felon in Sing Sing.

"That's all well and good," she told them, "but where does that get us?"

"It got us an appointment with the head of advertising for Westinghouse. We presented our findings to him and he reacted the same way we did. They want in on the act."

"Which act is that?"

"A whole new type of marketing. We're combining all three women—Adelaide, Betty, and you—with all three brands—Sunbeam, Betty Crocker, and Westinghouse—in a nationwide advertising campaign. We'll start a print blitz targeting the top ten magazines, and if that succeeds like we think it will, there will be a series of television ads in high-rating shows in the major markets. We're talking *Dragnet, Ellery Queen, Philco Television Playhouse—"*

*"Our Miss Brooks, Colgate Comedy Hour—"*

"You guys aim high."

"We've been waiting for NBC to lower the boom."

The full impact of *Window on Hollywood*'s cancellation began to hit home. The NBC money had been good, but it cost a lot to be "Kathryn Massey—prominent newspaper columnist and radio star." An extensive wardrobe; facials and manicures; twice-weekly hair appointments. And every couple of years she bought a new car and inevitably drove away in the most expensive model on the Oldsmobile lot.

There was also something else to consider.

Over the past month, she'd contacted FBI headquarters three times. On the first call, she'd given her name and asked to be put through to Mr. Hoover, but got the runaround. Call number two had taken her as far as the director's office, but no farther than the receptionist who'd blocked her every attempt to be transferred up the ladder of command.

Through sheer persistence and the ability to talk without stopping, the third call had landed her the assistant to Hoover's right-hand man, Clyde Tolson. But that was two weeks ago and she hadn't heard back. If she couldn't afford Dudley Hartman's thousand-dollar-a-week fee then, it was certainly out of the question now.

"And lucky for you," Kathryn told Pace, "NBC has lowered the boom you've been hoping for."

"With print ads and television in the mix, you'll reach more people than you did with your radio show. There's no downside!"

*Unless you're a girl with a father convicted of selling secrets to Nazis.*

An unexpected wave of relief flushed through her. Rather than trying to get through to Hoover, maybe a better approach would be an intermediary. The ideal candidate would have access to Hoover and credibility. Kathryn could think of only one person who fit that bill, and it was the person she trusted the least—but he was highly susceptible to flattery.

"What do you think?" Leo's eyes shone with hope.

Kathryn forced a perky smile. "Sounds like you know what you're doing."

"This will only work if all three of you girls participate."

In his most recent letter, Marcus had told Kathryn about *Subway People*. This was a rare opportunity for him to screw the studio who'd screwed him, so she didn't blame him for sticking around. For his own self-respect, he had to stay and fight for what was his, but that didn't mean she wouldn't give her last five NBC paychecks if it meant he could be here to hold her hand through all this.

"Sounds pretty great, huh?" Leo pressed.

Kathryn nodded. "Where do I sign?"

# CHAPTER 11

Marcus turned up his collar against the December air as he hit the sidewalk. He groped in his jacket pockets for the last pack of Camels. If he'd known how long he was going to be in Rome, he would have asked Kathryn to throw a dozen more into the care package she'd sent over the previous month along with the Bavarian mint chocolate bars from Schwab's, can of Barbasol shaving cream, tins of Ovaltine, and a batch of Doris's fudge.

Camels were available in Rome, but the ones Kathryn sent over were more satisfying—maybe it was because they'd sat on her kitchen counter at the Garden.

He pulled the second-to-last one out of the packet and headed toward Via Tuscolana, one of the main arteries that connected the heart of the city with Cinecittà. The Camels at the corner tobacconist tended to be old and overpriced, but they'd do in a pinch. He went to light up but decided it'd be smart to hold off. If Luigi had nothing for him, he'd have to hoard these final two.

As he drew closer to the *tabaccheria,* he spotted a familiar figure loitering in the doorway.

"Hoppy!" Marcus greeted him with a Continental kiss to both cheeks. "I didn't know you were staying around here."

Hoppy was pale with uncharacteristic solemnity. "I got a telegram first thing this morning. You're walking into a trap. They're planning to cheat you."

It had taken Arlene several weeks to confirm who held the copyright for *Ursula Goes Underground,* but when she had, it was exactly what he'd wanted to hear.

Cosmopolitan Productions had held the rights to Marcus's story *Subway People* for seven years, but when Hearst got into a shouting match with Mayer and stomped off to Warners, *Subway People/ Ursula Goes Underground* had stayed at MGM. But only for the term of the copyright, which ended in 1942.

"You own the rights to *Subway People,* and MGM are sitting ducks," Arlene had written. "To quote my esteemed boss, Mr. Geoffrey Tanner, Esquire: GO GET 'EM!"

Tanner had referred Marcus to a local entertainment lawyer. Salvatore Sabbatini was big on gold tiepins and diamond pinkie rings, and seemed to have learned English from watching Ricardo Montalban movies. But he understood Marcus's problem and promised "a pleasing outcome for all."

He had sent a sternly worded grievance to MGM Italia and Fratelli di Conti for copyright infringement, which had resulted in a hastily organized meeting in the offices of MGM's Italian lawyer.

"I'll have my guy with me," Marcus assured Hoppy now. The doorway smelled of vinegar gone sour. He pulled at Hoppy's sleeve so that they could escape the stink, but the guy resisted.

"Sabbatini, right?"

Marcus nodded. "A bit overly polished for my tastes, but—"

"He and the guy who heads up MGM Italia are second cousins."

Marcus slumped against the glass window. "But Arlene's boss recommended him."

"Tanner's a million miles away; he wouldn't know the family connection. I only discovered it by accident myself. It's a long story and this is one meeting you shouldn't be late for." Hoppy consulted his watch. "You need to walk into that room assuming that everyone there is colluding to ensure you get the minimum deal."

"Eight thousand miles away, and they can still grind you into dust."

"Remember: *Metropolitana* is deep in pre-production. You've got them on the hook, and they know it."

Even as the head of MGM's writing department, Marcus had been made to feel like he always had his back foot at the cliff's edge, one vicious uppercut away from being slugged into the abyss.

*But not today. There's a big, fat barrel and for once, I'm not the sucker bent over it.*

Hoppy poked at Marcus's chest. "Don't trust anyone in that room. Melody told me that those Conti brothers can get real dramatic, real fast. And if it looks like they're not getting their way, they become confrontational, explosive, and intimidating. So whatever happens, you're Mister Cool."

"Got it."

But anxiety still creased Hoppy's face. "She also said the Conti brothers are bullies. Napoleon Conti will have extra bodies on his side of the table—the more bodies, the more intimidating."

"Seriously?" Marcus almost wanted to laugh. "His name is *Napoleon*?"

"I had a script meeting with him the other day. Stand your ground, keep your head, and don't get suckered into their theatrics."

"Don't worry," Marcus told him. "I've waited a long time to be the one holding the cards."

* * *

Salvatore Sabbatini stood in front of the offices of MGM Italia holding a shiny briefcase the color of dark cherry wood. It matched his shoes and necktie, and the silk band around his Panama hat. The diamond in his pinkie ring glinted as he offered his hand for Marcus to shake. They climbed the steps and walked into the white marble foyer.

"This meeting will be short," Sabbatini said. "They have done the wrong and breaked the law. So they will present you with an offer most fair and an apology most sincere." They arrived at a pebbled glass door. "Remember: I do the talking."

The offices reminded Marcus of the executive floor on the Irving Thalberg Building: the jangling of telephones fighting for attention with the din of typewriters amid a maze of glassed-in offices stretching in all directions.

Marcus and Sabbatini were led into a conference room. Like its MGM counterpart, it had huge windows running down one side, and on the opposite wall hung framed posters of recent Roman Empire epics.

Fratelli di Conti had packed their side of the conference table with twelve men. It wasn't hard to tell who was who. The lawyers were dressed in conservative suits and the film people had teamed their stylish skinny neckties with modern-cut suits and wide lapels.

In the middle of the table sat a stern-faced thug with short-cropped hair and an aquiline nose that would have been more at home jutting out from under a centurion helmet. The guy had *Napoleon* written all over him.

At the left-hand end, Marcus saw a familiar face.

He had only seen Emilio Conti once—the day Melody caught him sneaking photographs of Ingrid Bergman. But once was enough to see that he was a disagreeable little shit with a chip on his shoulder the size of St. Peter's Basilica. And now he could see why. Emilio was a pallid imitation of his older brother.

Whereas Napoleon radiated the authority of a Roman general, Emilio was the squirrelly little nutcase who cowered alone in the corner at a party.

Napoleon's handshake was every bit as genuine as the unctuous smile that parted his lips. He took a seat, opened the folder in front of him, and pulled out a single sheet of paper. Spreading his fingers across it, he said, "Our offer is straightforward and will correct the unfortunate—" He rattled out a question to the associate on his right. When the assistant replied, he turned to Marcus again, slipping his glassy smile back into place. "Oversight."

He pushed the paper across the conference table.

*So much for the apology most sincere.*

Marcus skimmed the words until he came to the amount. "Three hundred?"

"We feel it is fair."

"Three hundred *what*?" Marcus kept his voice cordial.

"American dollars."

Marcus shook his head very, very slowly at Napoleon. *What a ridiculous name, even if it does suit you.* "No."

A flutter of discomfort rolled through all twelve men on the other side of the table.

"What do you mean, no?" Napoleon snapped.

"Not even close to the figure I had in mind."

Sabbatini's hand gripped his forearm. "Signore Adler," the lawyer whispered, "this offer is more than—"

Marcus wrenched his arm away. "The answer is still 'no.'"

Napoleon jutted out his lantern jaw. "What is your amount?"

Marcus wished Kathryn and Gwendolyn were here to witness this. And Doris, too. And Arlene and Bertie and Quentin and Domenico. *What the hell, let's throw in L.B. Mayer, Clifford Wardell, Ramon, and Hugo.* He glanced up at the posters for *Queen of Judea, Titus Flavius,* and *Rome Burns*, and realized they were Melody Hope films. It made him feel like at least she was with him.

"Ten thousand."

Sabbatini made a strangled wheezing sound. Someone else in the room dropped a pen. Nobody moved.

Napoleon Conti looked like a Michelangelo statue—minus the warmth. His jaw quivered as he sucked his lips inside his mouth.

"And," Marcus placed his fingertip on the allegedly fair offer and pushed it away, "ten percent of the gross box office."

Napoleon flew to his feet in a blur, planted both palms on the table like an alpha gorilla. He unleashed a Vesuvian eruption of Italian that sounded like a single super-long incomprehensible word.

Marcus had sat through meetings with Hollywood studio heads, script conferences with spoiled movie stars and egotistical directors, and he'd endured a cross-examination at the hands of the House Un-American Activities Committee in front of the national media. And each time, he felt like he was being hauled through the wringer. Squashed and squeezed. Pummeled and beaten. Gwendolyn had once told him that his soul was too sensitive for a dog-eat-dog town like Hollywood, and on occasion he suspected maybe she was right.

But not anymore.

The realization exploded with a dizzying rush. *I truly do not give a rat's ass what this man is saying. I could leave this room right now and not look back. Not even to give him my best stink-eye.*

Napoleon Conti was still spewing his tirade like a lava-vomiting Titan when Marcus stood.

"Those are my terms, so if you don't like them . . ." He gave an exaggerated shrug like an old Jewish yenta. Sabbatini looked like his voice box had been clean slapped out of him. "I'll see myself out."

Marcus's hand was pressed against the polished wood of the conference room door when the defeated General Conti moaned, "Yes."

Marcus paused for a heartbeat and turned to face twelve furious Italians. Thirteen if he counted Sabbatini. "Ten thousand plus ten percent of the gross."

Conti nodded stiffly.

"If you can get that contract retyped immediately, we can leave this room with a signed agreement tied up in a pretty pink bow."

Napoleon Conti handed the old contract to the nearest flunky with instructions to locate the fastest typist in the office. The room festered with resentment. Marcus passed the time by playing a mental game—assigning names as though they were characters in a screenplay and giving them backstories. He wasn't halfway to Emilio when the flunky slapped three sheets of paper in front of him—the new contract and two copies.

*$10,000 American, plus 10% of the gross box office revenues.*

"Anybody got a pen?" Marcus asked the room. Emilio Conti skimmed one across the table. "When can I expect payment?"

"By the end of the year."

It was now the first week of December; Marcus longed to see the red-and-green Christmas decorations lit up along Hollywood Boulevard.

"By Christmas would be better." Salvatore Sabbatini gave a low grunt: *Don't push your luck, Yankee Doodle Dandy.*

Marcus signed the three copies, thanked Conti in a voice dripping with smarminess, and left the building. He hurried down the steps and found a patch of lukewarm sunlight among the shade trees. He pulled out his copy of the agreement. "Look at you," he told it, "helping me to bend General Conti over his own barrel and force him to take one for the team."

"GREEDY *BASTARDO*!" Emilio Conti was shorter than Marcus remembered—barely five foot four to Marcus's five nine, and scrawny in a Wile E. Coyote sort of way. "You will regret crossing the Conti brothers. I guarantee it!"

"Let me guess: you're a fan of James Cagney." *And about as tall, too.*

"Nobody takes advantage of Fratelli di Conti. NOBODY!"

Marcus could see he wasn't about to convince this furious little gnome of anything so he changed tack. "We have something in common."

Emilio looked him up and down. "We have nothing the same."

"You're the *scattino*, right?"

"Si."

"Me too."

Another down-up-down. "You? An *americano*? Ridiculous."

"Remember that *scattino* photograph of Sophia Loren on the set of *Quo Vadis*?"

Emilio nodded warily. Marcus jacked a thumb toward his chest.

*"Impossibile!"*

"I first came here to work on the *Quo Vadis* screenplay, and later documented the production with my camera." Marcus let the words sink in. "And then there's Ingrid Bergman."

Marcus's surreptitious snaps had come out extraordinarily well. He'd sent them to *Epoca* magazine, who'd bought them for a generous fee and featured six in a double-page spread. Marcus's favorite caught Bergman laughing at her magazine. It wasn't the most flattering photo, but she came across natural and unposed. Two weeks later it had landed on the cover of *Look* under the caption: *LOOK AT INGRID LOOKING AT LOOK!*

Emilio curled his lip into a snarl. "Loren *and* Bergman? I don't believe you."

Marcus rattled the contract in his hand. "Ciao."

* * *

A half-hour later, Marcus met Hoppy and Domenico in a café across the Tiber from the Castel Sant'Angelo where old men argued about football and chewed over battles they'd fought during the war.

He ordered an espresso, then laid the agreement in front of them.

When Domenico read the part about the lump sum, he slapped his cheeks. "*Gesù Cristo!*"

"All that and ten percent of the gross?" Hoppy told Marcus. "*Gesù Cristo* indeed!"

When Marcus told him Emilio was there too, Domenico's eyebrows hit the ceiling.

"Ah, poor Emilio," Domenico tsked. "If he wasn't so obnoxious, I almost feel sorry for him. Their mother could not make the babies. She saw every specialist in Italy but they told her it is God's will. She went to Lourdes and prayed; three months later she learned she was having triplets. She told everybody about her visit to Lourdes and the Virgin Mary blessed her." Domenico started juggling invisible balls. "The newspapers made a big deal of it, calling them the 'Conti Miracle Babies.'"

"And what about Emilio?" Marcus asked.

Domenico shook his head mournfully. "Twenty years later, Signora Conti was pregnant again. But the new baby wasn't a miracle like his brothers; he was a nuisance. He has been angry since the day he rushed out of his mother."

Hoppy asked, "Did you read the whole contract?"

"Sure."

"Do you know what 'locked funds' are?"

"It's when the Italians declared that Hollywood's pre-war profits could only be spent on projects aimed at reviving the Italian film industry. It's how *Quo Vadis* and *Three Coins* were financed."

"They're paying you out of locked funds."

"Is that illegal?"

"No, but you can't stuff ten thousand dollars' worth of lira into your pockets as you board the *Ile de France*."

"Why would I do that?"

"Because you can't take it out of the country."

Marcus snatched the paper from Hoppy's hand but he was too panicked to read the fine print. "So what does that mean?"

"You ain't going no place till we figure out how to get your money back to the States."

"I'm *still* stuck here?"

The insipid December sun fought hard to warm Marcus's face as a cool wind blew across the Tiber.

# CHAPTER 12

Kathryn flipped through the albums next to her record player.

*Dinah Shore Sings the Blues*? Too depressing.

*By the Light of the Silvery Moon with Doris Day*? Too sweet.

She skimmed through Anita O'Day, Fred Astaire, Kay Starr, and Bing Crosby, but nothing seemed right. *Eddie Fisher Sings* felt too earnest, and she wasn't even sure how *Christmas Day in the Morning with Burl Ives* had got there.

She came to *Sinatra Sings His Greatest Hits.* What would Ava do if she walked in and heard her husband's music? Would she think it a cute gesture? Or would she let loose with a string of cuss words and leave?

Three sharp knocks rang out. Ava Gardner opened the door and strode in like she owned the place. "I love how people around here still keep their doors unlocked." With the barest brush of mascara and a hint of lipstick, she still managed to fill Kathryn's living room with a radiance that few women enjoyed.

"Come on in!" Kathryn blew her a welcome kiss.

Ava bunched her hands together, threading and unthreading her fingers like shoelaces. She was usually so laid back that she gave Tallulah Bankhead a run for her money. Every slink of her hips and smirk on her lips seemed to say, "Cast me in your movie or don't; renew my contract or don't; stay the night or get out of bed. It's all the same to me."

But there was no "Go on, baby, give it your best shot" in the way Ava let her handbag slip onto the coffee table.

Kathryn lifted up two albums. "Kay or Jo?"

Ava pointed to Jo Stafford, so Kathryn placed *Portrait of New Orleans* onto her record player and let a jazzy trumpet meander through the villa. As she crossed to her liquor cabinet, Kathryn watched how Ava knotted together her fingers again and wondered if asking for a favor might not be such a great idea. But the days had blurred into weeks.

"I was so glad to get your call." Nostalgia tinged Ava's voice. "There are times I wish I still lived here. Life seemed so easy, didn't it?"

Kathryn twisted off the top of a bottle of Bristol Cream Sherry and pulled out a matching pair of lead crystal glasses. "But you were with Artie Shaw back then. As I recall, that marriage wasn't any walk in the park."

"More like a walk off the gangplank."

Ava accepted Kathryn's sherry and they clinked glasses. "Good to see you, ol' neighbor of mine."

Kathryn led her to the sofa, where she made a point of slipping out of her shoes, hoping her guest would do the same. She wanted Ava to feel relaxed and at home when she asked for the favor she had in mind.

But instead of following Kathryn's lead, Ava crossed her legs and fidgeted with the hem of her skirt as her eyes skipped about the room like nervous crickets. She sipped the cream sherry and let out a long breath. "I gotta say that when you invited me to lunch, I wasn't expecting a home-cooked meal from one of America's most beloved housewives."

As far as Kathryn knew, the Sunbeam - Betty Crocker - Westinghouse advertising ménage à trois was still under closed-door negotiations. "Where'd you hear that?"

Ava shrugged slyly. "Around."

"Around what? Stonehenge? You've been in England shooting *Knights of the Round Table* all summer."

"You of all people should know that branches of the grapevine extend past the eastern seaboard." She flicked her wrist, sending the tiny music charms on her bracelet tinkling against each other. "I think it's funny—you're about as useful in the kitchen as I am. But if mum's the word, my lips are sealed."

"Thank you," Kathryn said, "but it'll be a minor miracle if this idea even clears the starting gate."

Although she came off sounding like she couldn't care less, Kathryn was desperate for Leo's idea to gain traction. Now that her show was off the air and she was back to being just another columnist among dozens, her income had plummeted. Leo had promised her "tons of filthy lucre" if this deal went through, and she would need all the lucre she could lay her hands on to pay Dudley Hartman.

"And by the way," she told Ava, "if by 'home-cooked meal' you mean a bag of nosh I hauled home from Greenblatt's Deli, then yes, I've prepared everything by hand."

Ava held her sherry glass out for a refill. "Is this lunch business or pleasure?"

"A bit of both," Kathryn hedged. She refilled Ava's glass and topped up her own, although she'd barely touched it.

"Ain't it always?" Ava didn't sound particularly miffed. "Let's get the business part over with first. *Knights of the Round Table,* I assume?"

Ava's movie was MGM's first CinemaScope film, and the first CinemaScope production shot in Britain. It was also the first one not produced by 20th Century-Fox. Under Louis B. Mayer's stewardship, MGM had always set the gold standard. The studio's acknowledgment that they were using a rival's technology flashed a neon sign that, despite Dory Schary's assertions, Hollywood's former leading studio was unlikely to regain its primacy.

Kathryn nodded.

Ava sighed. "It's the usual stuff. Robert Taylor's very nice, Mel Ferrer not so much. I could have had an affair with any number of people but I've got my hands full with ol' Frankie, so I didn't. The costumes are lovely. The scenery, too. It's all uncomfortable armor and clanking swords and lines like, 'It's the valley of death. The Devil himself has plowed it under.' I'm not even sure I know what that means."

"Do you care?"

Ava replied with a light laugh. "It was an excuse to run away to Merrie Olde England."

Statements like these presented Kathryn with an ethical juggling act. On the one hand, they were a pair of old neighbors getting together for an overdue catch-up. But on the other, she was a prominent gossip columnist clinking sherry glasses with a world-famous movie star married to an equally well-known singer.

From the glittering, shiny surface she presented, it would seem that Ava Gardner had everything that society deemed worth chasing: looks, talent, success, money, marriage, fame. And yet here she was confessing she wanted to run away.

The friend in Kathryn wanted Ava to feel she could confide in her, but the gossip columnist was aching to pick up her pad and pen, sitting two feet away.

"Don't look at me like that," Ava said accusingly.

"Like what?"

Ava drained her glass and set it beside Kathryn's pad, tapping it several times with a fingernail. "We're still talking on the record."

"I wasn't sure."

"You'll know when we're not."

They weren't sitting in public—surely that must have given her a clue that Kathryn's invitation to lunch had an ulterior motive. "So *Knights of the Round Table* was an excuse to run away from what—or who?"

"Frank's great in the sack, but oh brother! Outside the bedroom, he's exhausting. His career is on a downward spiral right now, while mine is all hands on deck and man the battle stations. Everything with him is such a drama. Even that cameo I did in *The Band Wagon* last year. I was on set for one goddamned day, and you should have heard him."

"So when you told him that *Knights* was a four-month shoot in England, I bet that went down well."

Ava cast her eyes over to Kathryn's kitchen. "So what did you get at Greenblatt's?"

"Tuna salad on rye."

"And pickles?"

"Why bother going to Greenblatt's if you don't get the pickles?"

"Any chance we could eat outside? I've spent all week watching Frank record *Swing Easy*. He's hoping to project a fresh, hip image so that the public will—Jesus! I'm already bored to death. Some wife I am, huh?" She jumped to her feet. "I don't mind if it's a little chilly. It'll be nothing compared to England. What those people call 'summer' is a joke. All two and a half weeks of it."

They had the entire patio area out back of the main building to themselves. The house painters had done a terrific job sprucing up the place. Its fresh coat of light terracotta glowed in the sun through the daisy bushes and lemon trees.

Ava set two bottles of Schlitz beer on a wrought iron table and cast her eyes around the pool area. "Is the bougainvillea still as glorious as I remember? The summer Artie and I lived here, I got it into my head that I needed to exercise my mind and my body, so I took up swimming. Marcus gave me some lessons. How is he, by the way?"

"Good, as far as I—"

"By the end of that summer, I was a swimming machine, plowing through the water like a goddamned mermaid! But I also decided to read every book on the bestseller list. I started with *Forever Amber*. Christ knows why. The damned thing was nearly a thousand pages long."

"Probably because everybody was reading—"

"So there I was, sitting in that villa." Ava pointed across the pool to number eight, where Arlene now lived. Next to it lay the rectangular patch of newly turned dirt where Gwennie's tulips should soon come into bloom, brightening the place with winter color. "I was reading about little orphan Amber when Artie comes in and says, 'What the hell is that?' He grabs it out of my hand, calls it 'a pile of stinkin' fuckin' trash' and throws it clear across the room. Like he's the goddamned Literary Police." She bit off half a pickle spear and chomped it with her mouth open. "That was the beginning of the end, let me tell you."

"*The Razor's Edge* might've been a better—"

"Do you remember who that bastard married three days after our divorce came through? Kathleen Winsor. Do you know who she is?"

Kathryn hadn't seen Ava rant like this before. Her hopes of guiding the conversation in a different direction ebbed. "The author of *Forever Amber*."

"Ain't that the limit? Husbands—blagh!" She raised her Schlitz. "You've got the right idea, honey. Keep yourself single and avoid the melodrama."

As Ava slugged herself with more Schlitz, Kathryn sensed it was now-or-never time. "I have a favor to ask." It wasn't until the confession was out that she realized Ava had spoken at the same time. "What did you say?"

Ava unleashed a honking laugh. "I said that *I* need a favor from *you*. It's why I jumped at the chance to come over. If I hear Frank warble 'Jeepers Creepers' one more time, I'm going to lose my ever-lovin' mind. If I go out for lunch without him, he hits the roof. The only reason I'm here is because it's you and the Garden of Allah. He's got fond memories of this place and he respects you. As soon as I could see the first hint of him relenting, I beat it out of there so damned fast."

"Is that why you've been so jumpy?" Kathryn asked.

"I could ask the same thing."

"What?"

"Take a look at your pickle." Kathryn's kosher pickle had snapped in half, but she couldn't remember doing it. "I guess we're both a bit distracted."

"You want to go first?"

Ava dropped her sandwich onto her plate. "I need to get out of LA."

"But you only just got back."

"Sinatra and his goddamned jealousy. It drives me batty! If I stick around, I'll end up planting a knife between his ribs."

"Let's try and avoid *that* scenario."

"You get the lowdown with what's going on around town before everybody else. I was hoping—I mean, I know it's a long shot and all—but perhaps in a movie that's shooting outside LA. Canada, maybe? Mexico?"

"What about Rome?"

Ava clamped a firm hand around Kathryn's wrist. "Perfect!"

Marcus had recently written about how Jean Negulesco told him that Joe Mankiewicz wanted to cast Rossano Brazzi in his next movie and so it might be in Marcus's interests if he took tons of photos of Brazzi on the *Three Coins* set. Recently, Kathryn heard that Mank had signed Brazzi, but was still looking for the female lead.

"How would you like to work for Joe Mankiewicz?"

It was a redundant question to ask any actress after what he'd done for Bette Davis in *All About Eve*.

Ava's face filled with excitement. "Is this the one about the naked duchess?"

"*Barefoot Contessa*. Would MGM consider lending you out?"

"If I beg the right people. Who else is in it?"

"Bogie."

"Oh boy!"

"Lauren will probably be with him and Marcus is still there. It'll be a mini Garden of Allah reunion."

Ava clapped her hands. "This gets better and better!

"I could put in a call to Mank's office and plant a seed. He owes me a favor after I wrote a positive item about his *Julius Caesar*."

Ava started strumming the patio table hard enough to chip a nail. "I'd really owe you one."

Kathryn put down the remainder of her tuna sandwich and wiped her mouth. "I've heard that Winchell is squiring you to the opening of *The Wild One*."

Ava shot her a side-look. "You can blame Harry Cohn for that. Frank's been nominated for Supporting Actor on *From Here to Eternity* and Harry doesn't get much of a crack at Oscar bragging rights, so he asked Frank to let me accompany Winchell to the *Wild One* premiere in exchange for getting fully behind a campaign to win Frank an Oscar."

"How do you feel about that?" Kathryn asked.

"I'm a Hollywood actress. I'm used to getting shoved around like cattle. The question is, what do *you* want from *me*?"

"I was hoping that perhaps when the conversation starts to run a little dry, you could suggest Winchell call me when he's in town."

"Is that all?" Ava jammed her cigarette butt into the remainder of her sandwich. "I could do that without getting out of bed."

"If he presses you for more information, tell him that I had you over for lunch and that I hinted at a story that's so big, you got the impression that I didn't know how to handle it."

"Why don't you call him up yourself?"

"Because I need him to think it's his idea. Plant the seed that I need someone with Winchell's status and influence, and he'll come running."

She lit up another cigarette, took a breath, and shook her head. "Male vanity. They make it so easy, don't they?"

"Ordinarily, I'd agree with you," Kathryn said, "but Winchell's a cunning little swine."

"Yeah, but he's still a man." She slouched in her chair and slung an arm over the back. "You leave it to me, honey."

# CHAPTER 13

Gwendolyn and Doris stood at the edge of their tulip bed.

"Maybe we dug too deep?"

Doris stabbed the bare ground with a rake. "Should we excavate and do an autopsy?"

Gwendolyn heard the patter of heels slapping the concrete that the construction workers had laid for the bar's remodeling. The Garden's new management had promised the residents more sunlight, more booths, more elbow room, and a dance floor. The re-opening was in three weeks' time; Gwendolyn wasn't sure that it was achievable, but at least the concrete was dry enough to walk on.

Doris slung the rake over her shoulder. "If they're not poking up out of the dirt by February, we'll know we've committed mass murder."

"Careful!" a voice behind them warned. "You could take an eye out with that thing."

Even in a frayed woolen dark blue coat, a nondescript dress that neither accentuated nor hid her figure, and ankle-laced espadrilles, Marilyn Monroe still managed to ooze a little something special.

"What on Earth . . .?" Gwendolyn cried out. "I thought you were hiding out until the whole *Playboy* ruckus blew over."

Marilyn brushed a lock of white-blonde hair out of her eyes. "Assuming it ever will."

Between her romance with Joe DiMaggio, her *Photoplay*'s "Hollywood's Fastest Rising Star" award, and her *Gentlemen Prefer Blondes* and *How to Marry a Millionaire* hits, Marilyn had been everywhere. And just when her fame seemed to be approaching saturation point, a new magazine had hit the stands.

*Playboy* touted itself as a men's magazine that would teach single professional men how to choose Bermuda shorts, shop for steaks, initiate a conversation with a pretty girl, and navigate modern politics, while exposing newly fabricated urbanites to Hemingway, the beat culture, and what was going on in an obscure country called Vietnam—all for fifty cents.

And to catch their attention, *Playboy* had acquired the rights to Marilyn's nude calendar photographs, dubbing her their "Sweetheart of the Month."

"I was going stir crazy at home," Marilyn said, "especially with Joe leaving for San Francisco." Marilyn peered at the bare patch of dirt behind Gwendolyn and Doris. "Whatcha doing?"

"We planted tulips but nothing's appeared."

Marilyn squatted and dug a finger into the ground. "This feels awfully damp."

Gwendolyn and Doris traded looks of we-drowned-'em regret.

"Well, that does it for me." Doris grabbed up the rake again. "I'm off to see *Beneath the 12-Mile Reef* at Grauman's." She bid them adieu and headed back to her villa.

"Do you like honey spice cake?" Gwendolyn asked.

"I don't know that I've ever had it."

"Betty Crocker sent Kathryn a ton of cake mixes. More than she could use in a year, so we each got a bunch. Want to help me bake one?"

Marilyn sighed. "That's the most normal question anyone's asked me in a year."

Inside Gwendolyn's villa, Marilyn shucked her coat as Gwendolyn pulled the cover off her Mixmaster—another perk of being Kathryn Massey's best friend.

With the tornado of publicity generated by the *Playboy* cover, Zanuck wanted an update on the possibility of a Monroe/DiMaggio wedding. But Marilyn hadn't been at the studio much now that retakes on *River of No Return* were finished, so Gwendolyn had nothing to report.

"See what you can find out," Zanuck had barked, then tempered his voice. "I'm not asking you to betray confidences." *The hell you ain't.* "And I'm not asking that you manipulate her." *That's exactly what you're doing.* "I need to know if she's going to marry DiMaggio. A marriage like that has repercussions. And you'll do well to remember who signs your paychecks."

Gwendolyn smiled at Marilyn. "Still wearing my Sunset Boulevard perfume?"

"Now that you're no longer in business, I have to ration myself."

Gwendolyn angled her head toward the bedroom. "I still have a hundred bottles. Any time you want more, just holler."

"Quelle relief! It's Joe's favorite."

Gwendolyn retrieved a couple of eggs from the refrigerator and returned to the counter, where she ripped open the box of cake mix and emptied its contents into the bowl.

"So Joe went back to San Francisco?"

"Uh-huh."

"In a huff over *Playboy*?"

"What's five notches above a huff?"

"Bad mood? Sulk? Rage?"

"Bingo."

She added the water to the batter but it sat there in a gluey lump. "How are you supposed to resolve a row if he leaves town?"

"That's what I'd like to know."

"He's rather traditional, isn't he?"

"And how. It's not like I asked them to publish those photos, but when the person you're going to marry is furious beyond furious, it makes life even harder than it already is."

Gwendolyn cracked the eggs into the bowl and inserted it under the beaters. "Are you going to marry him?"

"I love him, so why wouldn't I?"

Marilyn hadn't been using the breathy baby-girl voice that she used on screen—until just now. She pulled the Mixmaster toward her and flipped the switch to "ON." The noise prevented conversation.

Gwendolyn hated how she was being pressured into interrogating Marilyn like this, and for what? To keep her lousy job?

But it wasn't a lousy job. If Chez Gwendolyn had to close, this new situation was ideal. She was creating gorgeous outfits for television's best-loved fashion icon. Plus she got to work with Billy Travilla and Charles LeMaire, who knew everything about dreaming up clothes that would influence the course of American fashion for the next ten years.

*What's not to like?* She observed Marilyn's sadly beautiful but beautifully sad face as she watched the Mixmaster whip the batter into a maple-colored brew. *This,* she decided, *is what I don't like.*

Marilyn flipped off the Mixmaster and lifted the beaters out of the bowl. She ran a finger along one of the blades and tasted the batter. "This is good!"

Gwendolyn pulled her cake tin from her cupboard and set about greasing it. The words *I have a confession* hung on the tip of her tongue when Marilyn said, "You were right. Joe was furious about *Playboy,* which is hypocritical seeing as how he's never seen it. Then again, nor have I."

Gwendolyn plunged her wooden spoon into the cake mix. "You haven't?"

Marilyn's bright blue eyes flew open. "Have you?"

"I'm not the one featured in a controversial magazine."

"If I brought home a copy, it'd be the start of world war three."

"But you must be just a teensy bit curious."

"I'll say!"

"Do you want to go out and get one?"

Marilyn's lips formed a perfect "O" as she pressed her fingertips to her cheeks. "Where will we go?" Her question came out a hoarse whisper, as though DiMaggio might hear.

"Schwab's has a newsstand."

"No!" Marilyn blurted out. "Sidney'll be there!"

Sidney Skolsky was a journalist best known for his gossip column, *From A Stool At Schwab's,* and was one of the reasons why the pharmacy was still a central hub of Hollywood social life. He was also Marilyn's close friend and enthusiastic booster.

"There's a newsstand on Hollywood Boulevard," Gwendolyn suggested.

"The one near Musso and Frank?"

"But you're bound to be recognized."

"Oh, please!" Marilyn swatted away Gwendolyn's caution. "I walked down the Strip just now and nobody recognized me."

"How did you pull that off?"

"Confidence, posture, smile, makeup, hair, clothes, voice—you put it together and you—" she threw her arms out wide "—pop! But if you want to go unnoticed, you walk like someone who has no reason to fear getting recognized.

Marilyn dived into her pocketbook and pulled out a dark brown wig snipped into a pixie cut. "Come on, it'll be fun. I don't often get to walk around like Miss Anonymous."

Ten minutes later, with the cake mix in the Frigidaire and Marilyn in a pretzel-colored wig, they jaywalked across Crescent Heights Boulevard and headed along Sunset. Every passerby was preoccupied with their bag of groceries or energetic beagle straining at the leash and ignored her.

"I tell Joe all the time: Walk like a nobody and you are a nobody, but he's not willing to let me prove it. But if you ever meet him, don't tell him I told you that. He's super-private about everything. He doesn't like me bringing up anything we've talked about with other people, so keep all this between us, okay? I called him paranoid once. Oh brother, that didn't go over well."

They ambled past a line of old houses being razed to make way for apartments. By the time they were clear of it, Gwendolyn couldn't bear the weight of her conscience any longer.

"I have a confession to make. Zanuck wants me to report any information about you that I feel he ought to know."

Marilyn faced Gwendolyn with a thunderstruck look in her eye. "Spy on me?"

"He balked at my use of the word 'spy' but yes, that's the gist of it. But you and I have scarcely seen each other."

Marilyn lifted an overhanging honeysuckle vine to her nose. She breathed in deeply, hoping for some scent. "Do you think Betty Grable had to go through this nonsense? Or Alice Faye?"

"I think they were more content to do what they were told."

"So this is the price I pay for having an opinion and the guts to express it?"

They were heading into the commercial stretch of Hollywood Boulevard, where foot traffic was markedly busier. The lights turned green and they stepped off the curb.

"What'll we tell Zanuck the Panic?" Marilyn asked over the rumble of a passing bus. "You'll need to throw him a bone sooner or later. What would convince him that you're an obedient undercover agent?"

"He's all worked up over whether or not you're marrying Joe."

Marilyn sank back into her I'm-a-little-nobody posture as they approached The Hollywood House of Radio and Television. NBC had recently broadcast the Tournament of Roses Parade in color, but Gwendolyn hadn't seen it. Four TV sets lined up along the store window showed only a test pattern but it was arresting to see the vibrant colors.

"Joe didn't fly to San Francisco because he was in a huff over *Playboy*," Marilyn said, glued to the circle with eight colored panels, "but to arrange our wedding."

The eye-catching display attracted the attention of a pair of sales clerks dressed in Kress's five-and-dime uniforms. Gwendolyn nudged Marilyn along. "Congratulations."

"It's next week."

"But surely you don't want me to tell Zanuck that."

"As a matter of fact, I do." Marilyn sounded remarkably sanguine.

"He'll either sabotage it or turn it into a three-ring publicity circus."

"I want you to tell him, but wait until that morning. It'll be too late for him to round up a truckload of reporters, but he'll think you jumped on the blower as soon as you caught wind of it."

"Everybody wins." Gwendolyn wished the public knew how savvy Marilyn truly was, but audiences preferred their baby-doll blondes to be stupid.

They were at the newsstand now, where several copies of *Playboy* sat on display. The cover showed Marilyn sitting on white fur, wearing a black dress with a white collar and a neckline that plunged almost to her navel. Her mouth stretched into a mile-wide smile, she was waving like a beauty queen in a small-town parade.

Marilyn pulled the lapels of her plain woolen coat around her neck and sank her chin toward her chest. "I'll meet you inside."

The newsstand guy showed no surprise that a woman in her forties was buying a bachelor magazine. He slapped a copy into her left hand and took the two quarters she proffered in her right. Gwendolyn tucked it under her arm and stole into the restaurant.

Marilyn was seated in the second rear-most table, the large menu propped up in front of her. Gwendolyn passed the magazine over. She studied the cover for a moment. "I think they've shaded my breast to accentuate the curve."

"It *is* called *Playboy*," Gwendolyn pointed out.

Marilyn flipped open the magazine to the lead article and read the headline out loud. "'What makes Marilyn?' That's not even a complete sentence."

Gwendolyn pointed to the shot of Marilyn in a super-low-cut polka dot dress that made it look like her bust was about to spill out for all the world to see. "I doubt anybody's checking for grammar."

The roar of traffic swelled as the door opened and two men stomped inside.

Marilyn gave a little gasp. "Who's *that*?"

"Victor Mature."

"I mean his pal."

"The British guy from *The Robe*. Zanuck wants him to play the brother of John Wilkes Booth in *Prince of Players*, but he's refusing. Pretty ballsy, huh?"

*The Robe* was still drowning Fox in box office profits when Zanuck had offered Richard Burton a seven-year, seven-picture contract worth an astounding one million dollars. Hollywood had shaken its collective head when the Welshman turned him down and headed home to portray Hamlet at the Old Vic in London for a hundred and fifty pounds per week. They must have reached some sort of agreement, because Burton had returned to LA to start his contract.

Judy Lewis was happy to share what she'd heard on the studio's grapevine while Gwendolyn toiled on her mother's gowns. Gwendolyn, in turn, passed the best of the bunch onto Kathryn, who always appreciated a juicy squib.

After the red-jacketed waiter took their drinks order, they watched the stars of one of the biggest movies of the decade take over the room. These two didn't have to glad-hand patrons like a pair of politicians running for the Senate. By sheer force of personality, Burton and Mature were a pair of lighthouses shining their incandescence over a sea of spellbound faces.

"I think Joe is having me followed."

Lost in Burton's mesmeric presence, Gwendolyn needed a moment to take in Marilyn's admission. "Are you sure?"

She pulled at the edges of her wig. "Call it a hunch."

"You don't have to marry him, you know."

The waiter appeared with their martinis and asked if they were ready to order. Gwendolyn shooed him away.

Marilyn stirred her olive stick with resigned disinterest. She pulled it out of her cocktail glass then prodded the olive stick in Burton's direction. "I wish I could be more like him."

Burton and Mature sat halfway along the bar. It was a classic movie star move: force everyone's attention and pretend you don't care. They executed it with perfect nonchalance, but Gwendolyn wasn't fooled. *Of course they care. Everybody cares.*

Customers and staff alike watched Burton and Mature clink glasses and boom "BOTTOMS UP!"

*Clark Gable and his whole* Mogambo *safari could come thundering through here and nobody would notice.*

"Of course!"

"Of course what?" Marilyn asked.

"Clark Gable asked me to do him a favor and I've figured out how I can help him." Gwendolyn picked up the menu. "What do you think? The Chicken en Casserole Parisienne, or the Smoked Beef Tongue?"

# CHAPTER 14

Marcus chose a table in the sun outside Café Lombardia. He pulled out a pen and a postcard of the Spanish Steps.

*Dear Kathryn, I have taken an Italian lover! We just rode on his shiny black Vespa past these steps to a café on Via Veneto where we'll order espresso macchiato and biscotti. Delizioso! And so is he!*

Domenico joined him at the table, all smiles and windswept hair. He spotted the postcard and smiled. "To your friend, Katerina?"

Marcus wished he'd addressed the card *Dear Katerina*. He passed it across the table and placed their order.

Domenico smiled. "I am *delizioso*?"

"You are."

"*Delizioso* like espresso macchiato?"

"More like a biscotti."

"Because I taste like almonds?"

"Because you're so hard I'm surprised I haven't cracked a tooth."

The two men laughed. They did that frequently—it was one of the many blessings this fun-loving, joy-spreading, pleasure-seeking Italian had dropped into Marcus's lap. His short-lived victory over the Conti brothers had taught Marcus to take happiness where he could find it.

Ten grand was too much money to leave behind—not that he had seen a dime of it yet. So until the money came through, why not enjoy Rome and its delights: the food, the cafés, the history, the architecture—*and my Italian lover*.

"Why do you smile?" Domenico asked.

"I was wondering if you minded me describing you as 'my Italian lover.'"

"It is *molto* sexy. And it is the truth, no?" He ran his finger down Marcus's arm. "And I am your lover, *si*?"

Marcus nodded, and pulled away as the waiter arrived. The biscotti at the Café Lombardia were extra thick and extra long, leaving Marcus to wonder if perhaps he could break with tradition and dunk it into his coffee.

He went to ask Domenico if such an act was considered tacky when he caught a familiar figure slinking along the sidewalk. Dressed in a white woolen skirt with a vibrant butterfly print under a teal swing coat, she twirled her patent leather purse around her wrist with the abandon of a well-dressed prison escapee.

Marcus lifted his sunglasses. "Ava?"

Ava Gardner let out a piercing squeal and swooped in for an embrace, enveloping him in Gwendolyn's perfume. He breathed it in deeply. "Kathryn told me you were coming but not until the end of the month."

She dragged a seat from a neighboring table. "I had my reasons for leaving early."

A couple of times a week, Kathryn mailed off the latest *Hollywood Reporter*, and enclosed a letter detailing tidbits too salacious to print.

She described the quarrel when Ava had told Frank that she'd accepted the lead in *The Barefoot Contessa* and would be shooting in Rome for the first three months of 1954. The spat had disintegrated into a shouting match at Chasen's that ended with shattered glassware and broken crockery, rice pilaf sprayed across a neighboring table, and a champagne carpet stain the size of an LP record.

Ava took measure of Domenico. "And who is this handsome specimen?"

"Domenico Beneventi at your service, signorina." He gently kissed the top of Ava's hand.

"Holy cannoli!" Ava turned to Marcus. "Hats off to you, baby."

"How long have you been here?" Marcus asked.

She ordered a Campari from a passing waiter. "A few days."

"Enjoying the peace and quiet?"

"Chasen's has seen worse." Ava lit up a Lucky Strike and sent him a deprecating smirk. "We're in Rome, you're in love, Campari is cheap—why talk about that scrawny little shit? Tell me, Marcus, what's this I heard about you being a—a—what's the word? Scatinski? Scattalini?"

"*Scattino*," Domenico said. "Marcus is *molto famoso*."

"Get outta here!"

"I'm hardly famous."

Domenico slapped a hand on Marcus's back. "After he photographed Sophia Loren, everybody in Rome says, 'Who is this mysterious *scattino*?' And then Marcus, he took some photos of Ingrid Bergman—"

"I saw that cover!"

"Now everybody knows *Lo Scattino Americano*."

"Stop!" Marcus swatted Domenico's arm. He took any opportunity to touch the man.

Ava tapped a fingertip against her chin with a slow, purposeful rhythm. "How about you take a *scattino* photo of me? Right now!"

"I'm sure Joe Mankiewicz will have plenty of opportunities for you to pose—"

"This is for Cranky Frankie. He accused me of accepting *Barefoot Contessa* so that I'd have a chance at schtupping Rossano Brazzi. He said to me, 'You've obviously got a thing for wops. Three months oughta give you plenty of time to lure him between the sheets. And if you flunk out, you'll have a whole city chock full of drooling wops to choose from.'"

"I can see why you want to punch out the lights of your husband," Domenico said.

Marcus was impressed with Domenico's command of English, but the ways he mangled it brought a smile to Marcus's lips.

"Is there a park around here?" Ava asked. "Lots of trees and shrubs?"

"The grounds of the Villa Borghese are close by."

"Got your camera on you?"

Marcus had trained himself to always carry it with him. "I smell mischief."

Ava looked into the sky. "I'd say we have about an hour of sun left."

* * *

She spotted a thicket of umbrella pines surrounded by a ring of citrus trees. "Perfect!"

"Are you sure you want to do this?"

"I'll teach him to accuse me of wanting to seduce Rossano goddamned Brazzi!"

"The man *is* handsome," Domenico pointed out.

"That's beside the point."

They arrived at the ring of lemon trees alternating with orange that stretched twelve feet across and ensured absolute privacy. Somewhere between Café Lombardia and this quiet little nook, Marcus had warmed to Ava's idea. He was determined to return home with his *Metropolitana* nest egg intact. *Epoca* had paid him generously for the Bergman shots, so how much would they shell out for titillating photos of an American actress fresh off her Academy Award nomination for *Mogambo*?

He pictured Emilio Conti sneering at him. *Lo Scattino Americano.* "You know who will hate this?" he asked Domenico.

"I do."

"Who are we talking about?" Ava asked.

"A prick named Emilio Conti," Marcus told her. "He's Scattino Number One around here."

"He was," Domenico said, "until Sophia Loren and Ingrid Bergman. *Epoca* will be dancing with the joy over these photos, but Emilio will be furious like if you got to *La Speranza* first."

"Who is *La Speranza*?" Marcus asked.

"She was in one of our big Roman Empire films. It was a success, so she got another movie and it did better. Her next film earned the biggest box office. We saw her everywhere but now she likes to play the mystery woman, like *La Garbo*. If you can get a photograph of *La Speranza*, it will make you the most famous *scattino* in Rome. Conti will hate that."

Marcus removed the lens cap from his camera. "What about up against that tree?"

Ava let her coat slump to her feet. She cocked a leg against the tree trunk and pulled Domenico against her.

"Put your right arm over my head," she directed him. "Grab my ass with your left hand and don't be shy." Domenico stifled a giggle as he followed her instructions. "Angle your head away from the camera."

Marcus lifted his Leica. "Can I point out that Mank might not like this? It could have repercussions for his movie."

"I'm playing a poor girl turned man-eating diva, so this plays into the entire scenario. The possibility of causing Frank to spontaneously combust from jealousy is purely coincidental."

Marcus stood back to survey the tableau. "If you want to convince Frank, I suggest hitching your skirt. Or better still, Domenico, hitch it up for her, preferably as high as her panties."

"Who says I'm wearing any?" Ava laughed when Domenico jerked his hand away. "Relax, my European paramour. I am. Today."

Domenico pushed Ava's butterfly skirt up her leg. When a hint of lace showed, Marcus pressed his eye to the viewfinder. "Stop! Before I get jealous."

* * *

Ten days later, Marcus walked onto the Cinecittà studio lot with a copy of *Epoca* magazine rolled in his hand. He ran his eye down the blackboard inside the gates until he saw that *Barefoot Contessa* was filming on Stage Five.

The elaborate set of columns, arches, and frescoes was every bit as impressive as anything Hollywood could produce. At the center stood an artist's studio reaching two stories high. A life-sized sculpture of Ava's character stood on a pedestal, and to its right, resplendent in a sheer white gown of billowing gauze, Ava sat on a director's chair with Bogie on one side and Bacall on the other.

Marcus jiggled the magazine between his fingertips until Ava spotted him. She let out a scream when she saw the cover photo of herself, leaning against an umbrella palm, her head thrown back, her lips parted in an orgiastic moan as Domenico kissed her throat.

"Show me! Show me!"

Marcus hadn't seen Bogie since the shooting of *Sirocco* during his brief career as an extra, so he and Bogie and Lauren had some catching up to do. Soon they were bombarding him with recommendations for cafés, restaurants, and bars.

Ava pointed to the caption stamped across the bottom: *IL SUO AMANTE ITALIANO MISTERIOSO*. "Does this mean what I think it means?"

"Her mysterious Italian lover."

She let out a whoop that brought Joe Mankiewicz onto the set. She showed him the magazine. "Frank's going to flip his toupée when I send it to him anonymously."

"Save yourself the postage," Mank said. "He's already seen it. *Epoca* tried to sell the rights to *Look*. They were too spicy so they said no, but *Confidential* said yes. They're causing a sensation. And you're right—Frank has well and truly flipped his toupée. I just got off the phone from ten minutes of his caterwauling."

This news set Ava off into a laughing jag. "This is all too, too priceless!" She could barely wring the words out. "It couldn't be better if I'd planned it myself."

Mank examined the cover a little more closely. "Whoever took those photos has a great eye."

Ava pulled Marcus next to her. "Meet the photographer," she said, blotting her tears before the smudged mascara leaked onto her snowy-white dress. "Joe Mankiewicz, I want you to meet Marcus Adler."

Mankiewicz's handshake was firm. "Bette Davis has only the kindest words to say about you." He guided him to a window draped in diaphanous silk. "You took those stills on *Three Coins*, didn't you?"

"I hope you liked them. Negulesco said—"

"They helped me cast Rossano in this picture, so I have you to thank."

Ava let out a screech high enough to set dogs to barking. Marcus caught the word "panties," but Bacall's baritone laugh drowned out the rest.

"Those photos you took of Ava," Mank said, "they're the sorts of stills I want for this production, so I'd like to hire you for that, but there's also something else."

"You need help with the script?" Marcus asked, his hopes rising.

"Rossano's English was decent enough for *Three Coins* but I'm worried that American audiences might not understand him in this picture as well as they'll need to." Marcus didn't know what *The Barefoot Contessa* was about, but if Joe Mankiewicz had written it, it was likely to be a witty, sophisticated script. "He's especially self-conscious sharing the screen with Bogie and Ava, so I want you to coach him on pronunciation. If you're around as production photographer you can help out whenever he's feeling insecure. How does that sound?"

Mank was asking him to commit to the end of March, by which time he'd have been gone from LA for eight months, which was seven months too long.

"I can see you're hesitating," Mank said. "Is it a matter of pay? I have a discretionary fund I can draw from. Let's call it one hundred a week for production stills, and another hundred to help Rossano with his English. I can pay you cash, dollars, or lira—whichever you prefer."

*On the other hand, your Zanuck funds are running out.*

Marcus could draw on the *Subway People* windfall but he liked the "screw you, Conti brothers" quality to the notion of spiriting their money out of the country intact.

Across the set, Ava drew a line along her lips. "The identity of my clandestine Italian lover must remain secret!"

Marcus hadn't been the focus of someone's affection in a while. It was the little things that added up. Hearing the rhythmic breath of someone else in the bed. Looking for the pepper grinder and finding that someone was already passing it over. Knowing that his favorite Tuscan chianti would be waiting for him come dinnertime.

Marcus could hear Kathryn's voice in his head: *Three more months of that sort of treatment? A boy could do worse.*

Marcus held out his hand. "You've got yourself a deal."

Mank shook it with his right hand and with his left, pulled a compact English/Italian dictionary out of his pocket. "This is yours now."

Since that day in the Villa Borghese gardens, Marcus had been meaning to look up a word he hadn't encountered before. He flipped to the "S" tab.

*la speranza (noun) – the hope*

Domenico had described *La Speranza* as an actress who'd done well in a series of Roman epics.

Marcus smiled. He knew of an actress who fit that description.

Melody Hope.

# CHAPTER 15

Ciro's on the Sunset Strip had long embodied the pinnacle of Hollywood nightclub glamor. During that time, many clubs had sparkled brightly for a while, then fizzled into obscurity. Gwendolyn had a theory about why Ciro's had outlasted the competition: with its cream drapery and discreetly indirect illumination, everybody at Ciro's looked like they benefited from the best lighting professionals in the business.

But when she stepped into the club the evening of St. Valentine's Day, Gwendolyn let out a yip of surprise.

Judy Lewis peeked over her shoulder. "What's wrong?"

"It looks like Mocambo!"

Contrasting with Ciro's understated blend of creams, Mocambo was a riotous explosion of gay colors, as though Salvador Dali had been in charge of designing a Mardi Gras parade. Angelinos in search of an evening's entertainment could never confuse the two.

Until now.

Intertwined streamers of candy-apple red and Kelly green hung from the ceiling in low-hanging loops. A series of clown masks, each of them two feet wide, leered their frozen smiles over the audience. Three papier-mâché tightrope walker puppets with gangling long limbs decked out in gold-spangled tights danced along thick twine stretched across the top of the stage.

"Good grief!" The outburst came from Kathryn. "Do you think Kay knows about this?"

Officially, Kay Thompson was the reason the "Gwendolyn Brick Party of Eight" were at Ciro's. Their former Garden of Allah neighbor was now working the nightclub circuit as a solo and was making a splashy return to LA with a two-week run.

"Yes, Miss Thompson knows, and she's not terribly happy." The Ciro's maître d' was the usual sort of meticulously groomed and unflappable type that places like these needed to keep drunken shenanigans to a minimum. He waved a dismissive hand toward the kitschy decorations. "The circus theme is for Darryl Zanuck. What it has to do with St. Valentine's Day escapes me, but fortunately it's only for one night."

Leo gave a snort. "If self-generating rumor is anything to go by, Zanuck's bedroom prowess verges on the acrobatic, so there's that."

The maître d' smirked almost imperceptibly as he collected up eight menus. He led them to a table near the dance floor. Gwendolyn pulled at his elbow. "You should have a booking under Waterfield. Do you know where they'll be seated?"

The maître d' indicated a four-top directly opposite them on the other side of the dance floor.

Gwendolyn sat Judy Lewis at the center of the table, facing the room. "Kay is a force to be reckoned with and you don't want to miss a second."

Gwendolyn's date for the night was Quentin Luckett, who had recruited a suitable date for Judy. Jonathan Brady was a long-legged chap with an aw-shucks manner about him. Quentin had assured Gwendolyn that Jonathan was "suitable" because he had been the assistant choreographer on *White Christmas* at Paramount. "Assistant choreographer" was code for "gay as a goose," which meant he could show Judy a good time without Gwendolyn worrying about slow-dance groping.

Gwendolyn indicated that Quentin take the chair opposite her, with Brady taking the one across from Judy. Leo sat opposite Kathryn, and rounding out the party was Doris and her new beau, Emmett, a location scout at Columbia.

The six-man band on the stage started playing a leisurely version of "On the Atchison, Topeka, and the Santa Fe." Kay had done the original vocal arrangement for MGM, and half the crowd started humming along.

Gwendolyn looked across to the Waterfield table. It still sat empty with only thirty minutes to show time.

"Emmett," she prompted, "tell Judy about your work on *From Here to Eternity*."

Doris had told Gwendolyn that, if the conversation lagged, she should ask Emmett to recount his *From Here to Eternity* story. He was the guy who'd found the beach where the steamy Lancaster/Kerr kiss took place. It was an interesting story and Emmett told it well—especially the part where the two of them were supposed to clinch standing up until Lancaster suggested they do it horizontally. "No great surprise considering the two of them were going at it hammer and tongs in between takes." By the time he was done, the maître d' had seated the Waterfield party.

Bob Waterfield was married to Jane Russell and their guest was Clark Gable, whom Russell and Waterfield were wooing now that they'd formed a production company with the support of Howard Hughes. Waterfield and Clark rose to their feet when Clark's date, a vacant-eyed starlet with a jumble of Betty Hutton-esque curls piled on her head, arrived at their table. As he resumed his seat, Clark proffered Gwendolyn a quick smile.

The band changed to a jaunty "I Won't Dance." Gwendolyn pulled at an earlobe. It was the signal she'd arranged with Jonathan.

"Miss Lewis?" He extended his hand across the table. "Would you give me the pleasure?"

"Miss Brick?" Quentin extended his hand too. "A whirl around the dance floor, if you please?"

Gwendolyn and Quentin joined the Gary Coopers and the Randolph Scotts quickstepping around the Ciro's floor. She followed Clark's eyes as he watched Brady rotate his daughter into an effortless series of turns.

"Your friend Jonathan was a perfect choice," she told Quentin.

"He's a big Loretta Young fan, so I hardly had to talk him into it."

Quentin launched into a story about how James Stewart's wife was fretting that Grace Kelly would seduce her husband during the filming of *Rear Window*. But Gwendolyn listened with only one ear.

She watched Clark invite his giggling date to the dance floor as the band changed to "The Tennessee Waltz." When they swished past, Clark winked at her and mouthed "Thank you."

Quentin dug a knuckle into Gwendolyn's back. "What's going on with Gable? He thanked you for—wait a cotton-pickin' . . .!" His eyes bounced between Judy and Gable, then back to Gwendolyn. "Those rumors are true?"

The bandleader faced the microphone and asked that everybody take their seats as Miss Thompson's show was beginning shortly.

Gwendolyn led Quentin back to their table as loud rata-tat-tat laughter discharged from a large group swarming the entrance. Darryl Zanuck beamed like a victorious despot dressed in an expensive tux, his black silk bowtie already skewed to one side. On his left stood his wife, Virginia, a narrow-faced woman with the air of someone more suited to running a church bazaar and who was conspicuously no competition for the statuesque beauty in a snug gown of sapphire silk who stood at his right elbow.

Gwendolyn tilted her head toward Kathryn. "Is that Bella Darvi?"

"All thirty-eight, twenty-two, thirty-six of her."

The Zanuck party filed into the room, shrieking with laughter fueled by several robust pre-show cocktails. They tottered toward a pair of long parallel tables and took their seats, and the house lights dimmed to a drum roll.

"Ladies and gentlemen, Ciro's proudly presents the incomparable Miss Kay Thompson."

Kay strutted onto the stage dressed in white: a clinging long-sleeved top sprinkled with champagne-colored bugle beads, accented with chunky silver jewelry, white pants, and open-toed high heels.

"Hello, Hollywood!" she boomed into the mike. "Did you miss me?"

The crowd roared its reply. As it was dying down, a male voice yelled, "Like a dose of penicillin!"

Kay's head fell to one side, but she salvaged her composure in a split second.

"I've just come from Chicago, and I must say, that song got it right. It really is a toddlin' town. On my first night there, I—"

"—pushed the Williams Brothers into the river?"

It was common knowledge among this crowd that Kay had recently ended an affair with a member of her back-up group.

"Into the river?" Kay pursed her lips into a mock frown. "Why? Did the Chicago Police Department find any bodies?" The quip got a huge laugh. "So anyway, my first night in Chicago, I was in my hotel room—"

"Not for long, I bet!"

Kay shielded her eyes and peered into the audience. "The a-hole with the cake-hole—you wanna come up here and say that?"

Kay blinked several times as Zanuck stepped onto the stage. She'd called one of the most powerful men in Hollywood "an a-hole" and there he was, a huge cigar jammed into the side of his mouth, his arms thrust out wide, and a yep-it's-me grin on his puss.

"So, Mister Zanuck, is there a reason why you're stomping all over my act?" She ran a hand over her white-blonde hair. "Is it because I resemble Marilyn Monroe so uncannily that several pints of scotch has you a mite confused?"

He unplugged the cigar and blew a torrent of smoke into her face. She mugged clear of it by stumbling around the stage like a drunken hobo. The shtick brought some laughs but Zanuck frowned at her.

"You sayin' I can't hold my liquor?"

"Not at all," Kay replied. "I'm merely left to question whether your liquor can hold you."

Flummoxed by her rejoinder, he looked up at the trapeze hanging over their heads. "I bet I can do five chin-ups in a row."

Zanuck forced his cigar into her hand—she held it between two fingers like it was a lighted stick of dynamite—and looked on, horrified, as Zanuck shrugged off his jacket, undid his tie, and unbuttoned his shirt.

By the time he was naked from the waist up, the thirty people at his table were clapping their encouragement with a rhythmic beat. Virginia Zanuck sat with her hands in her lap, her face stony with disapproval. A chant revved up around her. "Go! To! Five! Go! To! Five!"

Eyeing his trim waist and firm chest, Gwendolyn was impressed with how well a guy in his fifties had kept himself—especially someone who smoked like a forest fire, drank like a whale, and feasted like an emperor.

He reached for the trapeze with one arm. "Single-handed!" He pulled his chin to the bar once. Twice. Halfway to the third try, his arm started to wobble. He hovered at the midway point, the muscles across his shoulder stippled with effort. He let out a raw moan and dropped onto the stage.

"A damn fine effort, don't you think?" Kay asked the audience.

They applauded, puncturing their approval with wolf whistles, but Zanuck kept his head down as he collected his clothes off the floor.

Kay swung around to the audience. "How about a song?"

The bandleader launched the orchestra into a number Kay had written called "Hello, Hello." The crowd identified it from the opening bars and endorsed it with a thundering ovation.

Gwendolyn watched Zanuck slink off to a dark corner where he could reassemble his wardrobe unobserved.

"Don't worry, Darryl dear," Kathryn murmured in Gwendolyn's ear, "you've impressed your mistress in front of your wife and that was the whole point."

* * *

Kay's act was fast and funny, punctuated with zingers and improvised put-downs that her audience devoured like starving paupers. Though not as vocally talented as the stars she coached, she could put over a song with enough zing to gloss over her shortcomings. By the time she finished, she'd wrung every laugh and gasp that could possibly be squeezed from her seen-it-all audience.

When the house lights came up, the first person to catch Gwendolyn's eye was Quentin. She turned away from him. "Hey Leo, Kathryn tells me you know how to cut a rug."

"You don't need to ask me twice."

Jonathan assumed that was his cue too, and asked Judy to dance.

The two couples joined the swirling floor to a cha-cha version of Peggy Lee's "Mañana (Is Soon Enough for Me.)"

Every eyeball in the place was trained on the next couple to join the floor: Clark Gable and Jane Russell. In three-inch heels, Jane perfectly matched Gable's six-foot-one, and together they capered like a pair of teens.

As the song drew to an end, Clark whispered into Jane's ear. She nodded and they broke apart. It took her three steps to reach Leo.

"I do like how you cha-cha!" He cast Gwendolyn adrift without fanfare. Clark gathered her in his arms and foxtrotted into a mirror-smooth version of "Summertime." Dimples pitted each cheek. "I appreciate this more than you could know."

"But why didn't you get Jane to cut into Jonathan and let you dance with Judy?"

The grin washed away. "I don't want to upend the girl's life. Her mother's a mighty fine woman but she's acutely aware of how this would look."

"Speaking as a girl who grew up with no father," Gwendolyn said, "I should remind you that flames can warm a girl instead of scorch her." He quizzed her silently with his gray-green Rhett Butler eyes. "I'm also fairly positive that she has no idea who her father is." Gwendolyn felt Clark's body jolt. "Are you prepared for when she asks you why nobody told her?"

The song came to an end and their momentum petered out. Someone behind her caught his attention. He collected up her right hand and kissed it. "A pleasure, Miss Brick."

Zanuck swept her into a waltz. A fog of Scotch whiskey hovered. "Are you fucking him?"

"No, Mr. Zanuck. I am not."

"Did you used to fuck him?"

"What you saw was simply a thank-you dance for a recent favor." She ignored his skeptical squint. "What's with the third degree?"

"I want you to do *me* a favor." He emphasized the word "me" by pressing his stocky frame to her body.

She angled away as best she could in his tight grip and told him, "When I found out Marilyn was marrying DiMaggio, you were the first person I called."

"I want to sign Gable to a two-picture deal. *Soldier of Fortune* and *The Tall Men* are perfect for him. His MGM contract still has months to run, but I'm told Gable hates Dore Schary with every fiber of his precious being. No amount of money will convince him to stay."

"He wouldn't listen to me," Gwendolyn insisted. "And why should he?"

"I saw the way he danced with you."

"He's a good dancer. That's all you saw."

"I saw more than that."

The last of Gwendolyn's patience leaked away. "You must have hundreds of people at your disposal—why pick on me?"

"Because I trust you."

Gwendolyn could perceive no agenda buried behind his eyes. "You and I have had a few conversations but I hardly think any of them were long enough for you to—"

"Between the Supreme Court anti-trust decision that forced the studios to break from our theater chains and the encroachment of television, my job gets harder and harder. I navigate all this purely on instinct. Screenwriters, actors, craftsmen—the only trait they have in common is that they're people. I form my opinions based on gut reactions and I go with it. And mine says that you're the person to help me get Gable. Talk him into coming to see me and I'll do the rest."

Through the tangle of dancers, Gwendolyn could see Kathryn and Quentin with their heads pressed together, watching her.

"And if I do?" Gwendolyn pitched her question with *What's in it for me?* bravado.

"You get to keep your job."

"Is my job at Fox dependent on doing you favors?"

"Everybody's job at Fox is dependent on doing me favors. But don't worry. I keep a detailed score card up here." He tapped his graying temple. "Memory like an elephant."

"I'll keep that in mind, sir. And thank you for the waltz."

He bowed his head gallantly. "Miss Brick."

Gwendolyn skirted the periphery of the dance floor, unsure what she should say to Kathryn and Quentin when she got back to the table. Halfway there, Judy and Leo glided past her. They slowed long enough for Judy to call out, "I'm having a marvelous time!"

Gwendolyn smiled and waved. For all his virile posturing, Zanuck had revealed himself to be the sort of person who put more stock in his feelings than she would have guessed. She had no idea how to convince Clark to hear Zanuck out, but her own gut instinct told her that until she did, she ought to keep mum.

# CHAPTER 16

After weeks of filming at Cinecittà, *The Barefoot Contessa* relocated to a mansion with a pair of fifteen-foot wrought iron doors set into a white stone archway that Marcus knew would make an arresting backdrop.

He felt a tap on his shoulder. It was Ava in a snug coat of dark gray with large buttons across her torso. It would contrast perfectly with the pale stone behind her.

Ava twirled around, flaring the bottom of the coat. "Do you think they'll let me keep it?"

He loaded a fresh roll. "There's a difference between 'stealing it' and 'forgetting to return it.'"

"Hmmmm." Ava ran her hand down her side.

He raised his camera. "Mind if I take a couple of shots?" A large copper vase sat in an alcove built into the wall. It held a tall fern with spindly shoots and spiky leaves that quivered in the cold breeze.

Ava posed in front of the stonework; the mid-morning light slanted onto her face. "Heard from Kathryn lately?"

"Not in a couple of weeks. Why?"

"I think I screwed up."

He prodded his chin to show her she needed to lift her face half an inch. "Why is that?"

"She asked me to convince Winchell to call her. Turns out, my charms ain't so red hot when I'm drunk off my ass. Please tell her I'm sorry if I let her down."

He guided her shoulders until they were at right angles to the wall. A wave of homesickness washed over him when he smelled Gwennie's fragrance. "You often wear that, don't you?"

"Oh yes, I love it. I was livid when Bullock's stopped stocking it."

A barrage of voices filled the still air. "AVA! AVA! AVA!"

There was no such thing as a typical *scattino*. Some of them were wild-eyed youths, barely out of high school, willing to jump any fence or hang from any rooftop to get a good shot. Others looked like war vets whose scoured faces had witnessed the worst that the human race could dish out. The rest of them hovered somewhere in between, wearing their fastidiously pressed One Good Suit as they tore around dusty streets. In the time Marcus had been in Rome, he'd noticed that they'd lost their good-natured camaraderie now that the plethora of magazines offered decent fees.

Fifteen of them were now approaching the low brick fence that bounded the mansion's grounds. "MIA BELLA AVA!" they shouted, "MIA BELLA AVA!" and fluttered a jumble of bright red, yellow, and green handkerchiefs.

An assistant director appeared. "We won't get any shooting done until we can get these guys to disperse, so Mank wants Ava inside."

"I'll see what I can do." Marcus slung his camera strap around his neck and marched toward them. "Sorry, guys," he told the group in his best Italian, "but Miss Gardner will be shooting indoors for the rest of the day."

A current of resentment rippled through the gang. One of them spat on the ground and hawked up a word that carried the weight of a cutting insult.

"Only one exterior shot today." He pointed out a sleek European convertible loaded with luggage parked off to one side. "Signorina Gardner and Signore Brazzi walk from the car to the door, turn to take in the view—"

A red ball splattered Marcus's shoulder. The *scattini* laughed as the stink of rotted tomato reached his nose. As the chorus of sniggering died down, someone taunted, "*Invasore americano*."

"American invader?" Marcus shouted in English. "Who said that?"

Emilio Conti sauntered forward. "You Americans, you come to Italy with your directors and your scripts and your stars and your crew. You make your pictures here because it is cheap. You wave your almighty American dollar in front of us like we are grateful peasants!"

The men started nodding and echoing specific words like a Greek chorus. "Cheap!" "American dollar!" "Peasants!"

"When will MGM and Twentieth Century-Fox come to Italy to shoot a movie with an Italian director?" Emilio started punching the palm of one hand with the fist of the other. "We have Rossellini! De Sica!"

Someone behind him yelled out "Fellini!" and someone else, "Visconti!"

"But you keep all the best jobs for yourself!" Conti pointed at Marcus's camera. "And now they bring their own *scattino*."

"I'm only here because of the Fratelli di Conti!" Marcus said, switching to Italian. If he was going to swing their opinion, he knew he'd have to do it in their language. "I'm still in Italy because the Contis tried to cheat me out of a pile of dough. I was forced to fight them for my money but have I seen one lira? Meanwhile, what am I supposed to live on?" Marcus should have known better than to trust Napoleon's assurance that he'd have his money by Christmas.

The resentful agitation Conti had whipped up began to subside.

"So yes, I take photos to sell to the magazines because I want to survive. Do you gentlemen want to know why Emilio Conti hates me? It is jealousy. *I* am the one who took those pictures of Sophia Loren." Several jaws dropped. "I took *Look*'s photos of Ingrid Bergman, as well as Ava Gardner and her mysterious Italian lover. I am *Lo Scattino Americano*!"

Marcus saw a shift from outrage to begrudged admiration in the faces opposite him.

"You are *americano*," Conti said. "You do not belong here."

"I propose a bet," Marcus said. "Let us see who can get the first photo of *La Speranza* into *Epoca*." The mention of Melody's nickname generated a chorus of hushed whispers. "If I win, you will get your brothers to pay up the money they owe me within one week of publication."

His challenge sparked a glint in Conti's eye. "And if I win, you must depart Italy immediately."

If Marcus accepted Emilio's terms, it could mean leaving Rome without ever seeing his money. It was a chance he was willing to take.

"I accept."

* * *

Melody's intercom chimed four times before it roused a response. "Who the hell is this?"

Her tone softened at the sound of Marcus's voice. She buzzed him in and opened the door wearing a red silk top and emerald cotton bottoms, no slippers, and hair that hadn't been brushed in a couple of days.

"I've got a question to ask you," he said.

"Shoot."

"Are you *La Speranza*?"

Her response was a shy smile that didn't last long. She pulled him inside and flopped onto her sofa. "When I first got here, I went the whole hog, publicity-wise. I was everywhere, always on display, but that kind of stuff gets old. So I decided to change my image. Add a bit of mystery. It worked for Garbo."

"But surely they'll want you to do P.R. on *Metropolitana*," Marcus said. "They've built the whole movie around you."

"They've pushed back the start date. I suspect your copyright showdown has gummed up the works."

"You want to help un-gum them?" Marcus asked.

A flare of the feisty spirit that American moviegoers had fallen in love with back in the thirties resurfaced. "What have you got in mind?"

"Pose for me like Ava did."

"WHAT?"

"And beat Emilio Conti at his own game."

"What game?"

Marcus told her about the bet he'd made with the self-proclaimed number one *scattino* in Rome. By the time he finished, Melody was on her feet, roaming around for cigarettes. "Oh Marcus, you shouldn't have."

"He's a mean little shit." He joined her in the kitchen and offered her a Camel. "You said so yourself that day we met at the café."

"That twerp needs taking down a peg or two, but you'll need to find some other way to do it."

"It's you or nothing."

"Sorry, Marcus. I'd love to help you out, but no dice." She took a deep drag. "I bought a new coffee pot because apparently I make terrible coffee. My downstairs neighbor told me it's 'jesterproof' but I assume he means 'foolproof.'"

"Is it because Emilio is one of the Conti brothers, and they're your bosses?" Marcus could feel his ten grand slipping away. "*Metropolitana* is a break from those costume dramas, and you don't want to endanger what could be a big boost."

"It's not that. Well, partly." She stirred the coffee grounds around the tin can as some sort of fight played out on her face.

He stilled her hand. "Forget I brought it up. Let's change the subject. Tell me about Trevor Bergin. What's he up to?"

She straightened, relieved that they'd moved onto a safer subject. "*Cross of Light* and *Lady and her Blade* were big hits. Then he had a few duds. But now he's in Greece on a seven-month shoot playing Paris in an epic called *The Grief of Achilles*. Last I heard, he was on some Greek island having the time of his life shooting arrows all day long."

"I'm glad to hear that." Marcus commandeered the coffee scoop. "Let me show you how Signora Scatena does it. First of all—"

"I had a baby." She kept her focus on the half-burned Camel between her fingers. "Italian men are such flirts—you must know that by now."

Marcus pictured Domenico's face. "I do."

"It was a regular textbook romance that started on *Rome Burns*. Banter led to flirting. Flirting led to stolen kisses and whispered sweet nothings behind sets. The sweet nothings led to . . ." She see-sawed her hands.

"Getting knocked up?"

"I launched myself into an affair with my eyes open—as well as my legs. I barely made it through shooting before I started to show. After that, I put myself into seclusion for the rest of my pregnancy."

"That's why you became a recluse?"

"It was his idea, because of course he was married as well. Oh yes, it was the full cliché!" Her voice had taken on a hysterical edge. "I hid myself away and waited for a little girl with the most delicate fingers you ever saw. They let me hold her for all of thirty seconds, then some bitch of a nun whisked her away." She stubbed out her cigarette in a dirty saucer.

"That must have been awful."

"Yeah, it was. But I didn't have much choice. These Catholics don't look too kindly on sex outside of marriage, or abortion, or unwed mothers."

Melody pulled another cigarette from the packet Marcus left on the counter. She tapped it several times but didn't light it.

"My second-wind Italian career has been all kinds of wonderful. If I mess this up too, I'm really screwed. By the time I gave birth, he'd unearthed *Metropolitana* and laid out this strategy that involved me going into seclusion and later reemerging with a new persona."

"The father? What's he got to do with *Metropolitana*?"

She let out a jagged sigh and crossed past him toward the picture window with the view across the Tiber. "He was the producer on *Rome Burns*."

"That was a Fratelli di Conti film, wasn't it?"

"Yuh-huh."

"You had an affair with one of the Conti brothers?"

"Yuh-huh."

"Please don't tell me it was Emilio."

"UCK!" Her disgust was so palpable it would have been funny if this had been a scene from *His Girl Friday*. "That pipsqueak? Give me some credit." She flopped down on the sofa beside him and let out a long, wet raspberry. "It was Napoleon. I know what you're thinking. Napoleon Conti has an ego the size of the Vatican, and thinks nothing of screaming the roof down to get his way. But he wasn't like that with me. He was kind and gentle and funny and romantic."

Marcus pictured the humorless bastard with the Caesar complex. "Until he got you pregnant."

Melody jackknifed into an upright position. "Much to my parents' eternal disappointment, I'm not the white-picket-fence type. Motherhood was never on my agenda, and I refuse to feel guilty about that."

Marcus was still juggling the conflicting images of Napoleon the bully with Napoleon the romantic. He risked a placating hand on her knee. "It sounds like you were railroaded."

Melody fiddled with a loose thread until she'd started to unravel the hem of her collar. "I was okay about giving up the baby until I came home to this empty apartment. He left me alone with nothing except my thoughts and regrets."

Marcus knew what came next. He'd written this scene in two or three movies. "Did you start drinking again?"

"Honestly, I tried not to. But there's no Alcoholics Anonymous over here; they expect you to pray the thirst away. So yeah, I hit the bottle. Oh, Marcus, I was a mess. Drunk and depressed and mean and resentful as hell."

"Because the Conti brothers took away your choice?"

She prodded an accusing finger at him. "I know what you're doing. You're trying to get me to turn against the Contis so that you can win your dumb bet."

"Doesn't mean I'm wrong, though."

She plucked the loose thread from her collar and wound it tightly around her left index finger. "I'll have you know that I got myself off the bottle." The thread broke and she flicked it away. "Napoleon came to visit me a couple of months later. It was in the morning so I wasn't completely bombed. Said he had this new picture."

"*Metropolitana*?"

"He told me how it was a chance to break out of the sword-and-sandals trap but only if I stayed in seclusion and got my act together. Then, when *Metropolitana* was ready to shoot, I could emerge as The New Melody Hope. He had this whole moth-cocoon-butterfly metaphor; it was very convincing."

Marcus pictured Napoleon Conti shoving his poetic moth-cocoon-butterfly theory down her throat until she cried uncle. "I'm sorry I missed it."

"If it wasn't for Napoleon rescuing me with *Metropolitana*, I might still be sitting here getting plastered morning, noon, and night."

Outside Melody's living room window, a juniper tree held a nest of European robins chirping together. It was an unpleasant, discordant sound that reminded Marcus of the *scattini* posse he'd faced on the *Contessa* location.

"So, to recap," he said, "he seduced you, knocked you up, and forced you into surrendering your baby, which sent you on a months-long binge, but he's your knight in shining armor because he wanted to cast you in his movie?"

"When you put it like that . . ."

"How would *you* put it?"

"I wanted to do *Metropolitana*. Desperately. It was my chance to reinvent myself—oh, stop it!" She slapped the upholstery as she jumped to her feet and disappeared into the bedroom.

The European robins stopped squawking as though the sound effects department had flipped a switch. The apartment filled with silence except for a methodical whooshing sound in the bedroom.

Marcus ventured as far as the doorway. Melody stood in front of a large semicircular vanity mirror, pulling a brush through her hair with gritted-teeth ferocity. "What are you doing?"

"Calming myself," she replied. "I found it helpful after I came out of the hospital."

"Lookit, Mel," he said, attempting to calm the mood with nonchalance. "I'm sorry if I upset you. I hate seeing you being taken advantage of—"

"I'm not mad at you." *Whoosh! Whoosh! Whoosh!* She swapped to the other side of her head. "I'm mad at myself for being so gullible." *Whoosh! Whoosh!* "For being such a wooly-headed puppet." She threw the hairbrush down; it hit the glass top with a loud crack. "Knight in shining armor, my ass!"

"All I meant was—"

"I have a slutty dress that makes my boobs look huge. Shall I put it on?"

"They'll need to recognize you, so no turban or sunglasses."

"Give me five minutes to change." She kicked him out of the room with her bare foot and slammed the door in his face.

# CHAPTER 17

Kathryn turned onto Petit Drive and thought it was odd that she'd encountered Clark Gable at nightclubs and premieres, and interviewed him on the sets of his movies, but had never visited his house, nestled high in the Hollywood hills above Encino.

She pulled up at number 4525. Leafy trees lined the red-brick driveway leading to an unpretentious ranch house. The press had dubbed it "The House of Two Gables" after Gable and Lombard got hitched, and somehow the name had stuck, even after Lombard's death and Clark's subsequent marriage to and divorce from Sylvia Ashley. Beyond a pair of whitewashed gates lay a path of large pale flagstones to a long porch that ran along the house to an open door.

*Oh, I see. It's his sanctuary.*

In her most recent column, *BEWARE THE IDES OF MARCH '54,* Kathryn had talked about how the sands under Hollywood's feet were shifting at an ever-faster pace.

In the same month that Errol Flynn had left Warner Bros., Hollywood's first official censor, Will Hays, had died, and the Academy had given his successor, Joseph Breen, an honorary Oscar before he retired. Over at MGM, Dory Schary was cleaning house with the vigor of a German hausfrau. Greer Garson—gone. Van Johnson—gone. But it was Gable's departure that had made Hollywood rear back.

Kathryn wasn't surprised, though. None of his recent movies had set the world on fire, but he refused to consider a shift to television like so many of his contemporaries. She had overheard Clark tell someone at the *Betrayed* premiere that he didn't approve of television because it was destroying the industry he loved. "I owe everything to the movies," he declared, "and I'm not about to desert them now."

She'd quoted him in her column, and the next day received an invitation to what Clark was calling his "Exit Party" to celebrate his freedom.

The smooth notes of Eddie Fisher's recording of "I'm in the Mood for Love" swam through an airy foyer that led to a long living room with all the windows flung open. The place was how Kathryn had always pictured it—wood paneling, firearms mounted on wall brackets, and even a matching pair of rocking chairs.

Following the laughter filtering from the back patio, Kathryn stepped onto a wooden deck and encountered Myrna Loy holding a filled champagne flute in each hand.

"One of these was for my husband," she explained, "but he's wandered off with John Ford and Victor Mature, talking about hunting." She gave one to Kathryn. They clinked glasses. "Clark asked me to keep an eye out for you."

Kathryn thought of the night when Zanuck showed off his virility at Ciro's. His antic had made the papers the next day and a few days later *Look* magazine published a photo.

While Zanuck had been performing for his mistress, Kathryn had been observing Clark as he watched his daughter take in the spectacle playing out in front of her. When Kathryn caught Clark's eye, he'd looked away, embarrassed at being caught out. She'd kept expecting him to look back, perhaps nod hello or offer up a you-caught-me shrug, but he didn't.

Myrna angled herself toward Kathryn's ear. "Are you and Winchell feuding?"

"I haven't laid eyes on him in a couple of years." *No thanks to Ava.*

"He'll be here today." Myrna sipped her champagne and eyeballed Howard Strickling, who'd headed up MGM's publicity department for more years than Kathryn could remember. He'd accompanied Clark to Carole's plane crash site, so it was no surprise that he was here today. But Winchell? Had he let it be known that he wanted to come and Gable had recruited Strickling as a chaperone?

*There's no such thing as "just a party" in Hollywood.*

"Did Winchell invite himself?"

"Clark said to send you into the den and he'll meet you there." Myrna pointed to a wing facing the stables. "And when you do, note how much MGM you'll see in the place."

"What do you mean?"

"The moment Clark got home from his last day, he got rid of every little bit of MGM paraphernalia." Myrna winked a knowing eye. "Except one."

* * *

Clark's den was a large square, and paneled floor to ceiling in light wood. An extra-long rifle hung from a pair of brackets over a window bordered with calico drapes with a dark green hedge pattern. A triangular cabinet sat snugly in the corner next to a small card table. On it sat a framed picture of Clark and Grace Kelly walking along a dirt road. From his safari hunter uniform, Kathryn guessed it had been taken on the set of *Mogambo.*

The photo was mounted in a frame made of deliberately rough wood to match the décor. A feminine hand had written the word "Memories!" below Grace Kelly's right foot.

Stars getting together after the cameras stopped rolling was virtually de rigueur—especially for movies shot on location, away from suspicious spouses. When Kathryn had caught wind of a hot and heavy rumor about Gable and Kelly, she had hardly been surprised. She supposed that once the company returned home, the affair had gone the way of its predecessors, but if this photo truly was the sole MGM souvenir he had kept in his home—

"We didn't get along too well at first."

In an open-necked shirt with a horseshoe pattern and a freshly lit cigarette, Clark looked more relaxed than he had in a while.

"You and Grace?" she asked.

"Me and Myrna."

Kathryn returned the photo frame to the triangular cabinet. "Her instructions were to meet you in the den. How very Hercule Poirot of you."

She meant it as a light jest to leaven the somber air that had followed him into the room, but it fell with a dull thud on the red Southwestern-style rug.

He said, "I want your advice."

"I'm flattered."

"Jane Russell and her husband are forming a production company, and one of their projects is called *The King and Four Queens*. Sort of a comedy-drama-western. They've asked me if I'd like to co-produce the movie with them and I want to know what you think."

*And give what could turn out to be the misguided advice that capsized the greatest screen career to have ever come out of Hollywood? No thanks.*

"Jimmy Stewart's the person you should be talking to."

"Why is that?"

"A couple of months ago, I was at Paramount to see Hitchcock's *Rear Window* set, and Jimmy Stewart told me that Universal first offered him two hundred thousand to make *Winchester '73*. But he decided to take a chance and countered with a smaller acting fee plus a cut of the profits."

Clark nodded thoughtfully, his eyes fixed on the drapes. "Did he tell you how much he earned?"

"Six hundred grand."

He blew out a plume of white smoke that reached the window. Every inch of his frame radiated relaxed geniality. Not all stars had managed to age this well. The last time she'd seen Errol Flynn was in *The Master of Ballantrae*. She knew enough about movie lighting to know that they must have spent a great deal of time getting him to look halfway decent.

Clark broke into a dimpled grin. "I knew you were the one to ask."

"Don't you have a manager or an agent?"

"Sure I do, but they have a vested interest in prodding clients toward the biggest paycheck. But you're a straight shooter with a good grip on what's going on."

She gazed up into his gray-green eyes. Like Gwendolyn, she'd grown up missing out on knowing who her real father was. It had left a man-sized hole in her life that she was only now getting around to filling. *Don't be that dad,* she wanted to tell him. *Don't wait until it's too late.*

His brows wrinkled together. "You're looking at me kinda goofy."

"I was thinking about that crazy night at Ciro's," Kathryn prodded. "After Zanuck did those pull-ups on the trapeze, you took to the dance floor with Jane Russell and every pair of eyes was on you."

Clark lifted a sardonic eyebrow. "I noticed you watching."

*Me watching you dance with Jane? Or you watching Judy watching Kay?* She was still formulating a clever response when Walter Winchell strode into the den like he was Lord Cardigan leading the charge of the Light Brigade.

"There you are, Gable, ol' sport. I've been looking all over for you!"

Clark stepped forward to greet Winchell, revealing Kathryn behind him.

Winchell smiled in anything but genuine surprise. "And Miss Massey. If you're the two birds, I must be the one stone."

Neither telephone, telegram, nor mail had helped Kathryn contact Winchell. She'd have tried smoke signals or carrier pigeon if she'd thought it would do any good, but now the man she liked the least but needed the most was within handcuffing distance. He presented her with a token nod as he spirited Clark away. Determined not to lose him, Kathryn followed the two men to the patio bar.

Kathryn lingered within direct eye contact as Winchell worked through the crowd. The guests greeted him with pleased-to-meetcha handshakes as though to prove Myrna's declaration that nobody says no to Winchell.

She stuck around through a long conversation with John Ford's wife, Mary, about their days at the Hollywood Canteen. Later, she endured a one-sided monolog from Clark's stunt double on *Mogambo*, who'd also been the location manager on *The African Queen*. He was still filling Kathryn's ear when the maid wheeled out an enormous chocolate cake frosted with the single word "FREEDOM" in large pink lettering.

Clark waved down the applause. "I'm very thankful for everything MGM has given me over the years," he told the group, "but times change and we must change with them, otherwise we risk getting stampeded by the onslaught of progress." He plunged his carving knife into the cake. "This isn't the freedom from MGM. It's the freedom to pursue opportunities."

John Ford led the group in a trio of hip-hip-hoorays for their host and wished Clark well on whatever successes awaited him.

It was a long time to be standing in heels on a stone patio, and Kathryn was looking around for a chair or a bench when she heard America's most famous radio voice behind her.

"The next time you want my attention, may I suggest you don't send Ava as your emissary?" Winchell made a pretense of contemplating the freshly filled glass of champagne he'd elevated to eye level.

"You could have replied to the myriad telegrams, letters, and phone messages I left with your secretary."

"I wanted to see how desperate you were, because I doubt that you trust me any more than I trust you."

A gravel path led down a gentle slope and into a grove of cypress pines. A bench of burnished copper slate sat in front of the largest one. She suggested they take a stroll, and said nothing until they were settled on the bench.

"As you know, Sheldon Voss admitted to me that he helped frame my father."

"But Voss is still AWOL," Winchell pointed out.

Kathryn nodded. "As I'm sure you can appreciate, I want my father to be exonerated. With Voss missing indefinitely, I need access to the files the FBI collected on Thomas Danford."

"What makes you think they have a file on him at all?"

Kathryn threw him a look that said *The FBI has a file on everybody*. Winchell didn't argue the point but instead nodded for her to continue.

"The fastest way to get a look-see on those files is via J. Edgar Hoover—"

"And he kind of hates you."

Kathryn knew Hoover wasn't her biggest fan, but it hadn't crossed her mind that he actively hated her. "That may or may not be true—"

"Believe me."

Kathryn wished she'd grabbed a drink from a passing waiter. At the very least, the flute would have kept her hands busy. "Here's my proposal: You go to Hoover and tell him about Voss laundering money through the FBI's LA office."

"Hoover has his finger in every pie in the FBI bakery. He'd know if the Los Angeles office had gone rogue."

"If he doesn't, it'll be quite a feather in your cap."

"You got proof?"

"Didn't you think it strange that Sheldon Voss handed his donations to the National Council of Negro Women?" The tentativeness in his eyes told her that he did. "Did you know that the offices of the NCNW are directly below the FBI's LA bureau?"

"Are you saying that the National Council of Negro Women are helping the FBI office to launder money?"

"God, no! They helped me fit the final jigsaw puzzle piece." He didn't laugh her off the bench so she faced him more squarely. "I'm no Hoover fan, but I do know he has a very strict moral code. A little twisted, in my view, but that's beside the point."

"What *is* your point?"

"He'll be horrified to know his LA office is involved in money laundering."

"We can agree on that, at least."

"You bring him this information and in return, you ask for access to Thomas Danford's files. When his innocence is proven, you can take all the credit for righting the wrong that befell an unjustly imprisoned American."

Up the hillside, someone had slapped Kay Starr onto Clark's record player; she was belting out "Wheel of Fortune" as though her life depended on it.

"What's with all this altruism when you could claim the glory for yourself?"

"I don't want to be publicly connected to Thomas Danford; I just want to see him released from jail. So will you do it? You'll get gobs of inches out of the whole thing."

"Yes, but do you trust me with the contents of your father's FBI file?"

"What if our situation was reversed?" she asked.

He gave her a down-up-down lookover: *Not a chance in hell.* But if this was what it took to get her father exonerated, it would all be worth it.

Winchell chewed over her offer for a few more seconds—longer than he needed, but enough time to make her squirm. "I haven't been on a juicy crusade in ages," he admitted. "What the hell. Sure. Okay." He shot to his feet and tipped the brim of his fedora.

She watched him amble back to the house as though they'd been discussing nothing more exciting than the recent renaming of the Pasadena Freeway.

The heat of a panic spread across Kathryn's chest like sunburn. *Is this what it feels like to make a deal with the devil?*

# CHAPTER 18

Marcus and Domenico wandered through the deserted theater foyer and onto the sidewalk. They stopped in front of a poster featuring a girl with her arms outstretched in alarm over the title "Destinazione . . . Terra!"

"It was *stupido*, no?" Domenico asked.

Marcus grinned to himself. It was the dumbest movie he'd seen in forever. The plot was illogical, the acting was overripe, the dialogue was wooden, and the special effects were anything but special. *It Came from Outer Space* represented the nadir of American cinema—but he loved it with an unprecedented level of patriotic fervor. Being six thousand miles from the nearest cheeseburger, large fries, and strawberry thick shake made Marcus yearn for anything American.

"It was very *stupido*," he agreed.

"We could have watched the new Roberto Rossellini instead. Why didn't we see that?"

*Because Italian movies are so gritty and earnest. I was desperate for some all-American nonsense.*

Marcus turned away from the poster.

"You miss them, don't you, my Marcus Aurelius?" Domenico asked.

"Who?"

"Signore Bogart, Signorina Bacall, Signorina Gardner."

The day before Joe Mankiewicz left for the States, he had taken Marcus to a bistro for lunch and told him of Zanuck's decision to film *The Egyptian* in Los Angeles so he no longer required the penthouse in Melody's building.

"I'm sure Zanuck was looking forward to banging that girl all summer, but the budget worked out better if they shot in LA so he was forced to zip it up." Mank sprinkled crushed chili peppers on his *quattro formaggi* pizza, "On the plus side, Zanuck was very happy with your production shots. You should also know that he's less than happy with the *Carmen Jones* screenplay and needs someone to punch it up. They start filming in June."

It was exactly the sort of opportunity Marcus had been hoping for to relaunch him onto the Hollywood scene. "Who's directing?" he asked Mank.

"Preminger."

"We worked together on *The Moon is Blue*, and I was instrumental in helping them blunt the power of the Breen Office." In truth, "instrumental" overstated Marcus's role, but Hollywood was a town that thrived on dramatics. "Maybe you could suggest to Zanuck that I would be the right guy for *Carmen Jones*."

Mank pulled a string of mozzarella out of his teeth. "You're better off aiming for *The Virgin Queen*. Bette Davis is doing Elizabeth I again and she'll be pulling out all the stops. It's a big-budget costume picture, so Zanuck's throwing buckets of dough at it. Henry Koster is directing because he made such a success of *The Robe*, but a reliable source told me the script is a disaster."

Marcus reminded Mank that he'd been gone a while, so he doubted anyone would hand him a prestige picture. Mank nodded as he chewed. "There's always a pile of projects going on, so don't worry."

They were encouraging words, but you were only as good as the last favor you did for someone.

Marcus and Domenico walked away from the cinema. "Sure I miss them. We've lived in the same hotel at one time or another. Being together again was like Old Home Week."

"What is 'Old Home Week'?"

"It's what you call a reunion with people you haven't seen in a while."

Domenico was always keen to improve his English and pounced on unfamiliar English phrases. Marcus gave him a full explanation, as he had also done with Rossano Brazzi, who had proved to be a diligent student. Fox had hinted that they were planning to bring him to the States and promote him as the next big thing in European lovers, so Brazzi was keen to master English as best he could.

But months and months of having to halt a conversation and explain what taking a rain check meant, or who Will Rogers was, had left Marcus wishing he could have a regular conversation with regular Americans. He'd got his fill being around Mank, Bogie, Bacall, and Ava, but their departure had opened a need in Marcus that even someone as thoughtful as Domenico couldn't fill.

They arrived at the corner of a busy intersection where a newsstand butted up against an ancient bank building.

Domenico pulled Marcus toward it. "Look!" he exclaimed, "they are still selling your *Epoca*."

In early February, *Epoca* had splashed Marcus's photos of Melody in front of the Triton Fountain in Piazza Barberini across a four-page spread and saved the best one for the cover. Everyone had talked about the photo of Melody holding her shoes aloft as she romped around the knee-deep water, her sunglasses skewed off her face.

A month later, *Epoca* featured an article proclaiming *Lo Scattino Americano* as the most skilled street photographer in Rome. "Perhaps it takes an outsider to capture post-war life," the article said, "in the city fast becoming the new European epicenter of film, fashion, and café society."

Domenico bid him *arrivederci* and told him that last-minute reshoots on the new Fellini movie, *La Strada*, were likely to go late into the night. It suited Marcus—he wanted to include a letter to the girls with the *Epoca* he bought at the newsstand. But when he returned home, Signora Scatena flung open her front door, a registered letter fluttering in her hand.

Inside his room, Marcus tore open the envelope. The one-page letter was from MGM Italia's attorney informing him that his *Metropolitana* check was ready.

The banks closed at four, so he had an hour to deposit it in his Italian account. Marcus made it to the lawyer's office by three thirty. The razor-sharp corners of the expensive parchment envelope pressed against his chest from his inside breast pocket as he hurried along the street.

The American Express office stood on a corner overlooking the triangular piazza spread out at the base of the Spanish Steps. A display in the window caught his eye, drawing him like a kid to a candy store.

A row of ten-inch gold palm trees stretched across the front. Behind them towered a backdrop, fifteen inches tall and painted in vivid mistletoe green. Near the top of the Hollywood hills, white letters the size of Marcus's thumb spelled out HOLLYWOODLAND, ignoring how the "LAND" part of the sign had been pulled down years ago.

A reasonably accurate facsimile of a movie palace marquee hung suspended above:

*Los Angeles – la città dei miti*
*Los Angeles – the city of myths*

The sight of this romanticized version of LA pricked Marcus's heart with tiny shards. Individually, they weren't barbed enough to draw blood, but collectively they held the power to thrust him through the doors and book the first Pan Am flight heading west.

He peered through the window. A line of desks ran along the right-hand side, each with a different sign:

*Mail Collection*

*American Express Travelers Cheques*

*International Travel Arrangements – Air, Sea*

*European Travel Arrangements – Train, Bus, Ferry*

His eyes flew back to *American Express Travelers Cheques.*

Italian banknotes were enormous, so smuggling ten thousand dollars' worth would be difficult. But what about travelers cheques?

He drummed his fingernails against the glass. *If the highest denomination is a hundred bucks, surely a stack of a hundred cheques couldn't be thicker than a comic book? Would it raise eyebrows if I went in and ordered ten grand worth? What if I came in twice a week? And what if I rotated between the three American Express offices?*

"I hate the sight of you!"

Marcus squared back his shoulders, then pivoted on his heel.

Emilio Conti was dressed in the same yellow suit he'd worn the day he accosted Gina Lollobrigida in front of Ristocaffé Colosseo. But today, it hung off him like a potato sack. One of the lapels was bent back at an awkward angle, a button hung by a limp thread, and either he'd forgotten to put on his cufflinks or they had fallen off.

The guy bunched his fingers into a fist tight enough to blanch the knuckles. "Why do you make my life a misery? Why don't you go back where you came from, *Signore Scattino Americano*?"

"I'm not responsible for that *Epoca* article," Marcus said.

"You loved it." Emilio treaded a semicircle around Marcus as he lifted his arms like a Pentecostal preacher. "Let us praise *Lo Scattino Americano*!" His voice bounced off the stone walls. "The most skilled in all Rome!"

"Emilio, don't do this. I'm only here because I'm stuck in Rome for the time being."

"You are an American. You can walk in there—" he pointed toward the American Express office "—and make a ticket on the *Cristoforo Colombo* or the Pan Am. Hello America! I have returned!"

"That was the view of one guy—"

"The top journalist for the top magazine in all of Italy."

"Trust me, Emilio, as soon as I can, I will walk into that office behind me and I will book a one-way ticket."

"Oh, yes! It is okay for you! You can leave. You can be whoever you want. Whatever you want. And you leave people like me stuck here." He waved his hands around wildly, nearly hitting a young woman pushing a stroller. "With these dusty ruins. All this history. All these families and their expectations."

*So he resents how I can leave any time I want.*

"Emilio," Marcus said, keeping his voice low and even, "if you want to go to America, just pack your bags and leave."

The guy's face curdled into a snarl. "It is not easy."

"Sure it is. There are so many Italians in America that you'll feel right at home."

Marcus attempted a friendly poke to Emilio's shoulder but he shoved Marcus's hand away. "I am not free. I can never be free!"

"I don't think that's true."

"YOU KNOW NOTHING!"

The guy began swinging wildly, struggling to land blows wherever he could. Marcus fended them off until he saw that Emilio was determined to cold-cock him. Marcus had to put a stop to this—the bank closed in less than fifteen minutes.

Marcus deposited his camera on the ground, then socked Emilio with a right hook that sent him staggering against the American Express window. It was the first time Marcus had ever slugged someone like that. The movies didn't show how punching someone hurt like holy hell.

* * *

If he hadn't run the last two blocks, he might not have made it to the bank in time.

For someone who had never even cheated on his income tax, the prospect of smuggling a large amount of money out of a foreign country made Marcus feel like he was in a Humphrey Bogart movie. He wished Kathryn or Gwendolyn were with him to play his femme fatale.

Was his American Express Travelers Cheques idea inspired? Or crazy? Was there a limit to how many they would sell him? Was anybody keeping track?

He turned the corner into the Piazza di Spagna to peek through the American Express window again but caught sight of a yellow smudge sprawled at the base of the Spanish Steps. Emilio Conti sat with his face planted in the palms of his hands. For a moment, Marcus wondered if he was crying.

Marcus crossed the piazza and sank to his haunches. "Let me buy you a drink. Maybe we can—"

Emilio let out a raw moan as he pushed Marcus onto the cobblestones and lurched to his feet. He pulled something from his jacket pocket but it escaped his grasp and crashed onto the ground, splintering into a thousand fragments. The smell of Scotch whiskey filled Marcus's nose as Emilio staggered past shocked onlookers. Marcus now felt like he really was in a Bogart picture, so he surrendered to an urge and followed this miserable little jerk.

Emilio reached the expansive Piazza del Popolo, skirted around the northern border of the gardens of the Villa Borghese, and lumbered deeper into the northern part of the city where Marcus had never ventured.

The main thoroughfares led to local streets, which gave way to a lattice of back alleys where cobblestones deteriorated into sparse gravel and the looks from passers-by grew wary.

Emilio abruptly stopped to brush the dirt from his suit and smooth down his hair. He reached for the brass handle attached to a door painted asphalt black. It squeaked in protest as it swung open; the shadows swallowed him whole.

Marcus wondered if he should get while the getting was good. He wasn't sure he could escape this maze of backstreets.

*Bogie would keep going.*

On the other side of the door lay a short corridor, its walls covered in peeling flocked velvet of dark pomegranate. The corridor opened into a large, semicircular room. The bar stood on the left, fanning out with stools crowding its lip. Waist-high cocktail tables lined the outer wall, each of them standing in a narrow pool of light cast by dim shaded lights dangling from a ceiling Marcus couldn't make out. Only a fraction of the tables were occupied; all the other patrons sat at the bar.

Emilio took a seat next to a man with bright red curly hair and motioned the bartender for another round of whatever-he's-having. The redhead asked Emilio a question and received a curt headshake in response. After a pause, Emilio let his shoulders sag and then gave them a well-maybe shrug, which made the redhead smile. He reached up and ran his fingers through Emilio's disheveled hair.

It was the sort of thing Domenico liked to do after they made love and fell back into each other's arms, panting and sweaty.

Marcus took in the rest of the bar more closely now that his eyes had started to adjust. In the city of the Vatican, where two thousand years of Catholic dogma condemned everything that certain types of men liked to do in the privacy of their pensiones, Marcus found himself standing in a queer bar.

Emilio closed his eyes and surrendered himself to the soothing sensation of his boyfriend's fingernails dragging across his scalp. A wistful smile emerged on what had been an angry, resentful face.

Marcus turned to leave, but Melody's warning came back to him. *Never trust a Conti.*

He removed his camera lens cover. The light in this joint was murky but Emilio's face was bathed in the light from the lamp directly above him.

Very, very slowly, Marcus pressed the shutter release button.

# CHAPTER 19

Kathryn stepped off the stairs leading down to the Beverly Hills Hotel pool and peered over the top of her sunglasses. Over the telephone yesterday, the guy had sounded like the smooth-talking European playboy Marcus had described, so she didn't think she'd have to look too hard. How many barrel-chested Italian hunks could possibly be lying around in the sun?

It was only late April but the hint of early summer already heated the air. Kathryn fanned her face with her straw pocketbook as she dodged around lollygaggers with nothing better to do on a Wednesday afternoon than sit around a hotel pool hoping to see Burt Lancaster.

She rounded the first corner and looked down the row of cabanas lined up along the ten-foot hedge. A man stepped out from between the white-and-gold-striped canvas flaps of the last one wearing only a bathing suit and a brilliant white smile.

If anyone deserved to be described as a "barrel-chested Italian hunk," it was Rossano Brazzi. He held out his hand. "Miss Massey, thank you so much for meeting me."

His grip was confident, manly. "Marcus has mentioned you in his letters."

Brazzi's cabana contained a glass-topped coffee table and two rattan chairs. A bottle of something bubbly rested in a pewter ice bucket emblazoned with the hotel's BHH logo.

Brazzi gestured toward the chairs. "I took a liberty to ordering refreshment."

Kathryn read the label. "What is prosecco?"

"Our version of champagne. I could have ordered Moët et Chandon, but I'm *Italiano*!"

It was only through Marcus that Kathryn even knew about the stateside publicity cavalcade Fox was planning for Brazzi ahead of the *Three Coins in the Fountain* launch the following month.

Now that she could see him for herself, she was grateful for this private meeting. Once Fox unveiled their "Europe's New Screen Romeo," he might not be so accessible.

He bent behind his chair and brought up a brown cardboard box tied with string. "From Signore Marcus. It is one jar of pesto sauce and one jar of pomodoro sauce made by his landlady."

Kathryn ran her finger along the edge of the box. She missed Marcus's laugh, his martinis, and his reassuring presence, but most of all, she missed his ability to listen. It wasn't until he had gone to Italy for *Quo Vadis* that Kathryn realized how rare a commodity good listeners were in a town filled with people hell-bent on pulling focus.

And boy, did she ever need Marcus's ears lately.

Her father's future, reputation, and freedom were at stake. Had she made a terrible blunder by convincing Winchell to approach the FBI on her behalf? Leo remained curiously noncommittal on the subject, and Gwendolyn had said it was a risk worth taking but acknowledged that it wasn't her taking the risk. Kathryn longed to hear Marcus's view, but a trans-Atlantic call would be exorbitant and letters weren't secure.

Kathryn took her first sip of prosecco. It was more bubbly than champagne, and drier, but refreshing in a cabana with no cross breeze. "Thank you for lugging this package all the way to Los Angeles."

"It was no trouble, and I must confess: I wanted a reason to see you."

"With this build-up Zanuck's giving you, I'm sure our paths would have crossed."

Brazzi knitted his fingers together. "There is somebody I want to meet."

Kathryn didn't need to hear any more. She already knew what was coming. The request grew more and more frequent as Marilyn Monroe's fame reached new heights. "I'll help if I can."

"I would like to meet Arthur Laurents."

Kathryn rolled the name around in her mind. "The playwright?"

"*Si*. United Artists will start shooting his play, *The Time of the Cuckoo* in Venice in July."

Europe's new screen Romeo had done his homework. "And you want to talk to him—why?"

"They have not cast the role of the antique storeowner, Renato de Rossi. I know they are considering Vittorio De Sica and Enzio Pinza, but I want to appeal to Signore Laurents himself. Marcus told me that you know everyone in Hollywood."

"Did you tell him what you wanted?" Brazzi shook his head. He'd done his homework, but not enough of it. "First of all, Arthur Laurents is a New Yorker, but that doesn't matter because his screenplay was rejected. The director is now writing it."

"You can connect me with him?"

"David Lean lives in London."

Brazzi's chin dropped onto his hands. "I am not in the correct continent."

"However . . ." She lifted his chin with a finger. "Katharine Hepburn *is* in Los Angeles. She hasn't made a movie since George Cukor directed her in *Pat and Mike*, and that was four years ago. This movie is sort of a mini-comeback, and my guess is that she'll have a big say in casting. It's Hepburn you have to impress."

"Can you introduce me to her?"

"George has been a bit of a recluse recovering from shooting *A Star is Born* for four months." She was trying not to get suckered in by his pleading hangdog expression, but the guy was just so gosh-darned handsome. "I can't promise anything."

* * *

Perino's on Wilshire Boulevard was the epitome of elegant European dining, as far as Angelenos were concerned. With its alabaster walls, bone ceiling, cream tablecloths, and eggshell carpet, it was saved from being bland as a vanilla milkshake by salmon upholstery and vases of roses, bright as Mercurochrome.

To Kathryn's surprise, Cukor readily agreed to set up a lunch the following Sunday with Hepburn and suggested she invite Gwendolyn and Leo as camouflage.

Kathryn had insisted that they all arrive at a quarter of one to ensure that Brazzi, Cukor, or Hepburn weren't kept waiting at an empty table. And thank goodness she had, because Hepburn arrived seven minutes early, leaving poor George to scurry along in her wake as she issued orders for iced water but no ice, and garlic in her mashed potatoes, even though she knew that Alexander Perino hated the stuff.

By one o'clock, they were seated at a central table, drinks ordered, and menus in hand.

"I must say, Mr. Brazzi," Hepburn said, "your English is excellent. Do all of your countrymen possess an equally fine command of our language? I ask because I'll be heading over there this summer. Shooting a movie, you know. My first in a while and I don't mind telling you that I'm looking forward to it. Working is vital; otherwise, everything atrophies."

Brazzi looked at Kathryn bleakly.

"She means 'weakens' or 'wastes away.'"

"That's right!" Hepburn thumped the table. "The gray matter, the reflexes. Good golly, it all goes if you don't use it. So, do they?"

Brazzi beseeched Kathryn again. *Do they what?*

"Your fellow Italians." Kathryn prompted. "Do they speak English as fluently as you?"

"I'm afraid they do not, Signorina Hepburn. When I was filming *The Barefoot Contessa*, Mister Zanuck employed someone with whom I could practice my English. Ah, but you must know him. He worked at MGM for many years."

"Oh yes?" Hepburn mused.

Gwendolyn brought her hand to her mouth and whispered "San Simeon!" under the light minuet waltzing through the loudspeakers.

A number of years before, Marcus had scored an invitation to Hearst's castle retreat up the Californian coast. Unfortunately, he had gotten horribly drunk and embarrassed himself in front of Hollywood's elite, including Katharine Hepburn.

"I can recommend the Oysters Rockefeller and the Breast of Capon," Kathryn exclaimed. "And I like the Antipasto Italiene, but perhaps Mr. Brazzi might be a better judge."

The tactic worked, and the conversation veered away from the poor impression Marcus had made that weekend.

When Kathryn had called Brazzi to tell him the luncheon was on, she'd instructed, "Feel free to ooze the European charm, but don't drown her in it. She's sharp as a carving knife, but she's still a woman. And ask her about her experiences. Actors love to talk about themselves."

"Please tell me about filming *The African Queen*," Brazzi said. "Was it very difficult?"

Hepburn's experiences in the Belgian Congo and Uganda led to a free-ranging discussion about the rewards and potholes of international travel, unfamiliar food, foreign customs, and the uselessness of guidebooks that are more than a year old.

By the time the appetizers arrived, Brazzi had managed to bring the conversation around to Venice. He had Hepburn in the palm of his well-manicured hand as he spoke rapturously of his favorite restaurant.

"Cantina Do Spade has been open since 1448," he enthused. "Casanova himself entertained his potential conquests there. More than five hundred years of Venetian history pours from every brick."

"You sound like you know Venice very well." Hepburn couldn't pull her eyes off Brazzi long enough to look at her Consommé Bellevue.

"I visited it many times when I attended university in Florence. I am very at peace there and think of it as my second home."

"Tell me, Mr. Brazzi—"

"Please call me Rossano."

"If you call me Katharine."

"I would be delighted."

"So, Rossano, what did you study at the university of Florence?"

"I am a lawyer by training."

"My goodness! Aren't you a man of many talents?"

Kathryn's eye started to wander. At places like these, she often spotted someone with someone who was married to someone else.

A striking woman entered the dining room. It wasn't her looks that caught Kathryn's interest—statuesque though she was; it was the way she made her entrance.

A beauty entering a prominent Hollywood restaurant like Perino's usually paused at the doorway, radiant smile in place and bosom on display, waved to some unseen acquaintance across the room, then walked to her table with swaying hips enfolded in a dress designed to highlight every asset.

But this woman didn't do any of that.

Her fitted suit of aubergine poplin showed her impressive measurements without drawing attention to them. Except for a silver starfish brooch on her left lapel, she eschewed the usual payload of glitter and sparkle.

Kathryn followed the woman's progress as she trailed the maître d' to an empty corner table without making eye contact. She sat down, pulled off her gloves, placed a drink order, and surveyed the menu with a world-weariness that made Kathryn wonder whether she was going to spend her entire lunch alone.

She didn't have to wonder for very long.

Darryl Zanuck charged into the room, followed by a man in his late sixties, his near-bald head shining in the lights of the crystal chandeliers. After both men greeted the woman with European kisses, Zanuck snapped his fingers to attract a waiter and ordered champagne.

"Who's the stunner?"

Hepburn's question brought Kathryn back to the table.

"It's Bella Darvi," Gwendolyn said.

"That's Michael Curtiz with them." George raised his eyebrows at Kathryn as high as they would go.

Two plus two started adding up.

Curtiz had directed *The Egyptian* for Zanuck. A recent letter from Marcus had detailed Zanuck's affair with the girl playing Nefer.

*Zanuck is using Curtiz as camouflage exactly like I'm using Cukor!* Kathryn tried to mask her unintentional giggle by sending it down her wine glass, but Hepburn wasn't fooled.

"I feel like I'm the only chump who doesn't get what's going on here."

"I suspect we're seeing a romantic rendezvous," Kathryn whispered, "and Zanuck is using Curtiz as cover. Whether or not Curtiz knows it is hard to say."

"He would have to be very foolish to still be in the dark," Brazzi said. When George asked him why, he replied, "Our *Barefoot Contessa* cinematographer, Milton, said they think they're getting away with nobody knowing, but we all knew."

"It's only a matter of time before all of Hollywood does, too, if that's how they're going to carry on in public." Hepburn pressed a light hand to Brazzi's arm. "Tell me, Rossano, do you have a hotel in Venice you can recommend for me during the *Summertime* shoot?"

Zanuck patted down his pockets and winced when he found himself out of cigarettes. He interrupted Curtiz's monolog to bum one, but the director merely pointed to the cigarette vending machine in the foyer. Zanuck looked around for a waiter, but every one of them was busy elsewhere. He pushed his chair away from the table in a juvenile huff and stomped out of the room.

"Excuse me," Kathryn told the group, "but business calls."

Zanuck didn't see her until she slid an arm along the top of the vending machine. "That's quite a table you've got there," he said, grim as an undertaker. "I was planning to drop by when I had a chance, but I—uh—"

"—didn't want to leave Curtiz too long with your new discovery?"

Zanuck mulled over her sly smile. "What's on your mind?"

"I've come to do you a favor."

"Why? Do you need one in return?"

"It's more like a warning." A pack of Camels fell to the tray at the bottom of the machine, but Zanuck left it there. "You're fooling yourself if you think nobody knows what's going on between you and your protégé."

Zanuck closed his eyes as he pressed his chest against the machine.

"It was the talk of the *Contessa* shoot. You might want to try and be a bit discreet."

"Thank you." A silent nod, a guarded eye. "What's the catch?"

"No catch."

"Why do I feel like I'm being cornered?"

"Okay, so maybe there's one little thing."

"Here it comes."

Kathryn bent down and retrieved Zanuck's pack of Camels and dropped it on the top of the machine. "It's about Marcus Adler."

Zanuck needed a moment to place the name. "Is he back in town?"

"No, but when he returns, he'll need a job."

"He's got a great eye. Those shots he took of Rome? Exactly what we needed."

"I meant more along the lines of a screenplay."

Zanuck took his cigarette pack and started to turn it over in his hand. "We'll see."

Kathryn wasn't sure if she was meddling where she shouldn't, but the longer Marcus was away, the harder it would be for him to jump-start his career.

"You ever been to a place called Amagansett?" he asked.

Kathryn wasn't sure what to make of this non-sequitur. "Never heard of it."

"I was in New York last week. Had dinner with Winchell."

"I bet that was fun."

"I arrived late, which didn't impress him. He was already three Tom Collins in."

"Pissed *and* drunk?"

"He's usually so focused and articulate, everything thought out and deliberate. But that night his conversation was scattered, like he was having trouble sticking to one idea at a time. He also mentioned someone called Pastorius."

"Sounds like a Roman general."

"He brought your name up several times. His whole tone was 'I know a secret.'"

"Should I have heard of this Pastorius guy?"

Zanuck eyeballed his table. Curtiz had inched closer to Darvi. "I got the idea that you should." He tossed his Camels into the air and caught them again. "I better get back to my table before Bella drowns in drool."

Kathryn scooted into the ladies' room and sat down at the last vanity. It was now over a month since Gable's party and Kathryn hadn't heard a word from Winchell. She wasn't worried about it, though. She figured it took time to suck up to Hoover and convince him to gain access to FBI files. But now his silence gnawed at her.

*What if he's already tracked down my father's file and has gone through it himself?*

She dropped her lipstick into her purse, left a quarter in the tip dish for the attendant, and walked slowly back toward the dining room.

*What were those names again? Agamasetts? Amagansett? Pretorius? Pasteurize? Jesus, I've already forgotten. I bet Winchell's got them written down in a little notebook. I bet he's sitting at the Stork Club right now, congratulating himself because he thinks he holds all the cards.*

Katharine Hepburn's voice cut through the air. "Oh, Rossano! You devil!"

*Problem is, if Winchell's gone and pawed through my father's FBI file, he really does hold all the cards.*

# CHAPTER 20

Gwendolyn knocked on the portable dressing room parked in a darkened corner of the soundstage. "Marilyn, honey, it's me. I got your note."

When a messenger from Stage Nine had arrived with a summons to the *There's No Business Like Show Business* set, Gwendolyn wasn't surprised. There were murmurs on the lot that filming had been problematic. Dan Dailey was dating Donald O'Connor's ex-wife, which made shooting awkward. Marilyn was upset over being forced into a supporting role after *Niagara, Gentlemen Prefer Blondes, How to Marry a Millionaire,* and *River of No Return* had been such huge hits. Meanwhile, Ethel Merman was furious at Marilyn for stealing the "Heat Wave" number away from her, even though the decision had been Zanuck's.

If anything, Gwendolyn was surprised that she hadn't been summoned before now, so when she'd read Marilyn's note, she'd hurried right over.

The bolt on the other side snapped. Gwendolyn turned the silver handle and cracked open the door. Catching a glimpse of leg, she pushed it wider.

Marilyn sat at her makeup mirror dressed in the costume Gwendolyn had spent two weeks working on. The huge white straw hat that went with it lay on the sofa opposite.

Gwendolyn closed the door. "Nervous about the number?"

Marilyn played with the black and white bangles hanging from her wrist. "The front gate called to tell me Joe's arrived with one of his pals. They've come to watch the filming but look at what I'm wearing!"

Marilyn jumped to her feet. Her torso was bare and her chest was lashed into a black-and-pink strapless bra. Fuchsia silk lined her voluminous skirt, which featured a bold pattern of large black leaves on a white background. The ends met two inches above her crotch. It weighed a ton and Gwendolyn didn't envy how Marilyn had to dance in it.

"Joe's going to have a fit when he sees me!" Marilyn cried.

Gwendolyn pressed an arm around her shoulders. "Not in public, he won't."

"He knew I was filming 'Heat Wave' today. He saw Billy's sketches. It's like he's come here to torture himself—and me."

Outside the dressing room, the volume of chatter increased until someone exclaimed, "Say, ain't that DiMaggio?" Marilyn's doe eyes glazed over.

"How about I go out there and distract them, keep them happy?" Gwendolyn suggested.

"Would you? Could you?"

Back in the costuming department, Billy Travilla's designs for Marilyn's next picture filled Gwendolyn's work desk. *The Seven Year Itch* was to be directed by Billy Wilder, who had very specific ideas about costuming. Wilder had rejected all of Travilla's designs, so they were starting to fall behind schedule. Meanwhile, the second season of *The Loretta Young Show* was starting in August, which gave Gwendolyn only two months to work up a slew of ideas. Gwendolyn didn't have the time to sit on a set all day, but nor did she have the heart to desert Marilyn when she needed her so desperately.

A knock on the door told Marilyn that they were ready.

"What's the name of Joe's pal?" Gwendolyn asked.

"George Solotaire. He's one of those hanger-on types, but very nice. He grew up in an orphanage just like I did."

Gwendolyn took Marilyn's hands. "Your job isn't to humor your husband. You've worked very hard on 'Heat Wave.' Focus on Jack Cole. He'll help get you through this, and leave Joe to me."

The set for the "Heat Wave" number was a nightclub stage, thirty feet across, draped with huge bolts of red velvet and studded with leafless papier-mâché trees. On the left sat a wagon constructed out of weathered poles painted pink and white, and held together with twine and ribbons. DiMaggio, face grim and eyes darting, paced along its periphery near a line of eight visitors' chairs.

"Mr. DiMaggio, I'm Gwendolyn Brick. Why don't you take a seat? Filming requires interminable stretches of time so you might as well make yourself comfortable."

The Yankee Clipper chewed a wad of Juicy Fruit like it was his final meal.

"C'mon, Joe, sit down, why doncha?" Solotaire was a round-faced guy with prominent ears and a drinker's belly, who was resigned to his role of playing circus clown to a volatile friend.

Gwendolyn eyed the six empty chairs next to Solotaire. "You expecting more people?"

"I think they're meant for us."

Sidney Skolsky stood behind Gwendolyn with drama teacher Paula Strasberg and her teenage daughter, Susan. With them was Marilyn's ubiquitous acting coach, Natasha Lytess, a plain woman on whom Marilyn depended to an unhealthy degree and whom nobody at Fox liked.

Marilyn was nervous enough having to appear in such a skimpy outfit, but to perform in front of her angry husband, astringent coach, a serious acting teacher, and a columnist? Gwendolyn feared it would send Marilyn back into her dressing room.

"Is she wearing that costume?" DiMaggio growled. "The one where you can damn well see nearly everything?"

"She—uh—" Gwendolyn cast around for support from Jack, who had choreographed this entire number and who was in charge today.

"Gwendolyn!" Dorothy Dandridge walked through the soundstage door waving a large white purse. "What a lovely surprise."

Gwendolyn knew Dorothy from her Chez Gwendolyn days and was the perfect distraction. Relieved, she greeted Dorothy with a kiss. "I want you to meet Joe DiMaggio. Mr. DiMaggio, I'd like to present Miss Dorothy Dandridge."

Dorothy's eyes widened, her smile bright as meringue. "Mr. DiMaggio!"

The guy looked at her as though she was a tree stump.

"Dorothy is about to start filming *Carmen Jones*," Gwendolyn persevered. "Her director is Otto Preminger."

That got a rise out of DiMaggio, which was why Gwendolyn had brought it up. Marilyn's feuds with Preminger had become grist for the gossip mill.

"Good luck with that Hungarian ham."

"Otto's so magnetic!" Dorothy gushed like a sophomore. "So charismatic! So hypnotic!"

Gwendolyn had heard this sort of effusive praise before and knew that Dorothy would soon be sleeping with her director—if she wasn't already.

"Jesus Christ! Look at her!"

DiMaggio charged toward Marilyn, who was practicing her climb out of the rickety wagon with as much grace as she could muster. "Joe," she pleaded. "Don't. Please."

"Did you even stop to think how it looks with my wife parading around with her dress cut up to there?" He pointed below the belt designed to hide her navel. "And what the hell are you wearing around your chest? Sneeze and it could fly off." He waved his hands around and squealed in a patronizing falsetto, "We're having a tropical heat wave that's so hot I'll have to take off my top!"

Jack Cole stepped forward. "Mr. DiMaggio, please, we're trying to work here."

Marilyn had once confided to Gwendolyn that Cole was one of the few studio people whom she trusted explicitly. He had an elfin nimbleness about him coupled with the stamina of a dancer.

DiMaggio wheeled around. "And as for you, you goddamned fairy. I suppose you're the one getting her to do all those high kicks and pelvic thrusts."

"JOE! PLEASE! NOT HERE!"

"I want to see *you* in *that* dressing room!"

A stealthy movement to the right caught Gwendolyn's attention.

Ever since Marcus had found work as a production photographer, Gwendolyn had become aware of the consequences of behaving badly on set. She watched the guy take shot after shot. Nobody was going to come out looking good—not Marilyn pleading with her husband, not Joe DiMaggio screaming at everybody, and not Jack Cole being called a goddamned fairy.

Gwendolyn inserted herself between Joe and Marilyn, with her back to the rickety wagon built for Marilyn's entrance. "Could I remind you—"

"AND I MEAN RIGHT NOW!"

DiMaggio thrust his hand out toward Marilyn's dressing room, but his fist connected with the side of Gwendolyn's face. The brute force sent her staggering backward into the wooden cart, filling her head with blurry images and slivers of blinding light. She felt a sharp pain crack her skull. Her feet skidded outwards and she crashed to the concrete floor. As she did, the cart toppled onto her.

Dazed, she heard muffled yelling. An excruciating pain shot through her ankle. More yelling. One of them was Marilyn, all traces of her baby-doll voice now gone. But there were others—male, deep, angry. The pain in her ankle was agony. Sharp needles of torture, shooting like fireworks. The weight of the cart grew heavier and heavier and heavier.

* * *

Gwendolyn let her head fall back onto the hospital pillow. She closed her eyes against the clinical glare and listened to the regular beeping from a room on the other side of the corridor.

*Joe DiMaggio thwacked me so hard that I landed on Marilyn's entrance wagon and then . . .*

The subsequent details became lost in fuzzy confusion.

All she knew now was that broken or sprained, her ankle had blown up like a beach ball and screamed every time she moved.

"There you are!" It was Kathryn's voice, but from the heavy footfall on the linoleum, Gwendolyn could tell she wasn't alone.

*Please don't tell me Joe DiMaggio is with her.*

"Maybe she's asleep? Should we come back later?"

It was a man's voice but it didn't belong to DiMaggio. Gwendolyn opened her eyes. "MONTY?!"

His face was more weathered now, but his eyes were still the color of the Pacific. The first hints of gray were creeping in at his temples, but he stood with the erect posture of a career military man.

"I came to the studio to surprise you, but when I walked into the soundstage I saw some guy sock you in the jaw."

"It was an accident," she told him.

"All I saw was this big bruiser deck you, and I thought, Not with my sister you don't, so I clocked him."

"You popped Joe DiMaggio in the face?" Gwendolyn started to laugh but it sent needles of pain up her leg.

"How was I supposed to know it was him?"

"Because he's the most famous baseball player in the world?" Kathryn suggested.

Gwendolyn squeezed her brother's thumb. "My hero."

"You're welcome."

"But why didn't you let me know you were coming?"

He grinned, deepening the gash that carved a line from under his right ear, across his cheek, to the middle of his chin. "Because I wanted to tell you my news in person."

Gwendolyn noticed Monty's plain gray Brooks Brothers suit. "Why aren't you wearing your uniform? Monty! Have you left the service?"

He patted her hand reassuringly. "I'm a navy man, through and through. They've got me till I curl up my toes."

"What's with the civvies?"

"I've been transferred to LA to be a landlubber, if you can believe that."

A single tear oozed out of the corner of Gwendolyn's eye. "You'll be living here? In LA? Full time?"

Monty laughed. She'd forgotten how deep his laughter was—like a roll of thunder. "It's a five-year appointment."

"Oh, Monty!" Gwendolyn wished she could leap up and squeeze every last molecule of salty air from her brother's lungs.

Kathryn dropped her handbag and gloves on Gwendolyn's tray table. "You're not going to believe this!" She pointed to Monty, who straightened to his full six foot four. "Your brother is the new liaison officer between the navy and the studios."

Monty bowed stiffly. "I wanted to tell you in person but when I socked DiMaggio, studio security appeared like Aladdin's genie and hustled me out."

"But Mo-Mo," Gwendolyn said, "how did this happen? I mean, why you?"

"About a year ago, I was on overnight radar duty with our newest recruit. To keep each other awake, we took turns talking. I told him about my experiences during the war when I was serving under Admiral Halsey, and during Typhoon Connie, and the surrender of Japan in Tokyo Bay on the USS *Missouri*. When I finished, this guy says I should write it down, like in a memoir, because his brother-in-law is one of those literary agents. I told him I'm not the writing type. He says to me, 'You got some better way to fill in these long navy voyages?'"

Gwendolyn peered into Monty's earnest face. "You've written a memoir?"

"Yeah! He sent it to his in-law, who loved it. A while after that, I get a letter saying he's sold it to Simon and Schuster."

"What?!" All this news coming at once made Gwendolyn's head spin. It might also have been the dose of painkillers the nurse had just fed her. "When does it come out?"

"It takes forever so who the heck knows? But about a month ago, I got hauled in front of the head of navy public relations who tells me recruitment is on the decrease since the war in Korea ain't going so good. They need to improve P.R. and figure my memoir might be it. Before you can say 'kamikaze,' I'm the new navy liaison officer!"

The fresh fog of painkillers drifted through Gwendolyn. She felt like she was lying on a bed of cotton candy nestled in a drifting cloud. "I'm so proud of you."

"My office is in the Taft Building. D'you know where that is?"

"Corner of Hollywood and Vine," Kathryn said. "The Academy of Motion Picture Arts and Sciences have their offices there."

"Is it near the Garden of Allah?" Monty asked.

"Easy drive down Sunset. You thinking of moving in?"

"Got room on your sofa till they get a vacancy?"

"Better yet," Kathryn said, "Marcus's place is empty. God knows when he'll be back, so why don't you just move in there? I'm sure he won't mind, especially if you take over the rent."

Beyond the capability of producing sound now, Gwendolyn managed to nod her head before slipping into a dreamy netherworld of cashmere, eiderdown, and angels.

# CHAPTER 21

When Rossano Brazzi returned from Los Angeles, one of his first calls was to Marcus. Rossano thought he'd impressed Katharine Hepburn enough to consider him for the lead in *Summertime*, but much of the sophisticated chatter between Hepburn and Cukor escaped him.

"I must not be in the same situation again!" he told Marcus. "I want to increase my English lessons to three times a week, plus one extra day to remove my accent."

Marcus pointed out that if Fox was promoting him as "Europe's New Screen Romeo" he should sound like he was "from Italy, not Inglewood," but conceded that a softened accent might make him more comprehensible to American audiences.

The Rome premiere of *Three Coins in the Fountain* was approaching, followed by *The Barefoot Contessa* in the fall. Every Monday, Tuesday, Thursday, and Friday, Marcus walked across Rome to Brazzi's apartment near the Victor Emmanuel II monument. Romans detested it, but it reminded Marcus of the more extravagant sets in Hollywood movies such as *Intolerance, Ben-Hur,* and *Citizen Kane*, and now that Hollywood had gone widescreen, *The Robe*.

Rossano lived on the top floor of a five-story building, far enough removed from the chaotic piazza to dim the traffic noise. The place had no elevator, so by the time Marcus reached the apartment, he needed to catch his breath. With no Garden of Allah pool to keep him in shape, it was a daily reminder that Rome's chianti-and-pasta lifestyle could take its toll on his waistline if he wasn't careful.

He rapped the doorknocker twice, paused, then twice again. It was their secret knock, alerting Rossano that it was Marcus and not an intrepid *scattino* or emboldened fan.

"COME!"

Marcus walked down the long corridor lined with Brazzi family portraits of long-past generations and into the spacious living room that smelled of freshly cut flowers, olive oil, red wine, and ancient history. The furniture had been pushed aside to make room for five matching traveling trunks in black leather and polished brass arranged in a semicircle; each of them was angled open. Rossano stood at the middle one, a tangle of neckties gathered in his hand.

"What's all this?" Marcus asked.

"Lydia and I are going to Florence for a law-school reunion. It will last the whole weekend with many parties." He rapped his knuckles on the trunk in front of him. "This is mine. The others are for Lydia. She is staying for one month."

Marcus inspected the trunk at the end. Its innards were a beautifully designed arrangement of drawers upholstered in red Chinese silk featuring a stork motif. Instead of handles, each one had a small crystal ball. "These are pretty."

Rossano pointed at it. "What are they called in English?"

"I'd probably call it a knob."

"Nob?"

"With a 'k.'"

Rossano rolled his eyes. "The infamous silent k. You have a ridiculous language."

Marcus ran his fingers down the spine of the trunk until he got to a large hinge at the top. "What do we call these?"

Rossano tried to force out the word like a cough. He gave up.

"It's a hinge."

"Hinge," he repeated thoughtfully.

"Use it in a sentence."

"My *trahveling troonk* has a large hinge."

"'Traveling' is with a short a, as in 'cat,' and 'trunk' is a short u, as in 'cut.' Say it again."

In the weeks they'd been working together, Rossano's English had improved but his accent stubbornly fought correction. He repeated the sentence, sharpening his vowels. The progress was marginal, so Marcus got him to repeat the sentence until he grew bored with it and joined him at the trunk.

He squatted onto his knees and pulled the ball attached to the lowest drawer. It glided out noiselessly. He flicked his wrist and a box upholstered in the same red silk dropped into his hand. He lifted it out. "I cannot think of the English word for this."

It was about the size of a cigar box. Marcus turned it over in his hand. "Where did this come from?"

"There is a little space hidden with a trigger. Clever, no?"

"Very. We call this a secret compartment."

Rossano forced back a mordant smile. "My wife, she is in love with expensive jewelry. What she cannot wear, we hide in these secret compartments."

"There is more than one?"

"*Si*. Three in each trunk. Lydia is like all women. Everything that—mmm, *brilla*."

"Sparkles."

Rossano turned to his neckties and started hanging them from a mahogany rod. "Sparkles. I like how this word jumps around the mouth."

Marcus pressed his hand to the black leather as his mind started churning. "Where can I get luggage like this?"

"From a luggage maker near the Vatican. He has helped refugee aristocracy and runaway fascists and banished clergy for many years." Rossano hooked his neckties into his trunk and crossed his arms. "You have something to smuggle out of Italy?"

Marcus nodded.

"Before the war, many people with assets to hide, they used trunks like these. But now customs officials know all the tricks. They search every trunk. If they find many monies, they seize it and charge a heavy fine. Until it is paid, they do not allow you to leave the country, and sometimes put you in jail."

*Oh well, it seemed like a good idea.*

"However."

A yelp of hope caught in Marcus's throat. "Yes?"

"First, you convert the money to gold bullion. Small bricks, the size of your finger. You have your tailor sew them into the lining and pockets of your clothes. I can send you to the same tailor that King Farouk uses."

The last king of Egypt was now a permanent fixture in the café society culture springing up around Rome. The guy was richer than Solomon, so his tailor probably charged accordingly. Still, if it let Marcus get his money out of Italy . . .

"This tailor," Marcus said. "Is he as discreet as your luggage maker?"

"He will sew the tiny bricks into your suit so that nobody will notice the bulge or hear them clink together."

"But if the customs officials are onto all the tricks, won't they know about the gold-in-the-hem scam?"

"In the main ports like Rome, Genoa, or Venice, yes. But if you travel alone with a small suitcase to Sicily, you can catch a freighter from Palermo to Casablanca, where I know a man who will buy your bullion in American dollars. From there, you sail to the Canary Islands. A Portuguese shipping company has regular voyages from Tenerife to the Azores, and then Puerto Rico."

Marcus could see now that he should have been thinking more like Orson Welles' Harry Lime in *The Third Man*. "I need to write this down."

* * *

Domenico squirmed in his seat at a Napolitano restaurant near the Castel Sant'Angelo as Marcus related Rossano's solution. By the time Marcus finished, he had burned through two Nazionale cigarettes. He crushed the butt of the second one into the ashtray and motioned to the waiter for a third round of prosecco. "Smuggle gold out of the country? If that is the kind of lawyer he was, I understand why he is now an actor."

Domenico's joie de vivre was one of his most appealing attributes. The whole time they'd known each other, Marcus had never heard anything remotely scornful come out of his mouth.

It was evening now. Lights bathed the circular castle in a buttery luster. "Ten thousand dollars is a lot of money."

Domenico snorted a begrudging agreement. "So King Farouk's tailor fill your suit with little gold bricks and you sail to America via a hundred stops?"

"It's not as bad—"

"Tell me again the route."

"Rome to Palermo to Casablanca, where I'd catch a boat to the Canary Islands. And from there the Azores—"

"Do you know where are the Azores?"

"In the middle of the Atlantic."

"So you are in the middle of nowhere, and then?"

"Another boat to Puerto Rico, which is near Cuba, which is off the coast of Florida. And from there I'm practically home."

As he said it out loud, Rossano's solution sounded fraught with places where it could go horribly wrong. "Okay," he conceded. "I see your point."

"I said nothing."

"I know when you're upset."

The waiter placed their freshened glasses of prosecco in front of them, bubbles pushing to the surface.

"*Si,* Marcus, I am upset, but not for the reason you believe."

"You're right. It's a crazy plan. I could get robbed or stabbed anywhere along the route. It sounds like a B movie that George Raft rejected ten years ago. Let's forget it."

"The crazy plan of Rossano Brazzi is not why I am unhappy."

Marcus was glad that they were two and a half glasses into this conversation. "Say what you need to say."

"I think you are not ready to leave Rome."

A passing priest tossed a heel of bread at a flock of seagulls. They squawked and shrieked, fighting for a chance to nip at the crust. Except one, smaller than the others. He dragged behind him a wing bent at a graceless angle. Another seagull joined him on the rough cobblestones. Together they watched the rest of the flock tussle for scraps.

"Domenico," he said gently, "you and I weren't meant to last forever. I told you when we met that I was never going to be—"

"You talk in your sleep."

"Since when?"

"More and more. You do not mumble. You are very clear."

Marcus lit the last of the Camels Kathryn had given Rossano to carry back to Rome. "What do I talk about?"

"Oliver."

The name dropped on Marcus like a felled sequoia.

*I should have seen this coming. God knows, Oliver has been popping up in my dreams enough.*

In his first few weeks in Rome, Marcus had thought of Oliver whenever he wore his lucky purple tie, or the cufflink he'd had made to duplicate the one he'd lost in the Trevi Fountain, or when he saw Oliver's favorite wine on a menu.

But as the weeks had dissolved into months and Domenico had taken Oliver's place in Marcus's bed and his heart, thoughts of his former boyfriend had grown less frequent.

But in his dream life, Oliver still came calling. Often he'd be standing in the distance watching Marcus eat dinner with Kathryn or Gwendolyn, usually at Mama Weiss's Hungarian Restaurant on Beverly Drive.

More often, he'd be sitting around the pool at the Garden, knowing that Oliver lurked behind the elephant palms. Sometimes the pool was transformed into the Trevi Fountain and Marcus would find himself wading in the freezing water, looking for that blasted cufflink.

"I see."

They finished their meal in silence.

During the stroll back to Marcus's place, the air of uneasiness grew more awkward with every passing block. By the time they arrived at Signora Scatena's front door, Marcus knew Domenico wouldn't be joining him upstairs.

Signora Scatena threw open her door. "Signore!" She had her hands clasped together as though beseeching the Good Lord above. "Two men were here looking for you," she told him in machine-gun Italian. "They asked me questions: What sort of person are you? How long have you lived at my pensione? I answered their questions, but they were not satisfied and said they would return at ten o'clock this evening."

It was nearly that time now. Marcus thanked Signora Scatena and sent her inside. "You should go now," he told Domenico.

"Nothing good happens at this time of night. I will stay."

* * *

Three sharp knocks on the door set Marcus's nerves on edge. At his landing stood two middle-aged men in careworn suits, no hats, and shiny ties. They held badges identifying them as officials of the Immigration department.

The older, pudgier of the two asked Marcus to identify himself. When Marcus did so, he said, "We are here to seize your passport."

"What for?"

"There have been allegations that you are planning to smuggle a large amount of money out of the country."

"Allegations from who?"

Signore Pudgy stuck out his hand. "Until we are able to make a full investigation, we command you to surrender your passport.

"Do they have the right?" Marcus asked Domenico, who nodded silently.

Careful not to show his heart pounding in his chest, Marcus retrieved his passport from its hiding place in the bookshelf and handed it over. Signore Pudgy's partner wrote out a receipt and told him they would be in contact.

Marcus closed the door behind them, then slumped against it with his face pressed to the wood.

"What was he talking about?" Domenico asked.

"I've been buying a hundred dollars' worth of American Express travelers cheques three times a week."

Marcus felt Domenico's hot, anxious breath on the back of his neck. "Do you go to the same counter?"

"I don't even go to the same office. I rotate them."

"For how long have you done this?"

"Couple of months. The first time I walked past the American Express office was the day I got my MGM check, and I was hurrying to the bank to deposit it. I walked past their bureau on Piazza di Spagna. It was the day when—SHIT!" Marcus walloped the door with the palm of his hand.

"Shit what?" Domenico asked.

"That was the day I punched Emilio Conti to the ground."

# CHAPTER 22

Kathryn typed the period on the final sentence of her next column and reread what she considered one of her best efforts in nearly twenty years.

On the day she had seen Warner Bros.' latest addition to the "atomic blasts give rise to mutant bugs" genre, Senator Joe McCarthy had self-destructed at the hands of army counsel Joseph Welsh during the nationally televised hearings.

When she heard that she had missed Welsh demand of McCarthy, "Have you no sense of decency, sir?", she'd set about conflating the thin plot of *Them!*, in which giant man-eating ants threatened civilization, with the threat that the bloated egomania of a morally bankrupt US senator represented to the American way of life.

She pulled the paper from her typewriter. *Not too shabby, if I do say so myself.*

"Kathryn Massey?"

The Western Union delivery boy looked at least forty-five but had the weathered complexion of a sixty-year-old. He thrust an enveloped cable into her hand and asked her to sign his receipt.

She should already have been halfway to the Taft Building. She tore open the envelope and read the originating station.

*Rome! Is he coming back at last?*

> PASSPORT CONFISCATED STOP NOT SURE WHY STOP
> BIG MYSTERY STOP KNOW ANYONE IN THE STATE DEPT?

*What did he do? Rob the Italian Fort Knox? Do they even have a Fort Knox?*

"That's not a happy face."

When Mike Connolly had joined the *Hollywood Reporter* a couple of years ago, Kathryn's gut told her to mistrust the guy. Though clever with words and well connected, he was also glib, opinionated, smug, and an ugly drunk. However, when push came to shove the night of Voss's MacArthur Park broadcast, he hadn't hesitated to help Kathryn expose the guy as the phony he was.

"Unexpected news." She folded the cable back into the envelope and collected up her pocketbook.

She ought to have been driving along Sunset right now, but Harlan McNamara and the girls would have to wait. She hurried up the corridor and into the boss's office.

Billy Wilkerson was at his desk proofing a four-page spread that he, Kathryn, and Mike had worked on for the upcoming release of *On the Waterfront*. It was getting the royal treatment because the movie was a Columbia picture and because, the previous weekend, Wilkerson had lost a substantial poker game to Columbia head Harry Cohn and this was how he repaid the debt without Mrs. Wilkerson knowing.

"You still working on that?" Kathryn asked.

Wilkerson nodded. "What's up?"

Kathryn showed Wilkerson the cable.

"Yikes."

"Do you know someone at the State Department?"

Wilkerson pulled the reading glasses from his face. "No, but a few telephone calls might change that. Shouldn't you be over at Hollywood and Vine by now?"

Kathryn thanked her boss as she flew out the door and toward the stairs that led down to the lobby. She reached her car in under a minute, cranked the engine to life, and swung into traffic. She hadn't gone a block when she regretted telling Wilkerson.

What if Marcus had inadvertently committed a major crime? He wasn't in jail, so it couldn't have been *that* bad. Or did it mean they didn't have enough evidence to arrest him yet?

Thoughts of evidence caused Kathryn's mind to turn toward Winchell. It had been five weeks since her encounter with Zanuck at Perino's, and three months since she had nervously confided in Winchell at Gable's party. She had attempted to contact him via telephone, telegrams, letters, and cards, but he hadn't returned a single one. On his radio show, he'd announced a three-week trip to London. But he was back from that now and still nothing.

Instinct told her that he'd tracked down Thomas Danford's FBI file, but what was he doing with the information? And had he shared it with anyone? She'd already told him that he could have all the credit, so what was with this silent treatment?

She arrived at the Taft Building. If she'd had the time, she would have dropped in on Monty's office. She had planned on stopping by to see how his landlubber job was going, but she was twenty minutes late, so she'd have to do that another day.

She rode the elevator to Harlan McNamara's photographic studio on the top floor. Today was her first photo shoot with Adelaide Hawley and Betty Furness for the Sunbeam - Betty Crocker - Westinghouse blitz. A three-way advertising campaign had never previously been attempted, so negotiations over the sharing of costs, expenses, and scheduling had become unexpectedly complicated. But now the contracts had been signed, the paperwork filed, and the corporate lawyers paid, so it was time to start posing.

Adelaide and Betty were more experienced than Kathryn with this sort of photo shoot: "Hold straight, hold smile, hold cake, hold pose." In the company of such pros, Kathryn was glad she had Harlan to guide her through today's session. Although short on stature, he was long on the charming knack of putting people at ease.

"Sorry I'm so late," she announced to the group, pulling off her hat and gloves. "It's been one of those days."

A long kitchen counter, shiny with faux-marble Formica, was strewn with a range of cooking utensils, most of which Kathryn couldn't even name, let alone use. At one end was a triple-layered chocolate cake bigger than the wicker birdcage her mother kept in the corner of her living room. It sat next to a Mixmaster and in front of a Westinghouse refrigerator that dwarfed anything installed at the Garden of Allah.

"We took bets on you," Harlan said.

"How late I would be?"

"Whether you would show up at all," Adelaide replied, with a laugh.

"Is my reputation that bad?"

"Haven't you heard yet?" Betty asked. "About Sheldon Voss?"

"What about him?"

"It came over the radio just now. He's turned up."

"Alive?" Kathryn was drawn between hoping the bastard was dead and praying he was chained down somewhere so that she could drill him like a sadistic cop.

"Some poor janitor discovered him passed out in a cut-rate vacation apartment at Laguna Beach," Harlan said. "They managed to bring him around, but he's claiming amnesia."

"What?!"

"Says he doesn't remember anything of the past twenty years."

Kathryn jammed her fists onto her hips. "That's awfully convenient, I must say. And where is he now?"

Harlan started switching on the lights placed strategically around the kitchen set. "They transferred him to LA General but they've put him in isolation due to his—ahem—delicate state of mind."

Kathryn rummaged around her pocketbook for a last-minute lipstick repair. *We'll see about that.*

* * *

Los Angeles County General Hospital was a snow-white monolith that looked like a Howard Roark design from *The Fountainhead*. It was fifteen stories tall, with wings buttressing into the stark California sunshine and more entrances than Kathryn could count.

The information-desk volunteer directed her to the top floor of a wing that looked out over a hundred acres of railway tracks. The circular nurses' station stood to the left past an open waiting area filled with the mingled droning of men's voices. Kathryn approached the nurse behind the desk. A trace of recognition twinkled in the woman's eyes—sometimes it helped to be high profile.

"Miss Massey," the woman said, rising to her feet, "I was a big fan of your radio show. I miss hearing you on the air each week."

"Thank you—" Kathryn checked the nametag. "—Nurse Foster. I miss being on the air each week, too."

"May I assume that Sheldon Voss brings you to our floor?"

"I was hoping to see him."

"You and a thousand others."

"What number in the line am I?"

"There is no line. Doctor's orders are stricter than a Catholic boarding school. Nobody but family."

Kathryn was tempted to confide in this nurse, but the fewer people who knew, the better. "Is his doctor here right now?"

"Yes, but I have my orders—"

"I want half a minute of his time and not one second more."

"I'll see what I can do."

The doctor supervising Voss's case was a beanpole of a man who had the sharp-eyed wariness of someone who'd heard every type of sob story. The only ace in Kathryn's hand was the truth—or as little of it as she could get away with.

"I understand that you're only allowing family members to see Sheldon Voss."

"That's correct. So please understand that it's impossible—"

Kathryn angled her body away from the nurses' station. "The thing is, doctor—and I'm placing my trust in you to show the utmost discretion because it's not widely known—but I'm his niece." He went to make an objection, but she cut him off. "I'm very aware of how far-fetched it sounds, especially in view of your waiting room packed with bloodthirsty press. Nevertheless, it's true, and all I have to offer is my word."

She maintained her most modest smile as Doctor Beanpole chewed over the options available to him. "Take a seat, but modify your expectations."

Kathryn counted seventeen reporters lounging around the waiting room, ties loosened, ashtrays filled, and all out of small talk. She took a seat in the corner where the clanking of trains reverberated through the open window.

A copy of *Look* dangled in the tired paws of a shabby journalist who hadn't shaved in at least two days. By his sallow complexion, it seemed unlikely that he'd eaten anything more substantial than an apple danish during that time, either. Normally she would avoid catching the eye of someone like that, but the magazine's cover story made it impossible to look away.

*OPERATION PASTORIUS*
*A DOZEN YEARS LATER.*
*WE REVISIT THE SCARY NIGHT*
*THAT CHANGED THE*
*TOWN OF AMAGANSETT*

Below the headline, a photograph showed gentle waves lapping onto a windswept beach hemmed in by a long strip of knee-high grass. The idyllic scene looked like the last place that anybody could spend a scary night.

Zanuck's voice from that day at Perino's came back to her: *You ever been to a place called Amagansett?* And the name of the guy who sounded like a Roman general—wasn't it Pastorius?

The reporter took an agonizing hour to finish the magazine and cast it aside. Kathryn scooped it up and dived back to her seat. She rustled the pages until she came to the cover story and forced herself to read each word in case she inadvertently skipped over an important fact she might need later.

Operation Pastorius, she learned, was a German plan to sabotage a dozen strategic targets during the summer of 1942. It was the unfortunate fate of Amagansett, a town near the eastern end of Long Island, to be the spot where the Nazis chose to land their first U-boat. When one of the saboteurs decided to betray the mission, he alerted the FBI and the campaign ended disastrously. But it did bring the German navy uncomfortably close to New York, as well as a national spotlight on an otherwise sleepy hamlet.

If this was the "Amagansett" and "Pastorius" that Winchell had referred to during his drunken rant to Zanuck, it confirmed he'd had read through Danford's FBI file.

She shoved the magazine into her pocketbook and went to the window to watch Union Pacific engines shunt around Piggyback Yard. The article failed to mention Thomas Danford by name, so what did all this have to do with him?

"Miss Massey?" Nurse Foster kept her voice to a whisper. "If you will please follow me."

Kathryn trailed her down a long corridor until they arrived at the final room on the right. The nurse pulled at a ring of keys attached to her belt and selected one. "The doctor has authorized five minutes."

"Thank you. I'm very—"

"The patient is non-responsive, so I wouldn't get my hopes up if I were you."

*Don't tell me you people are buying this cockamamie act?* "Does he know I'm here?"

"No. However, the doctor is hopeful that the shock of seeing someone familiar might serve as a catalyst."

*It'll serve as something, all right.*

The nurse opened the door. "Mister Voss?" she called in a light sing-song. "You have a visitor." She motioned for Kathryn to follow her in.

The room was painted white and contained only a narrow bed along one wall and a metal toilet behind the door. At the far end of the room, a narrow window let in sunlight but a grille of bars muted the effect.

Voss stood with his forehead pressed against the glass, gazing vacantly over the railway yards. Very slowly, he turned his head toward Kathryn. Had she not been watching carefully, she might have missed the slight flaring of his eyelids.

He turned back to the window. "I prefer to be alone."

"But Mr. Voss," the nurse said gently, "this lady is family. Why don't you sit together on the bed? You never know what may pop up."

Kathryn sat down and patted the mattress. It was lumpy and sagged in the middle. "Come, Sheldon, let's have a chat."

Voss lifted his upper lip to suggest a snarl; it was the only movement he made.

Kathryn turned to the nurse. "Perhaps if you could leave us alone?"

"Sorry. Doctor's orders. You've been allowed five minutes and—" she consulted the watch pinned to her bosom "—you've got three and a half left."

Kathryn wasn't going to get the full confession that she wanted, certainly not in less than three minutes. But maybe she could get proof that all this was an elaborate hoax.

"Francine?" she asked. "Philadelphia? Boston? Sea to Shining Sea? Voss Vanguard? Quarter Cans?" None of these elicited the response she needed. Nor would they, she realized. They were all too obvious and had probably already been tried on him.

Kathryn reached into her pocketbook and pulled out her pilfered magazine. She held it up folded in half so he couldn't see the cover. "Uncle Sheldon?" she asked, sweet as treacle. She unfolded the cover to reveal the shot of the beach and held it out so that only he could read the headline.

His jaw muscles tensed as he swallowed hard.

"Remember that summer during the war?" Kathryn pushed. "The one we spent on Long Island? The cute little village called Amagansett? Oh, and that German bakery. The one with those delicious pastries. Do you recall the name? Pastorius Bakery, wasn't it? Does *any* of this ring a bell, Uncle Sheldon?"

He hadn't blinked once during her whole speech but remained glued to the cover of *Look*. "No," he said flatly.

"Your time is up." The nurse stepped to the door.

While her back was turned, Kathryn looked at Voss. "See you real soon I hope, Uncle Shel."

He closed his left hand into a fist and slowly lifted his middle finger.

# CHAPTER 23

The strip of chrome under Gwendolyn's elbow caught the morning light as Judy Lewis turned off Sunset and onto Doheny. "This is new, isn't it?" Gwendolyn asked.

"What?"

"Your car." She ran her hand across the dashboard. "It has that fresh-out-of-the-factory smell."

Judy smiled, but it was a grim effort.

"A Chevrolet Bel Air, right?" Gwendolyn persisted. "It certainly is a real smooth ride."

Silence.

"Aqua blue is such a pretty color. I made a gown this shade for Alfred Hitchcock's wife. She said it reminded her of the sea at Saint Tropez where they used to vacation each summer."

Judy kept her eyes on the road as it dipped into Beverly Hills. "Uh-huh."

"You ever been? To Europe, I mean."

"No."

The morning peak-hour drive from the Garden of Allah to Twentieth Century-Fox was starting to take longer and longer, but this stony silence made the trip insufferable. If Gwendolyn had known Judy was going to be like this, she wouldn't have accepted the offer to drive her around until her ankle healed.

The x-ray showed that it wasn't broken but had sustained a serious sprain, so the doctor ordered Gwendolyn to stay off it for three weeks "regardless of what your boss insists to the contrary." The orthopedist had assumed he was talking about Darryl Zanuck, but it was Loretta Young whom Gwendolyn had to deal with.

The new season of Loretta's show called for thirty-five episodes, which meant building thirty-five gowns from scratch. Loretta could have gotten someone else to do them, but she remained loyal to Gwendolyn.

"Of course she is," Kathryn had told her over pumpkin soup. "She knows class when she sees it."

Stuck at home, Gwendolyn became dependent on Kathryn, Doris, and Arlene to rotate mealtimes. Doris and Arlene always made their contributions themselves, but Kathryn preferred to stop in at Greenblatt's or Schwab's. Considering she was on the precipice of becoming America's new domestic queen, the irony was lost on neither of them.

"That dramatic entrance through the doors at the top of every episode? I thought it was just a gimmick," Kathryn had said, "but what a winner it's turned out to be. Everyone's tuning in to see what she'll be wearing when she flings open those doors. And that's because of *you*, my dear. Time to ask for a raise."

Kathryn was probably right, but with a messed-up ankle, Gwendolyn was thankful that Loretta hadn't pushed her under the bus and hired somebody else. In fact, she had outdone herself: she had conscripted her daughter into ferrying the designs, material swatches, and gowns between the studio and the Garden where Gwendolyn worked with her ankle up.

Consequently, Gwendolyn saw a lot of Judy, who would often linger for a chat or make them a sandwich. She was more relaxed away from her mother's watchful gaze. She chatted with girlish enthusiasm about the smorgasbord of possibilities that lay ahead for a fun-loving nineteen-year-old.

But today she was a different girl.

"Judy," Gwendolyn asked, "are you okay?"

"I have something I want to ask you but it's harder than I thought it would be." Judy ran a red light, realized what she'd done, and slowed down as the tall, white studio walls came into view. "How long have you known Clark Gable?"

Gwendolyn sorted through the various reasons why the girl would ask this particular question. In all their chats over tuna salad sandwiches or bolts of chiffon, they'd never talked about that night at Ciro's.

Gwendolyn pressed a hand to her chest. "Do any of us remember a time when we didn't know him?" The silence in the car evolved from stony to anxious. "Why do you ask?"

"Because he's going to be working at the studio soon."

The last time Gwendolyn had spoken to Clark was when she'd put in her dutiful phone call suggesting he might want to hear what Zanuck had to say. Not long after that, Zanuck had called Kathryn with the scoop that they'd made a two-picture deal and that *Soldier of Fortune* was due to start filming in November—two months away.

Judy slowed her Chevrolet to a crawl. "Did I ever tell you about the day I got home from school and he was sitting in Mother's living room?"

"I don't think so."

"I walked through the door and there he was! It's not like I'd never met movie stars before, but this was *Clark Gable*! Waiting to meet *me*!" Judy panted as she marshaled the strength to push the words out. "But that night at Ciro's, I noticed him staring at me. He wasn't being rude or anything. It was like when you see someone who reminds you of someone else, but you can't put your finger on who. At one point I waved at him, but he pretended not to see me."

"Maybe he didn't."

"He saw me, all right. Soon after that, I saw the two of you on the dance floor and—I dunno . . . I thought I'd ask. It's been playing on my mind but just forget I said anything. Sorry to come across so cranky."

It sounded to Gwendolyn like Judy was starting to grope around in the dark without the sort of flashlight Gwendolyn could provide.

The studio was coming up on them fast.

"Billy and I have started work on the *Soldier of Fortune* costumes for Susan Hayward and Anna Sten," Gwendolyn said, "Billy has also asked me to put together options for Gable and Michael Rennie. You could happen to be around when the guys come in." She realized she had pushed too hard when Judy hit the brake at the security gate.

The guard leaned out the window.

"The big guy's office called down here. Mr. Z. wants to see you straight away."

He lifted the boom gate and waved them through.

Judy gave a long whistle. "Does he think you're gonna sue him for getting popped on his lot?" She parked outside the administrative building and pulled out a copy of *The Disenchanted.* The novel was a biting attack on life in Hollywood—an interesting choice for a nineteen-year old. "I'll be here until Zanuck's finished with you, then I'll run you over to Costuming. Mother's chomping at the bit to have you back."

* * *

When Zanuck told her to take a seat, Gwendolyn gave up any ladylike pretense of lowering herself into the visitor chair with poise and dignity. She half-threw herself into it, landing with a soft groan.

"I was sorry to hear what happened to you on *No Business.*" Deep furrows wrinkled his brow with what appeared to be candid concern.

"Thank you, Mr. Zanuck."

"I assume your foot or ankle or whatever is okay now?"

"Getting better every day."

He let out a yelping guffaw as he pulled on a half-smoked cigar. "Man, oh man, but that damned DiMaggio guy can be a hothead, huh? I sure hope he apologized to you."

Gwendolyn weighed up the pros and cons of pointing out that the only two people she hadn't heard from during her convalescence were Joe DiMaggio and Darryl Zanuck. Marilyn was the one who'd sent cards and letters and flowers and books and magazines and apologies and regrets. But her ankle was healing nicely and she was keen to get back to work.

"How may I help you, Mr. Zanuck?"

"I'm taking you away from costumes."

Gwendolyn felt a jolt. "Why would you do that?"

"You're too valuable to me to waste your time stitching frocks together."

"I do more than just—"

"I'm creating a new job. You're going to be a special assistant."

"A—what?"

"You'll be doing special projects for me."

"What kind?"

"As needed."

Gwendolyn didn't like the sound of this. No sirree, not one little bit. Zanuck was a man with a well-earned reputation of keeping tabs on every aspect of the movie-making process. "As needed" sounded suspiciously vague. But he said it with such decisive finality that she felt as cornered as she had when he'd recruited her to snoop on Marilyn.

"Why me?" she asked him. "I'm handy with needles and threads, and, I suppose, I have an appealing bedside manner when it comes to handling insecure actresses like Loretta and Marilyn. But that's about it."

Zanuck snuffed out the cigar in a square copper ashtray with his initials, DFZ, stenciled in complex, intertwining calligraphy. He fixed her with a look that bordered on wistful.

"You have the darndest habit of popping up like a jack-in-the-box. You stopped me from getting poisoned that night at Chasen's. You reconnected me with Hilda. And when that nude calendar debacle blew up with Marilyn, there you were, giving her safe harbor. Who stepped in to stop DiMaggio when nobody else was shutting him down that day? And who helped bring Gable to Fox?"

"I'm sure I was one of a whole chorus of crickets chirping in his ear."

"Being too modest will get you no place in this town."

"I'm just a gal who's trying to get along."

"Of course," Zanuck continued, "this does mean a pay increase."

Gwendolyn doubted that Zanuck had any idea of her salary. On the other hand, he was King of All Details.

"It does?" she asked, feigning nonchalance as best she could.

"I'm doubling your pay."

It meant halving the time it would take to pay off her Chez Gwendolyn bank loan. "That's very generous."

"Effective immediately."

Gwendolyn pictured the mound of half-finished gowns waiting for her in the costuming department. She could only accomplish so much at home with a throbbing ankle hoisted onto pillows. The vision of inchoate outfits vanished, and in its place rose Loretta Young, her face flushed with irritation, demanding to know why she was being left in the lurch.

"When you say 'immediately,' you don't mean today, do you?"

"Why not?"

"Miss Young's show starts again in a couple of weeks. I haven't completed any of her entrance gowns."

"We have a whole costume department."

"The relationship between a performer and their costumer isn't about needles and threads. It's about trust, and support, and—"

"How long do you need?"

"I'll have to butter her up. Of course, it would've helped if you'd cast her in *A Woman's World*."

"June Allyson was a much better fit, but point taken."

"I've got six gowns lined up and with help, I can probably finish one every other day. So, two weeks?"

"Three days."

"But Mr. Zanuck—"

"That's all I can give you." He pushed aside a stack of scripts and dragged across a folder with a bunch of pages jammed inside. "I want to talk to you about a new project. It's called *On the Deck of the Missouri*, and I need your help to land the screen rights."

Gwendolyn's ankle started to throb. "On the deck of the what?"

"Don't look at me like that—I know the author is your brother."

As far as Gwendolyn knew, Monty had called his memoir *My Summer in Tokyo Bay*. She thought of all the times Monty had visited with her, often first thing in the morning or when he got home at the end of the day. *I wish I could say I knew that he'd changed the title.*

"Yes, he is."

"It has the earmarks of a damn fine motion picture, so all the major studios are putting in bids."

"And you want me to persuade Monty to give *you* the rights."

"See? You're one smart cookie."

"You don't need to involve me, Mr. Zanuck. Just offer Monty more money than everyone else."

The rosy hue of Zanuck's lips disappeared as he pressed them together. "Your brother's literary agent is one taciturn bastard."

*You think Monty shares all this with me? If you're willing to double my salary to get the rights to a book whose name I didn't even know, the joke's on you, mister.*

A generous offer from a Hollywood studio could set Monty up very nicely should he decide to quit the navy. The last thing Gwendolyn wanted was to inadvertently sabotage the deal. She'd spent more than enough years watching Marcus getting pushed and pulled by the studio system to know what it thought of writers.

"Mr. Zanuck," she said, "I've only seen my brother a handful of times in the last twenty-five years. He's a military man who plays his cards closer to his chest than your gold tiepin. I doubt my poking around in his business will do either of us much good."

He opened his mouth but she raised her right hand and showed him her palm.

"Which isn't to say I won't try," she continued. She made an exaggerated movement of looking at her watch. "I've been away from the department for three weeks. I've fallen behind with Miss Young's gowns and *The Seven Year Itch* is coming up. Now that you've only given me three days, I'll need every minute I can get."

Zanuck pushed his chair away from the desk and rapped a knuckle against his window. "The girl in the convertible down there—is that Judy Lewis?"

"It is."

"You planning on taking her to the *Solider of Fortune* set?"

"Already suggested."

A knowing look passed between them. "And *that* is why I'm promoting you to special assistant. Now get along, and if Loretta kicks up a stink, tell her to come see me."

Gwendolyn hauled herself to her feet and made the long trek from Zanuck's desk to his office door as soundlessly as she could. By the time she got there, he was already in his seat, blue pencil in hand, eyes darting across a new script as though he'd already forgotten she'd been there.

## CHAPTER 24

Kathryn drove into the parking lot of the Moulin Rouge nightclub on Sunset Boulevard and pulled into the first space she came to.

"If you're not feeling well," she told her mother, "I can put you in a taxi."

"Not a chance." Francine tugged a handkerchief from her purse and dabbed at her face. In an attempt to cloak her pallor, she'd applied so much rouge that it approached clown-level color. "I shouldn't have told you how I was feeling."

"Dizziness and nausea aren't symptoms you should be ignoring. Especially not—"

"If you say especially not at my age, I'll clock you with my handbag."

Francine said it with a smile, but Kathryn knew she meant it.

"I am glad you're here," she said. "I'm nervous as hell about what I have to do in there."

If Leo's Sunbeam - Betty Crocker - Westinghouse idea had remained a slight reinvention of Kathryn's coast-to-coast tour from a couple of years back, Kathryn wouldn't have been twitchy about taking the stage with Betty Furness and Adelaide Hawley. But Leo had turned into Florenz Ziegfeld and now it was the sort of show that people might see at the Desert Inn in Las Vegas with musicians, back-up singers, and a sophisticated set covered in glitter, mirrors, chandeliers, and spotlights.

Kathryn wasn't sure what she was walking into this morning, but she half-expected to see the Rockettes executing a military-precision kick line.

Francine jammed her handkerchief up her sleeve. "But you've been performing in front of audiences for years. Why is Suncrockerhouse any different?"

At some point, everybody had tacitly agreed that "Sunbeam – Betty Crocker – Westinghouse" was too big a mouthful so they'd adopted the more convenient shorthand "Suncrockerhouse" when referring to the show.

To Kathryn, the doors of the Moulin Rouge now looked like Rodin's Gates of Hell. "I have a sneaking suspicion that Leo's going to ask me to sing."

Francine's eyes bulged. "Do you remember that audition you did for Eddie Cantor?"

Cantor had announced he was putting together a nationwide tour and needed a child performer. Francine had forced an eleven-year-old Kathryn to audition with a maudlin song called "Baby Shoes." She had been so bad that she'd left the stage in tears without stopping to retrieve the sheet music.

"Why do you think I never sang on my radio show?"

The two of them sat in Kathryn's Oldsmobile as the seconds ticked by, until Francine said, "Are we going in, or are you taking me out to that expensive lunch you promised?"

"In, I guess."

Francine propped her handbag on the edge of her knees. "If you're truly terrible, I'll let you know and you can tell Leo to come up with a substitute. Deal?"

Kathryn smiled. *Why weren't you this nice when I was growing up?* She risked a light kiss on her mother's cheek. "Deal."

* * *

A sign in black with gold lettering hung twelve feet over the curved stage.

*Sunbeam Mixmaster & Betty Crocker & Westinghouse Presents!*

Leo stood with a stagehand in front of an elaborate kitchen set checking through a list with the diligence of a brain surgeon. Once they were done, he cupped his hands to his mouth and called "Okay, Jim. Let's have it."

A string of enormous key lights blazed to life, drenching the stage.

"What the hell?" Kathryn muttered. "They're as bright as the ones on a movie set."

Francine pointed out a huge camera in the semi-dark of the audience seating. Stenciled on a side panel was a sign that read: *Property of 20th Century-Fox Studios.*

Kathryn dropped her handbag on a nearby table. "LEO!"

"You're here!" He pointed out the side stairs leading up to the stage. "I've got the most wonderful news!" He met her at the top of the steps. "I got a call yesterday from Fox Movietone Newsreel. They want to film the first show! Isn't that marvelous? You couldn't buy that sort of publicity!"

Kathryn nodded in feigned agreement.

"Not only that, but the newsreel is set to play ahead of Fox's big holiday release."

"*There's No Business Like Show Business*?"

"I don't know why Zanuck's okayed this, and I didn't stop to ask."

After her encounter with Zanuck at Perino's, Kathryn had received a cryptic thank-you for alerting him to how his affair with Bella Darvi wasn't as clandestine as he assumed, and a promise that he would pay back her good turn.

Leo searched Kathryn's face for excitement. "Aren't you thrilled?"

"Sure. It's just that—"

Kathryn pulled out a square sheet of white cardboard she'd found under her front door the previous night. It contained four lines of what looked to her like song lyrics written in Leo's pristine penmanship.

*Sunbeam's new Mixmaster*
*Mixes my Betty batter faster*
*It makes my baking more ambitious*
*'Cause everything turns out so delicious.*

She held the card up to face height. "What is this?" *Please don't say lyrics. Please don't say lyrics.*

"Lyrics to the big song! What do you think?"

Another crewmember with another clipboard approached him for his authority to pay the band. She caught sight of three words—"ten-piece orchestra"—and waited until the crewmember departed.

"An orchestra?"

"Nothing but the best, baby!"

She waved the card in Leo's face. "Please tell me I won't be singing."

"Each of you gets a verse and then you'll harmonize the chorus together." It took him an infuriatingly long moment to notice the frown on Kathryn's face. "Is that a problem?"

"Betty and Adelaide are professional performers. This sort of stuff comes naturally to them."

"But you're Kathryn Massey!" Leo took a step back and crossed his arms. "You've got more moxie than anybody I know. I assumed you'd be up for anything."

"Normally I would be, but singing? In front of hundreds of people? *And* a newsreel camera? That's where I draw the line. And nobody says 'moxie' anymore."

A shriek of laughter from Betty and Adelaide rang out from the rear of the cavernous auditorium.

"You're refusing to sing?" Leo asked.

*Not if you're going to look at me with those moon-faced droopy eyes.* "I didn't say that."

"How about we do a couple of run-throughs and see how it goes?"

Kathryn fanned herself. "Okay."

Leo pulled her into a hug and whispered several hurried thank-yous as her costars climbed onto the stage, brimming with all the verve and chutzpah Kathryn wished she possessed.

* * *

"Thank you, ladies and gentlemen," Leo announced in front of the footlights. "A few wrinkles to iron out, of course, but that was a wonderful first rehearsal. We'll see you tomorrow morning, ten A.M. sharp."

Kathryn descended the stairs, each step more wearying than the previous. She made it to Francine's table with very little left in her tank. "All those years I did *Window on Hollywood*," she said, plopping herself into the chair beside her mother, "I was never so drained as I am right now."

Even with no audience, no cameras, no microphones, and only the crew looking on, singing Leo's harmless little ditty was Kathryn's worst nightmare come to life. Leo had told her that she was fine; so had Betty and Adelaide.

But Kathryn paid them no heed. The opinion of the woman sitting next to her was the only one that mattered.

Kathryn had seen what happened when people surrounded themselves with sycophants. If "You're fantastic! You're so talented! You're one hundred percent correct!" was all they ever heard, they start to believe it, and that's where careers fell apart. But "straight from the hip" was Francine's sole modus operandi, so she was the only person in this room whom Kathryn trusted.

The two of them seemed to be getting along better recently. Francine was sixty-six now, and Kathryn hoped perhaps her mom was slipping into a less feisty, less combative, less judgmental age. But she was still strong-willed enough to let fly with a brutal opinion.

"Leo has put together a very slick show." Francine's verdict lacked conviction, scuttling Kathryn's confidence. "Lots of lively razzle-dazzle."

"But how was I? Both barrels, Mother."

Francine dabbed at her forehead. "You didn't embarrass yourself. I mean, obviously, Betty and Adelaide know what they're doing. Meanwhile, you were floundering around like a beached marlin. But you've got gumption and it shows. Your audiences will appreciate that." She reached out and patted Kathryn's hand. "You were fine, darling."

Francine Massey wasn't a tactile parent, so this warm act was unprecedented. What a shame her hand was so cold.

"You're freezing. If you're not feeling well, we can skip lunch—"

"What did I tell you?"

* * *

Kathryn's Oldsmobile purred to life. "I haven't been to the Polo Lounge in a while and it's so nice during summer." She pulled onto Sunset.

Two blocks later, Francine said, "I've changed my mind."

It was a phrase Kathryn had never heard coming from her mother. Coupled with the hand gesture, this was turning into a red-letter day. "I didn't get around to making a booking, so we can eat someplace else."

"I'd like to go to the veterans' hospital on Wilshire."

"Are you sure?"

"Quite."

Kathryn headed south toward the military hospital set among sprawling grounds on the approach to Santa Monica.

A week or two after Kathryn's confrontation with Voss at LA County had come the announcement that he was being transferred for "an extended recuperation." Although how a coward like Sheldon Voss had managed to get into a military hospital was a mystery. It was enough for Kathryn to know that Francine wanted to face her brother. Regardless of what happened, being a witness to that was worth whatever fallout might result.

The visitors' parking lot was surprisingly small, but Kathryn found an open space and pulled into it. As Francine reached for the car door handle, Kathryn stopped her with a nip to the elbow.

The afternoon sun shone onto Francine's face, revealing that she looked paler now than back at Moulin Rouge. Kathryn wanted to reach over and swipe away the line of sweat following the contours of Francine's hairline, but thought the better of it. "Do you have a plan?"

Francine shook her head. "I don't believe this amnesia story any more than you do, so I don't expect to get a confession out of him. But I want to see that miserable son-of-a-bitch squirm when he sees me. And if I can get close enough to give him a piece of my mind, all the better."

"You did pretty well for yourself that night in MacArthur Park."

"I spent the next week thinking of what I *wished* I'd said. If I can get one or two out today, I'll walk away satisfied."

Kathryn had assumed that Voss would be locked away in the same sort of cell he'd occupied at LA County, but the cheery volunteer with the Joan Blondell face told them that they'd find him in the recreation room at the end of the hall.

It was two stories tall with windows on three sides that opened out to the summery air. A light breeze wafted across residents scattered around club chairs and card tables, reading or chatting or playing board games.

Voss sat by himself, his chin propped on the palm of his right hand and his gaze fixed blankly on the lawns outside.

Kathryn and Francine started walking toward him.

"He's a sitting duck." Francine murmured.

Kathryn let out a yip of a laugh. Voss visibly stiffened. He turned the jerky movement into a stretch and yawn. Pretending not to have seen them, he rose from his chair.

The Joan Blondell nurse called out to him. "Not so fast!" She sounded more like a kindergarten teacher. "This is your sister, Mr. Voss. Remember what the doctor said? Regain your memory and you regain your life. You never know which face or voice or perhaps even a smell will bring it back."

A muttering groundswell rolled through the place. Since the display ads using Harlan McNamara's photos had started appearing in newspapers and magazines across the country, Kathryn was being recognized in new sorts of places: the supermarket, the library, the beach. And now convalescent wards, apparently.

She tapped the nurse on her shoulder. "Perhaps we could move to somewhere more private?"

Voss opened his mouth to protest but the nurse ignored him. "The rose garden pergola." She pointed to French doors opening out onto a slate path that followed the slope of the lawn, then disappeared into a grove of acorn trees.

Kathryn didn't need to look around the room to know that all eyes were on them. She appropriated Voss's elbow, but he yanked it away. Francine walked ahead and opened the glass door. "We'll have a lovely visit—you'll see."

With Francine on one side and Kathryn on the other, Voss said nothing as they trudged along the path. It swerved right at the acorn trees, revealing a pergola covered in roses intertwined with ivy. Surrounded by a semicircle of hedges, it stood on a slight rise to catch the coastal breezes.

"I want to go back inside," Voss said.

"But fresh air is so healthful!" Kathryn prodded him toward the pergola, where three separate benches provided seating for six. Overhead, the ivy and roses offered rare tranquility, a reprieve from the commotion of the sprawling city surrounding them. Kathryn, Francine, and Voss each took a bench.

"It's okay, Uncle Sheldon," Kathryn taunted, "nobody can hear you. There's nothing to give you away."

"I don't know who you think you are or what you think you're going to accomplish, but you'll get nothing out of me."

"Why?" Kathryn pushed. "Because you can't *remember*?"

"For all I know, you might be wearing a wire."

*Only because it hadn't occurred to me.* "Why would you be worried if you had nothing to hide?"

"I've been hounded by every two-bit shyster in this town who wants to get their greedy paws on my—" He folded one leg over another and hunkered down into a ball. "When you don't know anybody, you learn to trust nobody."

"For crying out loud!" Kathryn barked. "The only people who know the real you are sitting right here, so cut the crap and drop the act."

"I don't know what act you are referring to—"

"The one that came to an end when you gave me the finger at LA County General." Kathryn watched a wall rise in Voss's eyes. "Look," she said, softening her tone, "I don't care if you've got millions stashed away, or secrets you're holding over someone, or whatever monkey business you're up to with this amnesia gambit of yours. All I care about is Thomas Danford."

"EXACTLY!" Francine's roar startled nearby magpies to flight. "How *could* you?! I loved Thomas with all my heart." She was on her feet now, her hands tightened into fists, and her black Sunday hat slanted to the left. "We would've figured a way out of our predicament, but no! Mister Savior had to charge in like he's Mister Fix-Everything. You stuck your beak in where it wasn't invited, wasn't welcome, and wasn't needed."

Voss stayed glued to his wooden bench, even as Francine stood over him with her arms flung out wide.

"It wasn't your life to dictate! I could've spent the last forty years with the man I loved, but that ceased to be an option the minute you jumped on your high horse. That was bad enough, but then you set yourself up as some phony-baloney preacher. You and your Sea to Shining Sea March, your redemption boards, and your Quarter Cans. What a load of manure. And now you're trying to squirm out of it by playing the amnesia victim? Well, screw you, Sheldon Voss. You ain't nothing but the worst kind of swindler. I'm ashamed and disgusted to be related to you."

Francine started rolling her jaw. *Look at her!* Kathryn thought. *She's working up a wad to spit on him.* She jumped to her feet and joined her mother. "Nothing gave me greater pleasure than to see that resentful look on your face as you handed over your Quarter Cans to those Negroes."

Voss was on his feet now, slowly circling them like a jackal. He jabbed a finger at Francine. "I saved you from a marriage born of obligation that would have been lived in misery and despair."

"So now you're a fortune-teller?" Francine bit back.

"You were a plaything to satisfy his lust. He would never have done right by you."

"He most cert—"

"The Danfords think themselves far too la-di-dah to accept some stray member of the rabble into their midst. You were just too naïve to realize it."

"It wasn't your call to make," Kathryn said. "Thomas Danford—"

Voss wheeled around, his eyes blazing with scorn. "Your precious Daddy Danford couldn't keep his lust in his pants for two goddamned minutes, so what kind of father would he have been?"

"You're one to talk," Kathryn scoffed, "cheating widows and embezzling factory workers. But you outdid yourself when you framed my father."

Francine gave out a little gasp. "He what?"

Even with that article from *Look* magazine, Kathryn knew the evidence she'd gathered was circumstantial at best. Why put Francine through the wringer when she wasn't sure of the facts? But it was a moot point now that she'd blurted out everything.

"Sorry to keep you in the dark," Kathryn told her mother, "but I wanted more evidence. That night at MacArthur Park, this little worm admitted to me that he framed Thomas Danford."

"I admitted no such thing!" he hissed. "All I said was that I waited years to exact my revenge. You were the one throwing around accusations that I framed Danford. You're going to have to do a damn sight better than *Look* magazine—"

"What *Look* magazine?" Francine's voice trembled but Kathryn couldn't pull her eyes away from Voss's odious sneer.

"I'll show you later." Kathryn stepped in front of Francine and faced Voss. "I'm still collecting evidence, but when I have enough, I'll come after you. And you know what? I wish I'd thought to wear a wire because everybody who's so concerned about your welfare should be hearing this."

"But you're not wearing a wire, are you?" Voss's sangfroid was unnerving.

"Listen, you heinous prick—"

"Kathryn? Kathryn?"

Francine's hand pressed against Kathryn's shoulder blade, then trailed down her back.

Kathryn reached out as Francine clutched her chest, but her arms escaped her grasp as she staggered backward, hit her head against one of the benches, and collapsed onto the concrete.

"Mom! MOM!"

Kathryn gently rolled Francine onto her back, tucking her handbag under her head. "What's happening? Are you in pain?" Francine's only response was to stare up at her daughter, straining for breath in ragged gasps. "Is it your heart? Are you having a heart attack?"

Francine nodded weakly.

"GO GET HELP!" Kathryn shouted at Voss. "NOW!"

He cannonballed out of the pergola.

Francine's eyes lost their focus.

"Hang on, Mom. We're at a hospital. There are doctors. Lots of them. They're only seconds away. Stay with me." She sucked in a lungful of air. "Keep breathing. Like this. In . . . out . . . in . . . out . . ."

*Where did he go? What's taking so long?*

Francine started to open and close her mouth like a goldfish panting for air. In between each pant, she slurred in guttural whispers. "I . . . did it . . . all for you. Everything . . . for you."

"Mom! Please! Not now. Save your strength."

"Never . . . showed it . . ." Her breath was hot and damp. ". . . like I . . . should've."

Kathryn squeezed her eyes tightly shut, willing herself not to fall apart. She wrapped her arm around Francine's shoulder and cradled her to her chest.

"So proud. So proud." Francine sprang up into a half-sitting position, unleashed a low groan that sounded like she'd summoned it from the depth of her soul, then fell heavily to the ground, pulling Kathryn down with her.

## CHAPTER 25

The dark magenta lace looked better on Bella Darvi than Gwendolyn expected. "Not many people can get away with that color, but you can."

Bella turned side on to the mirror to check her silhouette. "I know."

There was no irony in her comment. There never was.

This was now the eighth day into a three-week assignment to guide Bella through wardrobe fittings in preparation for a crammed schedule of interviews centered around the premiere of *The Egyptian*.

The word around town was that Zanuck had a $4-million turkey on his hands. To his credit, he charged full steam ahead, building up Bella Darvi with an expensive wardrobe for the American openings and the Rome premiere.

*In other words,* Gwendolyn wrote to Marcus, *I'm a glorified babysitter.*

And she wouldn't have minded so much but this woman was a walking iceberg who didn't seem to care about anything. No matter what Gwendolyn suggested, the girl would shrug as though to say, *If you like.*

Don't you think an extra-thick belt would define this ensemble? Shrug.

What about a bow here? Shrug.

Autumn orange or butterscotch yellow? Shrug.

So when Gwendolyn showed Bella her sketches for a cocktail dress to wear to her Rome press conference and Bella said, "Magenta will work, but make sure it's dark," Gwendolyn shot over to Kathryn's villa. "I think she might be starting to trust me!"

Kathryn responded, "It's time I interviewed this Polish man-eater. Can you help set it up?"

It was the first sign of the old Kathryn since Francine's passing.

For twenty years, Gwendolyn had watched Kathryn and Francine clash with jabs and put-downs, exchanging verbal right hooks and reaching uneasy détentes that quickly withered. But it had all changed when Kathryn cradled her mother in her arms and watched her life ebb away. Francine was gone before help arrived, and in the days that followed, the life seemed to drain out of Kathryn, too.

Ever since the funeral, she lingered in bed until noon. Food went uneaten, clothes went unwashed, letters went unanswered. Even her column had to be ghostwritten by Mike Connolly, who stepped up when Kathryn couldn't think of committing thoughts to paper.

Gwendolyn did whatever she could: cooked up a pot of chicken soup and dropped it off with poppy-seed bagels; took bundles to the Chinese laundry; listened to Kathryn catalog her regrets and self-recriminations; and advised Leo to sit it out when he admitted feeling useless in the face of Kathryn's overwhelming grief.

"Do you want to wear this for when Kathryn arrives?" Gwendolyn asked Bella.

"Who?"

"Kathryn Massey. From the *Hollywood Reporter*. It's nearly eleven o'clock, so if you want to change—"

"No." Bella pressed a hand against her three petticoats and observed how they bounced back into position. "This dress. That dress. It doesn't matter."

"It's a knockout!"

Kathryn passed a knot of seamstresses stitching beads onto a complicated Elizabethan gown destined for Bette Davis. Half a dozen steps in and Gwendolyn knew that Kathryn was tipsier than a lady should be when she's about to interview the mistress of a studio boss who had the power to rescue Marcus with a phone call.

Gwendolyn met her halfway and inhaled deeply, expecting a whiff of brandy or sherry, but smelled only the scent of fresh Chinese laundry.

*Ah, so it's vodka.*

"Kathryn Massey from the *Hollywood Reporter*." She thrust out her hand; Bella shook it limply. "You must be the gal who half of Hollywood's talking about. I'm referring to the male half, of course. Goodness gracious, *look* at you. No wonder Zanuck is—"

"Take a seat!" Gwendolyn pointed to a stool parked at her work counter.

Kathryn did as she was told. "You're about to make the sort of splash that beautiful girls like you swarm to Hollywood for. You must feel lucky to be the one that Zanuck *plucked* from obscurity."

If the Polish Iceberg caught Kathryn's innuendo, it didn't show. "I suppose."

"You sound like you don't care whether or not your Hollywood film career takes off."

"If the American public like me, I will be cast in another movie and another until they tire of me. If not . . ."

Bella's composed almond eyes opened wider and wider.

"Am I interrupting?"

Marilyn Monroe stood in the doorway wearing the cream dress Billy Travilla had designed for her current picture. With a snug halter neck that held her breasts in place, a tight bodice tied together into a bow, and a voluminous skirt, it was one of Marilyn's most flattering screen costumes.

Earlier that month, she and Billy Wilder had traveled to New York and filmed a scene from *The Seven Year Itch* on Lexington Avenue in which Marilyn stood over a subway vent and let the updraft blow this dress above her waist. Wilder planned to film the real scene on a soundstage at Fox so the whole spectacle was an elaborate publicity stunt, but nobody had told the hundreds of gawkers who'd packed the sidewalks.

One of them had been Walter Winchell, who'd called Joe DiMaggio and egged him into going to see the spectacle for himself, knowing that DiMaggio would kick up a terrible stink. The sap had stormed across the set as Marilyn stood over the vent for a shot that wouldn't make the final cut but might end her marriage.

"Marilyn!" Gwendolyn rose to her feet. "What are you doing here?" *And in that dress.*

Marilyn stepped forward. "Something's scraping my back. I don't know what but it sure is annoying."

"You're reshooting the subway scene today?" Kathryn asked.

If Kathryn had been a teensy bit more sober she would have realized that Marilyn wasn't in full makeup.

"They're still building the set. When we were in New York, my shoulder blades got all scratched up so it needs fixing."

"Does Billy know you're wearing that?" Gwendolyn asked.

"Travilla or Wilder?"

"Both."

Travilla had toiled forever over endless variations until Wilder was satisfied. The final version was currently the most famous dress in America—and not what Marilyn should have been wearing as she wandered the studio.

Marilyn turned to Bella. "I don't believe we've met."

"I am Bella Darvi."

Marilyn brushed a nonexistent lock of hair from her clear blue eyes. "The one who stole Nefer out from under me?"

For months, Marilyn had lobbied Zanuck for the part of the Babylonian courtesan in *The Egyptian.* After he'd cast Bella, Marilyn dropped by Gwendolyn's place to unload her disappointment. It had taken Gwendolyn two full bottles of Dom Perignon to convince Marilyn that she couldn't expect to win every role. And now, six months later, *There's No Business Like Show Business* was set to do boffo box office and *The Egyptian* was shaping up to be dead on arrival.

Marilyn toyed with a stray white button sitting on the worktable. She set it on its edge and sent it spinning with a flick of her finger. She was no longer wearing her wedding ring.

"I did not steal your role," Bella said flatly. "If I had known, I would have said to Darryl, 'If Monroe wants Nefer so badly, give it to her.'"

"So it's 'Darryl,' huh?" Kathryn said under her breath.

If Kathryn hadn't been in such a fragile state, Gwendolyn would have swatted her. And if Marilyn hadn't been in an equally fragile state for a whole different reason, Gwendolyn might have swatted her as well.

"His name is Darryl. What other name would I call him?"

"Most people call him Mr. Zanuck," Kathryn said.

"Even *I* call him Mr. Zanuck." Marilyn added. "The only people who call him Darryl are his wife and—his—" The white button rolled off the edge of the table.

"I know what they think of me," Bella announced. "All these gossips with big mouths and empty heads."

"Say!" Kathryn straightened up. "I resent that."

Bella ignored her. "I am not stupid. People say 'She wants to be a movie star so she takes the short cut. She sleeps with the boss and bingo! She has a part in a picture. An expensive wardrobe. She flies to Europe for the premiere. First class. Parties. Interviews.' PAH!"

It was the longest speech the woman had said in days.

Kathryn propped her elbows onto Gwendolyn's workbench. "You *are* sleeping with him, right?"

Bella gave a blasé shrug. "Of course I am."

The matter-of-fact tone made Gwendolyn wonder if Zanuck had given her this assignment to see if there was any reason why he couldn't trust this woman. "Gee, Bella," she said, "I give you points for honesty."

The woman's eyes crinkled at the edges, her chin puckering as she strained to preserve her poise. Tears glazed her eyes. "I was flattered at first," she blurted out, "but his attentions, they are overwhelming. I feel trapped."

"Did he force himself on you?" Gwendolyn asked.

"No." She wiped away an escaped tear. "Perhaps a little, but I didn't mind. I found him attractive. He has the charisma, you know? And very determined."

"I hope it was worth it," Kathryn said.

"The sex is very—what is that English expression?" Bella asked. "He gives it his all?"

Kathryn started giggling. "Yep, that's the expression."

"Are you faithful to him?" Gwendolyn asked.

"No."

"Good for you!" Marilyn chimed in.

"I am not married. I date other men and women."

A hush blanketed the group. Gwendolyn looked at Kathryn, who looked at Marilyn, who looked at Gwendolyn.

Kathryn asked. "Does Darryl know about your predilections?"

"What does it mean, predilections?"

"Does Mr. Zanuck know that you date other people?"

"It is none of his business what I do in other beds."

*Everything is Zanuck's business.* "Have you told anyone else?" Gwendolyn asked. "Friends, for instance?"

Bella frowned. "What friends? Nobody in this town gives their friendship. They don't want to be near me in case they say the wrong thing and I tell Darryl."

*Or*, Gwendolyn mused, *because you're so aloof and detached.*

"Well," Marilyn said, clapping her hands together, "now you do. And in fact, next week, Ella Fitzgerald is playing at the Tiffany Club. Who's up for a girls-only outing?"

* * *

The Tiffany Club at the corner of Eighth and Normandie was shaped like a slice of pizza. The small stage stood at the narrow end, with twenty-two tables fanned out in concentric rows. The wallpaper was patterned with piano keyboards slanted on 45-degree angles and peppered with musical notes and shiny 78s. The foyer wasn't much bigger than a telephone booth.

"I feel positively scandalous!" Doris exclaimed.

"Why?" Kathryn asked. "This is a respectable club."

At the last minute, Kathryn had tried to bail. It seemed to Gwendolyn that she had turned a corner that day at Fox, but she should have known better. Grief doesn't dissipate in one neatly composed movie scene. It was a progression. One day you're asking a mogul's mistress about her penchant for women, and the next you find yourself heating chicken soup that you have no intention of eating. Gwendolyn managed to coerce her into coming only ten minutes before they were due to leave.

"We've got no men, no escorts, no chaperones," Doris exclaimed. "We look like a bunch of scarlet women!"

The room was only half-filled, but buzzy with anticipation. Gwendolyn caught sight of a table toward the back. Frank Sinatra and Ava Gardner sat alone. Gwendolyn alerted Kathryn with a discreet nudge.

After Marcus's photos of Ava and his Italian boyfriend, Sinatra had taken no pains to hide his displeasure, in private and public. During a particularly ugly spectacle at The Luau on Rodeo Drive, he demolished several bamboo bar stools and shattered an astonishing seven full bottles of high-class rum onto the floor behind the bar. A week later, Mike Connolly's *Rambling Reporter* column reported that the "Sparring Sinatras" had attended a press preview for *The Barefoot Contessa*, where Frank had gone out of his way to play nicey-nice.

Tonight, however, Frank contemplated the cocktail menu while Ava drew on a cigarette inserted into a long black holder; she looked bored as hell.

As the maître d' escorted them to a line of three tables pushed together, Gwendolyn scanned the place, though it was hardly necessary. Marilyn was easy to spot on a packed football field, let alone in a jazz joint not much bigger than the Garden of Allah's pool.

"You think she's going to show?" Kathryn asked.

Since that violent rant on the streets of New York, Gwendolyn had sensed that Marilyn and Joe's marriage was breaking down. Marilyn was getting to the *Seven Year Itch* set later and later each day, and when she did, she needed longer in the makeup chair. And that was when she showed up at all.

A commotion erupted in the foyer. Someone called out "Hello! Hello!" The flash bulb of the club's souvenir photographer glinted past the maître d' podium.

Marilyn broke free and entered the room. It was like the air suddenly blossomed with the perfume of night-blooming jasmine and tiny pixie-sprinkled flecks of tinsel that floated like golden dust motes. She wiggled down the aisle in a modest two-piece suit of dark brown without a trace of attention-grabbing sizzle. But even dressed in nutmeg, the girl sparkled.

She took one of the end chairs and smoothed her hair. "What a marvelous table!"

"Look at that one." It was the first time Bella had spoken tonight.

She indicated a table that was more likely to set tongues wagging than a group of women with no men. An older white woman sat with a well-dressed, much younger black one who, from the stiff-backed dancer's way she held herself, was clearly not the maid.

"That's Eartha Kitt," Gwendolyn said. "I think she's wearing one of my gowns."

"Who's that with her?" Marilyn asked.

"Charlie Morrison's wife."

"The guy who owns the Mocambo? Why would she be here? To see what Ella's like?"

"Surely everybody in America knows how talented Ella is," Gwendolyn said.

Marilyn waved to the bartender, who was heading toward them with champagne in a pewter bucket.

"My vocal coach told me to study Ella's method of interpreting a song. She's the absolute master and why she hasn't played Mocambo is beyond me."

"It's because she's not glamorous enough," Arlene said. "If Charlie Morrison's going to book a black singer, he'll get someone like Eartha. She performed at Mocambo last year so I'm betting she's nagged Mrs. Morrison into coming so that she can convince her husband to book Ella."

As the bartender set up the champagne, Marilyn turned to Gwendolyn. "Let's go over and say hello. I'd love to meet her."

Kathryn reached over and plucked the champagne bottle out of the bucket. "Meanwhile, we'll make a start."

As Gwendolyn and Marilyn drew closer, Mrs. Morrison's mouth fell open.

"Hello!" Gwendolyn pointed to Eartha's slinky emerald taffeta creation. "Looks familiar!"

"It's still one of my favorites." Eartha laid a brief hand on her companion's forearm. "This is the gal I told you about who used to own the boutique up on the Strip."

"And this," Gwendolyn pulled Marilyn forward, "is Miss Monroe."

"Gosh!" Marilyn gushed, "Miss Kitt, I've been a fan of yours since I saw you in *New Faces of 1952*." The girl let out a giggle that seemed to take even her by surprise.

"I'm flattered. It was hard to be noticed behind Paul Lynde, Carol Lawrence, and Alice Ghostley."

"Your song was a highlight."

"I'm heading back to Broadway in *Mrs. Patterson*. We'll be at the National Theater so please come see us."

"I'll certainly try." Marilyn turned her blue-eyed attention to Mrs. Morrison. "Have you ever seen Ella Fitzgerald perform live?"

"No, I haven't, I'm sorry to say."

"You're in for a real treat. Guaranteed!"

"Mrs. Morrison's husband runs Mocambo."

"He does?" Those golden motes seemed to hover around Marilyn's blonde halo—a sure sign that she was switching on the charm. She gripped Gwendolyn's arm with both hands. "Ella Fitzgerald at Mocambo? Can you imagine? I'd go every night!"

"You would?" Mrs. Morrison asked.

"Try and keep me away."

It dawned on Gwendolyn that Eartha had been on the Fox lot filming a thinly plotted version of New Faces of 1952 late last year. Getting Ella Fitzgerald booked at a place like Mocambo would be a significant step toward acceptance of black performers playing mainstream venues.

*This has all been a huge con.*

Gwendolyn's gaze settled on the Sinatra/Gardner table. They were watching this performance play out like it was a Hitchcock movie. Gwendolyn waved at Ava but received a pinched smile in return. She might have crossed the room to investigate, but the house lights dimmed, sending them back to their seats.

When Ella stepped out onto the stage, Gwendolyn hoped she might be wearing a Chez Gwendolyn original and was mildly crestfallen when she wasn't. But her disappointment lasted only until Ella sang the first line of "Stardust." Everything but the soulful voice struggling with regret and remorse melted away.

Two hours later, her hands aching from applause, Gwendolyn looked up to see Eartha and Mrs. Morrison heading for their table. From the other corner, Ava and Frank were, too.

Dropping his porkpie hat onto his head, Sinatra switched on his own brand of celebrated charm as he greeted "Mrs. Mocambo" with a kiss to the cheek. Ava broke away from him and circled the group until she came to Gwendolyn and Kathryn. She wavered in her high heels, her eyes dulled from too many whiskeys.

Ava hid her mouth behind her hand. "Frank and me are here as spies for DiMaggio!"

Gwendolyn didn't dare look at Marilyn. "Why?"

"Frankie and Joe have gotten chummy lately, especially since Marilyn filmed that subway scene. Ol' Joltin' Joe's got it into his wooden-headed noggin that she's cheating on him with her vocal coach."

Hal Schaefer often came up in Marilyn's conversation, especially after his attempted overdose of Benzedrine and Nembutal, washed down with typewriter cleaning fluid. Marilyn had been devastated and flew at once to Schaefer's hospital bed.

"Men and their jealousies," Gwendolyn sighed. "And people wonder why I'm single."

Ava huddled closer. "I don't suppose you know anyone who lives at 8122 Waring Avenue? It's a small apartment block on the corner of Kilkea Drive."

"That's six blocks from where we live," Gwendolyn said.

Frank jutted his head. Ava gave them each a parting hug. "It's been getting a lot of play in telephone calls that I may have been eavesdropping on. I suggest you ask Marilyn."

* * *

Halfway to Marilyn's latest address at the Brandon Arms Apartments six blocks east of the Garden, Gwendolyn asked her, "Do you know anybody on Waring Avenue?"

Marilyn rolled the window down to let the cool September air whip through her hair. "Sheila Stuart lives on the corner of Kilkea."

"Sheila's a contract player at Fox, isn't she?"

"She studies singing with Hal—or at least did until Hal tried—you know. Why are you asking? What's with all the funny looks?"

"Marilyn, honey, did you know that Joe's having you followed?"

The silence lasted until Gwendolyn turned onto Sunset.

"We're separating." Marilyn sounded like a ten-year-old.

The gossip columnist in Kathryn gurgled up from the murky depths she'd been wallowing in. "Really?"

"I'm sorry to hear it," Gwendolyn said.

"That night over the New York subway showed me I've been fooling myself for too long."

"Do you need anything?" Gwendolyn asked.

Kathryn turned around to face Marilyn in the back seat. "Anything at all? And I'm not asking as a reporter."

Gwendolyn wanted to reach over and give Marilyn's hand an encouraging squeeze, but she had to keep her eyes on the road. Although it was fairly late, traffic was getting crazier and crazier. These new freeways were supposed to alleviate street congestion, but they didn't seem to be doing much good. "Do you know when you'll make the announcement?"

"Sooner than he thinks." Ten-year-old Marilyn was gone. Movie Star Marilyn was back.

Gwendolyn pulled up at the red light on the Vine Street corner. She turned to the back seat. "Reached the point of no return?"

"I reached it the night we filmed the subway scene. Joe got so mad that I took my time going back to the hotel, figuring that he needed time to cool off. But he was still steaming mad, and I mean *steaming*. It was bad."

The lights changed and Gwendolyn had to face the front again. "How bad?"

"Things got—physical."

"He *hit* you?" Kathryn asked.

"We've had arguments. I mean, who hasn't?" Ten-year-old Marilyn had returned. "But for the first time since we got married, I was afraid of him. I didn't leave the hotel for days afterward."

"That *bastard*!" Kathryn thumped the top of the front seat. "I'd like to Yankee Clipper *him*!" Although perhaps under not quite the most ideal circumstances, Gwendolyn was glad to see the old Kathryn come roaring back.

# CHAPTER 26

As far as Kathryn was concerned, the summer of 1954 had been the Summer From Hell—and not because the newspapers were always saying how LA's smog was trapping heat in ever-increasing numbers. It was because a bank of dark, thick smog had descended over Sunset Boulevard between the Garden of Allah and the Chateau Marmont, obscuring Kathryn's vision and clouding her judgment.

She avoided the Chateau now. If she had an appointment west of the Strip, she took the long way around. She wouldn't go to Ciro's again if it meant walking past the place where Francine had lived and worked for nearly twenty years.

Dorothy Parker had come to town for the opening of Judy Garland's *A Star is Born*. Moss Hart had based his screenplay on Dorothy's 1937 version, and George Cukor had arranged to fly her in for the premiere. She insisted Kathryn meet her for drinks at her hotel before they started rerouting traffic outside the Pantages Theatre. Kathryn had agreed, but when she'd learned that Dorothy was staying at the Marmont, she'd backed out at the last minute. Miss Parker had been none too pleased.

Kathryn had reneged on most of her engagements. Sometimes she'd get as far as putting on her lipstick, but when she saw herself in the bathroom mirror, she found that she didn't have it in her.

She was spending too much time alone. She knew that. But in the weeks following Francine's death, she didn't think of herself as being alone. Not when she had a bottle of Four Roses bourbon with her.

In the muddied backwaters of her mind, she equated Four Roses with being near Marcus. Since that day at the veterans' hospital, his absence felt like a hunting knife slicing across her chest, leaving her heart to flop out onto the floor.

She kept his cable – WOULD JUMP ON NEXT FLIGHT HOME IF STILL HAD PASSPORT – taped to the wall behind her typewriter, where she banged out the bare minimum required to keep her job. If Marcus couldn't be here to comfort her, his favorite booze was the next best thing.

And she might have gone right on fooling herself if Gwendolyn hadn't coaxed her into the Tiffany Club.

Kathryn was glad she'd given in to Gwennie's cajoling. She would have missed Ella's tingling performance; she wouldn't have heard about DiMaggio hiring a private eye to tail Marilyn, and she would also have lost out on nabbing the scoop of the year: Marilyn Monroe was ending her marriage.

"You're in the business of scoop-getting," she told her reflection that night. "It's time to get your head back in the game."

And she was getting better. Slowly. She slept more soundly. A little. Every day she longed for a Four Roses later in the afternoon.

But going to the Chateau Marmont was unthinkable until she received a call from the hotel's manager. He started genially, offering his condolences at Francine's passing. But niceties gave way to a polite-but-firm reminder that they were unable to hold Francine's personal effects indefinitely.

It took Kathryn several days to work up the courage to reenter the grounds. When she was ready, she recruited Gwendolyn, Doris, and Arlene for support.

She led them around the side of the main building. When her mother's bungalow came into view, she looked the other way until they'd passed it. The path curved around to the right and up the hillside, ending at the hotel's storage facility. It was just a large garden shed with electric lighting. Over the brick fence that bordered the hotel's perimeter, Kathryn could see the top half of the Garden of Allah Hotel sign on Sunset.

"You know what's ironic?" she asked the girls. "My mother and I were always at war with each other. And where did she die? At a *military* hospital. Isn't that funny? Well, not funny-ha-ha, but—" She stared at three blank, patient faces. "I'm procrastinating, aren't I?"

"If you don't want to do this," Gwendolyn said, "we can do it for you."

"Thanks, but no. I need to."

The shed that held what was left of Francine's life was thirty feet by thirty feet. Everything Francine possessed had been packed into a large cardboard box and two steamer trunks. One of them dated back to 1908, when Francine, pregnant with Kathryn, had made the long train trip to California. The other was an old sailor trunk that Francine had used as a coffee table.

The cardboard box held a few pots and pans, an electric toaster, and cooking utensils. Kathryn pushed it aside and told the girls to take whatever they wanted.

Francine's clothes filled the steamer trunk, but it was all frumpy old-lady stuff that Kathryn wouldn't wear—touching the familiar blouses and jackets was hard enough. She told the girls to help themselves to anything that tickled their fancy, but hoped they'd reject the lot. Kathryn dreaded the thought of seeing Arlene or Doris walk through the Garden wearing her mother's clothes.

Kathryn felt a little foolish about getting worked up over a battered old chest. She knelt onto the cement and pulled open the lid.

The scent of Shalimar hit her like a slap in the face. She closed her eyes and drew back.

"How about you sit on the floor," Gwendolyn pointed to an empty section of wall, "and we'll hand you stuff."

Kathryn kicked off her shoes and scooted backward until she felt the wall.

The girls pulled out dry cleaning bills, income tax returns, and letters from people whose names Kathryn didn't know. She was starting to chide herself for getting worked up over an old sailor chest full of nothing when Arlene found a passbook for an account held with the Citizens National Trust and Savings Bank of Los Angeles.

Kathryn flipped to Francine's final transactions. "Holy moly! She had over five grand stashed away."

"That's a lot of money for a telephone operator," Doris said.

Francine had regularly deposited five dollars here, ten dollars there, right up to the week before her death.

Kathryn jumped to the first page, where Francine had written "RETIREMENT FUND." They were the saddest two words Kathryn had ever seen. Francine had only been a couple of months shy of her sixty-fifth birthday when she'd suffered that heart attack. *You spent your whole life saving for a retirement that you never got to enjoy.*

Gwendolyn slotted herself in beside Kathryn. "It's going to be okay. We'll get you through this."

"I wouldn't have picked her as the scrapbook type." Arlene hauled out a large album from the bottom of the trunk. The cover was light blue with a gold border. She passed it over to Kathryn with a grunt. "There's a whole pile of them in here."

The word "EIGHT" was inked in black near the top right corner.

The first article inside the front cover was the one Kathryn had written about Judy Garland's concert at the Philharmonic Auditorium when she'd made a triumphant return to LA following her record-breaking run in New York. Kathryn had taken Francine that night, and to the after-party at Romanoff's. Beneath it, Francine had written *April 21st 1952 - What a thrilling night!*

Kathryn turned the page and let out a strangled cry. She shifted the album onto Gwendolyn's lap and turned page after page. "The article I wrote about how more Americans go bowling than watch movies; the one about Howard Hughes suspending production at RKO to ferret out Communists; my column about the *This Is Cinerama* premiere."

Gwendolyn tapped a sheet. "Here's when you apologized for calling Audrey Hepburn a malnourished war waif with nothing to offer the movies but hip bones and a husky voice."

Kathryn shook her head as she scanned each page. "Every column, every review, every interview, every photo published in every newspaper and magazine—it's all here."

Her breath grew shallow until a lightheadedness blurred her vision. She squeezed her eyes tight shut, hoping to staunch the tears, but they leaked from the corners, collected in her lashes, and dripped onto her cheeks.

She felt Gwendolyn's hand grip hers. "My mother cared. All these years, through all those squabbles."

Kathryn opened her eyes. Gwendolyn's mouth gaped in astonishment, but that was all she could make out. The tears were flowing freely now, distorting everything. She nodded weakly.

"Who'd have guessed," Gwendolyn said, "that disapproving old biddy genuinely gave a rat's ass?"

Doris burst out laughing; Arlene joined her. It was exactly what Kathryn needed, and she started laughing, too. It was the first time she'd done that in weeks. How incongruous that she should do it with a lifetime's evidence that her distant, critical mother had taken the time and effort to document everything she'd done in eight enormous scrapbooks.

"What was her last entry?" Arlene asked.

The most recent pages were filled with variations of the magazine ads for the upcoming Suncrockerhouse stage extravaganza.

Doris hauled out the scrapbooks until she came to the bottom one and passed it over. "When did she start?"

Kathryn expected to see her debut *Hollywood Reporter* column, but found instead a set of twelve photographs of her three-year-old self.

"They look like the photo you came across on the *Sunset Boulevard* set," Gwendolyn said.

"She told me my father only sent her that one photo."

"It's the same cutesy dress and oversized hair bow."

Gwendolyn pointed to a shot of Danford trying to stand Kathryn on his knee. They wore identical strained smiles, their eyebrows angling toward the middle. "If you needed more evidence that Thomas Danford is your father, I think you've got it." She pulled out a clipped newspaper article jammed into the folds of the scrapbook and handed it to Kathryn. It crinkled as she unfolded it.

"This is from the *Charlotte Observe*r, dated 1912, reporting that a vagrant named Camden Caldecott had been arrested for framing the mayor for adultery and blackmailing him for a thousand dollars."

"Did he get away with it?" Arlene asked.

"The mayor hatched a plan with his brother-in-law, the chief of police, and nearly nabbed him red-handed but—and I quote—'the slick perpetrator evaded capture and absconded from town in a stolen pick-up truck.'" Kathryn laid the article onto her lap. "Sounds like Mister Voss has been at it for quite some time."

Gwendolyn waved Francine's passbook in Kathryn's face. "How much did that private eye want to charge you?"

* * *

The lime-green neon sign of the Formosa Café blinked to life as Kathryn stopped to check her purse. She didn't need to, but rifling through the papers helped settle her nerves.

"I really am so sorry that I couldn't be there for you the other day," Leo said. "It must have been tough going through your mother's personal effects."

She pulled off her glove and stroked his cheek. "It's enough that you wanted to be there."

The front door to Dudley Hartman's office had a new sign out front.

*Melrose Detective Agency*
*By appointment only*

The door swung open to reveal Hartman's smiling moonface. "I had a bet with myself that I'd see you again."

Kathryn pointed to the sign. "Should I have called ahead?"

"We put that there to discourage time-wasters. Come on in."

Hartman indicated two chairs in front of the desk as he took a seat behind it.

Kathryn had forgotten about the pine-scented Air Wick that pervaded his bungalow-turned-office. "Melrose Detective Agency, huh?"

"Business has been very good lately so I decided it was time I gave myself an official name. Please, how can I help?"

"You'll remember that I came to see you about tracking down Sheldon Voss."

"I thought of you when I heard he'd surfaced."

Kathryn pulled out the article tucked into Francine's scrapbook and flattened it out carefully. The paper was dry as an autumn leaf and liable to crack into pieces.

When Hartman was finished, his genial face was a blank slate. "This article is forty years old."

Kathryn handed over the copy of *Look* magazine that she'd come across at LA County General.

Hartman nodded thoughtfully. "Operation Pastorius has a bearing on this case?"

Kathryn took him through the conversation she'd had with Darryl Zanuck about his dinner with a well-sauced Winchell.

Hartman's smile turned smug. "There's nearly always a connection, a clue, some scrap of evidence waiting for someone to find it."

Kathryn's heart started thudding against her ribcage. "Enough to send you to Boston?"

He tapped her copy of *Look*. "You've already done half my work."

"Will it cost me half as much as it would have when I saw you a year ago?"

"Grubby rags like *Confidential* have brought a flood of clients looking to bury facts from their past, or to get the dirt on wandering spouses in case *Confidential* does. I've got more work than I can handle so I'm taking on a partner. He starts on Monday. It's good news for me because I can finally have a weekend off, and it's good news for you because he can look after the office while I'm gone. Win/win all round." He pressed his fingertips on top of the copy of *Look*. "Mind if I keep this?"

* * *

It was a long walk to the Garden of Allah, but Kathryn felt like she could skip home. "Can you imagine if he finds enough evidence to overturn my father's conviction?"

"Probably not as straightforward as it happens in the movies," Leo cautioned.

"I know it'll be complicated and drawn out, and chances are more remote than Siberia, but oh! The possibility!"

Leo squeezed her hand into the crook of his elbow. "Even if it comes to nothing, at least you'll have tried."

*Forget skipping. I feel like dancing up Sunset like Gene Kelly in* Singin' in the Rain. "I wonder how Mom would feel if she knew I was using her retirement money to clear Thomas's name."

Leo halted in front of a jewelry store; the golden glow of its window presentation filled his face. The usual assortment of necklaces, earrings, bracelets, and bangles packed the display, and to one side sat a collection of men's watches and cufflinks. One pair in shiny chrome featured a lowercase 'b' in the style of an old-fashioned typewriter.

Leo clasped her hand. "When you're up on stage in rehearsals with Betty and Adelaide, I can't help but notice how they're dripping in jewelry."

"They have exquisite taste." Kathryn wondered if this jeweler also had a pair of 'm' cufflinks. It wasn't Marcus's birthday for months and months, but with his passport still confiscated, she figured he could do with a cheerful gift.

Leo said, "It's just that when you stand next to them, by contrast, you look like the poor country cousin who can't afford sparkling baubles."

"Anything more than a string of pearls and a brooch is too much for me. But you know that, so why would you think I'd want to start decking myself out?"

He pointed out a rack of diamond rings in the center of the window. "Do any of those appeal?"

"You silly goose!" Those are engagement rings."

The words thudded like rocks onto the sidewalk. She felt his hand loosen its grip around hers. She pulled it away. *A guy doesn't lead a girl to a jewelry store and point to engagement rings just to mention how nicely they twinkle.* "What are you saying?" Seconds crawled by, dense with apprehension. "We've already had this discussion," she said.

"What discussion?" He kept his eyes on the contents of the window.

"I know very few people who are genuinely happily married."

"You live in Hollywood, where the divorce rate is artificially high—"

"On one of our first dates you told me that you'd tried marriage twice and both times it was a disaster, so you had no intention of putting yourself through that again."

"Yeah, but then . . ."

"But then what?" A feeling washed over her that maybe she shouldn't have asked.

"I met you."

"Oh, Leo."

"Your mother's passing reminded me that life can be short and death can be random."

Kathryn pressed her hand to the glass. It was warm from the heat of the lights. She'd had much the same thoughts. Not those exact words, but a meandering version circling in an endless loop.

*The only family you have is Sheldon Voss, whom you hate, and Thomas Danford, whom you've never met. Francine was only sixty-five when she died. Your death could come fast and unexpected, too. Do you want to get to* your *deathbed with regrets—*

"So, anyway," he said, slicing into her torment, "food for thought."

He turned from the store and walked away from her toward the late-summer dusk purpling the sky. The streetlamps stippled the deserted sidewalk with dots of light that made the boulevard resemble a reel of film that went on forever and ever.

# CHAPTER 27

Marcus laid down Kathryn's letter and surveyed a statue of Triton shooting a plume of water out of his head.

The opening of Kathryn's letter startled him: "This summer has been hell!" Whenever Kathryn had wailed about what a pain in the ass her mother was, Marcus had thought, *She's the only family you've got. Wait till she goes.* But he always assumed that he'd be there to help Scotch tape her life back together.

The authorities had confiscated his passport in June, and here it was October and he was no closer to knowing why or what he needed to do to get it back.

His first visit to the US embassy had generated enough red tape to choke Hannibal's elephant. But he'd swallowed his frustration and filled out the forms.

He'd returned a month later and argued his way up to the office manager, who looked more like an Indiana cornfield escapee than a diplomat. "We're not sure why they're stonewalling us," he drawled. "You're not FBI, are you? CIA? On the lam?"

The lawyer that Arlene's boss had recommended was tied to the Conti brothers so he'd asked Doris if Columbia had a Rome office. They did, so Marcus had burned through a sizable chunk of cash to dig deeper. The guy had come up against brick wall after brick wall and eventually sat Marcus down for the "there's nothing more I can do for you" conversation.

His mind kept turning to Emilio. But wasn't he just a hotheaded twerp who took pictures of big-chested starlets and European jet setters? He didn't seem like the sort of guy with connections to high levels of government.

"No," Domenico commented, "but I bet his brothers do."

The thought took root like an aggressive fungus eating away at his innards.

When it got too crazy-making, Marcus would take refuge at Café Barberini, where he'd order the fluffiest gnocchi in town. When he could find an *LA Times*, he'd catch up on news from America: the first live color TV broadcast; the Supreme Court's ban on racial segregation in public schools; Monroe's divorce from DiMaggio; Joseph Breen leaving the Hays Office.

He felt as though he was standing on the bank of a wide river watching the parade of his life march along the other shore.

But only on the bad days.

On all the others, he had Domenico: "A glass of wine; a bowl of melt-in-the-mouth pasta, someone playing 'Quanto sie Bella Roma' on the violin. What else do you need?"

He was right, too, in his observation that Marcus wasn't ready to leave Rome. He still dreamed of Oliver, but Oliver could be in Timbuktu, so there wasn't much Marcus could do about it. In his dreams, they were always near water: the Garden of Allah pool, Santa Monica beach, the Trevi Fountain. At the start of summer, the thought of Oliver had been a dull ache. As the full force of Rome's heat scorched the city, the ache had evolved into a throbbing timpani until Marcus reached a breaking point.

He'd kept telling himself to get out of bed, but couldn't summon the will power. He'd thrash around the sheets like a caged panther until he exhausted himself into a fitful sleep that afforded him little rest and no respite from the fixations that preoccupied his waking hours: Emilio Conti . . . passports . . . Kathryn, Gwendolyn, Francine, Zanuck . . . travelers cheques . . . gold bars. If he forced down some food, he'd have three spoons of minestrone and couldn't stomach another bite.

After a couple of weeks, Domenico had demanded to know what was going on.

Marcus's explanation soon degenerated into an incoherent string of words that stumbled over each other like a clutter of cats scrambling to escape firecrackers. Perhaps, Domenico suggested, he should fill his days with a different activity: shooting *scattino* photographs.

*Metropolitana* had opened to enormous box office, provoking rumors that Marcus's photos had been a publicity stunt. In the press, Melody was playing coy, and Marcus wanted to distance himself from the whole episode. He had a better idea.

His frustration stemmed from knowing that his opportunity to work on *Carmen Jones* and *The Virgin Queen* had come and gone, so the next day, he started work on a new project that he had full control over.

Nearly every original screenplay Marcus had ever worked on started with a pebble dropped into the pond of his imagination—an image, a comment, a headline. He knew he was on the right track when he felt a euphoric flurry stir his guts.

The success of *Quo Vadis* had triggered an avalanche of doppelgängers: *The Robe, Demetrius and the Gladiators, The Egyptian, Julius Caesar, Androcles and the Lion*. Paramount had sent Cecil B. DeMille to Egypt to remake *The Ten Commandments*, and the big rumor at Cinecittà was a new Fratelli di Conti film called *The Gates of Rome*.

If Hollywood couldn't get enough of togas and sandals and chariots and pagans, who was in a better position than he to give them what they wanted? Especially now that he'd uncovered a valiant hero forced to face a malevolent villain in the cinematic climax of a spectacular bridge collapsing into a river. The entry in Domenico's *Compendium of Roman Heroes* was only two sentences:

"Horatius Cocles was a foot soldier from the sixth century BC who became a hero when he chopped down a bridge across the Tiber to prevent an Etruscan invasion. Without him, Rome might never have evolved into a mighty republic that lasted 500 years."

Marcus could already see the marquee: *Horatius at the Bridge*.

He could have worked on his idea in his pensione but he needed to be on the streets, surrounded by Romans, absorbing the history bestowed by countless generations of their ancestors. Every day, he'd headed to the café at the end of Via Veneto with the view of the Triton Fountain. Hollywood was going to eat this up!

But now it was October and Marcus had nothing to show for his summer.

No returned passport, no evidence that Emilio Conti was responsible, no solution to smuggling out his locked funds, no way to track Oliver down, and no screenplay—just a notebook filled with half-baked ideas, clichéd situations, and cardboard characters mouthing corny dialogue stuffed with "thee," "thou," and "thy."

Lunchtime customers began to fill the café. It was almost one o'clock. If his lunch date was the reliable type, he ought to be showing up right about now. However, a host of adjectives could be used to describe his guest, but "reliable" wouldn't make the top one hundred.

The waiter, Adriano, delivered Marcus's prosecco and asked if he was ready to order. Marcus told him he was waiting for someone. "Let's wait till one-thirty."

"Certamente," Adriano said with a slight nod, and stared at a figure across the other side of the piazza.

"You've got whiskey back there, haven't you?" Marcus asked. "Make it a double. American if you have any. On the rocks. Wait five minutes, then bring another."

"Si, signore."

Marcus rose to his feet. "Mine eyes have seen the glory of the coming of the Lord."

Errol Flynn broke into the smile that had been setting hearts and groins aflame for twenty years. But the face that went with it was no longer a roguishly devil-may-care study in handsomeness.

He hadn't seen the Aussie swashbuckler since his trial during the war so he had been taken aback the previous week when Errol had telephoned to say he'd filmed a movie called *Crossed Swords* at Cinecittà last year, and that he was back for the premiere and wanted Marcus's services.

He'd produced this picture through Errol Flynn Productions. They'd made three movies, "but if this one bombs too, it'll be the last, so I'm going all out in the publicity department."

"You're a sight for sore eyes, ol' matey!" He flopped down into a chair, tossing his white Panama hat and dark glasses onto the table. Adriano approached with a filled tumbler. Errol sniffed it. "Wild Turkey?" He let out a whoop.

Errol's face used to glow with the vitality of a persona that only a forty-foot-wide screen could contain, but now it sagged at the edges. Blotches and wrinkles crisscrossed his forehead and cheeks, and early signs of a drinker's nose were surfacing. At forty-five, he was three years younger than Marcus, but looked ten years older.

A controlled environment like a soundstage, with lighting, camera, and makeup professionals, could hide flaws, but Errol wanted candid shots out and about on the streets.

He downed Adriano's whiskey. "What interesting setting have you come up with?"

"Did you see *Roman Holiday*?" Marcus asked.

"Yep."

"Remember when Gregory Peck takes Audrey Hepburn to a big stone mask?"

"That was a real cute scene."

"They filmed it at Bocca della Verità. It means 'Mouth of Truth,' so I thought—"

"Going for the irony angle, huh?"

Bocca della Verità sat inside an alcove that would protect Errol from the harshness of direct sunlight, but Errol didn't need to know that. "It's over near the Circus Maximus. We could walk, but if there's a chance you could be recognized—"

Errol picked up his hat and sunglasses. "Haven't you been around enough movie stars to know that we can turn it on and off at will?"

* * *

Bocca della Verità stood inside a brown-brick building of seven arches topped by a seven-story bell tower. The mid-afternoon sun slanted through the iron grillwork, casting planks of light on the stone floor.

Marcus looked through his camera's viewfinder. "Stick your hand in the mouth and declare a truth. If you're lying, the beast inside will bite it off."

Errol inserted his hand into the mask's cool marble mouth. "I declare that of all the hundreds of women I have slept with, I don't regret a single one."

Marcus started snapping rapid-fire. "Not even the two who accused you of rape?"

"Yes! Yes! A thousand times, yes!" He sounded like Robin Hood. "And as proof, I shall withdraw my hand unscathed!"

He extracted it with his fingers bunched like dead twigs. "Egads! I shall never play Beethoven's 'Moonlight Sonata' again!"

"This light's a bit low." Marcus replaced the used roll with a fresh one. "Let's try it with a flash."

Errol stuck his hand back inside the mouth. "It's cold and clammy in there. I wouldn't be surprised if some vicious scorpion was lurking—"

"There aren't any scorpions in Italy. Emote now; chat later."

Errol pulled a series of faces as Marcus clicked photo after photo, his flashbulb filling the nook with blinding light. He wasn't quite done when he heard a Midwest twang.

"Girls! Look! Errol Flynn in the ever-loving flesh!"

Errol yelled, "RUN!"

A huddle of women in elastic-waisted skirts shrieked as Marcus and Errol raced along the length of the Circus Maximus, veered hard left, and made for the Colosseum. Dodging four lanes of traffic, they shot inside the first archway and ducked around the corner.

Marcus pressed his back against the crumbling stone. "So much for turning it on and off."

"Sometimes it turns on by itself," Errol laughed. "But what's a guy to do when he hears the menopausal cries of the relentlessly frustrated?" He headed through the inner row of archways and gripped the metal railing. "You never did tell me what you're doing here."

Marcus took him through a truncated version of his run-in with the Fratelli di Conti over *Metropolitana* and how he was stuck in Rome until his passport reappeared.

"You want to go back to LA?" Errol asked.

*What an odd question.* "It's where my roots are. Kathryn and Gwendolyn, the Garden of Allah, everything."

"Hanging onto your past?" Errol winced as he turned back to the Colosseum's floor. "I've been holding onto mine for more years than I should've. When people see me, I feel like I have to give them Mister Movie Star; otherwise, they'll walk away disappointed. You know where it's gotten me? *Crossed Swords*, where I'm still playing the same old swashbuckler." He clamped a firm hand on Marcus's shoulder. "If there's anything from your past that's holding you back, let go of it."

Marcus had only ever seen the Errol Flynn that needed to be at the center of every party. This older and wiser but sadder version was hard to digest.

"What would you have said with your hand in Bocca della Verità?" Errol asked.

The answer came to Marcus without hesitation. "That I don't want to leave Rome until I've had a chance to say a proper goodbye to someone."

"Then do that."

"It won't solve my passport situation."

"They can't hold onto it indefinitely. But holding onto our past forever can grind a chap to dust. You need to track down—what's his name?"

"Oliver."

"You need to say your final goodbyes."

"Easier said than done. He joined the church, so he could be anywhere."

"But the Vatican must know where he is."

Marcus threw him a skeptical eye. "You got the Pope's phone number?"

"No, but Trevor Bergin played my wise-cracking sidekick in *Crossed Swords*, and let me tell you, ol' Trevor was a busy lad during filming. By the time we had our movie in the can, he'd burned through five guys, three of whom were in the church. Surely one of them will know somebody who knows somebody."

"Melody Hope told me he's in Greece filming *The Grief of Achilles*."

"He got back yesterday and lives five minutes from here. He's probably still unpacking."

* * *

Errol was right—Trevor was still unpacking, but it wasn't Trevor doing it. It was the ancient valet Trevor had brought back from Greece. Marcus and Errol barely understood his broken Italian but were able to get out of him that Trevor was at his favorite bistro.

Café de Paris consumed the sidewalk with two rows of tables, each covered in their signature peach tablecloth and placed under an awning to shelter its customers from the vagaries of the weather. Trevor Bergin sat by himself, drizzling olive oil over four large slices of bread.

He yelped when he saw Marcus beside Errol. "More champagne!" he called to the waiter. "And more bread!" He turned to Marcus. "This place has gotten a bit cliché since King Farouk made it his home away from home, but their bread is the best in town."

Trevor was still head-turningly handsome but his camera-ready jawline had softened and his dark brown hair was now flecked with silver. Though creased around the edges, his eyes remained clear and bright.

The conversation flowed from the impossible beauty of the Greeks, the temptations of love scenes with Gina Lollobrigida, and arrangements for the *Crossed Swords* premiere, to Melody Hope's post-Hollywood career.

"I can't believe you're *Lo Scattino Americano*!" Trevor told Marcus. "Wait till I get my hands on that *La Speranza* minx—I'm going to give her such a hiding, keeping you all to herself. And what about Oliver? How's he doing?"

"That's where you come in," Marcus said.

"Look out!" Trevor whispered. "Speak of the devil."

A pack of *scattini* gathered around the front of the café, checking their cameras and twisting their zoom lenses as a midnight-blue Bentley pulled up. The rotund figure of King Farouk lumbered out of the car as the *scattini* clicked as rapidly as their cameras would allow.

Trevor said, "He could teach Hollywood stars a thing or two about seeking attention."

"Farouk! Farouk!"

The banished king adjusted the tassel on his fez and strode past the *scattini* mosquitos and gaping diners without waiting for the quartet of pretty starlets who exited the car behind him.

Marcus knew that today's nameless hanger-on could be tomorrow's Gina Lollobrigida. The subjects of his photos had largely come to him. *Lo Scattino Americano* had happened with such little effort that he almost felt guilty that he'd never had to jostle and shove like those guys.

*Am I hanging onto my past?* His first reaction was to reject Errol's proposition. *Screenwriting is what I do. Screenwriter is who I am.*

Some screenplays took longer than others, but *Horatius at the Bridge* wasn't gelling at all. Meanwhile, every time he lifted his camera to take a shot, somebody laid out good money. *Maybe I'm not that person anymore.*

"FAROUK!" a *scattino* shrieked.

When he heard the voice, Marcus shot to his feet and stormed through the pack at the front of the restaurant. He throttled Emilio Conti by the collar and threw the guy against a telephone pole.

"You little shit!"

Conti blinked at him, panting hard.

"MY PASSPORT! I don't know how you did it, or what strings you pulled, but I want my passport back and I want it *now*."

Conti shoved Marcus in the chest. "I know about your passport," he jeered, "but you are crazy if you think I am guilty."

"Don't bullshit me, you little prick."

Conti's face reddened. He pulled at the hem of his jacket to straighten the creases, then gripped Marcus by the elbow and tugged him away from the *scattini* pack. They were almost nose-to-nose now. Marcus could feel the guy's breath on his skin. "Do you know why I hate you so much, Signore *Scattino Americano*?"

Marcus expected contempt and scorn in the guy's eyes, and he could see it lurking there, but behind a sheer screen of something else. Envy? Resentment? "Because I can leave and you think you can't?"

"I am desperate to get away from the Conti name and everything about it," he half-shouted. "I am so sick of Roma. Everything is old. The ruins and the dust. I want to go to America where everything is new and a man can be more than the accidental baby brother of the miraculous Conti triplets."

The photos Marcus had taken in that backstreets queer bar were sandwiched between the pre-war Italian romance novels Signora Scatena stored on the bookshelf in his room. "Remember that day we fought in front of the American Express office?" Marcus asked. "I followed you to a bar, somewhere north of the city in the back streets—"

Emilio's face flushed in pink blotches. "YOU WHAT?"

"I wasn't snooping, honest. I was just—I don't know what I was thinking. Anyway, I saw you meet up with a red-haired guy—"

"You FOLLOWED me?"

"It's okay!" Marcus held out his hands to pacify him, but Conti brushed them aside and shoved Marcus in the chest again.

"Let me tell you Signore *Americano*. I know why your passport was taken. All the *scattini* are talking about it."

He was so red-faced furious that Marcus wasn't sure he could believe anything that was about to come out of his mouth, but he had to ask. "Talking about what?"

"Those photographs of Ava Gardner? Frank Sinatra learned you took them and he make some telephone calls. Mafioso. Good luck getting your passport back. And if you tell *anyone* about that bar—" He broke into a string of Italian cussing.

Marcus thought of Sinatra as a member of the Garden family: Kathryn, Gwendolyn, Doris, Arlene, Bogie and Bacall, Dorothy Parker, Robert Benchley, Ava, Tallulah, Errol, Orson. They drifted in and out of each other's lives as circumstances dictated, but he'd never thought one of them would turn on him.

He was still shaky when he reached the table and related to Trevor and Errol what Emilio had revealed.

"Personally, I like Frankie," Errol said, "but I've always thought he wasn't one to cross. Tough break, Adler."

Trevor brought their conversation back. "We were talking about Oliver."

"Did you know he joined the church?"

Trevor's champagne glass halted midway to his mouth. "He's a padre?"

"Or similar. I need someone inside the church, and a certain Australian told me that you might know someone who could track him down."

Trevor confessed that Errol's rumors were true, "but none of the beautiful choirboys I've been bedding would rank high enough to access that sort of information."

*First Conti, then Sinatra, now this.* Marcus dropped his head into his hands, burning with a thirst that a hundred champagnes couldn't quench.

He felt the tip of Trevor's finger tap his wrist. "You don't need to contact the Vatican."

"No?"

Trevor placed the bottle of olive oil in front of Marcus with a flourish and rotated it until the oval label greeted him. It featured the smiling face of a monk in front of an olive tree laden with plump black olives. "Remind you of anyone?"

Marcus pushed his glasses onto his forehead so that he could inspect the picture more carefully. He let out a choked huff when he recognized the face.

"I think of Oliver every time I see it," Trevor said, "and I didn't even know he'd had a religious conversion. But this is where I'd start looking."

*Bottled at the Monastery of St Anthony of Padua, Tivoli, Italy.*

Marcus knew the shape of that face, the curve of that smile, the spark in those eyes like they were his own.

*All this time,* he told the bottle, *you've only been an hour's drive away.*

# CHAPTER 28

Kathryn dropped her script onto her kitchen counter. "Can't we just give Adelaide and Betty a duet and leave me out of it?"

Leo sighed. "You know why we can't."

"Because your stupid song is now our big finale." Kathryn regretted the insult as soon as she said it. She was being petulant and unprofessional, but her nerves were fraying. If they hadn't been standing in her living room she might have staged a walk-out.

Less than a hundred feet from her window, a bunch of new residents had gathered around the diving board where someone was playing the new Dave Brubeck album. Kathryn longed to be out there listening to *Jazz Goes to College* instead of trapped inside reciting the same lyrics over and over with no indication that she'd ever be word perfect.

But it wasn't only the lyrics that made her want to run away. It was being alone with Leo. Something had shifted since that night of the engagement rings.

Gwendolyn later pointed out that he hadn't delivered an ultimatum. "It wasn't like he said, 'Marry me by the end of the year or I'm calling it quits.'"

"I've never thought of myself as the marrying kind," Kathryn told her.

"But now?"

"I'm starting to wonder."

Gwendolyn's cracker snapped in two. "Where did *that* come from?"

It had come from Marcus's most recent letter. She'd had to read it a second time to make sure she understood it right. *Maybe I'm not a screenwriter anymore; maybe I'm a photographer. It's possible Errol is right: I'm hanging onto my past longer than is healthy.*

When Leo had turned up at the front door to her villa to rehearse his stupid song, Kathryn had noticed a lump in his coat pocket: the sort of suspiciously square bulge that a velvet-covered box might make.

Every time Leo's attention was distracted elsewhere, her gaze jumped straight to it. *Is it any wonder I can't concentrate with that elephant in the room?*

Leo opened her script to the finale. "Is there a line, or phrase, or combination of words that's throwing you?" He read them out loud. "Sunbeam's new Mixmaster. Mixes my Betty batter faster. It makes my baking more ambitious. 'Cause everything turns out so delicious." He pushed his reading glasses onto his forehead. "What, exactly, is the problem?"

THE PROBLEM, she wanted to scream, IS THAT YOU'VE GOT A RING IN YOUR POCKET.

He said, "I know 'Betty batter faster' is a bit of a tongue-twister. I thought it gave the lyrics bounce and pop, but we can change it if it's scaring you."

*I'm scared that you're going to ask me to marry you, and I'm even more scared that I'm going to say yes.*

She was saved by a knock on the door. She ran to it, hoping it might be the Dave Brubeck gang inviting her to join them.

It was a Western Union messenger.

These days, telegrams were more typically phoned through. The last time she'd received a paper telegram was when Marcus had cabled to say his passport had been confiscated. Had he learned more about the Sinatra situation? If Frank had been shooting a movie, Kathryn would have charged right over demanding to know what he thought he was doing. But the guy was playing the Palace in New York where he probably would have tossed her letters.

She sent the delivery boy on his way with a large tip, then sliced along the envelope with her nail and pulled out the telegram.

"Marcus again?" Leo asked.

She read the telegram out loud. "FBI contact confirms Danford file missing STOP Last person to view was WW STOP New partner has all details STOP" She skipped down to the sender information: Dudley Hartman, Lenox Hotel, Boston.

"Winchell!" She slapped the telegram onto her kitchen counter tiles. "I knew that slimy toad's fingerprints were all over this."

"Surely it's a serious crime to filch from the FBI."

"Depends on whether or not you're buddy-buddy with Hoover."

"I suppose you want to swing by Hartman's office and get the lowdown after we're done?"

"Leo, we *are* done."

"But you haven't got the words right—"

"I promise I will by the time we open."

"You know that's a week away, right?"

Kathryn jiggled her car keys at him. "Coming?"

Leo absently patted the square bulge in his jacket pocket, and nodded.

* * *

Kathryn pulled her Oldsmobile into the three-space parking lot.

"I still can't believe it," she told Leo. "For months, I've been trying to contact Winchell through every channel I can think of—his newspaper, secretary, radio station, agent—but I've been getting the runaround. Do you think I should tell Hartman to take the train down to New York and dog Winchell?"

She pulled her keys from the ignition and stepped out of the car. A cold November wind hit her in the face like a wet mop. "While he's at it, I could get him to pay Sinatra a visit. Rough him up a little, you know?"

Leo pulled off his hat so that he wouldn't lose it to the wind. "I don't think Hartman's the roughing-up type."

They headed toward the front door. "Maybe this new PI knows his way around a knuckle sandwich."

Leo smiled. "Hey, Capone, let's deal with one crisis at a time." He gave her a feather-soft right hook to the jaw and opened the agency's front door.

Kathryn laughed as she stepped inside. The new guy behind the desk leapt to his feet. "I've been expecting you."

The laughter dried on Kathryn's lips as her heart lurched up into her throat, pounded her voice into silence, then dropped into her stomach.

He extended his hand toward her, but she could only drink in his face like a nomad lost in the desert.

"The name is Nelson Hoyt." He kept his hand suspended in mid-air, his eyes fixed on hers.

*How could I have forgotten the shade of those gray-blue eyes? And where are his dimples? Ah. They've disappeared into those deep grooves etched around the sides of his mouth. And oh, those lips that look like they were carved by Michelangelo.*

Leo shook Nelson's hand and introduced himself.

Nelson's eyes crinkled in the corners. His skin had taken on a craggy quality, like he'd spent the last eight years standing on the bow of a whaler zigzagging the Pacific.

She forced herself to take his hand; it was warmer than she remembered.

"Please, take a seat." He pulled a thick file from his desk drawer and placed it in front of him. "Dudley has been a busy fellow."

"Have you been here long, Mr. Hoyt?" Kathryn's voice came out raspy. "In LA, I mean."

"Perhaps you might feel more secure if you knew a bit about me and my background, et cetera."

"No, no," Leo waved away the question "I'm sure Dudley did a thorough check—"

"*I* would like to hear Mr. Hoyt's story."

He smiled the way he used to whenever Kathryn won an argument, or caved in because it was easier. "I'm ex-FBI."

Kathryn swallowed hard. "Where were you stationed?"

"Nome, Alaska."

*So that's where Hoover shanghaied you. No wonder I never heard from you again.* "Who even knew the FBI had an office in the middle of nowhere?"

"It's right near the Bering Strait where only fifty-five miles separate Russia from the States. As you can imagine, with the Cold War and everything . . ."

"Did you enjoy your time there?"

"Hated every minute of it," he said. "There's nothing to do but sit around and think of loved ones. I stuck it out for three years, then quit the Bureau and headed to Seattle where I joined the Pinkerton agency. I liked the work well enough, but my dad fell ill, so I came to LA to nurse him."

"How is he now?"

"He died earlier this year."

"Oh!" It was too pained a cry for the father of someone she was supposedly meeting for the first time, but Kathryn had only the warmest feelings toward Wesley Hoyt. It was like hearing that a favorite uncle had passed away. "I'm sorry to hear that. I lost my mother recently, too."

Leo pulled back.

"Unfortunately, Pinkerton didn't have an opening in their LA office but I met Dudley at a private eye convention and he made me a partner. Life has a way of working out, doesn't it?"

Kathryn chanced a peek at Nelson's left hand—no wedding ring. But did he know that she and Leo were together? *Of course he does, you big dummy. The guy is a detective – and one of the sharpest people you've ever met.*

Leo cleared his throat. "Shall we review what Dudley has discovered?"

Nelson flipped open the folder. "The FBI started a file on Danford when he declared his candidacy for the Massachusetts governorship. Between Dudley's contacts and mine, we've been able to determine that Voss zeroed in on a disgruntled FBI agent who Voss knew would have access to Bureau files."

"That Voss sure is a crafty old fox," Leo said. "Right, honey?"

It was an effort for Kathryn to pull her eyes away from Nelson's naked ring finger. "What do you know about this disgruntled FBI employee?"

"He was a rising star at the headquarters in DC until he fell afoul of Hoover."

"Falling afoul of Hoover? That can't have been pretty."

A wry smile lingered on Nelson's face. "He was banished to Boston, which made him the perfect person for Voss to target in order to learn what the Bureau held on Danford."

"Do you know what was in my father's file?"

"We have a fair idea."

"Even though Winchell stole it?"

"Let's just say that disgruntled employees don't hold up to a touch of the strong arm. Evidently, it contained the details for all his business trips, which were the usual places around New England. But an odd one stood out.

"Your father went to Allagash, Maine, right up near the Canadian border, looking to buy a maple tree plantation, unaware that Voss had started taking tons of photos and developed the ones where he looked guilty or furtive or was meeting with men on the street. And when the perfect opportunity arose, Voss grabbed it."

"Operation Pastorius?" Kathryn asked.

"Correct. Evidently, Danford spent several idyllic childhood summers in Amagansett out on Long Island and had always wanted a vacation home there. So as he roamed New England hunting for maple plantations, he also made several trips to Amagansett looking for the right house. It was unfortunate timing that he was there on June 12th, 1942."

"When the Germans landed?"

"Voss must have danced a merry jig when he learned about that."

Metal clanged against metal from the Formosa Café kitchen next door. She could hear the manager reminding the staff "every last mother-humping pot needs to be scrubbed spotless."

Kathryn couldn't look at Nelson anymore. Her pulse thundered in her ears; she felt the color draining from her face and yet she was hot as blazes. *Say something, Leo. I doubt that I can.*

Five seconds of eternity crept by. "Photos can help build a convincing case," Leo said, "but surely that's not all Voss did?"

"He managed to get a hold of official letterheads from the FBI and the OWI, and forged reports describing Danford as a person of interest."

Kathryn crossed her arms. "Did the FBI know Danford's conviction was a frame-up?"

"We don't know that for certain. I'd say probably not at the time, but now they're aware of it. We do know that the FBI agent Voss befriended is the same one who gave Winchell access to Danford's file."

"What does this disgruntled agent do?"

"He's in charge of FBI records and archives for the state of Massachusetts."

"Voss sure can pick 'em."

"Our working theory is that he gave your father's file to Winchell, so Winchell knows about the frame job that got your father convicted."

Kathryn picked up one of the pencils strewn around Nelson's desk and started threading it through her fingers. "But I told Winchell he can take the glory of spearheading an investigation that will lead to my father's exoneration."

"Perhaps there's a reason why he's keeping you out of the loop."

The pencil snapped in half. Kathryn turned to Leo. "I need to go to New York and confront him."

"Our full dress rehearsals start in three days," Leo pointed out, "and the first public performance is next Friday. You can't pull out now. I'm sorry, but you just can't."

*My father's freedom is more important than standing on a stage singing about Betty Crocker's goddamned batter. I need room to breathe and time to think.* She looked down at the two halves of the pencil in her hand.

Nelson said, "I might have a way for you to corner Winchell without having to leave LA."

Kathryn noticed that he was wearing the same necktie he'd worn the last time she saw him. It was at the Radio Room the night he'd figured out that "the girl" Bugsy Siegel kept mentioning on the FBI-bugged phone was Kathryn. It was a beautiful tie, aquamarine, patterned with tiny alternating seagulls and anchors in white. "Let's hear it," she said.

"I have a pal who's pretty high in security at Fox. He told me that there's a plan to sneak Winchell into the studio to interview Marilyn Monroe."

Kathryn wondered why Gwendolyn didn't know about this. She was closer to Marilyn than most people. "If you've heard of it and I haven't, that meeting must be super-duper secret."

"My buddy owed me a big favor so I called in the chip for you."

"Thank you." Kathryn felt her face redden. "Does Marilyn know about this?"

"I got the impression that this is a mutual-back-scratching deal between Winchell and Zanuck. Marilyn's given no interviews since she announced her divorce and Winchell wanted her first one, so he traded Zanuck a big feature story on *The Seven Year Itch*."

Kathryn felt a twinge of envy—not so much that Winchell had hooked such a big story but that she hadn't thought of it first. "Do you know where this interview's taking place?"

"On the set of her current movie."

"He's a clever bastard, I'll give him that much. When's this happening?"

"You must have someone at Fox who can help with that. I suspect you know how advantageous the element of surprise can be."

Hoyt smiled. It wasn't a polite, lips-together-teeth-hidden smile, but a broad one, glowing with sincerity. He wasn't naturally given to smiley outbreaks, but when he did, it was like the whole room glowed brighter, the colors more vibrant.

She felt her heart melt and needed to look away before both men read her mind.

Nelson said, "Your best bet to get your hands on Danford's file is through Winchell."

Leo slapped his hands onto his knees. "Anything else we need to know?"

Nelson hesitated for a split second, but it was long enough to quiver Kathryn's antenna. "Ever heard of a guy called Barney Ruditsky?"

"Sure."

"Who?" Leo asked.

"Ex-NYPD, now an LA private eye, but he's always got a vague gangland stink."

"What about him?" Kathryn asked.

"I've heard that DiMaggio has engaged him to tail Marilyn Monroe. You might want to pass it along to interested parties."

"Thank you. I will."

Leo got to his feet and shook Nelson's hand. "You've done a first-class job. Thank you."

"Yes." Kathryn felt unsteady on her feet and short of breath.

When Nelson shook her hand, he clamped the free one on top and gave it an extra squeeze. It was almost imperceptible, but it nearly undid Kathryn completely. His eyes followed Leo to the door, then darted back to Kathryn. His thoughts shone like neon: *I've never forgotten you.*

"Thank you so very much." She hated how her voice shook. "For everything, Mr. Hoyt."

"Please call me Nelson."

Leo opened the office door. A broad strip of afternoon sunlight cut across Nelson's desk, illuminating the swirl of emotions playing out on his face. Leo stepped out onto the sidewalk to smoke a cigarette. She looked over her shoulder; her eyes glistened with stifled tears. "Nelson—"

"I know." His voice was barely above a whisper.

She attempted a smile, but it collapsed before she got very far. Wrenching herself away, she followed Leo outside. *Don't look back, you fool. Move forward.* She unlocked her car and climbed in.

But she had failed to close the door of the Melrose Detective Agency. Through the gap she saw Nelson's silhouetted shadow outlined on the wall behind him. It looked like he'd hadn't moved since she walked out.

# CHAPTER 29

Gwendolyn pushed aside the drapes covering Sheila Stuart's second-story window and peered up Kilkea Drive.

"Anything?" Sheila asked from the sofa.

"What color did you say Marilyn's new Cadillac is?"

"White."

The streetlights came on. "She should be here by now."

Sheila laughed amiably. "Punctuality is a negotiable concept for her."

When Kathryn had come home with the news that Joe DiMaggio had hired Barney Ruditsky, she and Gwendolyn had debated telling Marilyn. Poor Billy Wilder was forced to juggle a budget, schedule, and release date while patiently coaxing a charming comedic performance out of a leading lady who was falling apart on the inside.

Zanuck had hauled Gwendolyn back into his office. "I know her marriage crashed and burned," he told her, "but isn't there anything you can say? Hell, if it helps, tell her, 'Zanuck's waiting for you to fail so let's show him.' Just get her in front of the cameras with a minimum of dents in that cotton candy ego of hers."

Gwendolyn and Kathryn had decided that with only a few more days left on *Itch*, they'd tell her about this Barney Ruditsky situation once the movie was in the can. After the wrap party, Gwendolyn had driven Marilyn home. Unsure what sort of reaction she was going to get, it had taken some effort to muster the courage.

Marilyn had laughed. "Is that who it is? For a famous PI, he's terrible at his job."

"You don't sound too upset," Gwendolyn had remarked.

"Honestly, it's like being in a French farce. One day, I was driving down Wilshire and the lights at Rodeo Drive turned red so I had to slam on the brakes. We nearly bumped fenders!"

Gwendolyn had let Marilyn stew over the knowledge that this wasn't some two-bit gumshoe. If someone as high profile as Ruditsky was trailing her, word was bound to leak out, prompting magazines like *Confidential* to come sniffing around.

"I need to put a stop to this."

Gwendolyn had been relieved to hear the determination in Marilyn's voice. "You really do."

"But I don't want to be alone when I confront Joe and Frank."

"Sinatra?" Since hearing Marcus's news, Frank's name sparked ferocious outrage inside Gwendolyn. "What's he got to do with all this?"

"They're practically joined at the hip these days. If a private eye has been hired, then Sinatra is probably connected somehow."

"So what do you want to do?"

"Turn the tables on the lot of them," Marilyn had replied with a giggle.

The light bulbs and neon along Sunset crowded a late-fall dusk. "For the world's most famous dumb blonde, you sure are a smart little so-and-so."

"Don't clue the menfolk in. We all need an edge."

When Gwendolyn had returned home to the Garden and told Kathryn what Marilyn had in mind, Kathryn had declared that she couldn't wait to get her "hands on that skinny little Sinatra bastard. I don't care if Barney Ruditsky is there." She had been furious when she'd learned that Marilyn's trap was set for Friday, November fifth. It was the same date as Suncrockerhouse's debut at the Pasadena Playhouse, which Leo had now organized to be broadcast live on KNX.

"Don't worry," Gwendolyn had told her, "I'll scream loud enough for both of us."

The next week had flown by, and now Gwendolyn was standing at Sheila's window. She let the curtain drop back into place and checked her watch. It was getting close to a quarter of eight. Technically, Marilyn wasn't late yet, but Kathryn's broadcast was due to start soon. "Mind if we switch stations?"

Sheila waved her hand toward her old wooden Philco sitting on the bookshelf behind her.

It was an accepted fact in Hollywood that the more famous an actor became, the fewer people could be trusted. The ones that Marilyn let into her circle were often brainy academic types who wore thick glasses and read Dostoyevsky—probably in the original Russian—and could quote Ibsen speeches verbatim.

Sheila Stuart was the opposite of Marilyn's highbrows. With a pleasant, wide-open face and a mass of curls neither brown nor blonde, Sheila was like thousands of other girls Gwendolyn had met over the years: pleasant, but not memorable; talented enough to be cast, but not in a role that would let her shine.

She was, however, loyal to Marilyn and had readily agreed to let her apartment be the place where tonight's confrontation would play out. Assuming, of course, that anything played out. If Marilyn failed to show, Gwendolyn would be doubly disappointed. She wouldn't be at the Pasadena Playhouse to calm a jittery Kathryn, and she'd be denied the opportunity to berate Frank Sinatra and badger him into undoing whatever he'd done to Marcus.

She adjusted the dial to KNX, where Perry Como was singing "Papa Loves Mambo."

A flare of headlights brushed Sheila's lace curtains and Gwendolyn pulled them aside to see Marilyn park her Cadillac under the streetlight out front. She closed the door with a jut of her hip and hurried up the path to Sheila's door, her heels clattering on the stone. Gwendolyn opened the door as Marilyn arrived at the front step.

"Did they take the bait?" Sheila asked.

Marilyn's eyes gleamed. "And how!"

Gwendolyn joined Sheila at the window. A gray Chrysler New Yorker was now parked behind Marilyn's car, shining like a newly minted quarter. Five men piled out of it and gathered on the curb. Marilyn peaked over their shoulders.

"The two next to Joe and Frank are Barney and his partner, Phil Irwin. And the guy in the dark suit—I think he's Sinatra's manager, Hank."

Backlit by the streetlight, DiMaggio and Sinatra stood face to face. DiMaggio's hands were a blur of wild gestures as he worked himself up into a fury. Sinatra nodded slowly, rhythmically, but made no other movement.

Ruditsky stood off to the side, studying the apartment building. His partner shouted the odd comment, but Gwendolyn couldn't make them out.

Sinatra's manager kept trying to insert himself between Joe and Frank. His left hand pointed to an object hidden by the shadow Joe cast along the lawn until Joe hoisted a long tube over his head.

Gwendolyn gasped. "Is that a baseball bat?"

Marilyn let out a little cry. "I can't watch this!" She backed away from the window.

Sinatra pulled at Joe's arm. The bat vaulted out of his hands and bounced onto the lawn. He wrenched himself free from Sinatra's grip, collected the bat, and marched across the grass.

"What's happening?" Marilyn asked.

"Joe's walking toward the building," Gwendolyn craned her neck "but he's going to the left."

Sheila gasped. "He's heading for the wrong door! They must think I live at 8120."

Marilyn pressed her hands together tight enough to crack knuckles. "Who lives there?"

"Her name's Florence and she wouldn't say boo to a butterfly."

"Is she home?"

A crack of splintering wood ripped the tranquil night air. Muffled shouting followed, then the crash of shattered glass.

Gwendolyn held her breath.

Shrieking erupted, piercing the walls and filling Sheila's apartment.

All five men disappeared inside, roaring like bulls.

Gwendolyn pulled out one of Marcus's old cameras from her purse. She raced down the tiled stairwell and into the front yard. A porch light hung over the doorway to 8120, where fractured chunks of painted wood were scattered across the steps and into the passageway beyond. A matching pair of dented brass hinges swung in the porch light, and Florence was still screaming.

Gwendolyn tugged the lens cap off Marcus's Leica and took a couple of shots.

"Joe! We've screwed up! Come ON!" Sinatra's voice blasted through the empty doorway. "Someone's bound to call the cops."

Gwendolyn melted into the shadows and waited until DiMaggio and Sinatra stepped over the wreckage in the passageway and onto the porch. She started taking photos as fast as she could. *Click! Click!* She wasn't even sure if there was film in the camera—it was enough that they saw her taking photos of them running from the wrong door, which the Yankee Clipper had reduced to toothpicks. *Click! Click!*

"Who's that?" Joe yelled. "Who are you taking my goddamned picture?"

Ruditsky and Irwin joined them. "Let's *GO!*" Ruditsky pulled Joe along by the elbow and Irwin did the same with Frank.

"YOU IDIOT!" Gwendolyn stepped into the circle cast by Florence's porch light. "A baseball bat? What did you think was going to happen tonight?"

"I—just—I—can't—"

Joe slunk toward the silver Chrysler.

Gwendolyn followed him. "You thought Hal Schaefer was in there, didn't you?" That was enough to get the guy to stop at the curb. "You thought you'd hack down the door and race into the boudoir, catch Hal and Marilyn in flagrante delicto—and then what? Bash their heads in? Was that the plan, Mister Great Big Hero to the Nation? Well, guess what?" She lifted Marcus's camera and snapped a bunch more shots. "That's why people get sent to jail."

"I only wanted to scare her!" DiMaggio bawled. "Since the divorce, I've been all—"

"Gwendolyn!" Sinatra's tone was love-ballad smooth. He stepped out from behind Joe's shadow and into the street lamp, wearing an affable smile. "Howdy, neighbor! I haven't seen you since—was it some party at the Garden of Allah? Maybe for Bogie and Bacall? Anyway, all this fuss, it's not how it looks. Trust me."

"TRUST YOU? I'm here because of you."

"Me?" Frank pressed his hands to his diaphragm. "What did *I* do?"

"It's what you did to Marcus Adler. He's stranded over there. Without a passport. In a foreign country. Where he barely knows anybody. What kind of miserable heel does that?"

"Whoa! Gwennie!" Frank maintained his convivial smile, though from the way it twitched at the ends, she could see it was disintegrating.

"Okay, so he took some pictures," Gwendolyn taunted. "Big whoop-de-doo. You know they were staged, don't you? It was Ava's idea. And that guy? He wasn't her Italian lover; he's Marcus's. And you fell for it like a fool."

Frank charged forward. "He shoulda said, 'No, Ava, no.' A guy doesn't do that sort of thing to another guy, especially when he knows a photo like that would end up on half the magazines around the world. Humiliating me. Mortifying me. Y'know what? I hope he rots over there for an eternity, because you don't cross Frank Sinatra like that and get away with it." He turned his back on her. "Come on, fellas, we're leaving."

Gwendolyn felt a pebble scuff her shoe. She picked it up and took aim. It struck him on the left shoulder, causing him to stumble off the curb.

He reeled around. "What the hell's the matter with you?"

"I want you to call whoever it was you called and get them to give Marcus back his passport."

"And the way to do that is throw goddamned rocks at me?"

Gwendolyn realized too late that lobbing missiles probably wasn't the smartest tactic. "And I want it to be the first call you make tomorrow."

"Jesus Christ! I used to wonder why you never landed a man. A looker like you—great face, knockout figure, you've even got a wicked sense of humor. I didn't get it until now that you ain't nothing but an ordinary, garden-variety, loud-mouthed shrew."

*What did he – ? I'm a – ? Did he just call me – ?*

"Wait a second! I know who you are." DiMaggio looked like he'd stepped in something that would be unpleasant to scrub off later. "You're that dressmaker." He made 'dressmaker' sound like 'streetwalker.' "You pretend to listen to Marilyn, and then you go running off to Zanuck and tell him everything. I bet the next phone call you make will be to the boss telling him about what happened tonight." He slapped the thick end of his bat into the palm of his left hand. "You think you're so damned smart."

Joe's snide speech was long enough for Gwendolyn to find her wits again. "Says the guy who battered down the wrong door." She pointed to the jumble of splintered wood behind her. "Poor Florence has every right to sue you. And if I can help, I will."

It was a good exit line, so she spun on her heel, but then a more cutting remark came to her.

"Oh, and for the record, Marilyn was here, but she took off out the back. Her last words to me were, 'Tell Joe that if he was hoping for a reconciliation, it died when I saw his baseball bat.' In other words, you completely blew it, you stupid, *stupid* schmuck."

A block away, rotating red-and-blue lights mottled the night. The five men raced for the Chrysler; Gwendolyn flew back inside. Sheila stood at the window, alone.

"Where's Marilyn?" Gwendolyn asked.

"Gone."

She collapsed onto the sofa with Sinatra's words stinging in her ear. *I used to wonder why you never landed a man.*

"You could do with a drink," Sheila said. "Vodka okay?"

"On the rocks. Make it a double."

*With princes like Sinatra and DiMaggio treating their women like dirt, or playthings, or trophies, why would I want to tie myself down? Just because I've never wanted to get married doesn't make me a shrew.*

Sheila emerged from the kitchen with a matching pair of filled tumblers. "Boy oh boy," she said, dropping onto the sofa, "you sure gave it to them down there."

Gwendolyn felt the adrenalin bleed out of her system, leaving her heavy-limbed. The spiraling red-and-blue police lights threw a bizarre show through the lace curtains. "The cops will be up here soon."

"I smell a coincidence." Sheila ripped open a fresh pack of Pall Malls. "Back in the forties when film noirs were getting popular, Barney Ruditsky was a technical consultant at Fox on account of how he used to work for the NYPD. Ten years later, he's tailing their biggest star." She kicked off her shoes. "Could be nothing."

Her vodka was the sort of top-shelf stuff that slid effortlessly down a shrew's throat. Gwendolyn threw back a mouthful and thought about how Sheila Stuart had failed to make the big time, or even the middle time. But she was capable of delivering a line like *Could be nothing* when she really meant *I'd bet my last dime that it's not.*

# CHAPTER 30

Kathryn was pouring her six A.M. coffee when she heard *The New York Times* thump her doorstep. She didn't get up from her table until the *LA Times* joined it. She was halfway to the door when she heard a timid knock and "It's just me."

Gwendolyn stepped inside, holding Kathryn's papers. She dropped them on the table as Kathryn poured her a cup.

"Tell me everything. Did DiMaggio show? Did he see Marilyn? Did they reconcile—"

"Everything happened when your broadcast was on so I didn't get to hear anything. It went off okay, didn't it?"

By the time the curtain went up, Leo's extravaganza had included chorus girls dressed as boxes of Betty Crocker cake mix, a rotating Westinghouse refrigerator, and a live band that had almost drowned her out, which was a relief.

"Nothing dropped on my head, and nobody fell off the stage. I call that a win. The suits are hard to read, but they appeared to be happy."

Gwendolyn sighed. "When it comes to men, who knows what's going through their tiny little pea brains?" She crossed her arms. "Tell me, honestly, am I a garden-variety, loud-mouthed shrew?"

Kathryn would have laughed if not for the earnest look on Gwendolyn's face. "What the hell happened last night?"

"I'm not, am I?"

"Did DiMaggio call you that? He might be a world-class baseball player, but given how he's treated Marilyn, he's also a world-class cretin, so who cares—"

"It was Frank."

"I hope you gave it to him with both guns blazing."

Gwendolyn smiled. "You'd have been proud of me. I even threw a rock at him."

"You didn't!

"It was really just a pebble, but Trevor Bergin never had better aim."

Kathryn slotted two slices of bread into her toaster. "Start at the beginning and leave out nothing."

Her jaw dropped open little by little as Gwendolyn relayed the disgraceful events of the previous night.

"I can't believe I missed it!"

"I wish I had," Gwendolyn said.

"You know it's not true, don't you? That business about being a shrew."

Gwendolyn gave off an evasive shrug. "Getting married wasn't something I yearned for. Does that make me some kind of freak?"

Kathryn clamped her hand over Gwendolyn's. "Who cares what that skinny little twerp thinks? He's lost one of the most beautiful women on the planet, so who's he to hand out marital advice? And the same goes for Joe DiMaggio. How was Marilyn during all this?"

"You should have seen her when we heard Joe bust that door down. I thought she'd faint."

"You remember what's happening this afternoon, don't you?" It was the day Winchell was planning to sneak onto the Fox lot to interview Marilyn on the *Seven Year Itch* subway set.

Gwendolyn nodded.

"Do you think she'll show?"

"Marilyn's become so erratic, it's hard to pin her down." Gwendolyn drained the last of her coffee. "I'd better get going. Charles has petitioned Zanuck to let me assist on Bette's *Virgin Queen* costumes. They're as complicated as hell and we're slipping behind."

"What happened to you being Zanuck's special-projects assistant?"

"Lately I've been doing trivial stuff that anyone could do, so I told Charles to ask for me. I don't want to waste an hour in case Zanuck changes his mind."

After Gwendolyn left, Kathryn shoved her dishes into the sink and flipped open the *LA Times*. It was a slow news day when the big story was how the 100th citrus tree had been removed from the site Walt Disney was excavating for his planned amusement park.

She shoved the paper aside, turned to *The New York Times*, and gripped the edge of her kitchen counter when she read the headline.

*EXECUTION DATE SET FOR*
*SUPPLIER OF SECRETS TO NAZIS*
*Danford to face electric chair in February*

All this time, she'd assumed that Danford got a prison sentence, not a death sentence, so she thought she had time. Lots and lots of it. But now she had less than four months and the exoneration process could take years.

Halfway down the page was a photo of her father leaving the courthouse, his wrists manacled together, his head bowed and turned away from the cameras.

*I should have been doing more. I should have flown to New York and cornered Winchell. Or to Boston and demanded to see my father's file. Or Washington and pleaded my case to Hoover. They knew it was a frame-up. They have to serve justice. It's their job.*

A sharp knock on her front door startled her.

"GWENNIE!" She pulled at the brass doorknob. "You saw the paper?"

Frank Sinatra's lids drooped over bloodshot eyes, his hair wild and uncombed. He ran a hand over two-day growth; the stink of a thousand cigarettes radiated from him. "Gwendolyn's already told you, huh?"

"Yep."

"I screwed up. Real bad. I need to make amends. I know, I know. I tried to do the right thing. Honest." He made the sign of the cross. "But the whole situation got out of hand." He stepped past her.

"I didn't invite you in."

"Don't make me stand out there where half the Garden can hear us."

Kathryn slammed her door with all the force she could muster. "I'm sure they heard *that*."

"I haven't had a hit since *From Here to Eternity*, and that opened a year ago. I've got a lot riding on this new movie with Doris Day."

"You land on my doorstep at six in the morning to talk about *your career*?"

"Hear me out. I need *Young at Heart* to open big, but after last night I'm scared I'll be dragged through the mud once word gets out."

"Maybe you should have thought of that *before* you jumped into the mud."

His ears reddened. "Someone had to talk him down. None of those other slobs were doing it. But when Joe gets mad, he gets crazy mad. You gotta believe me, I tried to stop it."

"For crying out loud, Frank, I'm not mad about what happened last night—wait, yes, I am, but that's not all."

He blanched. "The Marcus thing?"

"YES, THE MARCUS THING!"

"Gwendolyn's already ripped into me about that."

"She told me your reply: 'You don't cross Frank Sinatra and get away with it.' Of all the unmitigated ego—"

"One lecture is quite enough, thank you," Frank bit back. "I sure as hell don't need yet another one from yet another furious dame who—"

"—who you've ambushed asking for a favor to prop up your failing career." She pressed him against the wall of her foyer with a sharp fingernail. "Marcus Adler is my best friend, and you screwed him over."

"He had it coming. His photos wrecked my marriage."

"No, Frank, *you* wrecked your marriage. *You* had it coming. But you used Marcus as a scapegoat. He's stranded in a foreign country with no proper identification and roadblocked at every turn."

She rolled the *Times* into a truncheon and brought it down on his head.

"HEY!" He tried to swat it down but was fighting fatigue.

"I am sick—" *whack!*

"—and tired—" *whack!*

"—of men like you—" *whack!*

"—who think they can do—" *whack!*

"—whatever they want—" *whack!*

"—just because they're men!"

"Christ, Kathryn!" Frank yelled. "Get a hold of yourself."

She backhanded the *Times* across his chest.

"You're all the same!" *Whack!*

"You!" *Whack!*

"DiMaggio!" *Whack!*

"Zanuck!" *Whack!*

"Winchell!" *Whack!*

"Voss! *Whack!*

"Hoyt!" *Whack!*

"Enough already!" He wrestled the bludgeon away from her and flung it across the room. "Who the hell is Hoyt and what the hell's *his* crime?"

She pressed her forehead against the wall. It was still cool from the previous night. "Never mind. Not your problem."

"Is he a problem I can help with?"

She opened her eyes and mustered a droll look. "Your sort of help, I can do without."

He pulled his chin away as though she'd punched him in the jaw. "I deserved that."

"Count yourself lucky I wasn't holding a hammer."

"How do I make amends?"

Frank sounded sincere but he'd had years of practice putting across mushy ballads. *He's got that movie coming out,* she warned herself. *He needs a hit.*

Kathryn headed for the Chesterfields on her kitchen counter. *I can't believe Hoyt popped out of my mouth like that.* "Marcus has been through so much," she said, lighting up. "Why did you have to kick him while he was—"

"Tell me how I can fix it." Frank helped himself to one of Kathryn's Chesterfields and started tapping it against the back of his left hand. "And don't tell me to call whoever I called in the first place. The—guy's—dead." His admission came out in strangled syllables.

"What did he die of?"

"Don't ask."

Kathryn dropped onto a chair and rested her head on her palms. The surprise attack with Winchell on the *Seven Year Itch* set this afternoon was more than enough to deal with; she didn't need this crap, too. "Are we talking about the Italian Mafioso? Because I've been hearing rumors."

"Remember three seconds ago when I said don't ask?"

Kathryn had had enough gangland dealings with Bugsy Siegel, and wasn't prepared to go another round.

"So you can't set things right for Marcus?"

"I'm saying it's not as easy as making a phone call."

"You better go to Plan B."

"There isn't one."

"You need to make one."

"And if I do, will you plug *Young at Heart*?"

*Everybody's always selling*. "Let's see: my best friend's future versus a plug for your movie. Yeah. Sounds fair."

The chair scraped across the tile as Frank lumbered to his feet. "I'll see what I can do."

Kathryn waited for a full two minutes before she opened her front door. Feeling slightly paranoid, she wanted to be sure Frank really had left. The November night chill still lingered in the air as the Garden of Allah stirred to life. She waved to Marcus's sister, who was walking past Gwendolyn's tulip bed. That girl must be doing well at Columbia—it seemed like she left for the studio earlier and earlier these days. And those tulips! They'd taken their time to appear and had been pretty to have around, and would soon be pushing up a fresh crop.

The vision of *The New York Times* headline jumped into her head. February was only four months away.

* * *

Kathryn walked into Stage Ten on the Fox lot and onto an exact replica of the corner of Lexington and 52nd Street where the world's most famous subway grate ran along the sidewalk. She scraped her heel on the grit that Wilder's art department had strewn over the phony concrete.

"Realistic, isn't it?"

Marilyn was dressed in a pair of nondescript brown slacks and a loose-fitting cream cashmere sweater. She had wiped her face clear of the heavy filming makeup that would have hidden the puffiness around her eyes and the pasty hue of her skin. The ensemble struck Gwendolyn as surprisingly casual for someone who had an interview with America's most influential columnist.

"Aren't you a little early?" Marilyn asked.

"Tomorrow's column wrote itself, so here I am."

In truth, Kathryn had arrived at the office too distracted to work, so she'd slogged out her column like Livingston through the jungle, cobbling together a bunch of emergency items, and called it a day.

"Did Gwendolyn tell you what happened?" Marilyn asked.

"Must have been awful."

"The worst."

"I had Sinatra on my doorstep this morning."

"What a rat."

"Claimed he was trying to talk Joe out of it. For what it's worth, he seemed contrite."

"Okay, so he's a contrite rat, but he's still a rat."

Marilyn stepped onto the subway grate and looked down through the gaps to where wind machines would blow her white dress around her waist. "There are some good ones, I suppose."

"You mean men?"

She dug the tip of her shoe into one of the slits in the grate. "Leo's one of the good guys, isn't he?"

"He is." *But The One Who Got Away has come back and now I don't know what I want.*

"It gives a girl hope to know there are some around."

"Speaking of rats, are you ready for Winchell?"

"Is anybody ever ready for the king of the rats?" Marilyn let out a mournful sigh. "This interview is a three-way pact between Wilder, Zanuck, and Winchell. Filming that scene in New York was a great boost for the movie, so Wilder benefits. Winchell inserted himself into the drama by egging Joe on until he blew a gasket, so Winchell benefits. Meanwhile, Zanuck scores maximum publicity for his star, his director, his picture, and his studio, so he benefits. But what about me?"

Marilyn sauntered over to the shop window, where an elaborate display of paste jewels shone in the lights.

"Those were *my* panties on show," she declared. "*My* marriage falling apart. What do *I* get out of it?" She thought for a moment. "If Winchell wants to use me, he gets the bare minimum."

"Good for you. Don't let the rats get you down." Kathryn joined her at the window. "But what are you going to say if Winchell asks you about last night?"

Marilyn let out a breathless squeak. "Do you think Joe would've blabbed?"

"Stiff drinks loosen lips."

Marilyn bunched her hands together. "I don't know that I can do this. He's too intimidating."

"Miss Monroe?" A security guard stood at the entryway into the soundstage. "You wanted to know when Mr. Winchell drove on to the lot."

Marilyn's eyes turned wild with panic.

"Where is he now?" Kathryn asked the guard.

"I can see him from here, walking in this direction."

Kathryn thanked the guy and shooed him away.

"What if he brings up last night?" Marilyn's voice was now a hoarse whisper. "I'll fall apart."

"No, you won't," Kathryn said, soothingly. "You're an actress; you know how to fake it. Tell him that your personal life needs to stay personal. You—"

"I can't have this conversation right now. I'm still shaking like an earthquake from last night." Marilyn started to back away. "You came here to confront him; he's all yours." She disappeared behind the liquor store.

Kathryn's plan was to lurk behind the *Seven Year Itch* set until Marilyn gave a pre-arranged signal. Every time she'd stood up to Hoover or Wilkerson or Hearst it was for a high-flying principle, but this time it was about as personal as it could get and she felt her determination wilt around the edges.

"Jesus fucking Christ," Winchell barked. "Zanuck promised me Monroe. Is this an ambush?"

"Not exactly."

"What does that mean?"

"It means I wouldn't be here if you'd returned any of my messages, but instead you give me the silent treatment. I need to hear what you've tracked down about my father. I know about Amagansett and Operation Pastorius, and I know that his FBI file is missing. I assume you have it?"

Winchell started fanning himself with a battered Homburg. "Yeah, I've got it."

Until now, Kathryn had pinned her hopes onto a slippery handful of ifs and maybes. But now she knew there really was a file, and everything she needed to help set her father free was inside it, and it was in the hands of someone she trusted less than Jack the Ripper.

Winchell ushered her into the recessed doorway of the liquor store even though nobody was around to overhear them.

"I have a contact at the FBI."

"The disgruntled employee with a grudge to bear?"

"I don't know how you know that, but yes. And he told me that I'm not the only one asking about Danford. I didn't want the information I saw in the file to get into anyone else's hands, and I knew you wouldn't, either, so I took it."

Kathryn had always prided herself on her ability to distinguish between authenticity and bullshit, but today it failed her. She wasn't sure what to make of this version of Walter Winchell: kind, considerate, selfless. Was he putting one over on her? What was the end game? Expose her as the illegitimate daughter of a convicted felon? Or was this the real deal?

"Did the disgruntled FBI guy say who's been snooping around?"

Winchell nodded until the caution in his eyes capitulated into resignation. "Robert Harrison."

The last name Kathryn wanted to hear right now was Harrison's—he was the notorious owner of *Confidential*, the smutty rag that ignored truth in favor of giving the insatiable public more of what they thought they wanted, regardless of how it destroyed careers and reputations.

Winchell continued, "That odious little turd is not someone you want sniffing around your private business."

"I thought the two of you were the best of pals."

"He likes to think we are, and that suits me. For now."

"Why not just tell me that? I already said you could have the credit."

"Because Harrison isn't above tapping my telephone, or intercepting my letters and telegrams."

Kathryn's first instinct was to write him off as paranoid, but the guy wasn't without enemies.

"Harrison knows I've been working on a big story. He keeps badgering me about it."

"It must be killing him."

"I need to put him off the scent."

Whatever had strained their friendship must have been serious if Winchell wanted to distract Harrison from a big story. Kathryn saw that keeping those two apart was to her advantage.

"I want you to give me something," he said. "And it needs to be big."

Kathryn wanted to laugh in his face. "Stories like that don't fall into your lap like oranges off a tree."

"But you're Kathryn Massey." His tone had turned supercilious—more like the Walter Winchell she hated. "You've always got an orange or two."

She looked at him blankly. "Is that what you think?"

"Don't insult me with this Rebecca of Sunnypuke Farm act."

"I'm sorry but I don't—"

"What happened last night?"

"This is LA. Something happens every night."

Winchell ripped off his eyeglasses and massaged the bridge of his nose. "DiMaggio and I had plans for a drink at the Beverly Hills Hotel. He arrived two hours late, completely at sixes and sevens. Could barely keep the conversation going. I asked him what was wrong but he kept changing the subject."

"I'm not a sports writer," Kathryn replied. "I wouldn't know the first thing—"

"He's separating from Monroe, who I was supposed to meet here, but instead I find you looking distraught. I want you to tell me what happened—and don't leave out a single detail."

Winchell was too astute to fool for very long. "It's not my story to tell," she said.

"Yes it is."

"I wasn't there."

"Since when has that stopped either of us?" He bored into her with his pitiless eyes. "Isn't your father's freedom worth more than some lover's tiff?"

"It was more than a tiff!" Kathryn looked down at her shoes. They were scuffed from the dirt and grime that the art department had applied to their Lexington Avenue reproduction.

*Please forgive me, Marilyn. It's for my father.*

* * *

Leo already had a double Four Roses waiting for Kathryn when she arrived at Musso and Frank Grill.

She slipped into the red-upholstered booth. "How did you know I'd need one of these?"

"I read *The New York Times*." They clinked glasses. "I'd have called, but I had so much to deal with after the show last night."

Standing on the stage of the Pasadena Playhouse seemed like eons ago. "Not my favorite newspaper headline." She took another whiskey slug and tried to catch the eye of a passing waiter.

"I told him to line up another one as soon as you sat down."

*It's like Marilyn said – you're one of the good guys.*

He crinkled his nose. "You look like you have something to share."

The waiter set down her second Four Roses and removed the empty glass.

*I've betrayed Marilyn so that someone as heinous as Robert Harrison can be put off the scent. Maybe someday I'll tell you, but not today.*

Leo lifted his martini. "Here's to us."

Their glasses clinked gently over the gypsy violin music. Kathryn tipped the glass to her lips. Something touched them. She held it up. A twinkle caught the overhead light.

"What the hell— " Kathryn dipped her finger into the whiskey and fished out a gold ring topped with a marquise-cut diamond ring.

Leo took it from her and rubbed it dry with his napkin, then held it between his fingers. "Will you marry me?"

Kathryn thought of her mother. She'd only had one love, and circumstances had driven her clear across the country, where she'd spent the rest of her life alone.

*Don't be like her. Don't turn away when happiness is right in front of you, holding an engagement ring. Nelson Hoyt was yesterday. He was a lost opportunity. And he's too late. Look at that brave smile. If Leo can take a leap of faith, you can, too.*

Kathryn smiled. "Yes," she said. "I will."

# CHAPTER 31

Gwendolyn drove up the main gate of the Fox lot and waved to the security guard.

"Got a message for you, Miss Brick." He passed a slip of paper through her window. "Marked *URGENT*." She thanked him and headed toward the executive tower.

Her "Assistant in Charge of Special Projects" title sounded grand, and her increased salary was helping to shrink the hefty sum she owed the bank, but Zanuck's idea of a special project was somewhat elastic. Mostly it was organizing outfits for stars like June Allyson, Lauren Bacall, and Arlene Dahl to wear at premieres, or shepherding visiting VIPs around the lot.

Sometimes he called on her to drive a top-secret script to the home of an actor or agent so they could read it while she waited. During the filming of *Désirée*, Zanuck had ordered Gwendolyn to look after Merle Oberon after she'd dozed off under a sunlamp, forcing her director to redesign her close-ups until the sunburn healed.

When Zanuck had nothing for her, she helped Billy Travilla or Charles LeMaire, or the woman who now did Loretta Young's wardrobe, which gave her a chance to catch up with Judy, who was still drifting around the studio.

What made today's directive different was Zanuck's own scrawl. That was a first.

She exited the elevator, flicking the message across the tops of her fingernails. When Zanuck's secretary, Irma, spotted her, she motioned for Gwendolyn to go right in.

The first rule of seeing Zanuck inside his domain was: Don't sit down unless specifically invited. She stood on the lush carpet, breathing lightly, until he was ready to address her.

Behind him stood mockups of forthcoming posters for *There's No Business Like Show Business*, *Prince of Players*, and *The Racers*. The last movie wouldn't be coming out until well into 1955, but it starred Bella Darvi, who was about to jet off to Rome for the opening of *The Egyptian*.

Whenever she saw Bella's name, Gwendolyn thought of Marcus. As the autumn leaves began to fall across Los Angeles, his letters had subsided to a trickle.

"So," Zanuck closed a script with a sharp slap, "today's the day." He turned around to see what had caught Gwendolyn's attention. "You don't like the poster?"

Gwendolyn presented what she called her "Zanuck smile": bland, sweet, detached. "Today is what day?"

"What were you thinking just now?"

"Bella's all set for her trip to Europe."

"Great job on managing her wardrobe. She's going to make the biggest splash Rome has seen since Cleopatra."

"Are you sending her there by herself?"

"If you're angling for a free trip, forget it."

"I was thinking about my friend Marcus Adler," Gwendolyn replied. "He knows the lay of the land pretty well."

Zanuck frowned. "Adler's still there?"

"He could escort Bella around town. Look out for her. Look after her."

Zanuck nodded thoughtfully, tapping his blue pencil on the *Carousel* script in front of him. "That's a good idea. Set it up as soon as you can."

"Will do." Gwendolyn waved the note. "You sent for me?"

"Today's the day Gable starts work on *Soldier of Fortune*."

"That's quite a coup," Gwendolyn said. It was the sort of ego-stroking she'd learned men—even astute ones like Zanuck—found irresistible. "Dory Schary must be steaming mad."

He emerged from his vast desk and planted his butt on the edge.

"Back in 1947 when we out-grossed MGM for the first time, Mayer gave me such a pile of shit about it being a blip on the radar, and that they would be back on top. I vowed I'd do whatever it took to steal the King of Hollywood from them. I knew I had to play the long game. I had my strategies and I put them in place like a trail of candy, luring him onto the Fox lot. And here we are."

"Edward Dmytryk, too," Gwendolyn said. The director of *Soldier of Fortune* was one of the Hollywood Ten, but he had rehabilitated his career by testifying to HUAC. So this movie was also Zanuck's "Screw you!" to the blacklist, which was another reason why Gwendolyn had brought up Marcus's name. "It's a big day."

"I'm gathering together a welcome party to make a fuss when he arrives. You know, the usual movie star ego stuff."

"I don't know that Gable's the sort who responds to—"

"I want you to be a sheepdog."

"Excuse me?"

"Discreetly, of course. There's going to be at least twenty people there, so I need someone to herd them together. Not too close, but not too spread out, either."

"Okay." Gwendolyn wasn't sure if she had any herding skills.

"But before that whole circus starts, I wanted to talk about Marilyn."

*This is why I've really been summoned.*

"If I can get the King and Queen of Hollywood together in the same picture, the marquee value alone would be worth a couple of million in box office. I had to give him co-star approval, so I want you to convince him to replace Susan Hayward with Marilyn."

"But they start in about an hour."

"The public only cares about the finished product. A week or so to get Marilyn up to speed is nothing in the long run."

Gwendolyn went to ask him if that was a wise move considering Gable was in his fifties and Marilyn was only twenty-eight. But she kept her trap shut when she realized the age gap was roughly the same between Zanuck and Darvi.

"I hate to be the one to break it to you, boss, but Marilyn has hightailed it to New York and she's not likely to return any time soon."

"New York? What the hell's she doing there? Jesus Christ, why didn't you tell me?"

"I assumed—"

"Your job isn't to assume. It's to apprise me of any major decisions Marilyn makes that might affect my shooting schedule."

"Including pictures she isn't cast in?"

"INCLUDING EVERYTHING!" He walloped the top of his desk. "You should have kept a shorter leash on her."

"She's a grown woman, not a *CHIHUAHUA*." Gwendolyn could feel the thin ice cracking below her feet but she didn't care. *I'll find some other way to repay the bank.* "Besides, it's your own fault."

"What is?"

She plunked her handbag onto his desk. "Aren't you the one who suggested DiMaggio use Barney Ruditsky to trail Marilyn?"

His smile was part surprise, part impressed, part arrogance. "I suggested it to Sinatra."

"Well, it worked out peachy-keen, didn't it?"

"How do you mean?"

"The night of the fifth? At Sheila Stewart's apartment?"

Blank face.

Gwendolyn laid out for him the events of the previous week. "So you see," she finished up, "you're going to have to work hard to get her back to Hollywood."

He rubbed his hand along the rigid line of his jaw. "Who else knows about this?"

*You mean apart from Kathryn Massey, Walter Winchell, and probably Robert Harrison by now?* "It was just us three girls in the apartment, and poor old Florence downstairs. Beyond that, I couldn't say."

"Shit! *SHIT!*" Zanuck returned to his side of the desk. "Why is this business so hard?"

"You'd prefer to run a paintbrush factory?" Gwendolyn asked.

"THAT'S NOT FUNNY!" Zanuck exploded. "Everyone thinks it's easy massaging egos, juggling schedules, begging for bank loans, staying up all night to fix a story only to be told the next morning that your leading lady doesn't like it because the rain storm is going to muss her hair."

Gwendolyn heard a piercing crack in the ice beneath her. "I'm sorry, boss. I didn't mean to—"

"I brought you in as a special assistant. I never said, nor did I imply, that the job came with the privilege of telling me I've fucked up."

"Yes, boss."

"And quit calling me that. I want to hear 'sir' or 'Mister Zanuck.'"

"Yes, sir."

He started straightening piles of papers that didn't need tidying. "As far as *Soldier of Fortune* goes, I'm assigning you to keep Gable happy during the shoot."

The almost imperceptible way he hesitated before the word "happy" set Gwendolyn on edge. "What do you mean, 'keep him happy'?"

"Whatever he needs, take care of it."

That pause. *Whatever he . . . needs.* "Could you be more specific?"

"I had to move heaven and earth to get Gable here, and I want to ensure he's glad that he signed on with us. You're a woman—you know what it takes to keep a man satisfied."

Zanuck's office door swung open and Edward Dmytryk walked in with the studio's head of P.R., along with a pair of flunkies and a photographer. Gwendolyn slipped on a bland smile and retreated to a wall while Zanuck greeted them with a round of handshakes. They were going over the morning's plan when Hedda Hopper arrived.

Unlike Louella Parsons, who was now well into her seventies, strongly conservative Hedda was hitting her stride amid the post-war, post-HUAC, post-McCarthy, mid-Eisenhower era. Consequently, Zanuck couldn't afford to piss her off. He reassured her that it was wonderful to see her, and that her inclusion in "our little welcome wagon" delighted him.

Although Hedda had contributed to the demise of her store, Gwendolyn wasn't sure Hedda knew what she looked like. In case she did, Gwendolyn tried to fade into the background, mulling over Zanuck's last statement.

*You know what it takes to keep a man satisfied.*

She wanted to think that Zanuck meant *Make his coffee how he likes it and ensure a supply of his favorite cigarettes is always on hand,* but those words—"keep a man satisfied." It was hard not to interpret them any way but horizontally.

* * *

Zanuck's eighteen-member cheer squad applauded when Gable walked onto the Chinese restaurant set.

Zanuck grasped Gable's hand. "Welcome! Welcome!" He sounded like a circus ringmaster playing to a crowd of thousands. "We're so pleased to have you here on what I know will be a thrilling picture. Let me introduce you around." He presented his prize pig to Dmytryk and Hedda and the principal actors: Susan Hayward, Michael Rennie, Gene Barry, Anna Sten.

Gable had arrived on his own: no agent or assistant, publicity person, manager, or hangers-on. If he was anxious about making his first picture since escaping MGM, Gwendolyn saw no signs of it. He exuded all the charm and self-confidence that had made him a major screen star for the past quarter-century.

"And finally," Zanuck said, "this is Gwendolyn Brick. You know each other, I believe."

Gable smiled. "We do." He gave a slight bow. "Nice to see you."

"Gwendolyn is the girl I mentioned," Zanuck said.

"She is?"

"If you need anything, Gwendolyn is your point man—er, point girl, as the case may be."

Gable continued to stare at Gwendolyn, more than a little disconcerted, as Zanuck turned back to the gathering. "It's time I left things in Ed's capable hands. I wish you all well!"

He swept out of the soundstage like an emperor.

Gwendolyn ran after him. "What am I supposed to do? Hang around in there?"

"Yes," he barked. "You're to do exactly that."

* * *

Gwendolyn took a seat at one of the tables on the Chinese restaurant set and tried to look interested as Dmytryk led his cast through their first table-read of the script.

If she'd known she was going to be sitting around for hours on end, she could have brought along a sewing project, or written a letter to Marcus, or finished the new Edna Ferber book, *Giant*.

But no.

She was a well-paid piece of *objet d'art* waiting until somebody wanted something that she wasn't sure she was willing to give.

*Surely he didn't promise Clark that he could just . . . After all, their womanizer reputations aren't unwarranted. But I'm forty-four years old, for goodness sake. If Zanuck was going to offer up the services of a companion, surely he'd have enlisted any one of the kewpies under contract.*

Gwendolyn tried to put questions she couldn't answer out of her mind and focused instead on watching the cast work through each page, stopping to clarify a motivation or polish a line. The tactic worked for short intervals but her thoughts kept straying.

Clark's first wife had been seventeen years older than him, and so was his second. Lombard had been younger, but Sylvia Ashley, whom Gable had divorced a couple of years ago, was five or six years older than Gwendolyn.

When the company broke for lunch, Clark wandered away from the table. Gwendolyn expected Dmytryk would corral him, but his cinematographer waylaid him. Gwendolyn marched up to Clark as he was putting on the jacket of his impeccable gabardine three-piece suit. "I imagine you're hungry?"

Those famous Gable dimples dented his face as he grinned. "Famished."

"The commissary makes out like it's French, but it's more like American-French. Let me take you there."

He lifted his hand in the direction of a cabin standing in a corner of the soundstage. It was painted an unobtrusive dark blue; Gwendolyn hadn't even noticed it. "I ordered lunch for two to be served in my dressing room."

A combined living room/dining room made up nearly half the space. The other half contained a bathroom and makeup table, and beyond that a bedroom with a double bed. A pair of large paintings of Half-Dome at Yosemite and Old Faithful at Yellowstone filled the back wall.

"Cozy," Gwendolyn commented.

"It was Zanuck's idea," Clark said, "but I chose the décor."

She ran her finger down the wall that separated the living room from the bedroom. "What color do you call this paint?"

"Californian Avocado. I find it calming. If Zanuck's going to the trouble to build me a whole bungalow, I figured I might as well get what I want."

The dining table was set for two: Caesar salad, cold meats, cottage cheese, and sliced tomatoes.

Clark pulled out a chair for Gwendolyn. "You have the whole menu to choose from," she said. "Nothing hot?"

"Not during the daytime. That's dinner to my way of thinking, but if you'd prefer a hot dish, I could call—"

"Mr. Gable—"

"When it's just us, the name is Clark."

"Clark, it appears that *I* am the person you call when you want a hot dish."

A warm blush prickled her face. If a program of pre-war love songs hadn't been playing on the cathedral radio set in the corner, the silence mushrooming between them would have been unbearable. He broke it first.

"Can we clear the air?"

Gwendolyn clutched her fork like a spear. "I sure hope so."

"I was told to expect an assistant to attend to my every need, but I didn't know it would be you. I must say, though, I was pleasantly surprised."

"That's very nice of you to say."

"I'll always be grateful for how you organized Judy to be at Ciro's that night. I was able to watch her for hours."

"I'm glad I could make it happen. I could bring her to the set."

"No! I'd be self-conscious with her around. And I'm insecure enough working at a new studio."

"You? Insecure? I find that very hard to believe."

"Because I'm Clark Gable?"

His withering tone made her realize that the man sitting opposite her could play self-possessed newspapermen, aviators, and big-game hunters better than anybody else in the business, but that didn't mean he was one himself.

She finished her final bite of Caesar salad and pushed the plate away. "My instructions are to do whatever is necessary to keep you happy. So if there's anything I can do to alleviate anxiety, let me know."

The smile that surfaced on Gable's face was hard to read. Smug without arrogance, relief tinged with expectation.

"Including . . .?" He glanced at the bed in the room behind him, then turned back.

Conflicting emotions avalanched over Gwendolyn, stifling her breath, choking off her voice.

*I'm not a hooker. I'm not a chess pawn. I have a choice. I can say no. I can get up and walk out. But Zanuck'll fire me. And then what? Go out and get a regular job for a quarter of the dough? Spend the next ten years paying off my debt? Or I could go in there. Sure I could. I'm not married. It's not like I haven't had casual flings. I've been around. But this is different. It feels like business. Will I walk out afterwards feeling like a cheap slut?*

Gable finished his salad. He pulled the napkin from his lap and slowly wiped it across his lips.

*On the other hand, you've got Clark Gable sitting in front of you, offering a tumble in the hay. Thousands – no, millions – of women would have jumped as soon as he said "including." What the hell are you waiting for? Zanuck's permission? I don't think so. This one's for ME.*

Gwendolyn uncrossed her legs and pushed away from the table. "They give us an hour for lunch," she told him. "We've still got forty-eight minutes."

# CHAPTER 32

Marcus stood in the middle of the Piazza Adriana on the outskirts of Tivoli and surveyed the church facing him. Soaring four stories high, it held a ten-foot oval stained-glass window depicting a monk dressed in a brown Franciscan habit with a golden aura extending from his shaved scalp. In one hand he held a small child bearing a similar aura; a bouquet of lilies rested in the other. A pair of bell towers rose overhead with pyramid-shaped roofs painted fire-engine red.

St. Anthony was the patron saint of the poor, so Marcus had been picturing a squat building of dreary bricks, disintegrating speck by speck as penniless monks fed the unfortunate with thin gruel and three-day-old bread. But the marble façade depicting St. Anthony's life, its wooden doors carved with flowers, trees, and plants, with brass bells polished to a high sheen, wasn't what Marcus had been picturing, but that was okay. This majestic church might have intimidated him if he'd taken this trip a month ago, but he was different now.

* * *

Errol's question—*Are you hanging onto your past?*—had preoccupied Marcus for days. He hated to admit it, but the answer was "Yes."

Domenico was everything Marcus wanted from a boyfriend: loving, funny, honest, uninhibited, tactile when they were alone, and ingenious at finding ways to express his affection when they weren't. But it was Oliver who continued to haunt his dreams and Marcus was getting sick of it.

"Forget about him," Trevor had said. "Let him rot in his scratchy monk's robe."

It sounded like sensible advice, but every time Marcus sat down at a café, the waiter would bring a basket of bread and a bottle of olive oil with the Franciscan monk on the label. He would stare at the damned thing wondering, *Am I not letting go of my history, or is it not letting go of me?*

After Gwendolyn's letter had arrived, with the news about DiMaggio and Sinatra busting down the wrong door and how she'd torn into Sinatra, he'd lived in daily hope that those two Immigration department officials would come knocking.

Days ticked by. Nobody knocked.

Rumors of Sinatra's connection with the mafia had been circulating Hollywood. Domenico had mentioned that Napoleon Conti had mafia connections too. Was it such a stretch to draw a line connecting Sinatra to Napoleon?

The longer he'd dwelled on it, the angrier he'd got. Soon, he was throwing cigarette lighters across a room when they ceased to work properly, and yanking typewriter ribbons out of their spools when *Horatius at the Bridge* refused to coalesce into a workable screenplay.

His dreams had grown more intense. In a particularly heated one, he and Sinatra were standing on the Garden's diving board having a sword fight using billiard cues made from rigid rattlesnakes. If they fell into the pool, the snakes would come alive. Halfway through the dream, Sinatra had turned into Oliver, and Marcus had become doubly angry and fought doubly hard to force Sinatra-Oliver into the water.

Anger-fueled fantasies filled his waking hours. He would imagine pounding on the monastery doors until they permitted him inside. They would bring Oliver to see him and Marcus would unshackle his frustrations.

*What was so wrong with us that you had to go and join a monastery?*

*Did a life without relationships, without sex, without companionship, seem like the better choice than a life with me?*

He would scream as he cornered Oliver in some over-decorated church.

*How could you say goodbye in a goddamned note?*

*After everything we'd been through, you ended us with a Dear John letter?*

The depth of his fury alarmed him, but when he thought of Oliver, a steaming geyser of resentment would rise inside him.

*I deserved better. I want an explanation and I'm here to get it.*

Every time he acted out the scene in his head, it ended with Oliver dissolving in guilty tears, begging for forgiveness. *You're nuts*, he would tell himself later. *Even if that's Oliver on the label, the chances that he actually lives at St Anthony's are dim.*

So like any man in his position, he hid this emotional turmoil from his boyfriend under a steady flow of lunchtime prosecco, afternoon whiskey, chianti with dinner, and brandy afterwards.

Marcus knew what he should do: *Jump on that goddamned bus to Tivoli and pound on that goddamned monastery door and insist on seeing the goddamned guy on their goddamned olive oil bottle*. But did he want Oliver's final image of him to be angry-eyed and spittle-mouthed? The bus ride would have to wait, he'd told himself, until he'd drained that reservoir of resentment.

Everything had changed when Gwendolyn's cable arrived, telling him her plans regarding Bella Darvi. She instructed him to steer the glacial beauty through press interviews and photo shoots in the lead-up to *The Egyptian* premiere.

Between Kathryn's letter detailing Bella's candid admission that she slept with men *and* women, and the on-set gossip during *Barefoot Contessa,* Marcus had expected an elegant ice queen who uttered as few words as possible—and it's exactly what he got. Even smiling for the press seemed like a herculean effort for her.

One day, Bella had announced she wanted French food. This was the first time she had expressed a desire for anything, so Marcus had prayed that their lunch wouldn't be a repetition of every stilted meal he'd endured with her. But she was as detached as ever, forcing Marcus to cast around for topics of conversation that might elicit more than a monosyllabic response. They'd burned through Mae West's revue at the Sahara Hotel in Las Vegas (she hadn't seen it); Allen Ginsberg's Beat Generation poetry (she'd never heard of him); and those new-fangled TV dinners (she couldn't think of anything worse.)

Exasperated, he had given up—and observed something far more intriguing.

Federico Fellini, Anthony Quinn, Giulietta Masina, and Richard Basehart had become the most famous quartet in Italian films after *La Strada* had triumphed at the Venice Film Festival. They sat at a corner table, but nobody was paying them the slightest attention.

Marcus never left home without his Leica, so when the quartet got up to leave, he called after Fellini and asked if they would mind if he took some pictures.

Six feet tall, with a lion's mane of black hair and an animated face, Fellini asked, "*Lo Scattino Americano*?" When Marcus admitted that he was, Fellini responded, "This is the wrong name for you. *Scattini* always shove and demand, but they do not ask permission."

That's when Marcus had heard Bella laugh for the first time. "You are now *Lo Scattino Simpatico*," she called out from their table, "The Nice Scattino!"

An elaborate Louis Quatorze desk stood in the restaurant's foyer. The *La Strada* foursome posed in front of it until Marcus ran out of film. By the time Marcus had returned to their table, Bella was a different person.

An impish smile played on her lips. "Your friend Gwendolyn, she painted a different picture. 'He knows Rome. He is so much fun. He will show you a good time.' I thought, Good. I need to escape Hollywood and have fun. But instead I get this angry man."

Marcus was shocked. "Is that how I come across?"

"I thought you resented the burden of a glamor girl who was only here because she is sleeping with the boss. But with those *La Strada* people, I saw a different person. That man with the camera, it is the real you, no?"

Marcus apologized if he'd made her feel uncomfortable. "It's my job to do the opposite."

She giggled like a drag queen's version of Doris Day. "It doesn't help when I am Miss Icicle, no?"

Over espressos, Bella had divulged her conflicted feelings about Zanuck.

"He loves me, but it is too much. I live always with fear that the telephone will ring and it will be Darryl saying, 'I am in the hotel lobby!'"

"Sounds suffocating."

"Why do you think I volunteered to come to Rome for his idiotic movie? Tell me," she waved her long fingers at Marcus, "what is this anger I am sensing?"

"You have a lover who won't leave you alone. I had a one who ended our relationship with a note."

"Did he leave you for another lover?"

"He joined the church."

She tsked. "Even worse."

"I have a new lover now, and he's terrific."

"However . . .?"

"Whenever I think of the old one, this boiling anger surges up inside of me. Domenico tells me I say his name in my sleep."

She plopped a sugar cube into her coffee. "Ah!"

It felt nice to unburden himself the way he would to Kathryn or Gwendolyn. "My friends tell me to forget it. 'You've met someone else. Move on.'"

"Your heart says 'But! but! but!'"

"I feel like Miss Haversham in *Great Expectations.*" His reference met with a blank look.

Bella tasted her coffee but frowned and pushed aside the cup. "During the war I was sent to a convent in Toulouse that the Nazis converted to a jail. I was lucky that they didn't send me to a concentration camp like my brother Robert, may he rest in peace. Still, it was not pleasant. What kept me going was the other young girls. We shared food, confidences, love. We relied on each other for our survival. One day, the guards told me I was free to go. Just like that."

"That must have been wonderful," Marcus said.

"It was," Bella agreed, "but for two years those girls were my whole world and I lost the opportunity to tell them what they meant to me." She tapped her chest. "Your heart wants what your heart wants. What your friends say is not relevant."

*If she could survive a Nazi prison,* Marcus had told himself, *surely I can knock on a church door*

* * *

A flock of large dark birds flew across the Piazza Adriana and landed on St. Anthony's rooftop. They squawked like a Greek chorus announcing his arrival.

Marcus rapped on the monastery's door. An old priest appeared, his face lined and weary. Marcus asked about their olive oil but the guy simply pointed to the right.

On the southern side of the building a pair of doors opened into a large room. Along one wall stood long tables, each of them piled with second-hand clothing. Along the back wall, people of all ages lined up for bowls of gazpacho and chunks of bread meted out by monks in brown Franciscan robes. A scattering of tables and mismatched chairs offered them a place to eat.

Overseeing everything was a monk in his sixties with the same weather-beaten face of the one at the door. Marcus approached him and asked about their olive oil.

"This is a place of God and charity, not business."

"I don't want to buy it; I am searching for the monk on the label."

"Ah!" The priest smiled. "Brother Bernardino."

Marcus's heart fell. *A wild goose chase.*

"We have a small store." The priest pointed to a laneway on the far side of the square.

Marcus nodded his thanks and returned to the piazza. With two hours to kill until the next bus to Rome, he walked back to the terminal where he'd spotted a ristocaffé.

The place wasn't much cheerier than the monk's soup kitchen, but Marcus was hungry now. On the far wall was a poster, very similar to the olive oil label, but blown up to life size. Marcus studied the face. *That monk isn't any Brother Bernardino.*

He headed for the alley.

The store had a doorway, a window, and a three-foot counter with bottles lined up along a shelf. Nobody was around.

Marcus heard the faint sound of singing. He strained until he could make out the melody: "Nice Work If You Can Get It." It was refreshing to hear a distinctly American song crooned with such clarity.

He lifted the hinged flap in the counter, let himself through the side door, and followed the singing past a storage room to a narrow path. Halfway along, he came to a wooden gate with an iron handle.

The handle squeaked; the singer continued.

The gate opened onto a thicket of mature olive trees arranged in six rows of twenty, hemmed in by a ten-foot wall. Three trees down on the second row stood a monk in a Franciscan habit with his back to him, plucking olives from the branches.

Marcus crept forward until he was one tree away. "Oliver?"

The figure in the brown habit stiffened. He let his hessian bag slide to his feet and turned around.

The label depicted him with his hood on, so it was a shock to see Oliver with his hair completely shaved off. It didn't suit him—especially with that slight bulge near the back of his head—but the sheer starkness served to highlight the green flecks in his light hazel eyes and the serenity that filled them.

*He looks like a Botticelli painting.*

"Surprise!" Marcus said weakly.

"That's an understatement."

The sound of Oliver's voice brought a sheen of tears to Marcus's eyes. He blinked it away. "You're not easy to find."

"And yet here you stand in my olive grove." Oliver's tone took on a sharp edge.

Marcus risked a step closer. "Your picture on the bottle of—"

"Why are you here, Marcus?" The dreamy Botticelli impression dissipated.

"I wanted—" What had seemed like a good idea in a fancy French restaurant now sounded trivial and selfish. "—to see you."

"And now you have." Oliver draped his bag over a shoulder. "I have a whole grove to harvest and I'm alone, so if you'll excuse me?" He turned back to the tree and recommenced picking olives.

Marcus had imagined this scenario dozens of times. Oliver was supposed to be so full of regret that tears brimmed over, apologies gushing out in wet sobs.

"Is there some place we could sit down?"

Oliver kept his focus on the branches in front of him. "Even monks keep a schedule."

"Perhaps I can help you." Marcus reached up to tug the closest olive.

"That one's not ready yet." The words came out peevish. "What is it you want?"

Marcus was glad now that he hadn't located Oliver while he still burned with resentment. This quadrangle with its three-hundred-year-old walls possessed a tranquility that he would have poisoned had he roared in here, eyes like Lucifer, screaming like Bette Davis, and throwing punches like Kid Galahad.

"I know it's been a long time," Marcus said. "I know I should forget about us, but I have to tell you, Oliver—I *need* to tell you that it bothers me—"

"The way I left?"

Marcus clutched the trunk of the closest tree. Its gnarled ridges were rough as sandpaper, but they kept him upright. "It wounded me. Deeply."

Oliver's eyes drifted across to Marcus's hand gripping the folds in the wood. "This life has brought me a calmness that Hollywood could never achieve."

His hands began moving among the branches with a methodical precision born of repetition, but his eyes were now weeping.

"I deserved more than a note."

"You want to know why I left?"

Oliver breathed in the still air until his shoulders relaxed. Finally, he was able to look Marcus in the eye.

"After I'd been at Cloverleaf a while, and those drugs started to leave my body, I became aware of a deep yearning inside of me. When you wanted me to come with you to Rome, where you'd be working on *Quo Vadis,* I took it as a sign. After all, it's the story of a man who succumbs to his faith in Christ. When I saw the photos you took of the scenes where the Christians are fed to the lions, I realized that if I didn't face the inevitable, I'd get eaten alive myself."

He smiled for the first time. But it was a sad sort of smile, not the joyful one Marcus missed so much. Marcus ached to reach out, but he clasped his hands behind his back.

Oliver continued, "*Quo Vadis* was originally called QUO VADIS? WITH A QUESTION MARK. IT WASN'T UNTIL I STARTED STUDYING LATIN THAT I REALIZED IT MEANS, 'Where are you going?' I had to find out where *I* was going."

"And have you?"

"My only wish is that you could also feel the profound contentment I experience every waking moment of my life."

"That sure would be nice, Oliver, but I'll settle for an apology."

Marcus wanted his riposte to come off flippant, but somewhere around the halfway mark it took a darker turn, belying the surge of anger that he was now struggling to constrain.

*Don't screw this up. We are two adults having a mature discussion intended to air grievances. Screaming like a banshee isn't going to get you the apology you came for.*

"I did what I had to do," Oliver said. "For my own sanity."

"You left me with a crummy note. What about *my* sanity?"

"I had to get away from you."

The quietude inside the olive grove took on a heaviness. "Living with me was so terrible?"

When Oliver answered, it was like a copper pipe to the sternum. "Yes."

He headed toward a marble bench built into the wall at the end of the row. Marcus followed him, determined to say nothing until Oliver explained himself. Nearly a whole minute dragged by.

"When we met, you were this big-time writer at MGM. Then you headed up the whole department. You were in a position of power that I could never dream of."

"Oliver, honey, I—"

"When HUAC and the blacklist came along, did you name names or buckle under? No! You got up in front of those clowns in Washington and you told them where to go. I was in awe of you."

This man he'd lived with, shared his bed with, and his life—Marcus wondered if he had ever known him at all.

"Then our car accident happened, and even as I descended into that murky hell taking those drugs, you refused to give up on me until I physically pushed you out the door. And then what did you do? You came charging into my rose garden at Cloverleaf and spirited me away to a fresh start. You're the most loyal person I've ever met. Nobody's ever shown me that sort of commitment; I felt like I didn't deserve it."

"Of course you deserved it," Marcus broke in. "You're a good person—"

"I've felt like a fish out of water my whole life: childhood, the Breen Office, in Hollywood, at the Garden of Allah. And then we got to Rome. You were completely absorbed making your big Hollywood movie so I enrolled in the language school with that teaching order—and everything fell into place."

They joined hands. Feeling the tremble in Oliver's fingers, Marcus held on tighter.

"It was your trajectory that made me realize I was trudging through the wrong life. The Latin classes, the bibles, the history, the theological arguments, the pageantry of the Catholic Church—it all felt like home. Look at me, Marcus!" He relinquished his grip to sweep his hands through the air. "I'm wearing a plain brown habit and second-hand sandals, picking olives from hundred-year-old trees until my back breaks, and I couldn't be happier."

"You are?" Marcus choked on his question. "Happy?"

Oliver nodded. "I knew that leaving you a note was the coward's way out, but telling you face to face would have led to a messy, emotional scene. I felt you deserved a clean break and decided a short note was best. For what it's worth," he added, "I can see now I was wrong."

Marcus fell against Oliver's shoulder and let his tears spill out in wet, heaving sobs until he realized Oliver was doing the same. Together, they cried and cried until at last they were spent.

Marcus took a deep breath and sat up straight. "Is this the sort of messy scene you were trying to avoid?"

Oliver laughed. "Pretty much. We should've done this three years ago."

"But I wouldn't have seen your olive grove—I mean Brother Bernardino's."

"Ah! You even know about that. When they asked me what new name I wanted to go by, the first one that popped into my head was San Bernardino. I didn't want to completely forget where I came from, so Brother Bernardino it was."

"And these olives?"

Oliver refastened the bag around his shoulders and returned to the tree to resume his work. "It started as a joke between me and the head of the monastery. He's the only person who knew my name was Oliver."

"Oh my God!" Marcus exclaimed. "Oliver—olives. That's where it came from?"

"Turns out, I'm a natural at growing, harvesting, and pressing them. I'd be proud of it, but of course pride is a sin, so naturally I don't indulge." It was nice to catch a glimpse of the old Oliver behind the curtain of this new incarnation. "We started getting orders from all over the country, so a commercial artist was commissioned to do the artwork. The first I knew of it was when the bottles arrived."

"And now your face is everywhere. The monk who ran away from Hollywood becomes famous."

Oliver lifted his eyes heavenward. "Such are the mysterious ways in which God works." He returned to his work. "Speaking of famous, Mister *Lo Scattino Americano*."

"You heard?"

"I'm not a hermit. Do you live here now?"

"It's more of a 'stuck here' type situation."

Oliver plucked handfuls of olives while Marcus described the convoluted saga of why he couldn't leave Italy.

"They can't hang onto your passport forever."

"Six months later I'm still here."

"You'll figure it out."

"I guess so. I mean, I *am* on a trajectory." They exchanged quiet smiles. "Mind you, I still have to figure out how to get my money out of the country."

"I might be able to help you there."

Marcus had a vision of being nailed inside a crate of olive oil addressed to Kathryn Massey, care of the Garden of Allah Hotel.

A mischievous smile emerged on Oliver's face. "When members of the clergy travel, those border officials barely look at our passports, let alone ask us what we're bringing into the country. They just wave us through."

He turned back to his olives and let Marcus wonder how many secret pockets he could fit into a monk's habit.

# CHAPTER 33

Kathryn braced herself as the lights on the Orpheum Theatre stage metamorphosed from baby pink to bright white. She knew the edge was probably ten feet away, but it still left her twitchy and insecure.

One more rousing verse, followed by an extended dance interlude, then a rousing chorus with all twenty members of the cast harmonizing like a Harlem Baptist choir.

She felt a bead of sweat collect at the bottom of her skull. It trickled down her neck until it hit the midway point between her shoulder blades.

She sang out, "Sunbeam's new Mixmaster!"

The dancer in front of her, a sweet girl from Des Moines named Renee, sank into the splits, her arms sheathed in red silk evening gloves. As she reached toward the ceiling, several of the diamantes glued at the wrist flew off. They caught the lights like microscopic stars as they scattered across the stage.

"Mixes my Betty batter faster!"

Kathryn stepped over Renee's leg and into a pool of blinding light, maintaining her smile and praying to a God she didn't believe in that he hadn't cast a tiny chunk of crystal in her path. But as she put her weight onto her right foot, she felt two of the little suckers skitter underneath her. She tried to pull back, but hesitated a fraction of a second too long—Renee had already started rising to her feet.

Kathryn felt herself falling forward. What should have been "It makes my baking more ambitious!" flew out as a series of shrill wails. A strong hand caught her by the armpits and returned her to upright position.

"'Cause everything turns out so delicious!"

Kathryn ran out of breath before the lyrics ended, so she mimed as best she could, maintaining her smile as the curtain came down.

"That was a close one!" Betty Furness exclaimed. "You okay, hon?"

"Yes," Kathryn assured her, "thanks to—" she patted the shoulders of the chorus boy with the pale blue eyes "—my quick-thinking knight in shining tap shoes."

"I thought we were done for when I caught sight of Renee's gems flying across the stage," he said.

Kathryn wanted to get back to her dressing room and forget the whole thing. She had bigger worries today. "It would take more than a few unglued diamantes to unglue me. Thanks everyone!"

Kathryn hurried into the wings, up a half-flight of stairs and into her dressing room.

Gwendolyn jumped up. "It's that cheap glue they made me use!" When Kathryn had suggested to Leo that Gwendolyn design and make the costumes for their extravaganza, he'd agreed but skimped on the budget. "You recovered so quickly, I doubt anybody noticed."

Kathryn pressed her hands against her chest. What had happened in front of two thousand people wasn't the only reason her heart was racing. "I don't suppose—?"

Gwendolyn shook her head.

Kathryn dropped onto the chair in front of her vanity. "This wait is killing me."

A month ago, when Kathryn had told Winchell about DiMaggio and Sinatra battering down the wrong door, she'd wanted to believe that he would hold up his end of the bargain. Winchell liked to think he had the scruples of Solomon the Wise, but she didn't delude herself into thinking that he was any more principled than Bugsy Siegel.

She didn't even give herself fifty-fifty odds that she'd ever see Thomas Danford's file. "More like ten to one," she wrote to Marcus. So she had been shocked, impressed, and elated when she arrived home a couple of weeks ago to find a note under her door telling her that Winchell was giving the FBI file to his ghostwriter, Herman Klurfeld, along with instructions to place the file directly into her hands. The note promised this would happen on Friday, December 10th but fell short on specifics.

The whole morning, Kathryn had busied herself with her column: the revenue for television broadcasters had surpassed radio; L.B. Mayer's long-time secretary, Ida Koverman, had died; and McCarthy had at last been condemned by the Senate.

She didn't know what Klurfeld looked like; every time someone approached her desk, she steadied herself. Two o'clock came and went. She'd hurried out of the office wondering if Klurfeld knew to find her at the Orpheum, and if he did, she hoped he'd appear before she went on stage. She didn't want to be preoccupied during a roadshow that now ran ninety minutes and featured half a dozen musical numbers, a chorus of twelve, a magician, a comedian, and four costume changes. The joke around the company was that it was now called "Cecil B. DeMille Presents."

Now that the show was over, she had to vacate the dressing room by seven to make Romanoff's by eight. Leo would be swinging by as soon as he had wrapped up in the control booth.

"Come on." Gwendolyn said. "Let's get you into your street clothes."

She was reaching for Kathryn's zipper when there was a knock on the door.

They froze, staring at each other.

Gwendolyn mouthed, "What are you waiting for?"

Kathryn pulled open the door to find a black woman dressed in a severe suit of gray wool and a plain cream blouse that barely contained the matronly swell of her enormous bosom. "Mrs. Wyatt! What a surprise!"

She steamed into Kathryn's dressing room like a battleship.

"May I present Gwendolyn Brick?" Kathryn stationed herself by Gwennie's side. "Cornelia Wyatt is the head of the California chapter of the National Council of Negro Women."

"Pleased to meet you, ma'am."

Kathryn checked the clock above her vanity. "How can I help you?"

"You're a busy woman, Miss Massey, so I'll come to the point."

*Holy hell! What if Klurfeld is waiting at the Garden?*

"Every February we award our highest honor to someone who has done much to elevate the status of Negro women. We wish to present you with our Woman of the Year award."

Gwendolyn stifled a yip.

"That's—unexpected," Kathryn said.

"So you accept?"

"It's just that, well, shouldn't your Woman of the Year be a—a—"

"Negro? Normally, yes. But we received that blessed windfall solely because of you, and it made an enormous difference to the lives of more women than you could possibly imagine."

Behind Mrs. Wyatt came another knock.

"What an honor. Of course I'll accept," Kathryn blurted out. "Perhaps you could contact me at my office with the details?" She shook the woman's hand forcefully. "Thank you so much."

Turning her around, Kathryn opened the door to someone whose face she was more familiar with than she cared to be. He was holding a large envelope.

Kathryn marshaled Mrs. Wyatt out into the hallway and waved her goodbye. Her smile fell away as she turned to face Felix Miller. He was Winchell's eyes and ears in LA, and Kathryn didn't trust a word that came out of his lipless pie hole.

Kathryn prodded him into the room as she scouted the hallway for Leo; he was nowhere in sight. "I was expecting Herman Klurfeld."

Miller winced. "The poor bastard came down with appendicitis. They raced him to Queen of Angels. Room 303 if you don't believe me."

"I'd believe Charles Ponzi before anything *you* said."

Gwendolyn picked up the telephone and asked the operator to connect her with Klurfeld's hospital.

Kathryn nodded at the envelope in Miller's hands.

"This is it," he said. "Whatever 'it' is." He showed her the adhesive tape secured across the back.

Gwendolyn hung up. "The third-floor nursing station confirmed that Klurfeld is recovering from an appendectomy."

Miller ceremoniously lowered his package into Kathryn's outstretched hands.

"You'll be okay to see your own way out, I hope."

They waited until Miller closed the door behind him. Kathryn tore along the top and pulled out the contents.

It was a regular-sized folder that anybody could buy at a stationery store; however, the label on the front looked official.

PROPERTY OF THE
FEDERAL BUREAU OF INVESTIGATION
CLASSIFIED: TOP SECRET
SUBJECT: THOMAS DANFORD

Kathryn gasped softly. "It's really his!"

"But honey?" Gwendolyn whispered. "Isn't it a little thin?"

Kathryn ran her fingernail across what couldn't have been any more than fifteen memos filled with boring Bureau-speak. "There's not enough here to exonerate a jaywalker." Kathryn said. "So the FBI doesn't have anything on my father?"

"Or," Gwendolyn replied, "somebody's lifted the juicy stuff."

* * *

The next day, Kathryn laid a hand on the door of the Melrose Detective Agency. "If Nelson is in there," she told Gwendolyn, "we're keeping everything strictly professional."

The office smelled of wood polish, as though Nelson had been expecting them and done a thorough spring clean. He'd treated himself to a better haircut, and had pressed his suit. Kathryn's heart kicked up a notch. *Damn you for looking even better than you did last month.*

"Hello," he said mildly, then recognized Gwendolyn. "Well, hello!"

Kathryn held up the FBI folder. "I have it."

Nelson called Dudley in from the other office and accepted the file from Kathryn. They took seats around Nelson's desk as he opened it up.

"A little on the meager side, isn't it?" Dudley asked.

Kathryn could feel Nelson's stare, begging her to look at him, but she couldn't bring herself to do it. "I fear we've been gypped," she told Dudley. "Herman Klurfeld took ill; it was Felix Miller who delivered the package."

"The plot thickens."

"Who is Felix Miller?" Nelson asked.

She longed to drink him in, if only to tell herself that she'd made the right decision accepting Leo's marriage proposal. But she was less sure now that she was close enough to hear him breathe. She opened her purse and extracted a cigarette. Nelson flicked his lighter and held it out for her.

She told him, "Miller is Winchell's man in Hollywood." His gaze scorched her face. "A real piece of work. Last summer, *Confidential* had a spread on the Garden of Allah—"

"'A Rainbow of Colors Dancing in the Garden of Eden'?"

"He took the photos."

"A real charmer, huh?"

"A peach," Gwendolyn chimed in.

"So he's tight with Robert Harrison?"

"That son-of-a-bitch is tight with anyone who'll pay him enough."

"Somebody's made off with the lion's share of your father's file," Dudley said, "and Miller is a likely suspect. Miss Brick, did you get a good look at him?"

When Gwendolyn told him that she'd seen Miller several times, Dudley asked her to accompany him into his office where he kept a folder with dozens of photographs of known tipsters around town. "We might get lucky," he said, ushering Gwendolyn out of the room.

Nelson asked, "What else can you tell me?"

Kathryn flicked ash into an ashtray with the Ciro's logo stenciled in black on the bottom. "I can tell you that Ciro's don't appreciate having their glassware stolen."

"Kathryn?" he said. She didn't respond. "Kat?"

He had to go and say the one word he knew would get a rise out of her: the nickname he used after they'd finished making love and were submerging into blissful slumber.

She summoned the courage to look at him, and wished she hadn't. Those blue-gray eyes she knew so well churned with emotion.

"Please don't," she said. "Let's stick to business. I can't—it's difficult for me to be here—"

"I never stopped thinking of you." His voice reached barely a hair above a whisper.

"Don't! It's too late—"

"Do you know what there is to do in Nome?"

"Not much, I'm guessing."

"Sweet F.A. I read a heap of books, and I got real good at Solitaire, but mostly I drove myself nuts thinking about you. I even started drawing you. I had to do it from memory because they gave me half an hour to pack and I didn't have a photo handy. So I sat there sketching you from memory over and over and over."

"I didn't know you were artistic."

He grinned. "I'm not. You wouldn't have recognized yourself, but it was all I had." He planted his elbows on the top of his desk and pressed his clasped hands to his mouth.

Kathryn longed to tell him that she thought about him too, usually over the silliest reminders like ugly lampshades and whenever she passed the Radio Room. "I'm engaged now. Let's leave the past—"

"I'd have thought you'd mention it in your column."

When Kathryn had accepted Leo's proposal, she'd reserved the right to make the announcement, telling him, "Timing is as important as the news itself." The tremor of annoyance in Leo's eyes had been hard to miss, but he agreed and she changed the subject. Six weeks later, she still hadn't announced their engagement.

"We're in no rush," she told Nelson.

"Maybe *you're* not, but I bet he's wondering what's going on." He rounded the desk to her side. Planting himself in Gwendolyn's chair, he took her hands in his. "You don't love this Leo guy the way you love me."

Kathryn tried to tug free of his grip but he had the strength of a gorilla. "You're not the last word in how I feel."

Those hands! So warm and firm, but calloused from manual labor. He could build anything with those hands. Cabinets. Picture frames. Doors. Window-box planters. Oh God, how she loved the way he'd run them over her body.

Abruptly, he released her. The chair scuffed the linoleum as he pushed it out from under him and retreated to his side of the desk.

Gwendolyn emerged from Dudley's office and placed a photograph in front of Kathryn. It was a blurry Felix Miller taken with a zoom lens, but it was him.

"Miller and Winchell go way back," Dudley said. "So do Miller and Harrison."

"No surprise there." Kathryn could still feel the goosebumps tingling her scalp. Leo didn't raise them like that.

Dudley took a seat. "Miller is also a known associate of Vincent Haynes."

"Should I know who that is?"

"Haynes was the lead Voss Vanguard member who coordinated Voss's LA meeting."

"You think Voss has a hand in the missing pages?"

"Always go with a person's motive," Nelson said.

Kathryn glanced at Gwendolyn, who was too preoccupied with studying Nelson's face to notice. "Last I heard, Winchell and Harrison aren't buddy-buddy anymore, so you have to wonder where Miller's loyalties lie."

Nelson tapped his cigarette lighter against the ink blotter on his desk. "With guys like that, it's best to assume they lie with their own best interests."

"In other words, whoever's willing to pay him the most."

"Exactly." Dudley ran his finger along the spine of the FBI file. "My hunch is that Miller believes his best interests now lie with Mister Amnesia."

Kathryn dropped her face into her hands. "I thought I was done with him."

"I wouldn't bet on it."

Kathryn looked up at Dudley. "Meaning?"

"I called the veterans' hospital yesterday. He checked himself out a few days ago, and nobody's heard from him since."

"So he disappeared around the same time that my father's drastically abridged FBI file arrived in LA."

Nelson stopped tapping his lighter. "Personally, I don't believe in coincidences."

She met his trenchant stare. *I know what you're doing*. "Neither do I."

"Miss Massey," Dudley said, "without the full contents of that file, it will be well-nigh impossible to build a case for exoneration. I believe our best chance to recover the missing documents is to find Voss."

"He's a slippery one," Gwendolyn warned.

"This could take some time, so I need your assurance that you're committed to the chase."

Dudley looked so much like Fatty Arbuckle that Kathryn wondered how she hadn't noticed already. "Absolutely," she assured him. "I want to see this through to the end." She yearned to look at Nelson, but didn't dare. "Wherever that may lead us."

# CHAPTER 34

Gwendolyn leaned on the rim of her bathroom basin and took deep breaths to alleviate the persistent ache south of her waistline.

It didn't work.

She had been feeling lousy for more than a week, but not so bad that she'd taken off time she couldn't afford to go see a doctor who would tell her that tenderness was the price she paid for an erratic menstrual cycle.

Since she was fourteen, Gwendolyn had dealt with periods that were as unpredictable as earthquakes, and about as much fun. She couldn't remember the last time she'd left home without a tampon.

But this ache was different. She'd never felt one buried so deeply in her pelvis. At first, it had felt like indigestion. But day by day, the discomfort had swelled into a twinge that became a throb, but not bad enough to call out the National Guard. Over the weekend, the throb had become a sluggish ache, but this morning it was now a conspicuous pain.

Promising herself that she'd make an appointment in the morning, she checked her face in the mirror. *God almighty, I am pale, aren't I?* She was halfway through brushing on extra rouge when she heard the squeak of aging hinges.

"It's just me," Kathryn called from the living room. "How come I don't see any canapés?"

"I'm a bit behind schedule."

Kathryn appeared at the bathroom door. "You okay?"

Gwendolyn shooed Kathryn toward the kitchen. After all the finagling she'd done to make tonight happen, she wasn't going to let a few stomach cramps get in the way. "We're making do with cheese and crackers. I've got pickles and some sort of relish. There's a green apple in the crisper. If we slice it very finely—" She caught sight of Kathryn's questioning look. "What?"

"You're going to have to pick up your culinary game now that you're dating Clark Gable."

"I'm not dating him!"

"What *are* you doing?"

Gwendolyn ripped open the top flap of the Ritz crackers box. "I don't know if there's a word for it."

After they had finished their dressing-room dalliance during *Soldier of Fortune*'s first lunch break, Gwendolyn and Clark had reassembled their outfits while stagehands banged hammers and connected electrical cords on the other side of the walls. As he zippered Gwendolyn back into her dress, Clark had kissed her neck and whispered, "They'd be jealous if they knew how lucky I got."

It was a flattering remark, but she'd thought no more about it. Clark had much to prove with his first picture since leaving MGM, and was fully absorbed by the task at hand.

So she'd been mildly surprised when the company broke for the weekend at Saturday lunchtime and he'd invited her into his dressing room. It was the same Caesar salad and cold cuts, but he'd wasted no time getting down to business. And what delicious business it was. Even better the second time around.

Afterwards, he'd said to her, "I'd enjoy myself more if we weren't—" He circled his hands around each other.

"Where did you have in mind?"

"You live at the Garden of Allah."

After that, they had started meeting there as opportunity and schedules permitted. Before Gwendolyn knew it, she was caught up in an affair with the King of Hollywood.

But 'affair' was entirely the wrong word.

They didn't go out for lunch or dinner. No gifts or flowers, perfume or jewelry. He proved himself an ardent, considerate lover and she hoped that he felt the same.

More than once or twice, Howard Hughes' stinging rebuke from a few years ago—"You're just too old"—revisited her, and she'd brushed it away with the satisfaction of knowing that Clark Gable disagreed.

After one particularly sweaty romp, Clark had kissed Gwendolyn on the cheek. "You're a rare oasis." She had no schemes to ensnare him with her womanly wiles, nor any interest in parading him down the aisle, and he knew it.

After that, their lovemaking had taken on heights of abandonment she hadn't enjoyed since Alistair Dunne, the artist who operated outside all cultural and societal norms. Whatever they were doing, it was casual, fun, satisfying, with no strings attached.

She sliced squares of cheese and pushed them across to Kathryn. "With the twists and turns my life has taken, this is the most unexpected one of all." A tremor of pain fired through Gwendolyn's innards and up into her chest.

The sound of two men breaking into belly laughs reached Gwendolyn's open doorway.

"I'd know that Gable laugh anywhere," Kathryn said, "but was that Monty with him?"

"Haven't you heard? Clark's got himself a new best friend."

Gwendolyn peeked through her living room window and watched Clark and Monty disappear into Marcus's villa. Clark was already in his tux, but Monty hadn't dressed yet.

"How did *that* happen?" Kathryn asked.

Gwendolyn's cheese squares weren't about to win any prizes at the LA County Fair but they'd have to do. Another shudder of pain screamed up her torso. *Just get through this evening.*

"Clark and I had finished up—you know—when Monty came knocking. He was home from work and walked straight in. I was mortified! Who wants to picture his sister doing it? But it was like water off a duck's back to him. Later on, he said, 'When you spend months cramped together on board ship, you learn not to judge anyone's love life. You take it where you can get it.' As Clark was still putting on his shirt, the two of them started jawing like a couple of Average Joes."

Kathryn slapped on pickle slices as fast as Gwendolyn could cover Ritz crackers with uneven lumps of cheese. "Monty wasn't the least bit intimidated?"

"Would you believe he's never seen a Gable picture? Clark roared when he heard that and said, 'Keep it that way!' And now it's Clark who idolizes Monty."

"No!"

"Standing in front of cameras has brought Clark gobs of money, but not much self-esteem. Especially during the war when he tried to be actively involved but Mayer pulled strings to stop him from getting in harm's way. He looks at Monty and sees a guy who's lived the life that he could've lived. And now they're sparring partners!"

"You mean like boxing?"

"Monty was a big deal on the navy boxing team, so now they punch the living daylights out of each other twice a week." The sound of a door slamming nearby bounced into Gwendolyn's villa. She didn't need to look up to know that it was Doris, who was included in tonight's group. "This is the first time in ages that Clark's made a non-film-industry friend, so he's tickled pink. And this is Monty's first civilian friend, so he's pleased as punch."

Kathryn let out a laugh. "Looks to me like the Bricks are in the Gable business."

"Who's in the Gable business?"

Doris had draped herself in a silver fox evening wrap over a low-cut gown of sapphire lamé that Gwendolyn was sure she'd seen on Rita Hayworth. "Somebody's been plundering Columbia's costume department."

"Is it too much?" Doris plastered her hands across her bust. "I've never worn anything quite so—"

"Trampy?" Kathryn suggested.

"Revealing. But this is Monty's first Hollywood premiere so I wanted to do it up right."

When Gwendolyn had put this group together, she'd never dreamed that Doris would take it so seriously. Did Doris really think of herself as Monty's "date" date? But the less people knew what was going on tonight, the better.

During one of their recent rendezvous, Gwendolyn could tell that Clark's mind wasn't in the game, so she'd brought their lovemaking to a halt. He'd told her that Zanuck had been leaning on him to attend the opening of *There's No Business Like Show Business*. He didn't mind the part about shoving it in MGM's face, but he hated being a pawn.

He'd rolled off her and tucked his hands behind his head. "Do you ever see Judy?"

"I do. Looking after your needs isn't the full-time job Zanuck imagined, so I've gone back to designing Loretta's gowns. She's become my unofficial assistant. I see her all the time."

"What are the chances of scoring her an invite to the opening of *No Business*?" He'd asked the question with the precision of an over-rehearsed scene. "I'd ask Zanuck, but I'd prefer not owing him a favor."

"Marilyn's coming from back East for it. Zanuck'll give her as many seats as she wants."

A longing filled his eyes. "If you put together a party that included Judy, I'd go."

"Okay," Gwendolyn said, "so there's you, me, Kathryn, Leo, Marcus's sister Doris, and Monty. Judy'll make seven, so we'd need a date for her. Perhaps that dancer who escorted her to Ciro's. We could orchestrate it so that you and Judy sit next to each other. How about I throw a little cocktail party beforehand? Low-key and casual. The eight of us can meet here—"

"No!" He had taken a deep breath like he was coming up for air. "I mean yes, that'll be nice, but we'll meet Judy there."

Gwendolyn left her motley plate of cheese and crackers and welcomed Doris with a hug. "Monty's eyes are going to bug out of his head."

Clark and Monty entered Gwendolyn's villa with timing worthy of a Moss Hart script. Thankfully, they each held a bottle of champagne. Gwendolyn had planned on buying some at Greenblatt's, but the cramping in her stomach had sent her to bed with a hot water bottle. The end of this evening couldn't come fast enough.

A popped cork sent bubbly champagne spilling out. Clark deftly caught most of it in the nearest flute and soon they were toasting the film's success.

"Hey, Monty," Kathryn said, "I keep hearing about this memoir of yours."

Clark turned to Monty. "You wrote a book?"

"It's hard to bring it up in conversation when you're always coming at me with an uppercut, but yes. It's called *On the Deck of the Missouri*, and—"

"That's *yours*? Well, I'll be a monkey's uncle," Clark exclaimed. "Zanuck's been stopping by the *Soldier of Fortune* set and dropping into the conversation the possibility of my playing the lead in the film version. He talks to me like I know all about it."

"Just to let you know," Gwendolyn said, "even though she lost out on *A Woman's World*, Loretta's hoping to get the female lead."

Clark and Loretta had managed to get through filming *Key to the City* a few years ago. From the way surprise flared his eyes, Gwendolyn could tell that he wasn't keen to repeat the experience.

Monty landed his glass on Gwendolyn's tiled counter. "What female lead? It's about life aboard the USS *Missouri*. There are no women in the entire book! That's the whole point—making a life for yourself *without* female companionship."

"Oh, dear sweet naïve brother of mine," Gwendolyn said, "half the audience for any movie is women, so there needs to be someone pretty who falls for someone handsome. But," she added quickly, to allay Clark's discomfort, "Zanuck is dying to put Gable and Monroe in a movie together. That's what he's probably angling for."

The room went silent as everybody pictured Gable and Monroe going at it in bed, because that's how most films were cast.

Pain jolted Gwendolyn from the pit of her guts and flared upwards, squeezing the breath from her lungs. She gripped the edge of the counter, praying it would pass quickly. Kathryn frowned at her; Gwendolyn subtly shook her head and asked the gathering, "Who needs a refill?"

* * *

Although movies had changed over the years—"Now with sound! In Technicolor! 3-D! CinemaScope!"—movie premieres had not. *There's No Business Like Show Business* opened at Grauman's with black-and-chrome limousines, searchlights scouring the night sky, bleachers filled with movie fans, press photographers, reporters, and a red carpet leading into the theater.

By the time she reached the foyer, Gwendolyn felt as though a fist-sized rock had lodged itself at the base of her spine.

Leo was waiting for them by the bar. He greeted Kathryn with a kiss, then turned to Gwendolyn. "You don't look so hot."

She scanned the crowd for Judy. "I'll be okay." A droplet of sweat trickled down the side of her face. "Perhaps a quick visit to the ladies' room. Keep an eye out for Judy and her date," she told Leo. "His name is Jonathan Brady."

Inside the gold-and-red ladies' room, Kathryn pulled a handkerchief from her pocketbook and dabbed at Gwendolyn's face. "I know you're up to mischief—" She pulled away. "Judy and Clark?"

"I think he's working up to telling her."

Gwendolyn faced the nearest mirror. She looked like she hadn't seen the sun in ten years. Her underarms felt damper than her face.

"Why don't you nab the seat on the aisle in case you need to make a hasty exit?" Kathryn suggested.

"Let's hope it won't come to that."

The corridor leading off the foyer was more crowded now but one figure stood apart. Darryl Zanuck stepped forward as Gwendolyn and Kathryn emerged.

"Hello Darryl!" Kathryn said brightly, stepping ahead.

Zanuck didn't bother to attempt a smile. "I need to speak with Gwendolyn. Alone." Kathryn dissolved into the crowd.

"I hear Clark and your brother are regular sparring partners at the Hollywood Athletic Club. You're even better at your job than I expected."

Gwendolyn didn't want to take undue credit, but she was feeling too lousy to correct him.

"Does your brother hunt, too?" Zanuck asked. "He and Gable could bond over that, and I'm going to need some help getting the navy's cooperation with *On the Deck of the Missouri.*"

Something in the back of Gwendolyn's mind snapped. "Did you pull strings to get my brother his navy liaison job?"

Zanuck beamed like a new father. "I admire your smarts for figuring it out. Nobody else has—not even your pal, and she's sharp as a switchblade."

*We're nothing but pawns in your chess game. Me, Clark, Monty, everyone. Little pieces of wood to finesse into doing what you want.*

Gwendolyn gathered her strength to give him a piece of her mind, but the rock in her belly burst into a ball of lava. Her head swam in nauseating waves as she crumpled to the floor.

* * *

Hours later, when Gwendolyn emerged from the fog of anesthetic, she was in the same hospital that had treated her ankle.

Kathryn and Monty's anxious faces appeared at her bedside.

"How you feeling?" Monty asked.

"The pain's gone."

Kathryn pressed the call button next to Gwendolyn's bed. "We'll let the doctor explain."

"Explain what?"

"It's probably best if we wait for him. I'll just get all those medical terms muddled."

"You're awake." In contrast to his brisk manner, he looked more like the sort of old-fashioned doctor that Andy Hardy might have visited. "Comfortable?"

Gwendolyn nodded.

"This pain you've been experiencing—it was caused by an ectopic pregnancy. Do you know what that is?"

The word "pregnancy" flashed in Gwendolyn's mind like a firework.

*But I'm forty-four. But I use protection. But the only person I've been with is Clark – oh jeez.*

"Miss Brick?" the doctor pressed.

She felt the sting of tears collecting behind her eyes. "You just gave me a bit of a shock."

The doctor replaced the chart hanging from the end of her bed. "In a normal pregnancy, a fertilized egg attaches itself in the uterus, but in your case, it was the fallopian tube."

"That explains the pain." Her voice sounded far away, like it belonged in a different room.

"Indeed. We had to go in and remove the embryo." *The embryo.* "It meant we had to tie off your fallopian tubes. I'm sorry, but it means you can never have a child."

An involuntary giggle percolated out of Gwendolyn. "That was never really an option. But I was wearing a Dutch cap. How could this happen?"

"You were using one manufactured by a company that delayed recalling a faulty batch." He pulled a slip of paper from the breast pocket of his shirt and deposited it on her portable meal table. "Here are the details if you want to join the class action suit."

"Thank you, doctor. For—everything."

"I'd like to keep you for forty-eight hours' observation. A couple of minutes," he told Kathryn and Monty, "then you must let her rest."

Monty waited until the doctor left the room. "I assume Clark's the father?"

Gwendolyn nodded.

"You going to tell him?"

"Hell's bells, no!" It wasn't Kathryn's question to answer but she did anyway. "If you hadn't lost the baby, it'd be different. But it's gone now; what would be the point? After all, this isn't Loretta, Part Two."

Monty frowned. "Who's Loretta?"

"Old news." Kathryn fluttered her hand. "We should go."

They each kissed Gwendolyn on the cheek and told her they'd be back in the morning after next to pick her up.

Gwendolyn turned her face toward the window. She could see only some clouds and the tops of elm trees lining the hospital's front lawn.

*You dodged what could have been a messy bullet. At least you weren't faced with Loretta's decision.*

A ripple of sedative splashed the edges of her mind. Loretta Young's face appeared. Gwendolyn felt a rush of sympathy toward the woman who had given into temptation and had been forced to live with the consequences. Loretta's face melted away; Clark's quickly supplanted hers.

*This isn't Loretta, Part Two,* she told him, *but it was close.*

She heard the echoes of a conversation they'd had once about fatherhood and how he wished he hadn't missed it. "But I'm fifty-three," he'd said with a resigned tone, "so that's that."

His face faded as her eyelids began to droop.

# CHAPTER 35

Cornelia Wyatt shook Kathryn's hand with the strength of a longshoreman. "I'm so glad to see you again."

Kathryn was still of two minds about accepting the NCNW's award. If the council hadn't occupied the offices below the FBI's Los Angeles bureau, they would never have been the charity that popped into Kathryn's mind in MacArthur Park.

"I'm still not sure I deserve—"

"Now, now!" Mrs. Wyatt scolded. "We don't abide false modesty here."

They walked down the side alley running along the Central Avenue YWCA and opened the door at the rear. Inside, Mrs. Wyatt pointed to a table where Kathryn could place her handbag. "We've already had our luncheon, so I'll make a speech, then you'll say something, and we'll have a meet-and-mingle afterwards, okay?"

Kathryn and her host stood in the wings of a small area separated from the main room by a curtain. On the other side, chatter filled the air.

"I know you're used to working with a microphone," Mrs. Wyatt said, "but down here at the YWCA, we're not that fancy. Speak loud and proud, and everyone'll hear you just fine."

She signaled to a young black woman standing on the far side, who pulled at a rope, parting the curtain. The chatter subsided as Mrs. Wyatt took her place center stage. With projection that Leontyne Price would have envied, she recapped for her audience the reasons why they were honoring today's recipient. "And so," she concluded, "it is my pleasure to welcome to the stage the 1955 recipient of our Woman of the Year award, Miss Kathryn Massey."

Kathryn walked to the center of the stage to join Mrs. Wyatt.

A hundred mouths gaped in confusion; two hundred gloved hands sat mute in laps.

Kathryn turned to look at Mrs. Wyatt. *You didn't tell them that you gave your award to a white woman, did you?*

"Ladies!" Mrs. Wyatt admonished. "Need I remind you that Miss Massey played a pivotal role in securing our Sheldon Voss endowment? When it came to deciding who we honored today, I felt it was an easy choice. If I was wrong, please let me know."

Kathryn scanned the crowd for a friendly face. She saw only puckered brows and resentment until someone in the back row started to clap. Slow and rhythmic at first, she gathered momentum, challenging the others to join her. Little by little, the applause grew.

The source of this encouragement was the only other white woman in the room. Her pale skin and copper-red hair shone like a stoplight. Her smile had a jarring quality to it but it was the only one in sight, so Kathryn took it gratefully.

* * *

At the meet-and-mingle after the presentation, precious little meeting or mingling took place. The good ladies of the NCNW were too ashamed, too embarrassed, or too daunted by the prospect of talking to Kathryn, so they avoided her like she was Jezebel dipped in the pox. Kathryn breathed a sigh of relief when the redhead approached.

"That was touch and go," the redhead commented drolly.

"You should have seen how it looked from my side of the footlights," Kathryn said. "Thank you for the support."

"Glad to help."

"I take it you're not a member?"

She shook her head. "I heard this was happening and thought it might have the makings of an interesting story. I'm a journalist. My name is Marjorie Meade." The redhead slithered her an enigmatic side-glance. "Truth be told, I have a second reason for coming today."

"Oh?"

"I've been asked to approach you with a proposal." Kathryn's intuition started flashing *Danger! Danger!* Marjorie angled herself away from the crowd. "I run Hollywood Research Inc. It's the intelligence-gathering arm of *Confidential*."

Kathryn wanted to tell the woman that the words "intelligence" and "*Confidential*" didn't belong in the same sentence.

Meade continued, "Robert Harrison is my uncle and he wants to meet with you." She swiped her hand through the air to silence Kathryn. "This is one meeting you'll want to take. Tomorrow night. Eight o'clock at the Bar of Music on Beverly Boulevard."

She disappeared into the crowd before Kathryn could tell her to take a hike.

* * *

Kathryn passed through the black lacquered doors of the Bar of Music and walked into a large room curved to resemble a grand piano. Nearly half the tables were occupied, but no one appeared to be paying attention to a quartet of dark-suited jazz musicians improvising a vaguely Cole-Porteresque melody.

Both photos that Kathryn had seen of Robert Harrison were grainy and unflattering, so she wasn't too sure what she was looking for. She ordered a Four Roses on the rocks in the hope it would calm her nerves from the ugly fight she'd just walked out on.

She and Leo rarely quarreled, but this one had been a humdinger.

He had insisted on coming with her to meet with Harrison. She appreciated his protectiveness, but had objected to his you're-just-a-woman tone. No, she'd told Leo. He couldn't come because he simply wasn't necessary.

"Not necessary?" He had thrown a sofa pillow, then his necktie. The *Examiner* soon followed. She'd hurled the bouquet of lilies he'd bought her and told him that surely by now he knew she wasn't a shrinking violet. The rest of the argument had been a blur of cuss words until she'd stormed out.

The bartender placed the Four Roses in front of her. "Are you Kathryn Massey?" He pointed to a table against the south wall, where a solitary figure nursed a highball.

Robert Harrison wasn't the outright sleaze she expected. He sported a professional shave and kept his hair carefully Brylcreemed in place. His white shirt was crisp and starched, and his dark gray silk tie with the light gray polka dots was the type of gift Kathryn might buy Marcus for Christmas.

But as soon as she sat down, she sensed the creep was greasy to the marrow.

"I thought you'd be more punctual." Kathryn bristled at his undiplomatic opening line. "No matter; you're here now."

"Why *am* I here?"

His smile was reptilian. "Because you're curious."

"Your niece mentioned a proposal."

He sipped his whiskey sour, sucking it through his teeth like it was industrial-strength mouthwash. "I want you to write for us."

"WHAT?!" Several heads turned toward their table, except for the beatniks, who were too steeped in ennui to bother. "You can't be serious."

"I never joke about business."

Kathryn knocked back a heavy slug and weighed up the pros and cons of throwing the remainder of her drink in his face.

"I want a stable of first-rate writers on my staff and I've long admired your work."

"You must know what I think of yours."

"Are you referring to that Garden of Eden article?"

"Among the hundreds of other appalling items you've published with no regard for truth." She swiped up her handbag and prepared to stand.

"I'll pay big bucks for the tips too hot for you to use."

"What on God's green earth makes you think—"

"I'm talking three."

Kathryn's handbag landed in her lap. "Three what?"

"Three grand. Per item."

Kathryn polished off the rest of her Four Roses. "How can you possibly afford to pay so much?"

"*Confidential*'s newsstand sales will soon pass five million. I make approximately half a mill per issue." He lit a Montecristo with the assurance of someone holding a royal flush. "What can I say? Scandal sells. And you can wipe that holier-than-thou look off your face. Dough like that is enough for Florabel Muir, Mike Todd, *and* Harry Cohn."

"If Todd and Cohn are your tipsters, it's because you've got the lowdown on them or the people who work for them, and you blackmail them into giving you dirt on someone else."

"I can't help it if the American public wants dirt and gossip—nor do I judge them for it. I simply report the news as I see it.

"The hell you do," Kathryn replied. "Let's talk about Rock Hudson."

The bastard didn't flinch. "What about him?"

"You bribed Jack Navaar ten thousand to spill the beans on Rock's personal life, but Jack told Henry Willson that *Confidential* was after Rock. I don't know what sort of deal Willson made with you, but I'm guessing he sacrificed some poor sap lower down the ladder."

Kathryn had caught wind of this from Quentin at Paramount, who'd been dating a guy in Universal's publicity department. He shouldn't have divulged the story to her, but they were at the post-premiere party for *Magnificent Obsession* at the Biltmore and he had been dreadfully blotto.

"You need to recruit new tipsters, Miss Massey. Your current ones are feeding you faulty information. And besides," Harrison waved his cigar around like it was some sort of surrender flag, "if Rock didn't want it to be known that he's a raging homo . . ."

Across the room, she spotted Nelson and Leo at a cocktail table.

Why the hell were the two men in her life sitting together? Who'd called whom and suggested they stake out the Bar of Music? They seemed cordial enough, but what were they talking about? Surely Nelson wouldn't let on to Leo about their past?

Kathryn cut through Harrison's attempt to whitewash the Rock Hudson situation. "You know where Sheldon Voss is, don't you?"

Surprise rolled across his face, but only for a split second. "As a matter of fact I do."

"Are the missing contents of Danford's FBI file with him?"

He took his time grinding the cigar into an ashtray. Its pungent smoke rose above their table in a choking cloud. "A convicted politician from Massachusetts seems far removed from your gay social whirl."

"He's more Winchell's interest than mine. I'm helping him out." He blinked slowly at her, unconvinced. "I want you to take me to Voss. Right now."

"And what's in it for me?"

Naturally there had to be something in it for him. "A three-thousand-dollar scoop."

"Oh?"

"For free."

"Go on."

"I don't have one right at my fingertips. But the next one I get, it's all yours."

"You want me to take you to Voss on an IOU?"

"It's the best I can do." She ached to look at Leo and Nelson's table. "Shall we go?"

Harrison's Cadillac Eldorado glowed nicotine yellow in the sole lamplight of the Bar of Music's parking lot. Harrison opened the passenger door.

Kathryn backed off. "I've got my own car. I'll follow you."

"If you want to see Voss . . ."

Neither Leo nor Nelson came charging out of the rear entrance.

She climbed in.

Beverly Boulevard led all the way into downtown, so Kathryn guessed Voss was holed up at some filthy dive where nobody would think to look for him. But they turned onto La Brea, then Wilshire.

Kathryn tilted her body until she had a full view in the side mirror. Two cars behind them could have been Leo's Buick Roadmaster, but it was difficult to see among the shadows. She was comforted to know she might not be alone, but it still unnerved her that the two men were together without her playing go-between.

"I don't suppose you'll tell me where we're going," she goaded cheerfully. "If I guess—WHOA!" The traffic lights ahead of them turned amber; Harrison hit the gas and roared through the intersection. "You always drive so recklessly?"

"I don't believe in caution."

Kathryn wanted to lecture the guy about taking other people into consideration, but this was the publisher whose recent cover headlines read, *WHEN LANA TURNER SHARED A LOVER WITH AVA GARDNER and ORSON WELLES, HIS CHOCOLATE BON BON AND THE WHOOPSY WAITER.*

The Ambassador Hotel had once represented the height of Hollywood chic, but had failed to keep up with the times. Ciro's, Romanoff's, and Mocambo had replaced the Cocoanut Grove, and the Beverly Wilshire and Beverly Hills Hotel were now the fashionable places to stay.

Harrison pulled into a deserted parking lot bordering the east wing. Paint splintered off the walls; newspaper was taped to a broken ground-floor window; the flowerbeds lay barren. Inside, the hallway carpeting frayed at the edges and smelled like a forgotten shut-in whose only companions were old cats and sepia memories.

They rode the elevator to the sixth floor, where Harrison let himself into room 617. It was an expansive suite with room for a quartet of love seats arranged in a square, and a dining area large enough for eight. Past the table, Kathryn could see a bedroom with two double beds and a blue-and-white tiled bathroom beyond that.

Sheldon Voss stood in the middle of the room wearing a dingy undershirt and baggy trousers that hung from his hips. It took him a heartbeat or two to register Kathryn's face. "You brought this bitch here without warning me?"

"If I had telephoned ahead, would you have answered?"

Harrison crossed to a bookshelf where seven or eight different bottles of booze stood in varying stages of consumption. He helped himself to a drink without offering Kathryn one. "I told you that if need be, I would bring her back here, which is why I suggested that you might want to clean yourself up." He dropped an empty bottle into the metal trashcan next to the desk, landing it with a loud clatter. "But finishing the Gordon's gin was more important."

Voss lumbered toward one of the sofas. "When I came to you—"

"When you came to me you were sober," Harrison shot back. "Big plans spouting out like you were the Bethesda Fountain."

Kathryn could tell this was the latest installment of an ongoing argument, but she was in no mood to stand in a room stinking of cigarettes and body odor, listening to another round.

"I'm here for the missing contents of my father's FBI file," she announced.

Voss thumped the back of the sofa, making a deep dent in the sun-faded upholstery. "What did you tell her?"

Harrison knocked off the rest of his drink and poured a second. "She's a sharp piece of work, which is more than I can say about you."

Voss pointed a trembling finger at Kathryn. "Did Little Miss Sharp Piece of Work tell you that she's my niece? And that I'm her uncle? Thomas Danford is her father." Voss lurched toward the bathroom, muttering about pissing himself to death.

Harrison waited until Voss kicked the door shut. "Is that true?"

*He's learned not to believe everything Voss tells him.* "When was the last time you guys cracked a window around here?" Kathryn fanned herself with her handbag. It wasn't very big and didn't make much of a breeze. "Information came to light indicating Danford and I might be related. I got a PI to look into it but nothing added up."

"This private eye you hired—that wouldn't be the guy sitting with your boyfriend at the Bar of Music, would it? Dudley Hartman's new partner? Ex-FBI, right?"

Running the red light had been a deliberate attempt to lose them, but she needed to reestablish her credibility if she was going to get her hands on those documents.

"For what it's worth, I was more than a little mad to see them there. Like most men, Leo seems to think I need protection."

"Louella, Hedda, Sheilah, Florabel—you're all much savvier than your editors give you credit for. I'd rather work with you girls than all the Winchells put together."

She would have been inclined to believe such candied words had they come from anyone but this ambulance-chasing bottom-feeder.

"Have you and Winchell had a spat?"

"It was a mutually beneficial friendship until it wasn't. I never fully trusted him—and vice versa."

"I assume it was Winchell who stole most of the contents of the file?"

Harrison nodded, preoccupied now.

"Are they here?"

He snapped out of his reverie with a vigorous intake of air. "Now that I know your interest in the Danford case, all this melodrama makes sense. I'm happy to give you everything—" Kathryn's heart leapt "—but—" he headed toward the bedroom "—Sheldon has stashed it in one of the drawers of his bureau. While I'm looking for it, come up with quid pro quo. And make it useful." He opened the door Voss had kicked shut and closed it with a quiet click.

Kathryn spotted a bottle of bourbon on the desk. It wasn't Four Roses but it'd suffice. She splashed some into the cleanest glass she could find and gulped it down as she tried to think of a juicy morsel.

She was pouring a refill when she remembered the increasingly persistent rumors about Frank Sinatra and his mob connections. They were only hearsay, but he'd failed to fix Marcus's passport situation, so the hell with him.

Then again, he was part of the so-called Holmby Hills Rat Pack that included a number of people she knew, like Garden of Allah'ers Bogie and Bacall, David Niven, and Robert Benchley's son, Nathanial, as well as Judy Garland, George Cukor, and Katharine Hepburn. She needed to think more carefully before she offered up Sinatra as a sacrificial lamb.

Something weighty thudded in the other room, followed by muffled shouting. Kathryn opened the door. The striped satin bed linen was half-tumbled onto the floor as though it had been thrown aside in a hurry. Room-service trays and dishes lay alongside half-empty bottles of booze and soda. Every ashtray was full.

The two men were tussling with an envelope similar to the one Felix Miller had delivered. Voss grew more and more red-faced and sweaty as he tried to pull it out of Harrison's grip. "Let! It! Go!" He released a catalog of cuss words that would've made his radio audience faint.

"Keep it down!" Kathryn hissed. "Someone might call management." The room stank like a city dump. "What a couple of pigs!" She opened the room's only window.

Voss swung more and more widely, trying to twist free of Harrison's grip, and almost managed to tip him off his balance, but the guy recovered quickly.

"I'm sick of your shit!" Harrison yelled. They reeled and scuffled all over the room. "You're a useless! Sloppy! Drunken! Has-been!" He let out an almighty grunt as he finally wrenched the thick envelope from Voss's grasp, causing Voss to stagger onto a satin pillowcase trailing on the floor. He skidded sideways, flinging out his hands. Kathryn caught the briefest glimpse of terror in Voss's eyes before he pitched backward through the open window and disappeared.

She stifled the scream that rose in her throat.

Harrison looked wildly around the room. "Where did he go?"

Kathryn ran toward the window; Harrison joined her. They leaned forward and peeked out. Voss lay face down, motionless among the weeds in the neglected flowerbed five stories down.

Harrison shrank from the glass. "This evening never happened. Except for my offer. It still stands."

He bolted from the room.

"Stop!" Kathryn whispered. "What if he's not dead?"

He halted, his hand gripping the knob of the suite's front door.

"If he's still alive, who knows what he'll say?" she pointed out. "And who he'll say it to. We need to go down there."

Harrison checked the corridor, then beckoned her. They said nothing as they raced down the stairwell at the end and onto the hotel's western lawn. Winter chill had cooled the night air. As far as Kathryn could see, nobody was rubbernecking out of their hotel window. She grew breathless as they approached the body.

Voss's arms and legs were flung out at awkward angles.

"Is he breathing? We need to be sure."

"Do you know how to do that?" Harrison's voice was as hoarse as hers.

"You want *me* to check his pulse?"

"I have an aversion to cadavers."

"You think I'm a fan?" Kathryn looked at Harrison but he had turned away. She bent down and touched Voss's right wrist. His skin was warm and the stench of liquor and tobacco still radiated from him. She pressed two fingers to his pulse. "He's gone."

"Okay, then," Harrison said. "I'm off."

"Shouldn't we get our stories straight?" Kathryn asked.

"We had our meeting at the Bar of Music where I made you an offer. The end."

"We were seen leaving together."

"Yes, but only by your boyfriend and the private eye. You can take care of them, can't you?"

Kathryn's breath grew shallow. "I guess."

"Good luck." Harrison pulled his Homburg down and took off toward the parking lot.

Dazed with panic, Kathryn turned away from Voss's body and considered her options. Her vehicle was back at the bar. Could she risk a taxi? Or call Leo? Or Nelson? Or Gwendolyn?

None of those options was ideal, but she couldn't stand there all night next to a cadaver.

A realization struck her so hard she nearly buckled at the weight of it.

The FBI envelope—where was it?

*Think! THINK!*

The two men had been tussling over it. Harrison had yanked it out of Voss's hands. Voss had fallen through the window. But what had Harrison done with it after that? He hadn't had it with him when they'd bolted out of the room.

Was it somewhere in that pigsty?

Five stories up, she reentered the deserted hallway. Twenty years ago, it would have been busy with revelers starting their evening's entertainment.

The door to Voss's room stood slightly ajar. Its hinges squealed as Kathryn nudged it open. *The faster you do this, the quicker you get out.* She tiptoed in and hunted around for the FBI envelope without switching on a light, but it was like combing through a junkyard at midnight for a house key.

It wasn't near the bar, or on the coffee table, or any of the sofas. Nor was it on the dining table or the sideboard that stood against the wall shared with the bedroom.

*Oh God, I'm going to have to go into the Stinkhole of Calcutta.*

Even with the window open, the smell lingered like smog. She picked among the debris of soiled sheets and discarded magazines, socks that reeked of foot rot, and apple cores furry with mold.

She found the envelope slouched against the wall opposite the open window. It was heavier than she expected. As she raced toward the exit, she passed the telephone.

*Should I call reception? And say what? Somebody fell out of a window and broke his neck but I wasn't there and I don't know a thing?*

Had Sheldon Voss been a decent person worthy of the adoration he'd desperately sought, she might have buzzed the concierge. But he'd been a two-faced charlatan and deserved the ignoble death he got.

She tucked the envelope under her arm, took one final look around the mess, then charged into the corridor.

# CHAPTER 36

Gwendolyn waited until Edward Dmytryk yelled, "CUT!" before she snipped off a loose end from the nine-foot rope of pearls she'd been threading.

Dmytryk stood up from his director's chair. "Break for lunch. Back at one."

As the crew began to disperse, he made his way to Gwendolyn. "Gable's scene is the first one we're tackling after lunch," he said. "Do you know if he's arrived yet?"

Gwendolyn straightened out the pearls along the length of her workbench. "I'm sorry, but I don't."

He eyed her handiwork. "What are these for?"

"They'll be looped across the front of a Queen Elizabeth costume that Charles LeMaire has designed for Bette Davis."

"Why are you doing this on my set?"

"*The Virgin Queen* starts filming the week after next and those complicated costumes aren't finished yet. I felt somewhat useless sitting around, so Charles asked Zanuck if I could assist with the costumes. He said sure, as long as I worked on the *Soldier of Fortune* set—"

"I don't care about Bette's pearls. I need Gable in front of my camera at one o'clock. Please tell me you can make that happen."

Gwendolyn jumped to her feet and tried to mask the agony throbbing her abdomen. The doctor had taken out her stitches but the residual pain they left behind attacked if she moved too quickly. She unclenched her teeth. "I'll do my best."

"Your best is only good enough if Gable's here by one o'clock."

She had been focused on Bette's pearls so Clark could have slipped into his dressing room. She knocked three times and called out his name, but got no response. She tried the door; it was locked.

The last time they'd lunched together was the day she'd reported for work after the New Year. As they'd sat down to their usual Caesar salad, he had asked if she was okay after that night at Grauman's. She told him it was an ordinary fainting spell but that Kathryn had panicked and called an ambulance. It wasn't hard to change the subject to how he'd enjoyed sitting next to Judy Lewis.

After that, he lunched with his visitors to the set, most often outdoorsy types from his MGM days. A couple of times she was invited to join them, but she was still very tender "down there" and wanted to discourage any advances until she was ready to take up with him again.

He seemed to sense it too, and didn't push to resume their liaison, but it meant she was no longer as in tune with his whereabouts as she'd used to be.

*Where would I be if I was Clark Gable?* The commissary was the most likely spot she could think of. She was only a dozen steps outside the soundstage when she heard someone call her name.

Loretta Young usually moved with the unhurried air of someone secure in the knowledge that people would always wait for her. But today she came running, her lips parted in distress. She gripped Gwendolyn by the hands and squeezed them tight. "I heard what happened!"

Charles LeMaire's final instructions were to be sure that his unwieldy string of pearls was finished by the end of the day. The job would take hours, so Gwendolyn hardly had the time to run around the Fox lot looking for Clark Gable. Or to be waylaid by Loretta Young.

Did she know about Clark sitting next to Judy at the *No Business* premiere, and, more to the point, did she hold Gwendolyn responsible?

"What did you hear?" Gwendolyn asked.

Loretta pulled her behind an acorn tree outside the fire station. "About your hospital stay."

"Much ado about nothing," Gwendolyn said lightly. "I fainted, is all."

A glaze of tears in Loretta's eyes glistened in the cool January sunshine. "I know what really happened and I want you to know that you have my utmost sympathy. I haven't lost a baby like that, but I—I've—"

*Unintentionally conceived a child with Clark Gable?* "Thank you, Loretta. That means a lot."

Loretta's trembling lips stretched into a smile. "Is everything okay now?"

"Yes, thank—"

"THERE YOU ARE!" Clark's voice hacked into their tête-à-tête like a machete. "I hear you're looking for me."

In an effort to disentangle herself from a sticky situation, Gwendolyn backed out from behind the tree and placed herself in full view.

"I am," she told him. "Dmytryk ordered me—"

"Why were you hiding?"

Loretta stepped out of the shadows. "Hello, Clark."

He looked at her, then back at Gwendolyn. "Am I interrupting?"

"A shared moment of empathy and compassion." The hostility in Loretta's voice was hardly the tone Gwendolyn would have used to divert Clark's curiosity.

"I don't know what that means," he said, "but—"

Loretta pushed her shoulders back. "Life just goes on and on for you, doesn't it?"

Clark turned to Gwendolyn. "What's she on about?"

"Don't talk like I'm not here!" Loretta's breath came in short rasps. "You're all action and no consequences."

"I'm *what*?"

"If you're not going to acknowledge your responsibilities, then I can't stand to look at you." Loretta faced Gwendolyn. "You know where to find me if you need me." She marched away without looking back.

"Why do I feel like the accused?"

"Don't worry about it," Gwendolyn said. "You need to be in costume and made up by one P.M." She stepped out from under the tree, but he pulled her back, obscuring them from view.

"I've heard that tone of hers before."

Gwendolyn fumbled around for a reply, but came up blank.

"That night of the premiere—it wasn't a fainting spell, was it?"

Gwendolyn swallowed hard. "What makes you think that?"

"It was something Monty said to me a few weeks back after one of our sparring sessions."

It may have been the sedative, or perhaps the shock of learning what had happened that had rendered her numb, but Gwendolyn had felt okay in the hospital. The news had been hard to hear, but the doctor had delivered it with calm compassion.

She hadn't fallen apart until she got home.

"It's not like I ever wanted a child. Or even get married," she'd blubbered onto Kathryn's shoulder. "I look at what marriage does to half the people in this town, and I think, 'No thanks!'"

She had drawn her blinds and taken to her bed until she was all cried out.

That's when Monty started dropping by. Who knew he made such a delicious duck-and-corn soup? He claimed he'd learned the recipe in Shanghai fifteen years before and had been perfecting it ever since. They would sit at her table and eat it, saying nothing, relaxing into the silence. When they were done, he'd clear the table, wash the dishes, kiss her on the forehead, and let himself out. He did that four or five times, and then one day he'd said, "It's the possibilities you're grieving for."

She'd asked him what he meant.

"I've met enough women to know that even the career gals, somewhere in the back of their minds they're thinking, 'Yeah, but what if my maternal instincts are slow to boil? I've still got time. It's not too late to change my mind.' But with you, that choice was taken away. And that's what you're mourning, if you ask me."

Things started to turn around after that. Not quickly—a decent night's sleep eluded her for weeks—but at least she was able to drag herself from her bed and report for work.

She looked up into Clark's glowering face, dappled by the leaves above their heads. "What did Monty say?"

"The subject of Carole came up." Carole Lombard often came up in his conversation. "And Monty said to me, 'Grief don't know no time limits. I hope Gwendolyn figures that out,' but I didn't think much about it at the time."

She wanted to take him by the hand, but somebody might see them.

"Well?" he demanded.

She stepped away from the tree and led him into his dressing room on the deserted *Soldier of Fortune* soundstage.

"You're scaring me," he said.

"Let's sit down—"

"If it's sit-down news, I'll take it standing up."

Gwendolyn began to feel like a gangly marionette whose arms wobbled and dithered with no comfortable place to put them. "I wasn't going to tell you this because it's over and done with, and I didn't see the point."

"What does this have to do with Loretta?"

"I didn't faint for no reason at Grauman's that night."

"Stop burying the lead."

She pushed the words out before she lost her nerve. "I had a miscarriage."

"You mean you were—? With my—? And you lost it?" Clark dropped onto the sofa where she joined him and took his big, meaty hand in hers.

"It was an ectopic pregnancy," she explained, although from the vacant expression she wasn't sure he was listening. "That's when the egg stakes its claim in a place it's got no business being. It was only a matter of time. Unfortunately for me, it happened while I was standing in a crowded theater."

A twitch jerked at his left eye. He bit down on his lower lip as though that might still it, but the way his fingers wrapped around her hand and squeezed them told her it was a losing proposition.

"Are you okay?" His words came out shaky.

"Yes, I'm fine."

"Are you still able to have children?"

"They had to go in and—" She let out a deep breath. "The upshot is that I won't be able to."

He relinquished his grip and buried his face in his hands. "I'm so sorry."

Gwendolyn hadn't told Clark about what had happened because she didn't want him to look at her as a narrowly dodged bullet. But nor had she anticipated this anguish.

"Don't be," she told him. "I'm nearly forty-five. Even if I wanted it, the motherhood ship has pretty much already sailed for me."

"Carole and I wanted kids."

"I'm sure."

"The chance to be a father—it's a precious thing."

His efforts to be close to Judy now made sense. Clark was ten years older than Gwendolyn, so if the motherhood ship had sailed for her, he was probably thinking fatherhood was too. This lost baby represented his last chance at being a dad.

"It wasn't meant to be," she whispered. "And besides, you and me? We're not that sort of couple."

His head shot out of his hands. His eyes were bloodshot. "What do you mean?"

"Oh, come on," she nudged him gently. "We weren't destined for a justice of the peace. The pressure was off so we were free to have fun. No harm, no foul. Especially seeing as how it all started with Zanuck and his instructions to keep you happy."

Clark twisted his shoulders toward her. "His instructions?"

"You know what I mean."

"Tell me what he said, exactly." His tone had changed from shaky to rigid.

"He said that he'd moved heaven and earth to get you here, and that it was my job to ensure you were glad you had."

"And that included sex?"

"He didn't come out and say it."

"But he implied it?"

"If I recall correctly, his words were, 'You must know what it takes to keep a man satisfied.'"

"THAT SON-OF-A-BITCH!" He launched to his feet.

Gwendolyn was touched that someone like Gable felt outraged at the thought that she had prostituted herself for him. However, there was a time and place for this conversation, and in his dressing room minutes prior to filming his final scenes on a crucial movie was not it.

"Maybe we could revisit this after filming's done—"

"He treated you like a hooker?"

"I saw your face when Zanuck presented me to you that first day of filming."

"All he told me was that he'd lined up an assistant I'd be very happy with. And when I saw it was you, I figured that he knew we were already acquainted and I'd feel more comfortable coming to a new studio."

"So when you invited me in here for lunch and . . . *dessert*?"

"It was because I think you're pretty damned gorgeous and hoped you might be up for a tumble or two."

"It wasn't because Zanuck led you to believe I had no option?"

Clark paced the floor as though looking for the best place to punch a hole in the wall. "I'm sorry if you ever thought that." He stopped abruptly. "Did you?"

Gwendolyn debated telling him that she had been threatened with losing her job, but after all, what kind of knucklehead would knock back the chance at landing Gable in the sack? "No."

"I've half a mind to march right up to that bastard and clock him right in the kisser. In fact, screw it. I'm going to—"

He charged toward the door but she hooked him by the elbow. "No, you're not."

"He can't treat people like that!"

"He shouldn't, but he can," she countered. "You are not going to punch Darryl Zanuck in the face."

"Why the hell not?"

"Let's be straight up about this," she coaxed him gently. "Zanuck likes to think he's the great and powerful puppet master, pushing and pulling us where he wants us to be, doing what he wants us to do. Okay fine, let him think that, but the joke's on him."

"How do you figure?"

"Because although something unfortunate came out of what we were doing, the fact is I was having fun with you because *I* wanted to. Not because I felt pressured."

He regarded her warily. "No duress, then?"

"None," she reassured him. "You said 'How about it?' and I said 'Sign me up.'"

"Okay. Well. That's different." He snorted. "I still want to punch his teeth in, though."

"But you're not going to do that because you've signed on to do *The Tall Men*, and Zanuck has the power to scuttle it as well as *Soldier of Fortune* if you give him reason to prove that without the MGM machinery, Clark Gable was just a product of studio hoopla. Don't give him that satisfaction."

She could see she was getting through to him; the red blotches of anger were fading from his neck.

"And don't forget *The King and Four Queens*," she continued. "Jane Russell and her husband have worked hard to put that movie together. Don't spoil your shot at producing. Remember: that's where the real money is."

It was now a quarter of one. He held up his hands in surrender. "But we can't let the bastard get away with this."

Despite her noble speech, Gwendolyn could feel the embers of her own anger start to glow. "We won't," she told him. "But wouldn't it be better if we managed to find a way that didn't wreck our futures?"

# CHAPTER 37

Marcus still had Gwendolyn's latest letter gripped in his hand as he turned the corner onto his street.

*Pregnant by Gable!*

He nipped inside the *tabaccheria* to stock up on cigarettes. He needed to read the letter a second time before he could compose a reply.

*Miscarried! In the middle of Grauman's!*

He added matches and a couple of ballpoint pens to his pile and handed over a fistful of lira. He had never felt so separated from Gwendolyn and Kathryn and life at the Garden of Allah.

He turned up his lapels against the chilled wind gusting up the street as he headed toward his pensione. A snifter of brandy, some biscotti, his one thick sweater, the armchair next to the signora's oil heater: he'd need them all to respond to a letter like that. If he'd known what was inside, he wouldn't have taken it to the café where he always read his letters from home.

The double doors into his pensione were pale wood, pock-marked from decades of weather and war, and tall enough to permit a horse and carriage to pass through. Marcus stepped through them and spotted a familiar figure standing next to the tiled fountain in the center of the courtyard. He ducked back into the shadows but was a half-second too late.

"Mister Adler? Is that you?"

He contemplated dashing out into the street and going into hiding for the rest of the day, but she would only come back again. He wiped his clammy hands down his trousers and stepped back into the alleyway.

At forty, Ingrid Bergman still possessed the beauty that had illuminated Hollywood movie screens, but up close, Marcus could see the last five or six years had seasoned her allure with a worldliness that sat on her like a favorite hat.

"Miss Bergman!"

She walked toward him, her hand outstretched. "Please call me Ingrid."

Her skin was soft but her handshake was firm.

"What can I do for you?" he asked.

She duplicated that reticent smile she'd used on Bing Crosby in *The Bells of St. Mary's*. "I was hoping we might have a chat. Perhaps we could get out of this cold?"

Up in his room, she unbuttoned her plain black duffel coat and pulled the gray knitted scarf from around her neck. "Your pensione is charming!"

Marcus set Gwendolyn's letter onto the mantel next to a framed photograph of Kathryn and Gwendolyn, Doris, Arlene, and Bertie crowded on the Garden of Allah diving board. Quentin took it when he asked Doris to be his date to the opening of *White Christmas*. The photo flattered all five of them, so he placed it in full view where he could see it every day.

"I was going to have some brandy to warm up," he told Ingrid, "but I could make us some coffee."

Ingrid beelined for the photo. "Either or." She ran her finger along the top edge of the frame. "Is this Kathryn Massey?"

"I met her the first week I came to Hollywood. I have limoncello someone brought back from Capri, if you'd prefer."

Her eyes, a delightful shade of blue, lit up. "I adore limoncello! Roberto introduced me to it during *Stromboli*."

Marcus lifted the bottle and two shot glasses from the shelf above his desk and told her to take one of his two dining chairs. "Is this about the *Look* magazine photos? Because if they caused you any trouble, it wasn't my intention."

She let out a disarmingly tinkling laugh. "Goodness me, no! I've come to beg for your assistance." The limoncello Domenico had brought back from a couple of weeks on location had a refreshingly tart bite to it. The shadow of the lace curtains covering the window behind Marcus speckled her face. "To be specific, the assistance of *Lo Scattino Simpatico*."

Marcus didn't think anything of Bella Darvi's joke until his *La Strada* photos started appearing in magazines across the continent, prompting a call from *Look,* who wanted to do a feature on him: "An American in Rome: *Lo Scattino Americano* becomes *Lo Scattino Simpatico*."

When Marcus asked how they came up with the idea, the guy said he had interviewed Bella Darvi in Paris as part of a press junket for *The Egyptian* and she talked about the *Scattino Americano* who took those *La Strada* photos.

The article had come out a couple of weeks ago, but Marcus hadn't seen it until Doris sent him a copy of the issue. It sat on the coffee table next to the heater.

"What can *Lo Scattino Simpatico* do for you?"

"Well!" Ingrid cupped her luminous face in her palms. "I recently finished *Journey to Italy.* My husband directed it but the film's having trouble finding a US distributor. I was complaining about it to Humphrey—"

"Bogart?"

"We have kept up a friendship since *Casablanca*. He's one of the few people who didn't desert me after I was denounced on the floor of the Senate. At any rate, he brought up those photos in *Look* that you took of me. He said Americans need reminding that I'm a real person, with real feelings, and your photos helped do that."

The vodka in the limoncello warmed Marcus's innards. Or it may have been the relief to know that his work hadn't been as intrusive as he'd feared. "You want me to take some more shots of you?"

Her smile turned impish. "There's a French play called *Anastasia* about a girl who is posing as the heir to the Russian throne. An English version is now playing on Broadway starring Viveca Lindfors."

"And you're angling for the film?"

"Fox have bought the screen rights. Naturally Viveca is lobbying for the lead, but I think I can do it better. Humphrey told me that you know Zanuck quite well."

"I wouldn't say that, but I do know someone with access to him." He thought of a particularly picturesque corner of the Cinecittà back lot that he discovered when taking photos of a strikingly gorgeous extra.

Not long after Bella Darvi left Rome, he got a call from Domenico. Warner Brothers were soon to start work on *Helen of Troy* at Cinecittà and the director, Robert Wise had asked if he knew an on-set photographer. The job paid well so Marcus took the assignment.

When he spotted one of the extras, the beauty of her unspoiled freshness made her stick out amid a sea of pretty girls. She carried herself like a ballerina, but at the same time seemed delicate as a dandelion.

When he approached her, she seemed faintly surprised. It could have been a ruse—she later confessed that she'd worked as a model from a young age—but it didn't matter. Marcus's photos revealed how much the camera adored the twenty-year-old.

Wise told him to take "as many pictures of her as you want" and arranged twenty-four hour access to Cinecittà. Later, his work turned up in *Epoca* and its equivalents in France, Spain, Germany, and Holland. He didn't receive any more money for them but he did gain extra *scattini* credibility being the guy that helped boost the career of Brigitte Bardot.

Marcus refilled their shot glasses. "How about we rummage through Cinecittà's costume department? I know of a particularly picturesque setting on the back lot where I could take some interesting shots and then send the best of them to Zanuck along with a suggestion that he consider you."

"*Perfecto*!" Ingrid clapped her hands together. "I'm desperate to get back to America and from what I understand, you know how that feels."

Gwendolyn's letter on the mantel glowed like an SOS beacon. She had written about the Gable situation in her usual self-effacing style, as though she'd accidently spilled coffee into his lap instead of falling pregnant by him. But he knew how to read between her lines, and he knew that she knew it too.

Despite the contented relationship he'd developed with Domenico and the success he'd made with this photography job he'd fallen into, Los Angeles sat like a golden bubble below the horizon, shining just brightly enough for him to catch a glimmer every now and then, beckoning him home.

"Yes," he admitted, "I do."

* * *

It took a warehouse the size of Union Station to house Cinecittà's costumes. The togas and uniforms of Ancient Rome filled two full aisles, but Marcus and Ingrid weren't looking for them.

Eastern European peasant girl?

1920s Parisian waif?

Turn-of-the-century Imperial Russia?

"I'll know it when I see it."

Ingrid pawed through dirndls, pinafores, sarafans, and 1920s couture until she pulled out a floor-length gown of white silk, stenciled with an ivy design in gold thread running in vertical bands from the waist. The bodice had a purple sash secured across it, with a tiny gold medal pinned over the left breast.

The stern signora who managed the costume department made it clear that Marcus and Ingrid were free to look around as long as they wished, but under no circumstances could she permit them to take anything outside the building. No, not even Ingrid Bergman.

"There must be a rear entrance to this building," Marcus whispered.

They found a fire escape in the far corner. It was locked, but the key hung from a nearby nail. The door opened directly onto the outer perimeter of a Tuscan village. It wasn't what Marcus had in mind, but the church façade gave Ingrid the privacy she needed to change into the gown.

She emerged five minutes later, lipstick reapplied, hair brushed, and looking more like "Movie Star Ingrid" than Marcus had seen in a while. She turned around so that he could zip her into the dress. It was made for someone with the waist of a twenty-three-year-old but they managed to squeeze her into it.

He steered her through the Roman Forum to a side alley that led to a town square dominated by a richly decorated façade that could be a church, a palazzo, a town hall, or the entrance to the home of an especially rich citizen of the Roman Empire.

"They used this as the outside of Nero's palace in *Quo Vadis*," Marcus explained, "but at the right angle, it can be pretty much anything."

He positioned her in front of a door off to the side. It was stained dark brown with black iron hinges and served as a stark contrast to her white silk. Wooden columns carved with interlocking blackbirds and ivy bordered each side of the door. They didn't look especially Russian, but the ivy in the design reflected the gold ivy in her dress.

With years of posing for portraits and taking direction, Ingrid was a dream model and within ten minutes, Marcus had burned through three rolls of film and was confident he'd caught a handful of images that might seize Zanuck's attention.

The door was still unlocked when they returned to the costume warehouse, and Ingrid was rehanging her gown as the manager called down the aisle, asking if they needed any assistance.

As Ingrid called out, "I think we've got a good idea of what you have," Marcus noticed that the rack opposite held the studio's collection of religious apparel: basic friar habits, cassocks, more elaborate ferraiolos, and up the church ladder to papal vestments.

"Do me a favor," he whispered to Ingrid, "keep her busy down the other end."

Ingrid launched into a speech about the elaborate headdresses for the wives of Roman senators.

Marcus ran his hand along the costumes until he came to a black ankle-length cassock with a tab collar and fuchsia piping. Its neighbor was almost identical but with purple edging, and the one on the other side had red. He knew that each color denoted a different rank within church hierarchy, but damned if he knew which color meant what.

The cassock with the fuchsia piping looked like it fitted him best, so he pulled it from the rack and returned to the rear entrance, where he opened the door and checked to see if anyone was about. He dropped the garment onto the ground and closed the door, locked it, and ran up the aisle.

* * *

Ingrid said nothing until they were three blocks past Cinecittà's main gate.

"I'm sure you have a perfectly reasonable explanation for what's under your arm," she said, "but I won't pry."

Marcus's heart was still beating like a bongo player hopped up on bennies. "I have a substantial amount of money stuck here."

"Locked funds?"

"It's been suggested that if I disguise myself as a clergyman, nobody will question me."

"Couldn't you have just bought one of those?"

"I tried, but they only sell to bona fide members of the church."

"So you'll be smuggling funds out of the country wearing *that*?" Ingrid laughed. "Oh my! What guts!"

Marcus had been sure he had the nerve to pull off this audacious plan back at the olive grove in Tivoli, but now that he had an actual cassock in his arms, the reality of what Oliver had suggested weighed more heavily. "Not that I can leave any time soon. My passport was confiscated back in June."

"Eight months? But how is that even legal?"

He gave her a rundown on Sinatra's reaction to the fake *scattini* photos he had taken of Ava and his lover.

"Have you asked someone to intercede on your behalf?"

"Kathryn cornered Frank but nothing happened. My lawyer got nowhere, and neither did the US embassy."

"Then matters must be taken in hand."

"I've tried everything I can think of."

"Yes, but now you've got me on your side, and in my years on the arm of Roberto Rossellini, I've learned how to handle these Italians. It's like dealing with Louella or Hedda. You have to *charm* them into doing what you want. Tell me, who's the mover-and-shaker in this scenario?"

"Napoleon Conti."

"What a snake! Now we need something we can hold over his head."

"I think I might have something," Marcus said. *Metropolitana* was Fratelli di Conti's all-time box office champ, which made Melody Hope the big meatball in their bowl of spaghetti. Now that she had successfully made the transition from historical dramas to twentieth-century stories, they were planning a new movie set in current-day Rome about a female *scattino*. "It involves Melody Hope."

Comprehension bloomed on Ingrid's angelic face. "So it's true? *Eccellente*!"

"I've heard he's got mafia connections."

"Who in Italy doesn't have those? And anyway, we have better ones. Have you heard about the Holmby Hills Rat Pack?"

Kathryn had mentioned it in one of her letters, but only in passing. "What do you know about them?"

"It's sort of a social group that's sprung up among a bunch of Hollywood celebrities who live in and around Holmby Hills. The Pack Master, as he's called, is Frank Sinatra. We need to prevail on Bogie to get Sinatra to use his connections to back off."

"According to Kathryn, he's already tried."

"Then he needs to try again."

"And what if he doesn't—or can't?"

Ingrid smiled. "Have you heard about the Wrong Door Raid?" *I know someone who was there, but how the hell do you know?* He nodded cautiously. "Sinatra has the whole debacle under wraps, but what if we each wrote to Bogie? Maybe together we could get him to find a way to convince Frank to directly persuade Napoleon to return your passport."

She didn't know that Kathryn had already given Walter Winchell the Wrong Door Raid scoop so that he could turn it over to *Confidential.* They hadn't exposed it yet, but surely that was only a matter of time. If he and Ingrid were going to act on this nutty plan, they needed to do it now.

Marcus asked, "But what if Napoleon refuses? I put one over on him; he hates that."

"In that case, we need to soften him up then attack at both ends. How well do you know Melody?"

"On a scale of one to ten? Pretty high, I'd say."

"We must get Napoleon and Melody together in the same place with you and me. It needs to be public."

The stolen cassock under Marcus's arm was growing heavy. He flagged down a taxi and opened the door for Ingrid. "I know just the place."

# CHAPTER 38

Gwendolyn peered at the afternoon sky through the willow tree at the northern end of the pool. The clouds congealing overhead were tinged with gray and would soon block out the sun.

"Should we move everything indoors?" she asked.

"Nah." Doris deposited her deviled eggs and celery stalks filled with Cheez Whiz on the table Monty had dragged from Marcus's villa. "Whoever heard of an indoor tiki party?"

"Don the Beachcomber." Gwendolyn peered over at Kathryn's villa.

"Where is she?" Doris asked. "Wasn't this party her idea?"

A few weeks ago, when Kathryn had suggested a 'Welcome Back to Hollywood' party for Bette Davis, Gwendolyn had been all for it. Shooting on *The Virgin Queen* was due to start on Monday, and with Bette being absent so long in Maine, she'd liked Kathryn's idea of easing her back into the Hollywood swim.

And then Kathryn had disappeared.

Not physically. Not immediately. But something had happened and she was keeping tight-lipped about it.

With Voss's so-called suicide following closely on Francine's passing, it made sense that Kathryn would be affected by the death of her sole remaining relative—even one she hated.

Gwendolyn knew what "sad Kathryn" and "angry Kathryn" looked like, but this felt different. Whatever the secret, it was occupying all of Kathryn's spare time. She left home only when the demands of her job beckoned. Otherwise, she kept herself cooped up in her villa with the blinds drawn.

When the time had come to organize the party, Gwendolyn quietly took on the task of inviting people, asking them to bring food, drink, and music. She'd asked Monty to see what he could do with Marcus's tree lights, which sat in a box in the main house's basement, and assigned Clark to bring six bags of ice.

"Yes," she told Doris, "it was her idea. Her only task was to tell Bette Davis when and where."

"And did she?" Doris asked.

*Darned if I know.* "When Monty shows up with the lights, could you give him a hand? I'm going to check on Kathryn." She eyed the drawn blinds. *Assuming she'll even answer.*

* * *

Kathryn stood in her living room and wedged her fists on her hips. "I've done it!" she whispered to the papers arranged like tiles, filling nearly every square inch of the floor. "My logic might be flawed or I could be fooling myself, but I think there's enough here to—" She didn't dare say the words out loud.

Getting this far without anybody the wiser felt like a major achievement. But what choice did she have? She couldn't let anybody know she'd been at the Ambassador that night. Not Leo; not Nelson; not Gwennie.

She had expected to find everything in that file arranged in chronological order. Instead, she had a hodge-podge of maps, newspaper articles, grainy photostats of telegrams, FBI memos, as well as dated and undated photos of Danford in various places across New England.

Night after night, Kathryn had laid out each piece of evidence on her living room floor and patched together a timeline. It took her nearly two weeks: the maple plantations in Maine, Operation Pastorius, Amagansett, as well as a whole litany of names, addresses, and telephone numbers of people connected with Jack Sheehan, the present Massachusetts governor and the man who had benefited most from Thomas Danford's downfall.

But was it enough to reopen the case? Kathryn didn't know, but Dudley would. And possibly Nelson. But seeing him again would only muddle her thinking and eat at her resolve. But it was now late February and Danford's execution date was March 31st. She didn't have time to pick and choose.

A knock on the door.

She ignored it.

The second knock was louder, more insistent. "It's me!"

Kathryn stood still, not sure what to do.

"You're getting ready, aren't you?" Gwennie called out.

Kathryn wedged her front door open. "For what?"

"Bette's 'Welcome Back to Hollywood' party."

"No, honey, that's tomorrow."

Worry narrowed Gwendolyn's eyes. "Today's the nineteenth."

*What happened to the eighteenth?*

"Okay. That's it." Gwendolyn pushed against the door until it was wide enough to squeeze through. "I want to know what's going on with you, and you better talk fast because in less than an hour Bette, Clark, Bogie and Lauren, Charles LeMaire, and a whole slew of others besides will be arriv—" She caught sight of Kathryn's living room with the furniture pushed aside and the carpet covered with sheets of paper.

Kathryn tried to pull her back. "It's better if you don't know."

Gwendolyn wrestled herself free from Kathryn's grip and looked down at a US Navy map of the coastline at the northern end of Long Island, pinpointing where the German U-boats were supposed to land.

"Is this what I think it is?" Gwendolyn asked.

Kathryn saw now that she should have done a better job of averting the curiosity aroused by holing up in her villa. "Uh-huh."

"Enough to prove his innocence?"

"I think so."

"Why didn't you tell me what you were up to?"

"I wanted to give you plausible deniability in case the *merde* hits the fan."

Gwendolyn crouched down to read an internal FBI memo that summarized Voss's background. It was the only one that mentioned Kathryn Massey by name. Gwendolyn looked up at her with skeptical eyes. "How did you all get this?"

"It fell out of the sky."

Gwendolyn stood up, unconvinced. "What happens now?"

"Show it to Dudley Hartman."

"Or Nelson."

Kathryn shook her head.

"You're avoiding him, aren't you?" Gwendolyn asked.

"It's easier."

"In the short run, maybe." She seized Kathryn by the shoulders and pointed her toward the bedroom. "Meanwhile, we've got guests coming."

* * *

Gwendolyn exited Kathryn's villa unnerved by what she had seen. Surely the punishment for possession of FBI property was significant? As she returned to the long table where Gardenites had deposited their contributions, Gwendolyn wondered if she was now an accessory after the fact. And what did "It fell out of the sky" mean?

Monty showed up with an armful of tiki torches. Doris trailed behind, holding a bunch, too. "Did you find Kathryn?"

"You know what she's like," Gwendolyn replied. "Work, work, work. She'll be out in a minute."

In her absence, someone had added Swedish meatballs, clam-cheese on crackers, and a pineapple upside-down cake. "Did you make all this?" she asked.

Doris pointed behind Gwendolyn.

She'd been so wrapped up in her thoughts that she'd failed to notice Bogie and Lauren sitting on the diving board, sharing a cigarette.

"You walked right past us," Bogie noted with a mocking grin.

"Like we weren't even here," Lauren added.

"Sorry!" Gwendolyn greeted them with a hug. "We're not quite as organized as I would like. I didn't even think about dessert, so thank you for the cake."

"It's not like you to be in disarray."

"It's all my fault! I fumbled the ball!" Kathryn hurried up the gravel path. "My plate's been even more full than usual lately. Can I make martinis?" She turned to Gwendolyn. *Do we have gin?*

Gwendolyn pointed out the patio table she'd designated as the bar where she'd set up an array of rum and mixers. "We're doing Mai Tais, but tonight they're called Bette's Bitch."

By the time Kathryn had made a batch of Bette's Bitch in the glass pitcher Gwendolyn had filched from Marcus's belongings stored in the basement, Monty had lit the torches, and Clark had arrived with the ice. Quentin Luckett showed up with a couple of friends from Paramount, one of whom had worked boom mics at Warners during Bette's 1930s and 40s heyday. Charles LeMaire arrived with his wife before Bette made her entrance through the French doors of the Garden's bar.

"Ta-da!"

Conversation halted as everybody took in the sight of Bette Davis in an orange pleated skirt, matching three-quarter-sleeved jacket, and zebra-striped blouse. But nobody was looking at what she wore because Bette Davis had shaved her head.

"Didn't anyone tell you people that it's rude to stare?" The flames of Monty's torches reflected in her pink skin, licking the sides of her scalp. "Think it'll catch on?"

Bogie asked the question that everybody was thinking. "Have you lost your ever-loving mind?"

Bette pointed to the cocktail in his hand. "I don't suppose there's a spare one for me."

Gwendolyn hijacked Kathryn's and brought it to her. Bette took a long, theatrical sip. "I'm playing Elizabeth I in *The Virgin Queen*."

"I never figured you for a Stanislavski girl," Lauren commented.

"When I did *Elizabeth and Essex*, I shaved off two inches from my hairline, but growing it back again was a nightmare. So I decided to get rid of the whole lot, figuring that once we were done, it would all sprout back uniformly." Bette bowed her head down. "Go on," she told Gwendolyn. "You can touch it if you like."

Gwendolyn ran her fingertips over Bette's disconcertingly smooth skin.

"It's like a baby's bottom, isn't it?"

Over Bette's shoulder a figure appeared on the gravel path that led to the parking lot. He stood outside the patches of flaming lights, but from his hands-in-pockets slouch, Gwendolyn knew who it was.

She caught Kathryn's attention and flicked a sly glance in the guy's direction.

* * *

Kathryn sidled up to Nelson Hoyt with a party-ready smile plastered on her face. "What are you doing here?"

"Call it a hunch."

She waved to Charles LeMaire, who'd just arrived with his wife. Charles had been tasked with designing Bette's ornate Elizabethan gowns, so it seemed appropriate that they invite him. But now that everyone was gathering disturbingly close to her living room, Kathryn wished she had suggested the back room at Chasen's for this party instead.

"A hunch about what?" she asked.

"According to Leo, you and Harrison drove around and talked after he lost us in traffic."

"You and Leo talk often?"

"The next morning, the papers were full of your uncle's snapped neck at the Ambassador. And then complete radio silence from you. Leo told me that he's barely seen you since that night."

"What else do you and Leo talk about?"

"So I say to myself, Hmm. I've got all the puzzle pieces: Kathryn, Voss, Harrison. Winchell must be in there somewhere, but nothing's adding up. I figure she'll be ready to talk sooner or later, but it's been two weeks, so the mountain has come to Mohammed."

"Sorry, but Miss Mohammed is hosting a party—"

"Where's Leo?"

"You tell me."

"You don't know where your fiancé is?"

Kathryn felt her face redden. She told Nelson to follow her, and took off toward her villa. Two minutes later, they were standing in front of the grid of papers.

"Did you push Voss out the window?"

The shock of his question jettisoned her reply before she had a chance to temper it. "It was an accident. There were these bed sheets—on the floor—silky ones—slippery—he fell out." Nelson didn't need to know that she was the one who had opened the window. "I swear!"

"And I believe you."

He wrapped his arms around her and she let her head fall against his chest. "God, it was awful."

He began to stroke her hair. She felt safe, protected. She caught the tang of freshly applied shaving cream. Had he cleaned himself up on the off-chance he'd find her at home? She was flattered, but none of this was right. She might not know where Leo was, but he was still her fiancé. Pulling away from him, she waved her hand over the arrangement. "I'm no legal expert but I think it's enough. So what now?"

"If you trust me with all this—"

"Of course I do. More than you probably know."

He smiled for the first time. "That means more to me than *you* probably know." The longing gaze returned, but a squeal of laughter near the pool broke the mood. "Here's the thing: only Governor Sheehan can pardon Danford. However, he benefited from your father's misfortune, so let's not count on him coming to the rescue."

"What about Danford's lawyer?"

"This is stolen evidence."

"He was already a goner. I simply picked it up as I left the room."

"It's inadmissible in court. This stuff needs to go back where it came from. And we need you-know-who's help."

"It was hard enough to trust Winchell in the first place. Now I have to trust him to get it *back* in the FBI vaults?" Kathryn slumped onto the doorjamb separating her living room from her foyer. The party noise outside felt so incongruous with what she was feeling. "All right, let's do that."

"We can't."

"We don't even have *that* option?"

"Hoover and Winchell have had a bitter falling-out and now Winchell won't have anything to do with him, or the FBI, especially if it means they could take the credit."

"Does that leave us with anybody?"

"Just one."

"Who?"

"Hoover himself."

Before Kathryn could gather her thoughts, Nelson leaned in.

* * *

Gwendolyn spotted Kathryn reemerging from her villa as the conversation shifted to one of Fox's big summer hopes, *Love Is a Many-Splendored Thing*, which would start filming next month. Bogie's new picture, *The Left Hand of God*, was due to go into production around the same time, and the month after that, Gable's *The Tall Men*.

"With all that going on," Bette exclaimed, "plus my *Virgin Queen* and Billy Wilder's *Seven Year Itch* in the summer, it looks like Fox has taken MGM's place at the top of the heap. Zanuck must feel like he's king of the world."

"He barely even cares."

Bella Darvi stood next to a huge mask of a Polynesian god called Ku. She wore a figure-hugging sheath in layered vermillion silk that Gwendolyn had made for her European press junket. At the time she hadn't been sure the outfit worked, but with Darvi standing with Ku on one side and a flaming torch on the other, it certainly made its mark.

Earlier that month, *The Racers*—in which Kirk Douglas played an Italian racing car driver to Bella's improbable ballerina—had bombed at the box office. Despite her implacably indifferent façade, Gwendolyn could tell Bella was despondent, so she had invited her to the party, never thinking she'd show up.

"I ain't buying it," Clark responded. "That guy lives, sleeps, and breathes Hollywood."

Bella shrugged. "He's getting sick of the day-to-day grind of churning out movie after movie. He wants to run away to Europe with me. Perhaps not tomorrow, but some day."

"Has he shared with you his idea of a possible replacement?" Kathryn asked.

"Buddy Adler."

Buddy was the producer on *Soldier of Fortune* and Bogie's *Left Hand of God,* as well as *Love Is a Many-Splendored Thing*.

"Trust me," Bella said with a smug smile, "he's dropping the ball on many fronts. He thinks of himself as Mister Movie Mogul and refuses to see that television production is a lucrative form of income. Even I know that, and I don't give two hoots about such things."

This revelation—that Zanuck might soon be leaving Twentieth Century-Fox as the studio was approaching its long-nurtured zenith—was the sort of news that could tip the balance of power within the entire industry.

Clark looked around. "Bogie needs to hear this. Where is he?"

Gwendolyn knew exactly where Bogie was: sitting with Kathryn in what looked like a confidential powwow behind the mask of Kahoalii, god of the underworld.

* * *

Kathryn didn't know where to begin. With everything that had been going on, she'd forgotten about Marcus's request. She felt like the world's most horrible friend when she saw Bogie and realized she'd done nothing.

"If I'd known you were going to take this long to talk," he said, "I'd have refilled my Bette's Bitch." He tried to loosen her up with a grin, but he only succeeded in looking like every gangster he'd played on the screen. "Who was that guy I saw you sneaking into your place with? The shifty-looking one. Handsome, though, in an offbeat sort of way. You're not stepping out on Leo, are you?" He lifted his hands. "Not that it's my business. When things started up with wife number four, I was still with number three, so . . ."

Things were complicated enough, but did Nelson have to plant that kiss? Telling her she needed to approach Hoover was like a left hook, but the kiss that followed was a one-two punch.

When Nelson had apologized, she'd told him it was only the high emotions running rampant. When he apologized again, she admitted that she enjoyed it, which prompted him to kiss her a third time. After they'd broken apart, she'd smoothed her hair while he adjusted the bulge in his pants. She told him to collect up the papers in order and let himself out and then left a little breathless.

"It's about Marcus."

Bogie pressed his pockets for cigarettes. "I thought I'd see him tonight."

"He's still in Rome—but not by choice."

Kathryn filled Bogie in on the saga of Marcus and his passport. When Bogie asked what the hell Marcus was going to do, she said, "That's where you come in."

Kathryn sensed a shift of mood in the party. She looked across the pool to see an arresting figure dressed in bright red standing alone, backlit by tiki flames. She was too far away to be sure, but if it was Bella Darvi, then Bette wasn't going to be happy about losing the spotlight to the stacked brunette currently bedding the boss of half the people at this party. She had to make this quick before the contents of Pandora's box were unleashed.

"It concerns the Holmby Hills Rat Pack."

"Does it also concern Ingrid Bergman? I got a letter from her the other day."

"Did she tell you how Sinatra exacted revenge by using his mafia connections to get Marcus's passport confiscated? And how we need you to prevail on him to use those same connections to undo what he's done?"

Bogie lit a match. The light flared in his face, revealing a wariness in his eyes. "That's pretty much the size of it."

"Will you talk to him?"

"From what I understand, Frank's already tried. And besides, we're talking the Italian mafia here, so I'm not sure what good will—"

"Ask Frank about what happened when he and DiMaggio went after Marilyn with a baseball bat."

"Christ on a cracker, do I even want to know about that?"

"*I* do."

Lauren Bacall stepped out from behind the Kahoalii mask and sat beside her husband. "Frank's our friend," she told Bogie, crossing her arms. "If he's committed an act of idiocy and we can help him undo it, we will. And sometimes a woman can get through to a man better than a man can."

"Oh, really?" Bogie sneered, half in jest, but only half.

She told him to shut up, then turned to Kathryn. "I've heard rumors but I want to know the whole story. I felt protective of Marilyn when we were filming *How to Marry a Millionaire,* so if she's suffered at the hands of one of our friends, I want to help put that right, too. What's the point of having a Rat Pack if we don't have each other's backs?" She fixed Kathryn with a very Bacall stare. "Tell me everything."

* * *

"You know," Monty said, holding the plate of Swedish meatballs skewered with toothpicks, "maybe this explains why Zanuck hasn't nailed down the screen option rights for *On the Deck of the Missouri.*"

Clark shot a quizzical look at Gwendolyn, who returned it with a this-is-news-to-me shrug. "What do you mean?"

Monty plucked a meatball off the platter and brandished it toward Bella. "This here gal is saying how Zanuck is starting to check out of the movie game, so I'm thinking maybe he's dropped the ball on the contract he's been promising 'cause I ain't seen hide nor hair of it."

Zanuck had launched his best charm offensive on Clark in an effort to get him to sign on for the movie version of Monty's memoir. He'd dangled the name of John Ford as a possible director knowing that Ford had directed Clark in *Mogambo,* his biggest hit since the war.

But Clark had been reluctant to sign on without reading the book first, so Monty had given him his author galleys. It was probably against the rules because the book wasn't due out for another month, but as Monty told Gwendolyn, "If I can trust the guy not to punch my brains out, I guess I can trust him with a book."

It was a shrewd move—Clark saw the book's screen potential and with Clark's name in the mix, Monty could jack up the price. Gwendolyn assumed that the deal was in place, but she could see from the blank look on Clark's face that nothing had happened yet.

"Let me get this straight," Gwendolyn said to her brother. "Zanuck hasn't ever made you an offer to buy the rights to *On the Deck of the Missouri*?"

"Nope."

"Written, verbal, or otherwise?" Clark asked.

"Not even on a banana peel."

Gwendolyn plucked a meatball off Monty's platter and turned to Clark. "Are you thinking what I'm thinking?"

# CHAPTER 39

The main dining room of the Café de Paris on Via Veneto bubbled with the chatter of Romans who'd performed their weekly penance of attending Sunday services and were now free to commit as many of the seven deadly sins as their urges dictated.

The menus were black with a line drawing of a large rooster in blue, yellow, and red. Marcus didn't dare peek over it. "Are they there yet?"

Domenico stole a glance. "The table's still empty."

"But it's past one o'clock."

"I hate to ask," Trevor said with a laugh fueled by a trail of Negronis that Marcus suspected led back to mid-morning, "but are you sure Ingrid Bergman can be counted on? I mean, you've already mailed those photos; what's in it for her?"

"She'll hold up her end of the bargain."

"She did help Marcus steal that monsignor cassock," Domenico pointed out.

The costume had become a point of friction as soon as he'd discovered it in Marcus's closet. Domenico's asking about the stolen vestment confronted Marcus with the reality that this also meant saying goodbye, and now he wasn't so sure he wanted to.

Life in Rome wasn't so bad: his pensione was comfortable; he had no trouble getting magazine work; the wine was delicious; the food was to die for; and Domenico was everything he'd always wanted in a boyfriend. *Why would I leave this?*

"It's my just-in-case plan," he told Domenico. "Regardless of what happens, I need my passport back. Without proper identification, I feel like a ghost. How about we focus on one issue at a time?"

"Wasn't Ingrid denounced in the Senate a few years ago?" Melody asked.

Marcus glared at her: *You're not helping*. She disappeared behind her menu.

"Look lively," Trevor whispered. "Incoming."

Marcus moved his menu aside enough to see Napoleon and Emilio Conti stride into the restaurant like they were Julius Caesar and Marc Antony invading Gaul. The maître d' led them to a four-top table set for three.

A waiter appeared beside Marcus and asked if they were ready. They weren't, but this was the most popular restaurant in Rome on their busiest day of the week. They couldn't sit there indefinitely. He ordered another round of Negronis and told the guy they would order lunch soon.

"What's happening?" Melody asked. "These damned sunglasses are so dark."

"The coast is disconcertingly clear," Marcus reported. *Now that Gwendolyn's put your photos in front of Zanuck, please don't bail on me. Don't be a flake. Don't abandon me.* He ran his eye down the menu but took in none of the choices.

Ingrid Bergman appeared at the front doors in a tea dress of gold sateen that flared out in sunray pleats. It swirled around her legs as she weaved around the tables. Around her shoulders was a gauzy wrap appliquéd with a pattern of gold petals.

The Conti brothers scrambled to their feet and greeted her with a kiss on the hand. They gallantly waited for her to be seated at their table. Napoleon called the headwaiter with a finger snap and loudly ordered a bottle of Moët et Chandon. It arrived at their table within seconds. The Contis let fly with a patently phony laugh designed to draw attention to their table. Not that it was necessary—all eyes were already on them.

The Negronis arrived. Marcus ordered a plate of bruschetta and another of prosciutto and figs. He trusted Ingrid's sense of timing, but it seemed to take forever. Finally, she removed her sparkling wrap and draped it on the back of her chair.

Marcus crossed the dining room. Without waiting for an invitation, he pulled out the fourth chair and sat down. Napoleon blinked rapidly and pulled his mouth into a scowl like he was forcing down a wad of rising bile. Maybe he was. Marcus clasped his hands together and rested his elbows on the table. "It's my understanding," he told Napoleon, "that you've been asked to call off the dogs and have them release my passport."

He wasn't sure what had happened back home. Kathryn's message wasn't clear, but someone—Kathryn? Bogie? Bacall?—had prevailed on Sinatra to try harder.

"You *what?*" Emilio rose half out of his seat. Napoleon told him to calm himself and reminded him that everybody was looking, but Emilio was beyond caring. "This *bastardo* is a thorn in my side since he arrived!" Spittle collected at the corners of his mouth. "I want to be rid of him and yet *you* keep him here?"

So Emilio really had no idea all this was his own brother's doing? It was a twist Marcus hadn't seen coming, but he couldn't afford to be distracted.

"When can I expect my—?"

Napoleon pulled out an American passport from his inside breast pocket and started to fan himself with it. Until Marcus got a look inside, he couldn't be sure it wasn't from the studio prop department. He made a grab for it; Napoleon pulled away.

"But why?" Emilio spluttered.

"Because this little *bastardo* cheated us out of ten thousand American dollars and I wasn't going to let him leave the country without getting it back."

"That ten grand was mine fair and square," Marcus said.

Napoleon waved the passport again. "You wrote a story twenty years ago that nobody wanted. Anything more than three hundred was greed. So I forced you to stay in my country until I can get my money back."

"*Metropolitana* was one of your biggest hits," Marcus countered. "You got your money back a hundred-fold."

Napoleon sucked at his teeth. "Listen to me, you little *americano* parvenu, nobody takes advantage of Napoleon Conti!"

Ingrid brought her hands together and smiled. "Gentlemen, gentlemen!" she said softly, "Everybody is watching us like we're the circus freak show. This encounter will soon be the talk of Rome, and not favorably. With so many people watching, Signore Conti, I would suggest you think twice before making a rash move."

Marcus thanked him for bringing his passport and went to take it, but Napoleon kept it out of Marcus's reach. In his other hand appeared a platinum cigarette lighter with the Fratelli di Conti logo engraved on the side.

"What are you going to do?" Marcus asked. "Burn it? Right here in front of everybody? The US embassy will issue me a new one now that it's been released."

Napoleon narrowed his eyes. "Unfortunately for you, the Immigration department does not know it has been released. As far as they're concerned, it is officially still under seizure. That means your embassy cannot issue a replacement. And this is why I carry it with me whenever I leave the house. I trust nobody."

"Mr. Conti," Ingrid maintained her sweetest smile, "what would it take for you to return Marcus's passport to him?"

"Ten thousand dollars."

"But you did very well out of *Metropolitana*. So tell me, what else?"

Napoleon started slapping Marcus's passport into the palm of his hand with a measured rhythm. Nearly a minute went by without him saying a word.

"Perhaps I can make a suggestion," Ingrid prompted. "Let's talk about *The Gates of Rome*."

All three men at the table sat upright at the mention of the Fratelli di Conti's hottest new property about a woman who returns to Rome after having fled the city during the war. Napoleon had taken a leaf out of David O. Selznick's book and had turned the casting of the lead role into a Scarlett O'Hara-type search.

"This character," Ingrid said, "she and I are the same age, no?"

Everybody in this restaurant knew that the Conti brothers would sacrifice their grandmother to cast Ingrid Bergman. While Napoleon launched himself into a flowery speech designed to convince Ingrid to do what she had no intention of doing, Marcus angled his shoulders away from the table.

"You'd better convince your brother to hand over my passport," he told Emilio.

"Otherwise what?"

"Did you see the table where I was sitting?"

Trevor picked up a large envelope and drew from it one of the photos Marcus had taken the night he followed Emilio to the queer bar. They had come out surprisingly well, and showed Emilio sitting intimately close to the redheaded guy. Trevor left it visible long enough for Emilio to recognize himself. Marcus had no intention of sharing those photos with anyone, but it was the best way he could think of to get Emilio's attention.

Torment and divided loyalties battled it out on Emilio's face in twitches and pained grunts. "I beg you."

"To immigrate to the US, you need a sponsor." Marcus wasn't sure if a non-relative or non-employer would qualify, but Emilio was desperate to escape to America, so if anything could get Emilio on his side, this might do it. "I'd be willing."

"After everything I've done to you?"

"I know what it's like to be on the outside looking in. We have more in common than either of us wants to admit."

He turned to look at Domenico, then back at Marcus, comprehension dawning on his face. He slapped the table. "Hand over the passport and let's be rid of this foreigner."

Napoleon glared at Marcus. "What did you say to my brother to convince him to go against the family?"

"The family?" Emilio cried out.

"Family comes first."

"My whole life I am Emilio the afterthought. Emilio the unwanted. Emilio the embarrassment."

"As long as I am the head of our family, you will not speak to me in such a way. You will give me the respect I deserve."

When Marcus smelled Gwendolyn's Sunset Boulevard perfume, he knew Melody had picked up her cue.

"Oh, for heaven's sake, Napoleon, stop being so dramatic."

Napoleon's face drooped when she slowly pulled away her billboard-sized sunglasses with one hand and her hat with the other.

The buzz around the Café de Paris changed to people crying out, "*La Speranza! La Speranza!*"

"You're going to hand over Marcus's passport," Melody told Napoleon, "and you're going to do it right now. Otherwise, I'm making a certain announcement to that crowd of *scattini* on the sidewalk."

The muscles at the corners of Napoleon's steel-cut jawline visibly clenched. He flicked open his cigarette lighter. The bright orange flame lit up his face as he brought it close enough to almost lick the bottom of Marcus's passport.

"I'm sure you don't need me to remind you that in our new movie I play a female *scattino*," she told him. "I guess that'd make me a *scattina*, wouldn't it? At any rate, I've become their mascot."

The flame stayed where it was, not close enough to set the passport alight, but not moving away either.

Marcus cleared his throat. "Whoever reaches the press first controls the story." He extended his right arm, flattening his palm so it was six inches from his passport.

When Napoleon tossed it to Marcus, everything that followed was a blur. Marcus vaulted to his feet; Melody laughed; Ingrid yelled "Screw you!"; a flash bulb went off; a second one; somebody screamed; Trevor's face appeared; Domenico pulled Marcus through the restaurant; everybody was shouting; a cork popped; a wine glass shattered.

Out in the street, the traffic seemed louder. Horns were blasting; men were shouting; the wind howling along Via Veneto had a colder bite to it. The *scattini* hovered and darted around each other like bees.

"I'll hold them off," Melody told Marcus.

Marcus, Ingrid, Domenico, and Trevor dashed up the street in a huddle and turned a corner into a side alley that stank like three-week-old garbage.

"Well!" Trevor exclaimed, laughing. "That was an adventure!"

"The passport?" Ingrid pressed her hands to her chest in an attempt to catch her breath. "Please tell me you've got it."

Marcus held it up.

"But is it yours?" Domenico's question cut a somber note through the uproar.

Marcus turned it over in his hand. The gold eagle emblem stamped into the teal leather looked genuine enough. He opened it.

"I'd forgotten how unflattering my photo was."

# CHAPTER 40

Gwendolyn walked into the foyer of the Moulin Rouge nightclub. Immediately, she felt the tension choking the air.

"Jeez!" Monty exclaimed beside her. "I thought the Emmy Awards would be a big ol' party, but this feels like a court martial."

Gwendolyn pointed out an NBC television camera parked inside the glass doors. "It's the first time the ceremony is being televised. I'd imagine everybody feels like they're on show."

"Aren't show people always on show?"

A surge of excitement ran around the crowd.

Lucille Ball and Desi Arnaz arrived amid a barrage of flashbulbs and applause. Lucille's red hair seemed to catch on fire in the portable spotlights. She shielded her eyes with her hand and pressed through the mob.

"She's looking for refuge." Kathryn waved, beckoning them toward her.

"Thank you," Lucille said as she approached. "Once we got inside, I panicked. Where do we go now? Who do we talk to?"

"It's the price you pay for being the most-nominated show tonight."

Lucille scrutinized Gwendolyn. "You're the gal who does Loretta's dresses, aren't you? I saw her coming in. She looked a bit awestruck."

"She's flattered to be nominated for Best Actress, but she's up against you, Gracie Allen, and Eve Arden, so she rates her chances very low."

In truth, the real reason for Loretta's nervousness stemmed from clinging to the perception that she belonged in feature films, and how she'd be considered "just a TV personality now" amid the sea of film people invited to tonight's ceremony. NBC was keen to get high ratings for the broadcast, so they'd lured as many celebrities as the Moulin Rouge would fit, which was how Gwendolyn and Clark had swayed Zanuck into attending.

Clark had told Zanuck, "I'll go if you go," knowing he would view film people attending the Emmys as slumming it. However, Clark also knew that Zanuck was anxious to keep him at Fox. Once Zanuck had capitulated, he decreed that the stars currently at Fox were commanded to accept the Television Academy's invitation—and that included Bette Davis, who arrived behind Lucille and Desi with her current director, Henry Koster.

Gwendolyn waved them over.

"Are we all here?" Bette asked.

"Waiting for the two main players."

Koster frowned at his date. "What does that mean?"

Bette told him, "Private joke," and pointed to the front door. "Look! It's Zanuck and his wife Virginia."

"With Gable behind him," Koster said. "But who's his date?"

The four of them emerged from the lightning storm of press photographers and into the foyer.

It had taken two weeks, a pack of broken needles, seven Band-Aids, three pounds of paillette sequins, and thirty yards of silk-backed lamé the color of lava, but Bella's strapless extravaganza with the plunging neckline and the mermaid silhouette was the most exciting dress Gwendolyn had ever created.

"Virginia and Bella in the same limo?" Lucille murmured. "Must have been a hell of a ride."

Gwendolyn caught Clark's eye as Lucille and Desi's production team beckoned them away. He charged across the foyer like Pecos Bill, forcing poor Bella to trail behind him.

"GREAT TO SEE YOU!" He greeted Kathryn and Gwendolyn with a bear hug, and Monty with a two-fisted handshake, then whispered, "Is he watching?"

Zanuck was used to playing kingpin to an audience of sycophantic brown-nosers, but these TV people were strangers. His smile was strained, and he wasn't sure what to do with his hands.

Gwendolyn waved at him and smiled. Relieved, Zanuck stampeded through the crowd as Clark had done.

"Well, well, well!" he exclaimed. "This looks like the fun group."

Gwendolyn did what introductions were necessary, saving Monty for last.

"Ah!" Bette exclaimed. "You're the remarkable memoirist I keep hearing about. A friend of mine at *The Saturday Evening Post* told me they're hoping to serialize *On the Deck of the Missouri* and what a marvelous picture it would make. I assume some clever producer has snapped up the rights?"

"Gee, Miss Davis, I'm awfully sorry." On the drive over, Gwendolyn had instructed Monty to pretend he was Jimmy Stewart, circa *Mr. Smith Goes to Washington*." Her suggestion had meant nothing to him, so she told him to play it hayseed. "None of the rights to my book have been secured."

Zanuck perked up. "Except the screen rights, of course."

"I have to contradict you there, Mr. Zanuck. My agent is still fielding offers from the studios."

"WHAT?" Clark wheeled around to square off with Zanuck. "You've been *lying* to me?" Confused, Zanuck started stumbling over half-syllables like Elmer Fudd. "You've been dangling this juicy carrot in front of me but you don't even hold the rights? Christ almighty! How the hell am I supposed to trust anything you say? I've got choices now that I've left MGM, and I'll be damned if I'm forced to work with anyone I can't trust."

He draped his arm around Bella, landing a hand near the top of her right breast. He hauled her off into the rubbernecking onlookers, who parted like rehearsed movie extras.

* * *

"Thank you!" Steve Allen boomed. "You've been a marvelous audience." He looked into the camera in front of him. "And that goes for you lovely people at home, too. I hope you've enjoyed our broadcast, but it's time for me to say good night and God bless." He froze until the house lights came on.

"What a shocking evening," Kathryn remarked. "*I Love Lucy* goes home empty-handed and Loretta wins Best Actress."

People were starting to circulate in the aisles and drift toward the foyer, congratulating, commiserating, schmoozing, gossiping. But no Zanuck.

Gwendolyn joined Kathryn in the aisle. "He left early?"

"I'm not sure what upset him more: realizing that he didn't hold the rights to Monty's memoir, or that his mistress was Clark Gable's date."

Virginia Zanuck battled against the tide of people ambling up the aisle. It was a good sign—if she was still here, her husband probably was, too.

Though reasonably attractive in her actress youth, Zanuck's wife looked ten years older than her fifty-three years. She was unfailingly pleasant, though, and nobody's fool.

"My husband needs to see you," she told Gwendolyn. "Immediately if not sooner, to quote him verbatim."

She followed Virginia to a side exit, which led to a corridor. Zanuck stood in the doorway that Gwendolyn guessed opened onto the wings. The end of his fat Montecristo glowed bright orange in the semi-dark.

"Your brother's memoirs—are they really still up for grabs?"

"The other day he commented on how surprised he was that movie negotiations took so long, especially considering you're going to have to deal with him if you want the navy's cooperation.'"

"I thought we'd locked down the rights months ago. I don't know what happened."

*What happened is that you're losing your grip.*

"Do you know how much the other studios have offered?" he asked.

She started fanning herself with her purse. "Goodness gracious me," she pretended to fret. "I'm not sure that I'm comfortable revealing—"

"Who pays your salary?"

"You do, Mr. Zanuck."

"Don't make me repeat the question." He obscured himself behind a veil of smoke.

"Monty doesn't share everything with me but I can tell you that MGM's price was $220,000."

"That much, huh?"

"Monty's agent told him it was high because Dore Schary couldn't stand the thought of losing to Paramount. So you can assume Paramount bid at least two hundred big ones."

Zanuck started pacing the width of the corridor like a skittish colt. "But why Paramount?"

"You must have heard the scuttlebutt about DeMille's remake of *The Ten Commandments*."

Zanuck shook his head.

*You really are losing touch.* "Kathryn's date tonight is head of writing at Paramount and he told her that filming on *Ten Commandments* has gone so well that it could be the biggest moneymaker of the decade."

Zanuck choked out a scoffing grunt. "The budget's twelve mill. It's the most expensive film ever made. They'll be lucky to break even."

"But if they're right, they'll be able to outbid everybody. You need to swoop in with a can't-say-no offer."

"Of how much?"

Gwendolyn started pawing at her handbag. "This is a conflict of interest. I'm not—"

"HOW MUCH?"

She threw him an outraged glare. "The phrase 'quarter of a million' will serve a whole bunch of purposes. My brother lives on a military salary, so he'll say yes; it makes for great P.R. copy; it'll shut out the competition; it'll almost guarantee you'll get Gable, which means you'll probably get John Ford. It's a ripping yarn right up Ford's alley, but you already know that."

The door to the wings swung open and a couple of performers ran past. In the light slipping in from the doorway, Gwendolyn caught the hesitation in his eyes.

"You have read it, haven't you?" she asked.

"Not exactly."

"You're prepared to shell out a quarter of a million on a book you haven't even read?" The Darryl F. Zanuck of ten years ago wouldn't have done that.

"I've been busy," he snapped.

"With Bella?"

Zanuck rolled the cigar back and forth along his fingertips. "Is she sleeping with Gable?"

Gwendolyn wanted to swat him across the face with her handbag, but it featured an oversized paste emerald that could leave a mark if she struck him in the wrong place. "That's a hell of a question to ask the girl you all but forced into having sex with Gable."

"Oh. Yeah. I did feel bad about that later."

"Careful, Mr. Zanuck, your conscience is showing."

He jabbed the burning end of his cigar at her. "From what I hear, you were having a damn good time."

"It wasn't the worst job I've ever had, even if it ended up—"

She cut herself off five words too late.

"I heard rumors," he said, more softly now.

This conversation was supposed to be about manipulating Zanuck into coughing up a fortune for Monty's book, but it had veered into territory Gwendolyn hadn't anticipated. "Sleeping dogs, Mr. Zanuck."

"Was it that bad?"

"I think Virginia's probably waiting for you out there—"

"Please tell me."

"If you must know, I had a miscarriage that resulted in emergency surgery and now I'm unable to have children. Glad you asked?" She regretted her catty tone when she saw his horrified look.

"Why didn't you come to me?"

"What's done is done—"

"I'll make it up to you."

*You can do that by making my brother a rich man.* "Lookit, at my age the question of kids is largely a moot point. So let's move on and make sure Monty's agent receives a generous offer."

"No, really, I'll make it up to you. I don't know how, but I will. But before I go, you still haven't answered my question."

The desperation in his voice said everything.

"No," Gwendolyn said, "your mistress isn't screwing Clark Gable."

* * *

Zanuck's $250,000 offer arrived on the desk of Monty's agent the next day. In a coincidence that usually only happens in a P.R. manager's wet dream, Monty signed the deal the same day that his book came out.

News of the screen rights, along with glowing reviews, helped *On the Deck of the Missouri* climb up the bestseller list alongside *Auntie Mame*, *Marjorie Morningstar*, and *Bonjour Tristesse.*

With his huge payday, Monty settled the outstanding debt for Gwendolyn's store. She told him he didn't have to, but he insisted, saying it was the least he could do. She accepted his generosity and felt lightheaded as she walked out of the bank with a statement that read, *"ZERO AMOUNT DUE."*

But while Zanuck had wasted no time fixing the Monty Brick situation, his promise to Gwendolyn went neglected—but that was okay.

As she'd half-expected, Gwendolyn's "special assistant" job dried up. She'd done for him what he wanted, so she returned full-time to the costume department, where her paycheck reverted to what it had originally been. But with her bank debt wiped away, it was enough for her needs.

Over the month that followed the Emmys, she assisted Billy Travilla and Charles Le Maire on a silly movie about two burlesque dancers hiding out in a college. Hoping to recapture some of the magic from *How to Marry a Millionaire*, Zanuck promoted its writer, Nunnally Johnson, to write and direct *How to Be Very, Very Popular*, and cast Betty Grable in what was going to be her last movie for Fox. Her reign was grinding down; an end-of-an-era feeling pervaded the whole production.

On the last full day of shooting, Grable charged into the workroom holding a dress that Gwendolyn knew she ought to be wearing in front of the camera right at that minute.

"This needs a repair job," Betty said. "The shoulder."

Gwendolyn took the garment from her. It was an ordinary dress that she wore under a coat in the chicken-eating scene and would barely be visible. She inspected the dress as Betty played with a zipper that Gwendolyn was about to insert into a blue dress she was making for Jennifer Jones in *Love Is a Many-Splendored Thing*.

Gwendolyn was used to an upbeat, chatty Betty Grable, not this nervous, distracted woman unable to look her in the eye. "You want to tell me what's going on?"

Betty dropped the zipper. "I'm in hiding from Zanuck's secretary."

Irma was efficient, loyal, diplomatic, and discreet, and knew how to tie her hair into the tightest bun in Hollywood, but she wasn't scary. "Why would you be hiding from her?"

"Because Zanuck's been hounding me with messages and telegrams to come see him once *Popular* has finished filming. But the closer I get, the harder it is for me to face the fact that twenty-five years are coming to an end, so I've been avoiding him."

Zanuck's secretary appeared at the costume department's doors. "There you are, Miss Grable." Irma held considerable power and had a fleet of runners to do her bidding. She rarely went out of her way to track down anybody herself.

Betty rolled her eyes at Gwendolyn and turned around. "I had a costume emergency and it seemed quicker if I came here myself. We're holding up filming, so perhaps it could wait until—"

"Mr. Zanuck has been trying to speak with you all week. He has an audition for you."

Betty's mouth fell open, and Gwendolyn didn't blame her. For two decades, she'd been one of the most famous women in America.

Irma approached Gwendolyn's workbench. "MGM has announced its first foray into television with a half-hour show called *The MGM Parade*. So now Mr. Zanuck feels like he's got to take action."

"Like what?" Betty's question sounded like it'd been throttled to within an inch of its life.

"He's calling it *Fox Fanfare*," Irma said. "They need a host and he wants you to report to Stage Nine at two o'clock. And don't worry, Nunnally is happy to shoot around you until you get back."

"I guess it's all set." Betty forged her most appealing musical-comedy smile, and waited until the swinging doors had stopped swaying behind Irma. "He's asking me to audition?" she demanded. "For *television*?"

"Look what it's done for Loretta Young," Gwendolyn rejoined.

"After twenty-five years, if that's the best he can do, I'm better off out of here."

"And fair enough, I guess," Gwendolyn said, "but are you really going to let the whole crew—and probably Zanuck himself—wait around until they realize you're not coming?"

"That would be unprofessional, huh?" Betty toyed with the zipper again as she paced the length of the workbench. "But I can't bring myself to—I mean, I just can't. I want to run out the door and keep running."

"Do you want me to fetch Irma and tell her?"

"Forget it. That woman is faster than the Super Chief. I don't suppose you could go for me?"

Gwendolyn looked down at the silk with white flowers embroidered onto it. The design wasn't quite right yet and Charles was waiting on her next sample. She hadn't encountered Zanuck since the night of the Emmys, which was fine by her. He'd delivered on his promise to Monty and that was enough.

Betty scooped up her costume. "This place is swarming with pretty girls who'd gleefully do backflips if it meant auditioning for a television show, so let them. We can finish *Popular* tomorrow. I'm o.u.t., out."

She dashed from the room.

* * *

The set was a den, if designed for a woman's use: frills around the lampshades and pink throw cushions. Twenty people milled around, adjusting lights and checking lists. Zanuck was conferring with a rotund gent in horn-rimmed glasses, who Gwendolyn took to be the director. She waved down an earnest girl in long braids and a Peter Pan collar, but it attracted Zanuck's attention. He crossed the set in seven long strides.

"I was with Betty Grable when Irma told her about this audition," Gwendolyn told him. "She was dreadfully insulted."

"What? Why?"

"There's a way to go about asking a star of her stature to audition for television, and sending your secretary wasn't it."

He rolled his notes into a baton and slapped his leg with it. "I'm not auditioning *her*. It's everybody else: the cameramen, lighting, sound. Nobody here's done TV. The guys are nervous as hell that we get this right, so I asked them who they wanted in front of the camera so that they'd feel comfortable. Down to the last man, they said, 'Betty Grable!' She's always been so kind to them, they've loved working with her. With her contract coming to an end, they figured it'd be the last chance they have."

"Why didn't you explain that to her?"

"She's been avoiding me like I've got leprosy. So now I have to send someone to the *Popular* set?"

"Too late," Gwendolyn told him. "She was so insulted that she's flown the coop."

"JESUS!" He slapped his rolled-up paper against his leg again; this time a loud *thwack* echoed across the soundstage. Every member of the crew froze. "We've only got a couple of hours. *The Left Hand of God* crew's gotta start building their hospital set today." He eyed her, tossing an idea around. "I need you to do me a favor. It's real easy. Just stand in front of the camera and read the cue cards. That's all. But you'll need to do it a bunch of times because like I said, we don't know what we're doing."

Gwendolyn fought back a rising urge to run screaming out the door. "Not on your life."

"Just smile and say the words. Is that such a big ask?"

She wanted to scream YES! but an explanation meant describing how her calamitous screen test for Scarlett O'Hara had led to becoming the laughing stock of private screening rooms across Hollywood.

He told the crew to stand by for the first take.

*It's a few words on cue cards. The sooner you do it, the sooner it'll be over.*

"I know you requested Betty Grable," Gwendolyn announced to everyone, "but she couldn't do it so you're stuck with me."

The makeup guy pulled out a pot of tar-black lipstick, and eye shadow almost as dark.

Gwendolyn reared back. "You're not putting that on me!"

"Television cameras need more light," he explained, "so there's greater contrast."

"I'll look like a panda bear!"

"Not on the TV monitor, you won't. Come on, honey, I've got five minutes to get this done."

He went about his work as Gwendolyn read through the lines on the cue cards carried by the girl in braids.

*Hello and welcome to Fox Fanfare. Each week we'll be bringing you one of the many Twentieth Century-Fox motion pictures that you've loved so much . . .*

When he was finished, he stepped away to assess his work.

"I look like Morticia Addams from those *New Yorker* cartoons, don't I?" she asked.

He admitted that she did as the portly gent called for quiet. "Could we get full lights now?"

Light flooded the set; Gwendolyn could barely see the cue cards.

"Everything okay?" Zanuck's voice came from someplace on her right.

Heat hit her skin like the flames of hell. "We'd better get going before I melt like a cheap candle."

"Attagirl," Zanuck chuckled. "You ready?"

*Yeah,* Gwendolyn thought. *Ready to get back to the costume department.*

# CHAPTER 41

Sammy Davis Jr. waited until a couple of *Ed Sullivan Show* stagehands had wheeled a balsa-wood palm tree into place before he approached Kathryn. "Nervous?"

"Me?" The squeak to Kathryn's response gave her away. "I did have a long-running radio show, you know."

"Live television's a whole different can of hairspray, baby." He snapped his fingers. "Oh! Wait! Maybe *I'm* the one who's nervous."

"Oh, please. You've been performing since you were knee-high to a duck."

Sammy tapped his left temple. "But now I got me this sparkly new glass eye. It screws with depth perception. I don't want to go falling over any of those cameras now, do I?"

Television cameras were the size of Shetland ponies; Kathryn doubted that he was likely to fall over one so obviously he was using it as a conversation icebreaker.

They were standing behind a beige velvet curtain. Its folds began to billow around them.

"How's Frank?" she asked.

Sammy broke into a wide smile that quivered at the edges. "He asked me to say hi to you but only if no sharp objects were within reach."

A laugh popped out of her, easy and natural. It was the first time she'd laughed like that recently. Her only hope to save her father's life lay with J. Edgar Hoover and she still hadn't heard from him.

Her readers thought she was in New York for *Ed Sullivan*. Getting on the show had been the easy part. The *Hollywood Reporter*'s New York office manager knew the guy in charge of booking talent and within an hour it had been set up.

But it was all a ruse.

Nelson had tracked down an FBI agent pal of his who worked out of the New York office. He'd gotten word to Hoover that Kathryn Massey wanted to see him and was prepared to come to Washington to make it happen.

The response had taken an agonizing eight days, and when it came, it was good news—sort of. The instructions were succinct: *Be in New York on March 27. Details of time and place by special messenger.*

March 27th was a Sunday; *The Ed Sullivan Show* aired on a Sunday. The timing would have been perfect had it not left four days until Danford's execution. But what choice did she have?

A second message arrived: *Return stolen information immediately.*

Kathryn was glad that only Nelson had been in the room when he'd delivered that information. No Leo, no Gwennie, no Wilkerson—nobody to see her collapse into a teary, sweaty, snotty, stuttering, blubbering mess.

Nelson hadn't told her to pull herself together, or to stop acting like a ridiculous female. He silently put his arm around her and gently guided her head to his shoulder and waited until she was done with her wretched self-pity.

"Stealing evidence from the FBI is a federal offense, so Hoover could have thrown the book at you," he'd pointed out. "But it seems like he's got bigger fish to fry, and perhaps he needs you to fry them."

Kathryn had nearly kissed him. She sure wanted to. They were alone and he was sitting right there, breathing heavier than she was. But Leo. It was always "But Leo."

She'd pulled away, thanked him, and left. The next day, she announced a week-long stay in New York, recruited Mike Connolly to supplement her column with late-breaking news, and booked a TWA flight to Idlewild Airport.

To the outside world, Kathryn Massey had been having a gay week of Broadway shows: *Cat on a Hot Tin Roof*, the opening of *Damn Yankees*, and a preview of *The Diary of Anne Frank*, written by her former Garden of Allah neighbors Frances Goodrich and Albert Hackett. On other nights, she went to the premieres of *East of Eden* and *Blackboard Jungle* and later rhapsodized over an exciting new actor, James Dean.

But in reality, it had been torture. It was just like the day she waited for the FBI file from Herman Klurfeld. Jesus, do all of these guys wait until the last minute just to torment a girl?

Every time her telephone at the Pierre rang or a message was delivered to her door, her heart gave a little start. But it was always "Paramount would love to take you out for lunch at the Grand Central Oyster Bar." Or "Dorothy Parker wants to meet for drinks at the Plaza but she can't afford it so they'll have to make do sneaking a flask into the Automat."

Now it was eight o'clock on the night of the 27th and still nothing. The desperate hope in her heart felt like a canary in a coal mine gasping for breath.

She and Sammy watched the stagehands set up four more palm trees.

"I'm singing 'Birth of the Blues' tonight," he said.

"Are those palm trees for you? Because 'Birth of the Blues' and California palm trees seem like an odd— " The perplexed look on his face sliced off the rest of her sentence. "What?"

"Birth. Of. The. Blues." He articulated each word with excessive emphasis.

"From your new album, right?"

"Aren't you supposed to ask me where?"

"Where's what?"

He unbuttoned the front of his black velvet jacket and started flapping it to cool himself. "Man, I'm just not cut out for this. A message was sent to your hotel this afternoon. Didn't you get it?"

"I was shopping at Bergdorf Goodman for this." She pawed at the voluminous black-and-white cocktail dress with the huge flower print. "It took much longer than I counted on so I came directly here."

"Great!" He slapped his sides. "My one chance to play Sammy the Spy and I blew it."

"What's the message?"

"*I* was supposed to say 'Birth of the Blues,' and *you* were supposed to say 'Greenwich Village,' and then *I* was supposed to say 'Eleven o'clock and don't be late.'"

*Thank Christ for that!* "And the location?"

Sammy shrugged.

A cold sweat tingled across her back.

"Miss Massey?" The stage manager was a nebbish called Irving. "This is your half-hour call. The green room is— "

"Thank you."

Sammy snapped his fingers again. "There's a jazz bar in the Village called Birth of the Blues, and it's a favorite of Frankie's."

Kathryn felt her body go damp beneath her Yves St. Laurent original. "And what does Frank Sinatra have to do with all this?"

"I'm not even sure what 'all this' is, but he did say to me that he's the one who made tonight happen and that he hoped it was enough for you to forgive him."

"I did that when Marcus got his passport back."

"Who's Marcus?"

Kathryn told him never mind and assured him that he'd done his super spy job perfectly. An assistant appeared, telling him that he was required on stage for camera blocking.

She blew him a kiss for good luck and billowed the petticoats under her skirt. National live television allowed no do-overs for a girl sweating like a hooker in a confessional.

* * *

Kathryn rushed into Birth of the Blues, handbag in one hand, hat in the other. The message had warned against tardiness and it was ten after eleven.

Following her appearance on *Ed Sullivan*, she'd left the building with plenty of time to get downtown. She had expected to encounter fans at the stage door, but assumed they'd be for Sammy. And some of them were, but the majority wanted to speak with her, tell her how much they admired her, and get her autograph. It was like the height of her radio days all over again.

Her first impulse was to push past them, smiling with a firm eye on the line of taxis at the curb. But she was now representing three national brands—Sunbeam Mixmaster, Betty Crocker cake mixes, and Westinghouse appliances—as well as the *Hollywood Reporter*, and couldn't ignore these people. She might still have been there had it not been for Sammy bursting through the stage door behind her.

Birth of the Blues was in the basement of a West Village brownstone. With walls painted velvety chocolate brown and matching table lamps, it felt like an old speakeasy, and reminded Kathryn of the Tiffany Club where she had seen Ella perform.

*Sinatra was at the Tiffany Club that night, too. Do all roads lead to him?*

She'd assumed she was meeting Hoover, but now wondered if it would be Winchell. New York was his turf. Had he and Hoover patched over their disagreement? Kathryn couldn't imagine Winchell consenting to be anyone's lackey—not even Hoover's—but she wasn't sure of anything anymore.

A cocktail waitress with Joan Crawford eyes approached her. "You looking for someone?"

"We were due to meet here at eleven." *Don't tell me he left because I was ten lousy minutes late.*

"What does he look like?"

She peered around the joint as best she could in the low lighting. "I'm not sure."

"Blind date, huh?"

"In a manner of speaking."

The waitress snapped her gum. "You ain't Miss Massey, are you?"

"I am, yes."

The girl looked at Kathryn like she was dumber than a lobotomized coconut. "Hardly a blind date then, is it?" She led Kathryn up a short flight of stairs to a small mezzanine level that overlooked the stage. Three tables were empty; at the fourth sat a solitary figure in a porkpie hat with his back to her.

"He's drinking whiskey and soda. Same?"

Kathryn nodded and approached the table. She didn't see who it was until she reached the other side.

Frank Sinatra scrambled to his feet and pulled out the chair next to him. "Hoover's been detained so he sent me to meet you." He tendered one of his unfiltered Camels. Ordinarily, unfiltered cigarettes were stronger than Kathryn preferred, but this scenario had taken on a surreal quality and she longed to feel the ground beneath her feet again.

She took a long drag and waited for the hit of nicotine to wallop her system. "What are you doing here?"

"Trying to get back into your good graces." He started flipping the gold lighter through his fingers. "Being in love with Ava Gardner, it's agony. She drives me to do stuff that I'd condemn in a second if some other dope did it."

"Are we talking about Marcus's photos?"

"Yep."

"And how you used your mafia connections to get his passport confiscated?"

"Yeah, yeah, all that."

"It makes you a prick, not a dope."

"And that whole debacle with DiMaggio and breaking into the wrong apartment."

"Okay, now *that* made you a dope."

"You'll get no argument here. So when the Bogarts took me aside and explained Marcus was still stuck over there, I thought to myself, Well Frankie ol' boy, you're going to have to go straight to the top."

"You called Hoover? Just like that?"

The waitress appeared with a couple of whiskeys and a bowl of peanuts, and told them the show would be starting soon.

"Not just like that," Frank said, "but I know people who know people. Please tell me Marcus got his passport back."

"He did, so thank you. I mean that."

"I bet he's glad to be stateside again."

Marcus had cabled confirming he had his passport, but hadn't mentioned booking a flight. She'd been expecting word every day since, but nothing had appeared.

"What did you have to do in return?" she asked.

He stiffened his spine and snatched the porkpie from his head. "Good evening."

J. Edgar Hoover had grown thicker around the waist since the last time she'd seen him. A little thinner and grayer up on top, too. But that menacing air still clung to him like leeches.

"Miss Massey," he said, nodding as he sat down and deposited a briefcase on the spare seat. "Sorry I'm late, but running the Bureau is a very full-time job."

"I can only imagine." Frank's Camel had stirred up a heady mixture of confidence and bluster. "Can we get down to business? March thirty-first is in four days."

The waitress appeared with another round of drinks. She started to ask if they needed anything else, but lost her nerve and fled back down the stairs.

Hoover reached into his briefcase and pulled out a folder. He let it fall from his hands, allowing it to thump the table. "I want to know how this information came into your hands."

"It proves my father's innocence, doesn't it?"

"Yes, but that's not what I asked."

Underneath the table, Kathryn gripped the bow-shaped metal clasp of her handbag. It started to hurt but she didn't care. She'd been working on the assumption that the contents of her father's FBI file were enough to exonerate him, but she had never been really sure until she heard Hoover's breezy "yes."

"There's a real case to be made for exoneration?"

"I asked you where you got this information."

Frank mouthed the words "Tell him." His eyes said *Don't leave anything out.*

"Winchell," she said, finally.

Hoover slammed his fist on top of the folder. "That slimy little fucker."

"I'm not his greatest fan, either," she added, "but he was my best chance of seeing Danford's name cleared."

"What gave you the idea that he was innocent?"

"Sheldon Voss."

"The evangelist?" Frank interrupted.

"Why would Voss frame him?" Hoover asked. "And why would he tell you?"

Kathryn wished they could get to the part where Hoover would agree to order the Massachusetts governor to issue a pardon. She should have guessed there'd be hoops to jump through first.

"Thomas Danford is my father." J. Edgar Hoover had the best poker face in America and was hardly likely to break it over news like this. Somehow, it gave Kathryn the nerve to keep going. "The night of Voss's MacArthur Park revival, we had a huge blow-up, during which he admitted that he'd framed Danford. I figured if that were really the case, you guys would have a file on him. I didn't know if it contained anything useful, but it was all I had. Winchell and I struck a deal. If he could wrangle access to information the Bureau had collected, then he was free to take the glory of getting Thomas Danford exonerated."

"I see." Hoover picked out a peanut from the bowl and started tearing away at the shell. "So Winchell gave you this information."

"No," Kathryn replied. "I didn't set eyes on it until—" *Crap, oh crap, oh crap. I'm going to have to admit everything.* In an hour's time there would only be three days left. "Until I was in Voss's room at the Ambassador."

"The night he died?"

Kathryn nodded. "Robert Harrison approached me—"

"That slob from *Confidential*?" Frank cut in.

Kathryn told him yes. "And by the way, he knows about the Wrong Door Raid."

"What's the Wrong Door Raid?" Hoover asked.

"Another discussion for another time." She tapped the folder in front of Hoover. "This was in Voss's room at the Ambassador."

"And tell me, Miss Massey, how is it that the file was in your possession when you left the Ambassador that night?"

"Harrison wanted to give it to me but Voss didn't. The two of them fought over it."

"Who won?"

"Voss was drunk. It was like fighting a sleepy toddler."

"And then?"

"I had what I came for, so I left."

"With Harrison?"

"No, he was long gone."

"Was Voss still alive when you left the room?"

"Yes." This time Kathryn paused, but wished she hadn't—it made her sound unsure of the facts. "There's no mystery and no skullduggery. It's just like the papers said: he was drunk and fell out the window. The end."

"The end indeed."

Kathryn wasn't confident that her version of the truth would hold up under scrutiny, but maybe if she moved things along fast enough, nobody would notice. "So," she said, tapping the file once more, "are you convinced Danford is innocent?"

Hoover nodded.

Kathryn drew in a deep breath. "Enough to present a case to the governor?"

Another nod.

"Even though he's the one who benefited from my father's conviction?"

"That won't be a problem."

"So you'll do it?"

"That's up to you, Miss Massey."

"In that case, I say let's go!" Kathryn could barely keep herself seated. "You have a car and driver. If we set out right now, we could be at the governor's mansion by dawn."

Hoover didn't stir.

*Don't be a fool,* Kathryn told herself. *There's always a catch.* "What exactly do you want, Mr. Hoover?"

A one-shoulder shrug. "What've you got?"

Kathryn turned away from the table, partly in disgust, partly in desperation. Once—just once—it would be nice if someone did someone else a favor without expecting payment in return.

Downstairs, the quartet of musicians climbed onto the stage. The drummer sat in the corner, and the bass player, guitarist, and pianist spread out along the front. The pianist was a Negro woman who held herself upright like a dancer; she launched into "Lullaby of Birdland."

Kathryn turned back to Hoover. "Isn't it enough I tipped you off about the LA bureau?"

"What tip-off?"

"About how they were laundering Voss's donations."

"I got that tip from Winchell."

"Oh yes, that'd be right. Mister Take All the Credit. Well, it didn't come from Winch—"

"Can you prove it?" Hoover asked quietly.

She jutted out her chin. "The National Council of Negro Women."

"What about it?"

"Their offices are on the next floor down. Mrs. Cornelia Wyatt heads up the California chapter. She's an honest, forthright woman who'll tell you what's been going on." She pulled out her address book. "If you have pen and paper, I can give you her phone number right now."

Hoover pulled a pad and pen and jotted down the number Kathryn gave him.

"So what happens now?" Frank asked, although nobody was looking at him.

Hoover asked, "You're staying at the Pierre?" Kathryn nodded. "A car will collect you at six o'clock tomorrow morning."

* * *

A gleaming black town car was parked at the 61st Street curb when Kathryn stepped outside. The chauffeur tipped his cap and opened the passenger door.

"How long will it take us to get to the Massachusetts governor's mansion?"

"My instructions were to take you to our destination without comment. Please step inside the vehicle."

Kathryn bent down, expecting to see someone—Hoover? Sinatra? Given the wildly improbable events of the past twenty-four hours, maybe even Marcus?

The cabin was empty.

She slid across the black leather.

*If we drive up Manhattan and end up on the I-95, that'll take us to Boston and the governor's office. If we head downtown on Park Avenue, that means the FBI's New York headquarters. But if we take the Queensboro Bridge, we're going back to Idlewild and I'm being run out of town.*

She watched the New York blocks slip by her window as they drove through the sixties, the eighties, and soon passed 110th Street. After they crossed the Harlem River she lost her bearings. She saw the turnoff for Yankee Stadium, but after that, the names meant nothing to her. Knightsbridge? Riverdale? Where the hell were they going?

Then she saw the sign for Yonkers.

*Upstate New York? What is there to do in the Catskills in March?*

It wasn't until she saw the sign for Tarrytown that her heart began to beat faster and she felt the color drain from her face.

"Are we going to Ossining?" she half-shouted. "I need to prepare myself. I'm not normally the hysterical type but there's a first time for everything and this might be it. Driver? DRIVER?"

"Sorry ma'am, but my instructions were strict—"

"Screw your instructions and screw you!" She ripped open her purse and groped around for a handkerchief. The heat of tears rose at the back of her eyes. They would soon be spilling out. Hot. Thick. Wet.

*There'll be splotches of mascara staining my face like soggy goddamn spider webs. And spit. And snot. Everything'll be leaking from everywhere. I'll look like an escapee from a nuthouse. I won't be able to string two words together. Where the hell is a handkerchief???*

"Driver? I'm sorry about that 'screw you' business. But I don't suppose you've got a spare—"

He was already handing over a freshly laundered men's handkerchief.

She mopped herself up and looked out the window again: *SLEEPY HOLLOW*

"The Headless Horseman," she muttered. "He's all I need."

She fanned herself with her purse and took slow breaths. For the next five miles she managed to hold herself together until she saw a sign welcoming her to Ossining.

Pressing the chauffeur's handkerchief to her mouth got her through the next mile, but the final sign nearly undid her completely.

SING SING
CORRECTIONAL FACILITY

She bent over and jammed her face to her knees. She'd read it was good for blood flow. "Don't lose it now, Massey," she whispered. "Don't lose it. Don't lose it."

The sound of tires crunching on gravel rose from below her. The brakes let out a thin shriek as the car came to a stop. The driver got out, rounded the front, and opened her door. Kathryn did her best to straighten up with a scrap of dignity. "Thank you." She smoothed her hair and took the driver's hand.

A raw breeze blew off the Hudson, but the sky stretched overhead in a clear blue arc. In front of the main gate a solitary figure in an ill-fitting dark suit stood with a brown paper package tucked under one arm.

Kathryn bit down on her lip to still her trembling chin. She placed one foot in front of the other. The gravel felt slick underfoot and her heels provided little comfort.

The man didn't move.

As she drew closer, single step by single step, she could make out his features. Round gold-rimmed glasses framed his eyes, but she caught a glimpse of the same shade of hazel she saw when she looked into the mirror. His hair was thin and graying, but retained enough of its original dark brown for her to know what it once looked like. And no amount of sagging, weathered skin could hide the determination of that familiar chin.

She was close enough now to see him swallow hard. He clasped his hands together to still the shaking.

She took another step.

He did, too. "Are you my Kathryn?"

His voice wasn't familiar like a father's should be. But it was warm, and it trembled with hope.

*My Kathryn. He said 'my Kathryn.'*

She opened her mouth but the words wouldn't come, so she nodded and threw herself against him as the tears gushed out of her in heaving sobs, soaking his shoulder.

She didn't care if she never stopped crying again.

# CHAPTER 42

Marcus hung up the last of the photos he'd developed on the set of *Too Bad She's Bad.* He particularly liked a shot he'd caught of the three stars, Vittorio de Sica, Sophia Loren, and Marcello Mastroianni, mid-laugh after their director had let out an Italian cuss word in the middle of a take.

He let himself out of his darkroom and pondered the monsignor cassock laid out on his bed.

Time felt different now that he had his passport back.

For nine months, he'd lost sleep worrying how he was going to get it back, whether he had overstayed his visa, and what the authorities might do when he left the country.

But after the excitement of that day at the Café de Paris had subsided, the urgency he felt to leave Rome had ebbed, too.

Life in Italy—with its chianti and its linguine allo scoglio, its Via Veneto and caffè macchiato, and especially its Domenico Beneventi— had taken on a charm that Marcus hadn't fully appreciated. It was as though a cinematographer had snuck new lenses into his glasses that bathed the Eternal City in romantic, golden light.

After he and Ingrid made off with the cassock, he'd stowed it in his closet and put it out of his mind. But now it had started to preoccupy him.

No, he kept telling it. Now that I can leave at any time, I'm not sure that I want to. No, he insisted, I'm not going to try it on because . . .

He didn't have any clear reason he could articulate about why he didn't want to. I just don't, he told it. That's all you need to know.

But after returning from the *Too Bad She's Bad* set, a burning curiosity enveloped him. He laid it out on his bed. The lace curtains cast a dappled shadow across the fuchsia piping.

*I'm going to try it on. See if it fits. Nothing more than that.*

He ran his fingers down the front. Smoother and more comfortable than he expected, he guessed it was cotton mixed with silk. He undid the six leather buttons from the waist to the collar and opened it up, exposing the large label that claimed it as the property of Cinecittà. He'd have to unpick it if he ever went through with this cuckoo plan.

He shucked off his shirt and pants and pulled the vestment over his head, letting it fall across his shoulders like a shirtwaist dress. The bottom hem brushed the top of his feet. He stretched out his arms like Jesus on the cross and wished he had a full-length mirror. Signora Scatena had one, but she'd probably keel over if she caught sight of him in this get-up. But it wasn't necessary to put her life at risk: from collar to ankles, wrist to wrist, it was a perfect fit.

It was kind of like being in drag, but the sort of drag you could cross oceans in and nobody would pay the slightest attention, except perhaps to genuflect.

He walked into his bathroom and strained to see as much of himself as he could in the oval mirror over the basin. Black didn't suit him, but with his horn-rimmed glasses and graying hair, he almost looked the part.

He pulled at the sides. Oh yes, plenty of room. Rossano's tailor could sew secret pockets for his cash and travelers cheques. If the tailor was as discreet as Rossano promised, this could work.

A knock on the door startled him. "It's me, Domenico! I have someone you must meet." Domenico was two steps inside before he caught sight of Marcus's costume. His gaze wandered up and down the cassock but he avoided meeting Marcus in the eye.

The chap behind him was in his mid-fifties, with a full head of gray hair and Cary Grant–level charisma. "You didn't tell me he was a monsignor."

Domenico frowned. "He's not."

Marcus couldn't separate the emotions coursing across Domenico's face. Disappointment? Anger? Desperation? He pulled at the edges of the cassock. "It's a costume."

Domenico drew the stranger forward. "Marcus Adler, may I present Clement Rousseau. Clement, this is Marcus Adler."

Rousseau shook Marcus's hand, but the hesitation in his smile broadcast *This isn't what I was expecting.*

"Please ignore everything from the neck down," Marcus told him. "It's a long story too complicated to go into." He gathered up his street clothes from the floor. "Give me two shakes and I'll change."

"I have a train back to Paris that I must catch very soon."

"Let's take a seat," Domenico said. Marcus's café-sized dining table had only two chairs. He dragged over an ottoman.

"Permit me to come to the point," Rousseau said. "I work for *Look* magazine."

"He heads up their entire European operation," Domenico put in.

"*Exactement*. Monsieur Adler, your photographs, they are very distinctive. *Vous comprenez?* They are not like the work of other *scattini*." Rousseau started counting off with his fingers. "Ingrid Bergman, Ava Gardner, Brigitte Bardot, *La Speranza*. Every one of them has a quality to them like no other. Perhaps because you bring an American sensibility."

"Are they really so different?"

The Frenchman nodded sternly. "I pass most of my day looking at photographs, and I always know when a Marcus Adler lands on my desk."

"I'm flattered." Marcus stole a glance at Domenico, whose desperate smile had turned hopeful.

"I want to offer you a retainer," Rousseau said. "Two hundred American dollars per month."

"In exchange for what?"

"I want first look at everything. If we don't accept it, you are free to sell on the open market. But we see them first. And I don't mean only movie stars and celebrities. I want everything—cities, country landscapes, churches, taxis, beggars in the streets, aristocracy walking their dogs, nuns feeding stray cats." Rousseau rested his elbows onto his knees and pressed his hands together. "Modern, post-war life. Whatever takes your eye, wherever you are, I want to see it."

"He is not talking only about Rome," Domenico broke in. "He's offering you all of Western Europe. Imagine it! Zurich, Stockholm, Madrid, Brussels, Majorca!"

Marcus turned to Rousseau. "That's quite an offer."

"You accept?"

"I'll certainly think about it."

"*Très bien.*" He deposited a business card on Marcus's table. "I hope to hear from you soon."

Marcus held open his front door as Domenico and Rousseau exchanged Continental kisses on each cheek. By the time Marcus closed his door, he already knew his answer.

"So," Domenico said, turning around and rubbing his hands together. "His offer! It is *fantastico,* no?"

"It's a head-spinner," Marcus said.

"'Head-spinner'? Is this good or bad?"

"It could go either way."

Down in the courtyard, Signora Scatena sang an old Italian song about unrequited love. Her off-kilter notes sailed through the open window as the two men gazed at each other.

Domenico was the first to pull away. He dropped down onto one of the dining chairs; it wobbled as it took his weight. "You will not accept, eh?"

"Dom—"

"You are returning to America."

"It's home." Marcus joined him at the table. "It's where my roots are. And it's calling me back."

"Oh!" Domenico threw his hands in the air. "So you make the offer to sponsor Emilio Conti to immigrate to America, but do you make the same offer to me?"

"I have no idea what the laws are. But if I can, would you? My sister works at Columbia. She does the same thing you do at Cinecittà. Maybe she could get you a job and we could live together at the Garden of Allah, and—"

But Domenico was already shaking his head. He sandwiched Marcus's hands between his own while he found the courage to look him in the eye. "Italy is my home. It is my fatherland. I cannot leave it."

"So you understand why I must go back to mine?"

They sat in silence and listened to the signora finish her mournful song. As her breath ran out on the final note, Domenico's eyes glistened.

"As I heard Mister Bogie say once, I gave it my best shot. Clement was my ace in the sleeve. He owed me a big favor so I called him."

"I'm sorry you wasted the favor."

Domenico pressed Marcus's hands even more tightly. "When you survive a war, you learn to play the gamble. You celebrate when you win, and also when you lose. So tell me, how much longer do I have you?"

"That depends on Rossano Brazzi's tailor."

"At least a week?"

"I'd say that's about right."

"We shall celebrate every night, my little Marcus Aurelius Americano Molto Simpatico."

As they leaned in for a kiss, Signora Scatena's reedy soprano warbled through the window, a new song, something about *arrivederci e buona fortuna.*

*Goodbye and good luck.*

It was almost as though she'd been listening the whole time.

# CHAPTER 43

Gwendolyn ran a finger along the panels of white satin laid out on her worktable and tapped her cheek with a finger. "I don't know," she told Billy Travilla. "A six-inch slit at the back will only let her take the smallest steps."

Billy nodded. "I've already pointed that out to Marilyn, but she said she was fine with it."

"I hope her limo isn't slung too close to the ground. She'll have a devil of a time getting out all ladylike."

"The press will have a field day if she can't."

"The press always has a field day at her premieres, but especially for this one. I hope *The Seven Year Itch* can live up to its publicity."

"It will if she brings—" Billy cut himself off and kept his eyes on the table between them.

"Do you know who she's bringing as her date?" Gwendolyn already knew, but wasn't sure if Marilyn had confided in Billy.

Marilyn had been AWOL from Fox for a year. It was a hell of a long suspension, but it was self-imposed—a declaration that she couldn't care less. She was glad to have escaped the stifling goldfish bowl that Hollywood had become and was thriving in New York. In her most recent letter, Marilyn had dropped one or two broad hints that she and DiMaggio weren't completely over and that she might bring him as her date.

"We spoke long-distance on the weekend," Billy said archly.

"I got a letter."

The two of them looked at each other, their eyes wide with unasked questions. They started talking at the same time.

"Joe DiMaggio?"

"What is she thinking?"

"With everything she's been through?"

"That night she filmed the subway scene—"

"I heard she got bruised—"

"And now she wants to start up again?"

"Sounds masochistic if you ask me."

The telephone rang in Billy's office. He told her to start with the bodice and they'll figure out the bust later.

He returned a minute or two later. "You've been summoned."

* * *

Irma sat at her typewriter, her back straight as a fence, her fingers a blur as she banged out yet another memo. When she saw Gwendolyn, her mouth melted into a smile.

Gwendolyn wondered if she was about to hear good news, or if Irma's instructions were to soften her up. "Reporting for duty."

Irma consulted the board of lights next to her intercom. "He's still on a call. Won't be long."

"I don't suppose you can give me a hint about why I've been subpoenaed."

"And spoil the surprise?"

After the events of the past six months, Gwendolyn wanted to settle back into her costuming job and sew attractive clothes for attractive people. Was that too much to ask?

One of the lights on Irma's board went out. "You can go in now."

Gwendolyn opened the door to Zanuck's office. Above his desk hung a grayish-white cloud of expensive cigar smoke. "Boy, oh boy! I'm about to put a great big smile on that beautiful dial of yours." He motioned for her to take a seat.

She lodged herself on the edge of the chair facing Zanuck's vast desk.

He drew a long pull of his cigar and let out one perfectly shaped "O" after another. "Remember when I said I'd make it up to you?"

*Of course I do, you big-talking clod. But that was weeks ago and I never heard anything. Not that I expected to.* "Yes, I remember—"

"Hold onto your hat, because I'm about to do it."

"Okay."

"That television test went better than we expected.

"I'm glad to hear it; the crew was pretty jumpy that day."

He beamed wider than the Hollywood sign. "Honey, you're a natural!"

"A natural what?"

"You came across like a goddamn real-life goddess. The camera loves you."

Gwendolyn fought off a sinking feeling. "Excuse me, Mr. Zanuck, but I find that hard to believe."

"What are you talking about?"

"I've seen myself twice on film and both times I was awful. No, honestly! I stunk."

"When you were acting, maybe. Could've been you were trying too hard, or could be you're just a lousy actress. But trust me: television cameras *love* you. When you're being yourself, you're adorable and lovable and so goddamned appealing. People are gonna eat you up, so I want you to be the host."

"Of what?"

"*Fox Fanfare*. You do a little spiel at the start, introduce the movie, maybe share some of the behind-the-scenes gossip—we'll figure it out later. You'll come back after the movie finishes, a few trivial facts, maybe show some stills, tell them what movie we'll be presenting the next week and boom, you're done."

Gwendolyn maintained a honeyed smile as she figured out a nice way to say *Not on your ever-lovin', pea-pickin' life, fella.*

"Thank you for the opportunity, Mr. Zanuck, but I'm going to say no."

He vaulted to his feet. "ARE YOU FUCKING KIDDING ME? I'm offering you the job of a lifetime. You'll be seen in more homes every week than someone like Marilyn Pain-In-My-Ass Monroe has been seen in her entire career!"

*And look where it's gotten her.* "Not everybody in Hollywood wants to be famous."

"What I'm talking about is a hand-in-glove perfect fit." He tapped the contract he'd pushed toward her. "This is your calling."

"My calling is a gorgeous white dress currently sitting on my worktable back in Costuming—"

"Bullshit! Listen, I've built my career by judging people on their ability to become other people. This business of being yourself on camera is new to me, but everyone I've shown your test footage to agrees: you've got it."

It was time to end this ridiculous conversation. Gwendolyn stood up, smoothing her skirt. "I appreciate the offer and the vote of confidence, but the answer is still no. It won't be hard to find someone else to—"

"Let me show it to you. Your audition, I mean."

"I wasn't auditioning; I was filling in."

Zanuck was on his feet now. "I want you to see what I saw. And that's an order."

Memories of her Scarlett screen test and *Maltese Falcon* cameo circled like hungry vultures, but as much as Gwendolyn hated to admit it, Zanuck's dogged insistence sparked the tiniest flame of curiosity.

She trailed behind Zanuck as he marched down a short corridor and into a screening room with seven rows of ten seats. He flicked the lights on. A large television set stood at the front. Zanuck led her to the middle seats in the first row and switched on the set.

Gwendolyn pictured herself in that frightful panda-bear makeup. *I should have said no on the basis of that alone.* She buried her face in her hands. The trumpets of the famous fanfare sounded woefully shrill through the set's tinny speakers.

"Hello, and welcome to *Fox Fanfare*."

Gwendolyn let out a tiny gasp. *Was that MY voice?*

"Each week, we'll be bringing you one of the many Twentieth Century-Fox motion pictures that you've loved so much over the years." She spread her fingers and peeked through the gaps. "But first, let me introduce myself. My name is Gwendolyn Brick and I do hope that we'll become the very best of friends as I present a new picture—that is, a new *old* picture—for you to enjoy. For all of us to enjoy!"

Parts of that had been ad-libbed. She couldn't say she was Betty Grable, nor could she say they were new pictures because some of them were twenty years old. So she had improvised, and after that, ignored the cue cards.

Gwendolyn's hands dropped away as she examined the girl on the TV screen. Where was that god-awful panda-bear makeup? This woman looked charming. Where were her trembling hands and twitching fingertips? She seemed relaxed and confident, and so very at home in that makeshift den. This warm, personable version of herself waved at the camera and told her viewers to be sure to tune in next week for *The Ghost and Mrs. Muir.*

The television screen went black.

Zanuck took a drag of his cigar. "And this is with an inexperienced crew. Imagine how it's going to look when the camera, lighting, makeup, and sound guys know what they're doing."

"I—I—" Gwendolyn groped for words, but they eluded her.

"You're floored that you could be so delightful that all of America will want to invite you over for dinner?" He turned to face her. "Here's my offer. Two-fifty a week, with an increase every season and a run-of-the-show contract.

"What about wardrobe?" The question popped out of its own accord.

"What about it?"

"I want full on-camera wardrobe approval." *Look at you,* Gwendolyn scolded herself, and suppressed a giggle. *Not even on the air and already making demands.*

"I suppose you want Travilla to design it, too."

He was being snarky, so she told him yes.

"Done." He reached out to shake her hand. "Welcome to television, Miss Brick."

# CHAPTER 44

Kathryn's coral suit with the white cuffs was the fourth outfit she'd put on in the last thirty minutes. The aquamarine suit was too bright for April. The green one made her look like a walking key lime pie. And the brown ensemble was too somber for a day like this.

She reread the enigmatic postscript in Marcus's letter.

*Don't be shocked when you see what I'm wearing. And don't jump to conclusions. Just brace yourself.*

"Brace myself?" she muttered out loud. "For what?"

His P.S. was the whole reason why she was so indecisive about what to wear. Normally, she'd choose a nice outfit, add a sparkly accessory, drag a brush through her hair, and be out the door in twenty minutes. What could he possibly be wearing that would cause her to faint?

The coral didn't seem right at all. She ran her hand along the contents of her closet until it landed on a skirt Gwendolyn had made for her a couple of years back when she'd found some poplin dyed the exact same shade as Francine's favorite dahlia—a dark terracotta that teamed perfectly with her reliable standby black silk blouse.

Kathryn pulled off her jacket and was about to unzip the skirt when she heard a knock on her door. Whoever it was had better be quick—she had to leave for LA International Airport in ten minutes. This was one flight arrival she refused to be late for.

She opened it to find Leo scraping his feet on her welcome mat. "Hello!" She stepped back to let him in, then headed toward her bedroom. "I've had the most terrible time choosing what to wear. Sounds silly, I know, but Marcus's P.S. threw me for a loop. I'm about to change into my fifth outfit!"

"I know this is a big day for you, but I've got a life to live too."

She watched the way he rolled the brim of his favorite fedora around his fingers. "Nobody's said otherwise, have they?"

He dropped his hat onto the coffee table. "I know the past week has been unprecedented for you. You got your father out of jail; you took him back to Manhattan and showed him a wonderful time. Nobody's happier for you than I am that it all worked out."

The past week had been a giddy blur of one emotional high stacked on another. *We both hate blue cheese! We both prefer Pepsi over Coke! Neither of us considers Red Skelton as funny as everybody else seems to think he is!*

They had had four glorious days getting to know each other before Winchell announced his release and the press had swamped him. Now he had the pieces of a life to pick up and she had pressing business back in Los Angeles—not the least of which had been Marcus's letter waiting for her when she got home.

"It's all been such a rollercoaster," she told Leo. "I'm only now starting to catch my breath."

"Which is why I've waited to have this conversation."

Kathryn knew what he meant. It was the same one she'd been putting off until after she got back from New York, and after Marcus returned from Italy, and after life resumed to some semblance of normal. But she hadn't counted on Leo beating her to it.

"I know about Nelson Hoyt," he said quietly. "That you and he had a past."

Kathryn felt wretched for not giving him more credit. "How did you find out?"

"I did my homework before I even approached you that first time. But he'd disappeared so I assumed the coast was clear."

"It was," she admitted. "When we walked into Dudley's office and I saw him there, I was floored."

Leo inched forward onto the end of the sofa. "Have you been—seeing him?"

She reached out to touch him but he recoiled. "Leo, honey, please believe me. There's been no sneaking around behind your back. Nelson and I have done nothing."

"But you've wanted to."

There had been that kiss during Bette Davis' welcome-back party, but it was just a kiss and nothing more. The truth hovered on the tip of her tongue, but pushing the words out took more courage than she possessed. "All our contact has been professional and above board."

"So it's just a matter of time?"

He wasn't going to let her off the hook, and he wasn't going to make this easy on her. *Nor does he have to*, she realized. *He's a decent guy who deserves the truth.*

It wasn't until she was an hour out of Idlewild that she had given any thought to how significant it was that the first person she'd called to share the news about her father with had been Nelson, not her fiancé. She tried to fool herself into thinking it was because he'd helped her on the case, so he deserved to know. But by the time she was over Colorado, she was ready to face the truth.

She folded her hands in her lap. "I expect so, yes."

His body shuddered inward as though he'd taken a punch to the chest. "Thank you for being honest."

"Please know that none of this is a reflection on you. You're a wonderful and thoughtful man—"

"—who doesn't get the girl."

She held off to let the comment evaporate. "Nelson fell afoul of Hoover and was banished from LA. I didn't know where he went and never thought I'd see him again. But then he popped up. And then you proposed—"

"I could see there was unfinished business between the two of you so I wanted to head him off at the pass. I thought if I could land that rock on your finger—"

"And I was so very flattered! And I wanted it to be right. Truly, I did." Kathryn tried to whip up some enthusiasm, but the words came out hollow. "And it was a beautiful ring."

"Right ring, wrong guy?" He let out a cross between a resigned sigh and a stifled grunt.

"Nelson and I do have unfinished business," she admitted, "and I need to finish it, whichever way it goes."

He looked at her for the first time since they'd sat down. "I hope you do, for your sake."

"Thank you, Leo. It's very kind of you to say so."

Another sigh-grunt.

"But I want you to know: this—you and me—us—the past five years, it wasn't nothing to me. I've cared for you deeply, and I still do. I'd hate for you to think what we've had has just been a lark for me. It hasn't. Anything but, in fact. Please know that."

He shot her a new look—less guarded but more resigned. They sat in silence until Kathryn asked, "So where does that leave our professional life? We've still got six more shows to do, and a possible tour beyond that—"

"You don't need to worry." He collected up his hat as though he was about to leave. "I've got nothing to do with the show anymore."

"You don't?!"

A rueful smile. "The Suncrockerhouse campaign has been so successful that Sunbeam have promoted me to head of national marketing."

"National? That's huge! Congrat—"

"In New York."

"But you hate New York. You said it's the ultimate Nice Place to Visit but You Wouldn't Want to Live There."

"Ain't nothing like a huge career opportunity to change a guy's mind."

"I suppose so."

"I had it all planned out. We'd get married here, then move to there to make a whole new life for ourselves. I even contacted a friend of mine at the *New York Journal-American* about you taking over the Cholly Knickerbocker column."

"I think Igor Cassini might object to that."

"There are ways to massage these sorts of situations. Lucky for Igor, though, you've got—" his eyes turned desolate "—other plans."

"I'm so very sorry." She reached for him but he stepped to one side. "Our time together has been incredibly wonderful," she said, "and under different circumstances—"

"Let's stop right there." He jammed his hat on his head. "You've got a plane to meet so let's not draw this out. You're one hell of an amazing woman, and I hope he knows it. Goodbye, Kathryn."

He headed out the door and into the dappled sunshine.

As the door closed, the inevitability of this moment cemented her to the rug. She had meant it when she went to say that under different circumstances they could've worked out. Leo Presnell was a caring, thoughtful guy whom she really had loved.

She fell back onto the sofa, her heart heavier than granite as she drew in one tattered breath after another in an attempt to steady herself. *Leo is great on paper, but he's not the one.* "Face it, Massey," she told herself, "Nelson is." Hearing it out loud, her heart gave a little flip. *He is! He really is!*

The urge to run and tell Nelson engulfed her, but the clock in the living room chimed the top of the hour. She should have been on the road by now. The coral suit was entirely the wrong choice but it was too late to change.

Kathryn gathered together her jacket, handbag, gloves, and hat and dashed outside, slamming her door behind her. She hurried along the path leading toward the rear of the Garden. "GWENNIE!" she called out. "ARE YOU READY?"

Gwendolyn appeared in her open doorway. "Do you realize how late we are?" Every inch of her was the perfect put-together picture that Kathryn had been trying for all morning.

Kathryn hustled her toward the main house.

"Aren't you parked in the side lot?" Gwendolyn asked.

Kathryn covered Gwennie's eyes and guided her toward Sunset. "Wait for it . . . wait for it . . ." At the right spot, she pulled her hand away.

Gwendolyn squealed when she saw the banner Kathryn had ordered a couple of days ago and paid the handyman to string up this morning across the back of the main house.

WELCOME HOME MARCUS!

When the banner painter had told Kathryn she could have any color combination, she'd been overwhelmed by all the options. In the end, she chose a white background with thick bold letters in candy-apple red, but wasn't sure how it'd look. "Do you think he'll like it?"

Gwendolyn clutched her arm. "Are you nuts? He'll love it!"

"I wanted him to know how much he's been missed."

"I think he knows that already. But if not, this will surely get the message across."

Kathryn pulled on her gloves and started heading for the Garden's parking lot on Crescent Heights. "We've got a little more than an hour. That should be enough time, right?"

"It'll have to be. We were at the gate when he left, and I want us to be there when he returns."

Kathryn's Oldsmobile was parked in the first space. They climbed inside and she revved the engine. "Okay," she said, "let's go get our boy."

*THE END*

**Did you enjoy this book? You can make a big difference.**

As an independent author, I don't have the financial muscle of a New York publisher supporting me. But I do have something much more powerful and effective, and it's something those publishers would kill to get their hands on: a committed and loyal bunch of readers.

Honest reviews of my books help bring them to the notice of other readers. If you've enjoyed this book, I would be so grateful if you could spend just a couple of minutes leaving a review on the website where you bought it.

Thank you very much,
*Martin Turnbull*

## ALSO BY MARTIN TURNBULL

***Hollywood's Garden of Allah novels:***

Book 1 – *The Garden on Sunset*
Book 2 – *The Trouble with Scarlett*
Book 3 – *Citizen Hollywood*
Book 4 – *Searchlights and Shadows*
Book 5 – *Reds in the Beds*
Book 6 – *Twisted Boulevard*
Book 7 – *Tinseltown Confidential*
Book 8 – *City of Myths*
Book 9 – To be announced

## ACKNOWLEDGMENTS

Heartfelt thanks to the following:

My editor: Jennifer McIntyre for her keen eye, unfailing humor, and the willingness to debate every last letter.

My cover designer: Dan Yeager at Nu-Image Design

My beta readers: Vince Hans, Nora Hernandez-Castillo, Bradley Brady, Beth Riches, Royce Sciortino, and Gene Strange for their invaluable time, insight, feedback and advice in shaping this novel.

My proofreaders extraordinaire: Bob Molinari and Susan Perkins

My thanks to Vilma Galano D'Aprano, Terese Scalise, and Jacqui Turnbull for their assistance in the Italian translations used in this novel.

And to Susan Milner and Andie Paysinger for providing verisimilitude. I can only dream of these lives but Susan and Andie lived it.

## CONNECT WITH MARTIN TURNBULL

www.MartinTurnbull.com

Facebook.com/ gardenofallahnovels

The Hollywood's Garden of Allah Novels blog

Goodreads: bit.ly/martingoodreads

Sign up for Martin's no-spam-ever mailing list, be the first to hear the latest news, and receive *Subway People* - a 1930s short story exclusively available to subscribers.
Go to: bit.ly/goasignup

Printed in Great Britain
by Amazon